"Phasers on stun!" Kirk ordered.

"Aye, sir."

Crouched beside the prone commissioner and his aide, doing his best to defend them with his phaser, Kirk used his free hand to pluck his communicator from his belt. He flipped it open with a practiced move.

"Kirk to *Enterprise*! We're under attack. Beam us back!"

Part of Kirk wanted to take the fight to the assassins, but his fi diplomats' safety. O   y back to the *Enter*   reinforcements—   this conflict on their own.

He ex   but got only static in re

"Spock

A fresh

Damn.

"They're jamming our signal somehow," Kirk called out to Bergstrom, shouting over the tumult. "We're on our own!"

STAR TREK®

THE ORIGINAL SERIES

NO TIME LIKE THE PAST

Greg Cox

Based upon *Star Trek*
created by Gene Roddenberry

POCKET BOOKS

New York • London • Toronto • Sydney • New Delhi

Pocket Books
A Division of Simon & Schuster, Inc.
1230 Avenue of the Americas
New York, NY 10020

This book is a work of fiction. Any references to historical events, real people, or real places are used fictitiously. Other names, characters, places, and events are products of the author's imagination, and any resemblance to actual events or places or persons, living or dead, is entirely coincidental.

First Pocket Books paperback edition March 2014

POCKET and colophon are registered trademarks of Simon & Schuster, Inc.

For information about special discounts for bulk purchases, please contact Simon & Schuster Special Sales at 1-866-506-1949 or business@simonandschuster.com.

The Simon & Schuster Speakers Bureau can bring authors to your live event. For more information or to book an event, contact the Simon & Schuster Speakers Bureau at 1-866-248-3049 or visit our website at www.simonspeakers.com.

Cover design by Alan Dingman

ISBN 978-1-4767-4949-5
ISBN 978-1-4767-4950-1 (ebook)

To my dad,
for letting me stay up past my bedtime
to watch Star Trek *on its original run.*

One

Captain's Log. Stardate 6122.5.

The Enterprise is taking part in a diplomatic mission to the planet Yusub, which has been providing safe havens for Orion pirates interfering with trade and exploration in this sector of the Alpha Quadrant. My mission is to assist Commissioner Santiago, a veteran Federation diplomat, in persuading the tribal chieftains of Yusub to stop sheltering the pirates in exchange for better relations with the Federation. . . .

They beamed into an oasis.

It was darker than the *Enterprise*'s transporter room and significantly cooler, too. A brisk night breeze greeted Captain James T. Kirk as his landing party materialized on the surface of the planet. Torchlight flickered at the periphery of his vision while his eyes adjusted to the nocturnal setting, which was a jarring contrast to the well-lit corridors of the starship he had been striding through only minutes ago. He took a second to orient himself.

Top-secret coordinates had landed them in the middle of a desert in a remote corner of Yusub. Endless sand dunes, broken up by monumental rock formations, stretched for kilometers in every direction. It was well after sunset in this hemisphere, and the light of a single crescent moon cast long shadows over the shallow ground of the torchlit oasis, where a grove of verdant palm trees had grown up around a rippling silver pond, defying the barren wastes beyond. A fresh-water spring bubbled at the center of the pond, providing a natural fountain that added to the tranquil beauty of the scene. An outdoor pavilion had been erected in a clearing by the edge of the pond. A feast, redolent of exotic alien spices, was laid out in anticipation of their arrival. Kirk's mouth watered at the enticing aroma. It was still early in the afternoon by the *Enterprise*'s reckoning. He was glad that he hadn't had dinner yet.

Bones is going to be sorry he missed this, he thought. *Too bad Santiago insisted on keeping the landing party to a minimum.*

The oasis struck Kirk as a congenial setting for to-night's conference, although he was aware that its isolated location and status as a neutral territory had also contributed to the site's selection. These negotiations were controversial to say the least; many of the Yusubi profited from their dealings with the Orion pirates and were in no hurry to see those lucrative arrangements sacrificed on the altar of Yusubi-Federation relations. He and Commissioner Santiago had their work cut out for them.

"Let me do the talking," Santiago said in a low voice. A conservative black suit matched his sober mien and bearing. He was stocky, but in a good shape for man his age. "At least at first."

"By all means," Kirk assented. His dress uniform fit the occasion. "I know you've come a long way for this."

The landing party consisted of Kirk, Santiago, the commissioner's personal aide, and a single Starfleet security officer. Frankly, the captain would have preferred a larger complement of bodyguards, if only for Santiago's own protection, but the diplomat had wanted to avoid anything that smacked of an excessive show of force. Factions among the Yusubi were already leery of the Federation's entreaties in this matter, seeing them as impositions on their own sovereignty. Kirk had deferred to his judgment; Santiago was the lead diplomat here. The man had spent many months setting up this meeting, via courier and subspace.

"Welcome, travelers," a guttural voice greeted them. "Accept the hospitality of our world."

A few dozen Yusubi were on hand to meet them, while more occupied the temporary tent city that had sprung up around the oasis, where a fleet of sand-schooners and sleds waited to transport the delegates out of the desert after the conference. The Yusubi were primates whose evolution had taken them in a more simian direction, so that they resembled early hominids, complete with sloping brows, long arms, and prognathous jaws. They wore hooded cloaks over loose, flowing robes whose colors reflected the environments of their respective territories: arctic white, sandy brown, jungle green, forest patterns, grassy stripes, and so on. Kirk assumed the tradition had its roots in camouflage.

As agreed, each clan leader was accompanied by a single assistant, along with a bodyguard armed with a primitive high-caliber rifle. The Yusubi had yet to make the transition to energy weapons, but even simple fire-arms could pack a punch, as Kirk remembered from his experiences on Tyree's world. In the right hands, gunpowder and bullets could be just as lethal as any phaser blast. More guards were posted on the surrounding dunes and rock formations, on the lookout for any hostile parties who might want to disrupt the conclave. Kirk hoped they would prove unnecessary.

Yusub itself was an oasis of sorts: a Class-M planet conveniently located along various interstellar trade routes. Although the Yusubi had yet to venture into space themselves, they had become familiar with extra-terrestrial visitors early in their history. A fiercely independent people, they had stubbornly refused to align themselves with any of the major galactic civilizations.

"The hospitality of the Yusubi is well known," Santiago replied smoothly. "And justly celebrated."

The diplomat was at least two decades older than Kirk and had a distinguished career behind him. His thinning hair had turned silver in the service of the Federation's diplomatic corps, while his careworn features, and the heavy pouches under his eyes, hinted at his personal tragedy. Kirk was well aware that Santiago had a very personal stake in these negotiations; his younger sister and her family had recently been killed in an Orion raid on a Federation science outpost in a neighboring sector.

Kirk sympathized with the man's loss. The death of his brother and sister-in-law, on Deneva four years ago, still stung.

"But perhaps your Federation finds us *too* hospitable? At least where the Orions are concerned?"

The speaker was an elderly female Yusubi, whose sandy yellow robe and burnoose matched the color of the deserts. The fine quality of her silken garments, with their ornate trim and embroidery, suggested that she was the leader of her clan. Bristly gray fur betrayed her age, but her silver eyes were as clear and bright as the moonlit surface of the nearby pool.

"That is what we are here to discus," Santiago

conceded. He stepped forward to introduce himself. "I am Commissioner Vincent Santiago. On behalf of the United Federation of Planets, I—"

She brushed past him to address Kirk instead.

"I am RoMusscu Dihana, Chieftain of the Cloudless Lands. By rank and privilege, the host of this conclave." She eyed Kirk curiously. "You are the master of the vessel above? The *U.S.S. Enterprise*?"

"I am." He tried to finesse the situation by directing her attention back to Santiago. "And Commissioner Santiago is one of our most respected diplomats."

"Diplomats? Respected?" She scoffed at the notion. "My people prefer explorers to bureaucrats, travelers to talkers. Explorers open up new territory and bring us wealth and wonders from the stars. Diplomats speak only of taxes and tariffs and treaties. . . ."

Diplomacy was hardly her own strong suit, Kirk noted. The chieftain was obviously one to speak her mind. *Not unlike McCoy,* he thought, *if Bones was an ancient alien matriarch, that is.*

"Commissioner Santiago is not just a 'talker,'" his aide protested, coming to his superior's defense. If anything, Cyril Hague seemed more offended by the snub than Santiago was. "He hasn't come all this way just to—"

"It's all right, Cyril," Santiago interrupted the younger man. "Our mission is what matters, not my ego." He stepped back, surrendering the spotlight to Kirk. "You must forgive my aide. He is loyal to a fault."

Hague fell silent. The aide was a pale, wiry young man with a slight Centauran accent. His dark suit matched his mentor's. Kirk had not had much contact with Hague on the way to Yusub. The aide had mostly been holed up with

Santiago, preparing for this meeting. The only impression Kirk had gotten was that Hague was a hard worker who took his duties seriously. And that he was perhaps a bit on the dull and earnest side.

"Loyalty is easily forgiven," Dihana granted, before turning her attention back to Kirk. "You have visited many worlds beside our own?"

"More than my share," the captain said with a smile.

Apparently it had fallen upon him to take the lead here, so Kirk resolved to make a good first impression. Anything he could do to make these talks go smoothly would improve their odds for success—and possibly deprive the ruthless Orion raiders of a safe haven from Federation justice.

"Then you must take with you a memento of your sojourn here, so you will not forget Yusub as you travel on." She beckoned to an aide, who came forward bearing a glazed terra-cotta sculpture. "Accept this gift as a token of our hospitality."

The sculpture was possibly a fertility idol of sorts, in the shape of a Yusubi nude of voluptuous propor-tions. Brownish-orange and roughly thirty centimeters in height, the idol was a bit simian for Kirk's tastes, but he accepted it diplomatically. It was lighter than he ex-pected, as though hollow.

"You're too generous," Kirk said, pretending to admire the idol. He wasn't quite sure where to put his hands. "I will treasure it, as I do your friendship."

He wondered briefly what on Earth he was going to do with the gift. Perhaps there was a Federation museum or university that would welcome such a donation?

"Let me take that for you, sir," Lieutenant Bergstrom

volunteered. She relieved Kirk of the cumbersome idol. "Just for safekeeping, of course."

Kirk appreciated her initiative. The young security officer had recently transferred over from the *Brandywine,* where she had received multiple commendations for exceptional bravery and service. She was a strapping redhead who was third-generation Starfleet. Kirk almost felt guilty for poaching her from the *Brandywine.*

"Thank you, Lieutenant." He tried to move the proceedings along. "I believe Commissioner Santiago has likewise brought a gift in appreciation of your hospitality. From the Federation to the Yusubi."

"That is quite right, Captain." Santiago accepted a rolled-up parchment bearing the embossed seal of the United Federation of Planets from Hague. He released an electronic latch and the sheet automatically unfurled to reveal a beautifully rendered star chart of the Milky Way. "Knowing of your people's long history of welcoming travelers from others worlds, we thought you might find value in this fine map of the known galaxy."

A click of a switch caused the chart to roll back up again. He offered it to Dihana, who deigned to accept it.

"A most thoughtful and appropriate gift," she declared, warming to Santiago somewhat, "which speaks well of your Federation and its intentions." She opened the map to admire it once more, chuckling to herself at the cleverness and convenience of the mechanism. "You will have to show me where to find your respective homeworlds on this lovely—"

A disruptor blast tore through her chest and set fire to the map.

Two

The murdered chieftain collapsed onto the ground in front of the landing party. Her lifeless body smothered the blazing parchment. The nauseating smell of burnt flesh assaulted Kirk's nostrils, overpowering the aroma of the now-forgotten feast. He didn't need McCoy to tell him that Dihana was dead.

What the devil?

Screams and angry shouts erupted from the startled spectators, whose alien vocalizations sounded like the squawks of agitated chimpanzees. It was unclear at first where the fatal blast had come from. Rival chieftains and their bodyguards glared suspiciously at each other and hurled accusations. Other Yusubi panicked and ran for cover, knocking over torches and tables in their haste to escape. Pandemonium spread like an out-of-control plasma fire.

"Wait! What's happening?" Santiago exclaimed. Frozen in shock, he presented a tempting target to the unknown assassin. "Who did this?"

Kirk had no idea, but he knew he had to protect the commissioner. He lunged forward and knocked Santiago to the ground. Hague dived for cover without any prompting.

"Keep your heads down!" Kirk ordered.

The captain reached behind his shirt and drew the

Type-1 phaser he had discreetly brought to the meeting, and he was not surprised to see that Bergstrom had already done the same. The idol lay discarded on the ground nearby. Bergstrom looked to him for direction.

"Captain?"

Before he could answer, a second blast took out a fleeing chieftain. This time Kirk spotted the origin of the shot: a sniper rising from the watery depths of the pond, accompanied by at least six accomplices armed with insulated disruptor rifles. Matte-black wet suits concealed the assassins' identities and species, although Kirk would have bet a week's pay that they were either Orions or local allies of the same. Compact breathing apparatuses explained how they had managed to stay concealed in the pool until the fatal moment. Kirk guessed that the strike force had been lurking at the bottom of the pool for hours, waiting to carry out their murderous mission. They fired at will into the fleeing crowd, adding to the chaos and bloodshed, and strode out onto dry land. Their leader spit his rebreather onto the ground.

"Over there!" Kirk called out to Bergstrom. "By the pool!"

"Got them!" Bergstrom acknowledged. She returned fire with her phaser, although the sheer tumult made it hard to target the enemy. Yusubi bodyguards, armed with rifles, joined the conflict. Gunshots rang out in the night. Ferns and palm fronds caught in the crossfire burst into flames. Fallen torches set the pavilion ablaze, while the forgotten feast was trampled beneath the feet of panicked Yusubi. Steam billowed where burning timbers crashed into the pool. In the confusion, it was difficult to tell who was shooting at whom.

"Phasers on stun!" Kirk ordered.

"Aye, sir."

Crouched beside the prone commissioner and his aide, doing his best to defend them with his phaser, Kirk used his free hand to pluck his communicator from his belt. He flipped it open with a practiced move.

"Kirk to *Enterprise*! We're under attack. Beam us back!"

Part of Kirk wanted to take the fight to the assassins, make sure they didn't get away with killing Dihana and the others, but his first responsibility was to see to the diplomats' safety. Once he got Santiago and Hague safely back to the *Enterprise*, he could perhaps return with reinforcements—unless the Yusubi insisted on handling this conflict on their own.

He expected an immediate response, but got only static in reply.

"Spock? Scotty? Do you read me?"

A fresh burst of static hurt his ears.

Damn.

"They're jamming our signal somehow," he called out to Bergstrom, shouting over the tumult. "We're on our own!"

By now, a full-fledged firefight was under way, turning the once-tranquil oasis into a war zone. Through the smoke and steam, Kirk glimpsed the marauders spreading out to wreak more havoc. Yusubi warriors, streaming from the tents outside the oasis, rushed past the landing party to engage the enemy. They shouted and squawked ferociously. Gunfire clashed with disruptor blasts. The attackers were outnumbered, but their superior weaponry gave them a definite edge. Rifle-toting Yusubi were disintegrated, guns and all.

"Stop them!" Santiago pleaded. "Don't worry about me. It's the Orions, I know it!" Anguish and frustration contorted his features. The smoldering remains of the torched star chart blew past his face. "They're ruining everything!"

That was for certain, Kirk agreed silently, but it was too late to salvage the conclave now. They needed to concentrate on surviving. He assessed their position, which was too exposed for his liking. Staying where they were, the landing party was likely to be shot or trampled or all of the above. Perhaps they'd be better off taking their chances with the desert?

"We need to get out of here," Kirk decided. He tugged Santiago to his feet and called out to the others. "Make for the dunes! Bergstrom, cover us!"

"Yes, sir!"

She took up a defensive position at their rear, even as Kirk hustled the diplomats away from the burning oasis. She fired back at the assassins to discourage pursuit. Soot blackened her fierce expression.

For a moment, Kirk thought they were all going to make it.

Then a lurking assassin, his glistening wet suit reflecting the bright orange flames consuming the oasis, darted out from behind the trunk of a blazing palm and fired at Bergstrom. A sizzling emerald beam vaporized her. She had time enough for only a single pain-tinged gasp before dissolving into atoms.

"Butcher!" Santiago cried.

Kirk fired back at the assassin, who ducked behind the tree trunk to avoid the sapphire beam. A different strategy occurred to Kirk, and he switched the phaser from stun to disrupt. A crimson beam sliced through the base of the tree, which toppled over onto the sniper. The man shrieked as the falling tree knocked him off his feet and pinned him to the ground. He squirmed beneath the heavy tree trunk, injured but obviously still alive.

Kirk had mixed feelings about that.

A stun beam took the trapped assassin out of commission. Despite the need to escape, Kirk paused long enough to take a closer look at the assassin. Olive-green skin peeked through gaps in the torn wet suit. A metal skullcap could be glimpsed beneath his rubber cowl.

Orion, Kirk thought. *I knew it.*

The pirates were obviously out to disrupt the talks—with extreme prejudice.

Kirk cast a pained glance at where Bergstrom had been disintegrated. No trace of her remained, and he still needed to get Santiago and Hague to safety, or some reasonable approximation thereof. He rejoined the civilians at the outer fringe of the oasis. Burning tents lit up the towering sand dunes and mammoth rock formations beyond the torched grove. Kirk heard furious fighting going on in what remained of the oasis.

Only a fool fights in a burning house, a Klingon commander had once told Kirk. Clearly, the vengeful Yusubi had other ideas.

"Come on," Kirk told the other humans. "Maybe we can get beyond the range of the jamming effect."

Santiago hesitated. He stared numbly at the empty space Bergstrom had occupied.

"They killed her . . . just like that."

"Yes," Kirk said tersely. He knew the commissioner had to be thinking of his murdered sister and her family, but they could mourn the dead later. "She'll be remembered, trust me."

Santiago's face darkened with rage. "Barbarians!" he snarled in a very undiplomatic fashion. "Bloodthirsty, murdering savages!"

"Please, sir!" Hague tugged on his superior's arm. "You need to listen to the captain. You're not safe here!"

Kirk appreciated the assist. He was suddenly thankful that neither the commissioner nor his aide was armed, otherwise Santiago might have charged back into the fray himself, which was the last thing Kirk needed right now. He wanted the diplomat safe, not out for blood.

"Truly, there is no safety to be found today!" a fierce voice intruded. "Only death . . . and retribution!"

A Yusubi warrior appeared between them and the beckoning dunes. His green burnoose indicated that he hailed from a more tropical clime. He brandished a smoking rifle.

Kirk lowered his phaser to avoid provoking the Yusubi, who was obviously (and understandably) on edge. He hoped the armed warrior didn't blame the humans for bringing the carnage consuming the oasis. He appealed to the Yusubi's fabled code of hospitality.

"These guests are under your protection!" Kirk reminded him. "Help me get them to safety!"

The Yusubi squawked derisively.

"You brought this on yourself, meddlers! You should've minded your own affairs!" He aimed his rifle at Kirk. "Drop your weapon, Federation!"

Kirk's heart sunk as he realized that this particular Yusubi was among those aligned with the Orions. For all Kirk knew, he had helped plan the attack and had revealed its location to the assassins.

"You don't have to do this," Kirk said, stalling. He weighed his chances of deploying his phaser before the hostile Yusubi squeezed the trigger on his rifle. Spock would be able to calculate the odds with mathematical precision, but even Kirk knew they weren't good. "We were here at the chieftains' invitation!"

The Yusubi's flat nose wrinkled in disgust.

"Fools and weaklings! Some Yusubi know who our true guests are . . . and who should be left buried in the sands!" He swung the muzzle of his rifle toward the commissioner. "I repeat: Drop your weapon!"

Kirk tossed his phaser aside. His muscles tensed, ready to jump the warrior the minute an opportunity presented itself. Perhaps he could buy the diplomats a chance at escape with his own life? It would be a pricy exchange, but he was willing to pay it . . . if required.

I'm counting on you, Spock, he thought. *Complete our mission—and get our passengers home.*

But salvation came from another quarter instead. Without warning, an azure phaser beam zipped over Kirk's shoulder, humming past his ear, to strike the traitorous Yusubi squarely in the chest. The warrior was flung backward by the impact of the blast. He landed unconscious at the base of a dune. Loose yellow sand poured down the slope to dust his head and shoulders.

Kirk was almost as startled as the unlucky warrior. He spun around to see who had saved him.

A statuesque female figure emerged from the fiery oasis, striding confidently toward them. The idol was cradled securely in the crook of her arm, while her other hand gripped a phaser pistol of unfamiliar design. Smoke and shadows partially concealed her identity.

Kirk blinked in confusion. "Bergstrom?"

For a moment, Kirk thought the murdered crew member had somehow come back to life, but then the woman stepped into a patch of moonlight and Kirk saw that she was a stranger. A skintight blue uniform flattered her attractive figure, which would have warranted closer attention under different circumstances. She appeared human, or humanoid, with alert blue eyes and upswept blond hair combed neatly atop her head. A badge in the shape of a stylized Starfleet emblem was affixed to her chest. Her striking features were adorned with metallic implants or ornaments that seemed to be embedded surgically in her flesh. One such implant partially framed her left eye, while another resembled a cybernetic spider lodged under her right ear. She regarded Kirk with a cool, quizzical expression.

"James Tiberius Kirk," she greeted him. "Captain of the *U.S.S Enterprise*. Designation: NCC-One-Seven-Zero-One?"

"That's right," he said, puzzled. "Who . . . ?"

"You're welcome," she said tartly. "I suggest we postpone any further introductions until a more suitable occasion." Falling in beside him, she turned to face the smoky oasis, where a furious battle was still being raged. She glanced pointedly at his discarded phaser. "Self-defense appears to be our current priority."

Kirk retrieved his phaser. "You may have a point there."

Sure enough, a party of Orion raiders and their Yusubi cohorts burst from the smoke and flames, only to encounter a volley of concentrated phaser fire from both Kirk and his enigmatic new ally. The marauders fell back, leaving their stunned accomplices where they fell. Kirk noted that the woman's phaser seemed to pack significantly more punch than his own Type-1 phaser, despite being even slimmer and more compact. He also wondered why she had bothered to rescue the idol, which she continued to hold on to with no obvious exertion. Her left hand, he observed, was augmented by the same sort of biomechanical implants visible on her face. He was starting to suspect they were not just cosmetic.

"You're stronger than you look," he observed. "And perhaps not quite human?"

She declined to address his query. "You should focus on your aim, Captain."

"My aim is fine," he retorted, proving it by stunning another Yusubi traitor, who dropped onto the sands beside his comrades. "As is yours, I must say."

She fired into the murky smoke and shadows. A dimly glimpsed figure tumbled backward onto the ground.

"I strive for precision," she observed.

"So I see."

To his relief, the tide of battle seemed to be turning against the raiders, who found themselves trapped between the phaser barrage and the remnants of the chieftain's bodyguards. Horns blared in alarm, summoning reinforcements. Rapid-fire gunshots popped like firecrackers.

"Retreat!" a burly Orion marauder bellowed. "We've inflicted enough damage tonight!"

Kirk wondered what their exit strategy was. Hiding in the pool before the conclave began had been a clever trick, but it wasn't going to get them away from the oasis in one piece.

The shimmering glow of a transporter effect partially answered his question. The raiders, including their fallen casualties, dissolved into atoms as the transporter whisked them away to . . . where? Kirk was certain there were no Orion pirate vessels in orbit around Yusub. Spock had carefully scanned the vicinity before the landing party had beamed down.

So where had they . . . ?

A loud motorized rumble shook a nearby dune, setting off a huge cascade of sand that flowed down the slope of the dune like a gritty yellow avalanche. The sandslide swept away a tent staked out at the base of the dune and came rolling toward Kirk and the others like surf at a shore.

"Run!" he shouted. "Get back!"

Santiago and the others, including the nameless woman, scrambled out of the way of the sandslide. Kirk didn't quite make it and was thrown forward by several kilograms of sand slamming against the back of his knees. He landed face-first on the desert floor, many meters from where he had been before. A wave of grit washed over his back, all but burying him. He scrambled to his feet, shaking the loose sand from his hair and shoulders.

That could have been a lot worse, he thought.

"Look!" Santiago shouted. He pointed frantically at the quaking dune. "There's something beneath it!"

The woman nodded in agreement. "A hidden vehicle, I surmise."

Her supposition proved as accurate as her aim. A tank-like ground vehicle, roughly the size of a Starfleet shuttlecraft, bulldozed out from beneath the collapsing dune. Armored treads carried the "getaway car" briskly across the desert, away from the torched oasis. Kirk kicked himself for forgetting that not only starships were equipped with transporters.

"Stop them!" Santiago cried out. "Don't let the butchers get away!"

Kirk had managed to hang on to his phaser during the sandslide. Chasing after the vehicle on foot, he fired his phaser at the treads, but the beam was deflected by the tank's ablative plating. He watched in frustration as the Orions escaped across the sands.

Another day, he vowed.

He had not forgotten Bergstrom. The young lieutenant had deserved better than to die in a firefight many light-years from home. He regretted that there wasn't even a body to be provided with an honorable burial in space.

The familiar whine of a transporter caught his ear. He whirled about, half-expecting more Orion raiders, only to spy a Starfleet landing party materializing on the sands only a few meters away. Spock, McCoy, and four red-shirted security officers arrived with phasers drawn.

Better late than never, Kirk thought.

"Jim!" Bones shouted, relief and anxiety both present in his voice. A medkit was slung over his shoulder. "Are you all right?"

"Most of us," Kirk said grimly. "See to the commissioner. He may be in shock."

McCoy did a quick head count. "That lieutenant? Bergstrom?"

Kirk shook his head.

"Damn it," the doctor swore.

Spock took the news of the fatality with his usual Vulcan reserve. He scanned the vicinity with his tricorder. "My apologies for the delay, Captain. Per your orders, I was reluctant to disrupt the conclave unless absolutely necessary. We mobilized a rescue party as soon as we detected signs of a significant armed conflict at the site of the conference. Communications difficulties prevented us from locking onto you with the transporters." He coolly observed what was left of the oasis. Wounded and wary Yusubi staggered from the battlefield. Wails and curses indicated that emotions were running high. Hostile glares were cast in the direction of the landing parties. "I recommend that we vacate this area immediately. The situation here appears to remain volatile."

"I concur," the mystery woman said. "We should relocate to your ship, Captain. There are matters that require our attention. It would be best to discuss them in a less chaotic environment."

Kirk wasn't sure whether to be impressed or irked by her presumption. He saw that she was still holding on to that damned idol as though it was the Holy Grail or the Crown Jewels of Paoli VI.

What was that all about?

Spock took note of the puzzling stranger. An arched eyebrow betrayed his curiosity.

"I am unfamiliar with this individual, Captain," he observed.

"Join the club," Kirk said. Now that the fighting was over for the time being, he wanted answers. He looked over the woman who had saved his life before. She was actually quite breathtaking, he observed. "You know, I don't believe I caught your name, Miss . . . ?"

She paused briefly before answering.

"Seven," she answered. "Call me . . . Annika Seven."

Three

Personal log, Seven of Nine. Stardate 53786.1.

    Voyager has detected an unusual signal from a lifeless planetoid in an otherwise unremarkable sector of the Delta Quadrant. The fact that the transmission appears to be an obsolete Starfleet distress signal, dating back nearly a century, poses a considerable puzzle. An away team has been mobilized to investigate the mystery, and Captain Janeway has requested my presence on the mission.

    I confess that I find the puzzle . . . intriguing.

"It doesn't make any sense," Captain Kathryn Janeway said as the away team gathered in the transporter room. "What's an old, defunct Starfleet signal doing this far from home? Starfleet hadn't even set foot in the Delta Quadrant the last time that signal was in use."

This was hardly the first time that the captain had voiced her bafflement, but Seven had observed that humanoid individuals often repeated themselves as a means of processing new data. She had become accustomed to such behavior during her stay on *Voyager*. It no longer offended her sense of efficiency . . . much.

"It appears Starfleet's historical records are incomplete," Seven stated. "It is probable that an earlier vessel, considered 'lost' by Starfleet, was displaced by some unexpected event and left stranded in this sector, its fate a mystery."

Such occurrences were not without precedent. *Voyager*'s own circumstances were proof of that, as was the case of the *Ares IV,* an earlier Terran spacecraft recently discovered lost in the Delta Quadrant.

"Perhaps we can fill in some of those blanks." Janeway smiled at Seven, clearly looking forward to engaging with the mystery. "You up to the challenge?"

"I completed a full regeneration cycle less than seventy-two minutes ago," Seven replied. "My faculties are at peak performance levels."

Janeway regarded her skeptically. "I'm going to give you the benefit of the doubt and assume that was a joke."

"Your confidence in my wit is gratifying," Seven responded.

The away team waited in front of the transporter platform while Lieutenant Torres manned the control console. Along with the captain and Seven, Lieutenant Tuvok had also been selected for the mission. The Vulcan security chief glanced at a nearby chronometer. His stoic features displayed a flicker of impatience.

"Mister Neelix is less than punctual," he noted. "As usual."

As if on cue, the doors whispered open and Neelix rushed into the transporter room. The Talaxian crew member was flushed and winded, as though he had run all the way from his quarters on Deck 8. The motley colors of his native garb were much more chaotic than the Starfleet uniforms worn by the captain and Tuvok, not to mention Seven's own skintight dermaplastic attire. She always had found Neelix's fashion choices to be contrary to conventional aesthetic standards, but she had come to tolerate them as evidence of his individuality. They suited him.

"Sorry to keep you waiting, Captain." He leaned against the control console while he caught his breath. "But I got caught up researching some fascinating myths and legends involving this sector. *Very* interesting, if I say so myself."

"No need to apologize, Mister Neelix," Janeway said. "We're still a few minutes out of transporter range."

Tuvok frowned slightly, nonetheless, but Janeway was evidently less concerned with the Talaxian's tardiness. She was more indulgent than Seven would have been. Like Tuvok, Seven valued punctuality. It was a sign of a properly organized mind and schedule. Anything less was inefficient.

"What have you learned?" Janeway asked. "Anything that might be relevant to our mission?"

"Very possibly," Neelix said with characteristic enthusiasm. "As you know, we're now far beyond the territory I knew back when I was an independent trader, but I've made a point of trying to familiarize myself with the lore and customs of each new sector in our path, in order to remain as useful as possible to *Voyager* and her crew . . . beyond my vital duties as cook and morale officer, of course."

Seven was aware that Neelix had originally served as a native guide, of sorts, to the uncharted expanses of the Delta Quadrant, but his value in this capacity had steadily diminished over the years, as *Voyager* left his former haunts behind. No doubt he was eager to maintain his relevance.

"Of course," Janeway said. "That's why I included you in this mission. You always have your ear to the ground, wherever our journey carries us." She gave him an encouraging smile. "So, you were saying . . . ?"

He practically beamed at her praise. "Well, during our recent layover at that rundown commercial space station in the Hokilee System, I made the acquaintance of a scaly old merchant-slash-smuggler who has been plying these space lanes since before any of us were conceived. He was quite the character, let me tell you. The stories he could tell, especially after several steaming mugs of hot Flibarian rum. . . ."

"The point, Mister Neelix," Tuvok interrupted. "If you please."

"Oh, right," Neelix said, only slightly abashed. "Anyway, he shared with me a curious folk tale regarding these parts. Seems the locals still tell stories about a 'wizard' from the other side of the galaxy who was said to be able to traverse space-time at will. The secret of his 'magic' is supposed to be hidden somewhere in this sector, but nobody really believes the legend anymore." He shrugged. "It's just an old story from centuries ago."

"How many centuries?" Seven asked. "Please be more precise."

"Depends on who is telling the story," Neelix said. "As I said, it's a tall tale, not a documented historical account. It might not mean anything at all."

"Perhaps not," Janeway conceded. "But what if this myth has some basis in fact? That misplaced Starfleet signal certainly seems to be from a distant time and place." Her voice took on a speculative tone. "Is it possible that this so-called 'wizard' actually possessed some form of advanced technology that might get us back to the Alpha Quadrant years ahead of schedule, perhaps by bending time and space in ways unknown to Starfleet? You know what they say, 'any sufficiently advanced technology is—'"

"'Indistinguishable from magic.'" Seven recognized the quotation. "Arthur C. Clarke. Earth, twentieth century."

Janeway nodded, looking pleased by Seven's erudition. "You're up on the classics. Good."

Seven ignored the compliment. Her knowledge of human literature was not at issue here. "Your optimism may be premature. In my experience, imperfect species and cultures often have overactive imaginations."

Unlike the Borg, she thought, *who found such fancies irrelevant.* She was no longer Borg, at least not entirely, yet she retained a healthy degree of skepticism where unconfirmed myths and legends were concerned. Wishful thinking was no substitute for an accurate assessment of probabilities.

"Guilty as charged," Janeway admitted. "Still, it's worth looking into. If nothing else, I want to find out the story behind that signal." She looked over at the control console. "What's our ETA, Lieutenant Torres?"

B'Elanna Torres had been too intent on her duties to take part in the conversation. Her ridged brow furrowed as she studied the readings on a display panel. The engineer's volatile nature sometimes brought her into conflict with her crewmates, but Seven had confidence in her abilities.

"Coming within range now, Captain," Torres reported. "I can't pinpoint the signal's precise point of

origin, but I should be able to beam you down somewhere in its proximity."

"Within walking distance, I hope." Janeway glanced
wryly at Seven. "Some of us haven't regenerated lately."

Seven took the quip in stride. "I shall do you the
courtesy of assuming that was a joke."

"Touché," Janeway said, chuckling. She took her
place on the transporter platform. "I guess we're off to
seek the wizard."

Seven, Tuvok, and Neelix joined her on the platform. Torres operated the controls and Seven felt a
familiar tingling sensation as the away team beamed
down to the planetoid, which was obscure enough to
lack a proper designation. Prior scans had indicated the
presence of a breathable atmosphere upon the surface,
so environment suits had been deemed unnecessary. A
Starfleet tricorder, customized to Seven's specifications,
clung to her hip, along with a standard Type-2 phaser.

The away team members found themselves in a rocky
canyon, hemmed in by high granite walls. Rough gray
boulders punctuated the rocky floor of the canyon, whose
steep walls provided a degree of shade from the hot noon-
day sun. Earth-normal gravity suggested that the planetoid's core was unusually dense. Spotty vegetation provided
the evidence of life. The air was dry, but sufficient.

Seven was unimpressed. Neelix stumbled slightly
on the uneven surface but recovered his balance without assistance. Tuvok surveyed their surroundings, but,
like Seven, discerned no obvious threats. This was to be
expected; *Voyager*'s sensors had detected no life-forms
on the planetoid, nor any evidence of habitation—aside
from the anomalous Starfleet signal.

"Pretty rugged terrain," Neelix commented, taking in the stark and barren scenery. "Reminds me of the Demon's Crack back on Uglogla Prime. I was almost ambushed by a band of Kazon renegades there several years back. Got away by the whiskers on my cheeks."

"Perhaps you can regale us with the story later," Tuvok said without enthusiasm. "At a more appropriate juncture."

"If you insist," Neelix replied. "You won't be disappointed, I promise!"

Janeway took a moment to check in with the ship. She tapped her combadge.

"Janeway to *Voyager*. We've arrived on the surface. Please thank Lieutenant Torres for the smooth landing."

"*Will do, Captain*," Commander Chakotay replied via the comm link. *Voyager*'s first officer would have no doubt preferred to join the away team, but duty and prudence had dictated that he command the bridge instead. "*Any answers to our mystery yet?*"

"None that I can see," Janeway said. Her keen eyes searched the desolate landscape. "But I'll keep you posted. Janeway out." The away team spread out to inspect their immediate surroundings. Nothing but unremarkable rock, dirt, and scrub presented itself. Given its remote location, Seven was not surprised that no species had apparently attempted to colonize or develop the planetoid. Sensors scans failed to detect any notable mineral resources as well.

"So what exactly are we looking for?" Neelix asked. "The wreckage of a crashed starship or shuttle?"

"Unlikely," Seven said. "Long-range scans detected no evidence of debris. I suspect the signal is emanating from somewhere beneath the surface." She consulted her tricorder and gestured north. "Readings indicate that we should proceed in that direction."

"Very well," Janeway said. "Lead the way."

They hiked up the canyon, carefully traversing the arid wasteland on foot. Neelix kept up a steady stream of irrelevant chatter that Seven did her best to ignore. The sun climbed higher in the sky, causing the temperature to rise more than was comfortable and limiting the amount of available shade. Seven decided she preferred the controlled climate aboard *Voyager*. The signal grew stronger as they rounded a bend in the canyon. She wondered how long it had gone unanswered. Slight-but-detectible evidence of signal degradation suggested that it had been broadcasting continuously for at least a century.

"I believe we are nearing the source of the transmission, Captain," she reported.

Janeway stopped and inhaled sharply. "I'm inclined to agree," she said in a hushed tone. "Look ahead."

Seven lifted her gaze from the tricorder. Her eyes widened at the sight of an enormous face, at least twenty meters in height, carved into the side of a cliff at the far end of the canyon. The immense countenance reminded her of the monumental sculptures on Earth's Mount Rushmore, which she knew of from *Voyager*'s databanks, or perhaps the towering funerary busts of Species 9591. Either way, it was an ambitious work of both art and engineering.

"By the Great Forest!" Neelix exclaimed. "How did our sensors ever miss this?"

"It is carved from natural granite," Seven pointed

out. "It would not register as an artificial structure on our scans."

"The craftsmanship is impressive," Tuvok said, "as is the scale of the sculpture."

Seven agreed with the Vulcan's assessment. The colossal sculpture expertly captured the likeness of a humanoid male, possibly of Terran descent, with wavy hair, clean-shaven features, and a resolute expression. The visage struck her as vaguely familiar, but, shorn of context, it took her a moment to place it.

"Captain," she said. "Unless I am mistaken, that is a portrait of—"

"James T. Kirk." Janeway gazed up at the monument with a rapt, but distinctly bewildered, expression. "Captain of the *Starship Enterprise*."

Four

Seven contemplated the looming granite sculpture. She was familiar with Captain Kirk's colorful career and reputation. Her recent encounter with the *Ares IV*, lost in the Delta Quadrant three centuries ago, had inspired her to make a thorough study of the history of human space exploration. James T. Kirk and his illustrious crew figured prominently in that history, even if some of the accounts of his exploits defied credibility. Hadn't Janeway once mentioned that Kirk claimed to have met Leonardo da Vinci—and not in a holodeck?

"I believe you are correct, Captain," Tuvok said. "The resemblance to James Kirk is striking."

Seven recalled that Kirk had been accompanied in his historic voyages by his Vulcan first officer, Spock. Her understanding was that Spock, who continued to serve the Federation as a roving ambassador and diplomat, was as respected by Vulcans as much as Kirk's heroism was celebrated by the next generation of human explorers. Seven herself had found Spock to be at least as intriguing a figure as Kirk, and rather easier to empathize with. Like her, he had struggled to reconcile his semi-human heritage with a more detached, scientific perspective. She would be interested in meeting him, should *Voyager* return to the Alpha Quadrant before he reached the end of his considerable lifespan.

"It's more than striking," Janeway said. "It's unmistakable. Kirk's career was required reading back at the Academy. I'd know those dashing good looks anywhere."

Seven conceded that the sculpture's literally chiseled features matched the recorded images of Kirk. And the edifice was appropriately larger-than-life as well.

"But what's a monument to Kirk doing on an uninhabited planetoid in the Delta Quadrant?" Janeway asked aloud. She sounded more intrigued than frustrated by the mystery. "This just keeps getting curiouser and curiouser."

Lewis Carroll, also designated Charles Dodgson, Seven thought, identifying the reference. The "Alice" books had struck her as singularly lacking in narrative logic. She hoped their current mission would not prove equally baffling.

Neelix tilted his head back to take in the entire mammoth sculpture. "You don't suppose this Kirk was the 'wizard' mentioned in the old stories?"

"Well, his opponents in battle sometimes accused him of being a sorcerer, but still . . ." Janeway sounded doubtful. "Kirk covered a lot of territory in his voyages, even venturing out past the Galactic Barrier, but there's no record of him ever setting foot in the Delta Quadrant."

Seven's own memory confirmed Janeway's recollections, but it raised a possible explanation.

"Was not Kirk's body lost in space during an encounter with an unexplained stellar phenomenon?" she recalled. "During the maiden voyage of the *Enterprise-B*?"

"That's right!" Janeway said. "Kirk is supposed to have died saving that ship from a strange, destructive ribbon of cosmic energy, but his remains were never recovered. It's believed that he was carried away by the ribbon—"

"All the way to the Delta Quadrant?" Neelix supplied. He gazed up at the towering monument. "Do you think this could be his tomb?"

Janeway considered the sculpture. "Well, its proportions are heroic enough, but we probably shouldn't get ahead of ourselves."

Seven agreed. Idle speculation was inefficient.

"In any event," she stated, "the proximity of this monument to the source of an archaic Starfleet signal is unlikely to be a coincidence." She advanced toward the sculpture. "I suggest we continue our investigation."

Janeway chuckled. "Try and stop me."

The away team approached the massive stone face. The canyon walls had helped to shield it from the elements, but it was clearly worn and weathered by the passage of time. The face dwarfed the party of explorers, rising high above their heads. Up close, Seven found herself at eye level with the sculpture's gigantic chin. Her tricorder scanned the petrified face of the cliff.

"I am detecting chambers and passageways within the monument," she reported. "The signal is definitely coming from somewhere inside the cliff."

Janeway scrutinized the cliff face. Her hands explored the rough, rocky surface of the sheer walls framing the sculpture. "There must be an entrance to the interior. Perhaps a hidden doorway?"

"Wouldn't it be easier just to have *Voyager* beam us directly inside?" Neelix asked.

"That would be unwise," Seven replied. "Impurities in the stone, including trace elements of magnesite, make it difficult to get precise readings. I would not be able to guarantee the safety of any coordinates."

Janeway nodded. "That explains why B'Elanna was unable to lock onto the exact origin of the signal." Undaunted by the complication, she brushed the gritty dust from her hands. "I guess we'll just have to do this the hard way. Keep looking around for a way in."

"Affirmative, Captain," Tuvok said.

"Too bad Jean-Luc Picard isn't here," Janeway mused, resting her chin on her knuckles as she considered the problem. "Amongst his other distinctions, he's quite the amateur archaeologist. A challenge like this would be right up his alley."

Picard.

The name provoked an involuntary flutter in Seven's cortical implant. Among the Borg, Picard was better known as Locutus. He was the first drone to regain his humanity after being assimilated by the Collective, and this unprecedented reversal had led to the Borg's momentous defeat at Wolf 359. Seven had likewise regained her individuality, some years later, but having been assimilated as a child, she'd had little in the way of humanity to return to. Picard's difficult transformation to Locutus and back again held unsettling parallels to Seven's own continuing evolution. . . .

"You all right, Seven?" Janeway asked with concern.

Seven experienced a flash of irritation at herself. Clearly, her momentary lack of composure had not gone unnoticed by the captain. Unwilling to admit to such a human imperfection, she chose to deny it.

"I am fine," she insisted. "I am merely intent on our task."

To her relief, Janeway did not press the issue. Erasing all thought of Picard from her mind, Seven redoubled her efforts to locate an entrance to the hidden caverns. While her companions employed their hands and eyes to scour the face of the cliff for seams or signs of entry, Seven chose to take a more efficient approach. Slowly and meticulously, she used her tricorder to scan one segment of stone after another. She watched carefully for any anomalies along the electromagnetic spectrum— until her diligent efforts yielded a provocative result.

"Captain," she said. "Over here."

Janeway turned away from her own visual inspection of the site. She hurried to join Seven to one side of the immense sculpture. Tuvok and Neelix followed her.

"What is it?" she asked. "Do you have something?"

"Perhaps." Seven double-checked her readings. "There appears to be a pattern of chroniton particles embedded in this segment of stone . . . and only here."

Janeway reacted with surprise. "Chronitons? Here?"

The subatomic particles were associated with time travel and other varieties of temporal distortions. There was no obvious explanation for their presence at this site.

"The chronitons are concentrated here," Seven explained, indicating a small expanse approximately the size of her palm. "Almost like a marker."

Neelix squinted at the coarse gray stone. "I don't see anything."

"The marker is slightly out of phase with these temporal coordinates," Seven stated. "Your eyes are not designed to detect such phenomenon. My ocular implant, however, possesses no such limitation."

She lowered her tricorder and applied her own

cybernetically enhanced vision to the marker. Concentration was required to adjust her focus to the proper temporal wavelength, but she soon discerned a pattern shimmering just beneath the surface of the stone. Its precise configuration took her by surprise.

"Curiouser and curiouser indeed," she said.

"What is it?" Janeway asked urgently. "What do you see?"

"Allow me to show you," Seven volunteered. Bending over, she plucked a random stone from the rubble at their feet and used it to scratch the outline of the pattern on the wall of the cliff. The familiar arrowhead shape of the Starfleet insignia drew gasps from both the captain and Neelix.

"Oh, my," Janeway said.

Tuvok arched an eyebrow. "Fascinating."

Seven discarded the stone she'd used to trace the insignia. She employed her tricorder to scan the marked area. "I believe there may be a passageway directly behind the symbol."

Tuvok drew his phaser. "It might be possible to carve an entrance to the passage."

"Not so fast." Janeway winced at the idea. "I'm reluctant to vandalize this site if we don't have to, especially when we have no clear idea of what's on the other side. But that insignia feels like an invitation to me."

Neelix compared the etched symbol to the combadge on his chest. "Maybe Kirk—or somebody else from your end of the galaxy—was just staking his claim on this site?"

"Possibly," Janeway said. "Or maybe it's a test." Her finger traced the outline of the insignia. "Seven, do you still have the old Starfleet response code to that signal?"

"Affirmative," she replied. "It is saved in my tricorder."

Voyager had transmitted the response code earlier, when it had first detected the anachronistic distress signal, but without apparent results. The planetoid had simply continued to transmit the original signal.

But perhaps now that they had located the site . . . ?

"Go ahead," Janeway instructed. "Ring the doorbell."

Seven took her meaning. Calling up the ancient response code and frequency from the tricorder's memory, she transmitted the code directly at the chroniton marker.

At first nothing happened, but then a hidden mechanism could be heard rumbling to life deep within the cliff. The accumulated dust and sediment of unknown years, decades, or centuries was shaken loose from the monument. The away team stepped back cautiously, wary of falling debris.

"I think you woke it up," Neelix said.

Imperfect beings also tended to state the obvious, Seven recalled. "That much is evident."

A slab of stone containing the chroniton marker sank into the ground, exposing a tunnel leading deeper into the cliff. Artificial lights flared to life inside the tunnel, which sloped upward into the monument.

"Open Sesame," Janeway murmured.

Seven's knowledge of human literature was getting a workout on this expedition. "Ali Baba," she acknowledged.

"Minus the forty thieves, I hope." Janeway eyed the beckoning tunnel with obvious excitement and curiosity. "I don't know about you, but I'm dying to find out what's at the other end of that tunnel."

"I recommend caution," Tuvok advised. "We do not know what risks that might entail."

"'Risk is our business,'" Janeway replied. "That's what Captain Kirk always said." She smiled confidently. "I think we know what Kirk would do in these circumstances."

"Kirk was famously reckless," Tuvok reminded her. "I am not entirely certain that his is an example we should wish to emulate." He regarded the open mouth of the tunnel warily. "At the very least, we should notify *Voyager* before proceeding further."

"Agreed," Janeway said. "Inform Commander Chakotay of our present location and intentions."

"Aye, Captain."

While Tuvok updated *Voyager* on the status of the mission, the rest of the away team inspected the mouth of the tunnel, which formed an isosceles trapezoid approximately two meters in height. Although the area just beyond the entrance was illuminated, the end of the tunnel remained cloaked in darkness.

"What do you think is up there, Captain?" Neelix asked.

"Answers, possibly," Janeway said. "Or perhaps simply more questions."

"I would prefer the former," Seven said. She took advantage of the gap in the cliff face to scan the interior of the monument. "I am detecting energy readings ahead, although I cannot identify the precise nature of the technology."

"Any life signs?" Janeway asked.

"Negative."

This did not seem to reassure Neelix, who regarded

the tunnel opening with ill-concealed trepidation. "You know, this whole situation reminds me of one of Mister Paris's favorite *Captain Proton* holo-adventures: 'Chapter Nine: The Curse of the Astro-Mummy's Tomb!'"

He shuddered vigorously.

"Lieutenant Paris's tastes in entertainment often lack sophistication," Seven stated, "and are of little relevance to this mission."

Neelix still looked apprehensive. "So you don't believe there's a curse?"

Talaxians were a superstitious species, Seven recalled, prone to flights of fancy and irrational beliefs. The Borg had always gone to great lengths to eliminate these imperfections from any and all Talaxians they assimilated. Seven could not say that she entirely blamed them.

"Curses are illogical," Tuvok said, before addressing Janeway. "*Voyager* has been informed of our situation, Captain. Do you still wish to proceed?"

"No time like the present," she said. "Let's look inside Kirk's head."

Tuvok insisted on leading the way. He kept his phaser ready, although this struck Seven as a possibly unnecessary precaution. They cautiously made their way up the tunnel, drawn upward by the overhead lights that switched on in sequence ahead of them, meter by meter. The air was stale but breathable, while the temperature inside the tunnels, away from the harsh sun outside, was cooler by several degrees. The lack of animal life on the planet meant that the tunnel was thankfully free of cobwebs and vermin.

Seven observed the décor. The curved gray walls of the tunnel were smooth and unadorned, as though carved out by an industrial phaser drill or an equally industrious Horta, but the sloping floor of the tunnel was decorated with inlaid tiles repeating the same distinctive motif: a disk divided into four intersecting wedges of alternating red and violet hues. The simple design offered little clue as to the monument's origin; Seven did not associate it with any known species or culture. The away team trod upon the disks as they advanced cautiously.

"Watch out for booby traps," Janeway cautioned. "Curse or no curse, whoever built this complex might have wanted to discourage intruders."

Neelix gulped. "Did I ever tell you about the time I went treasure-hunting in the catacombs beneath the Lost Sphinx of Sniilor the Eighth? I didn't find any gem-studded latinum, but I narrowly avoided a bottomless pit filled with flesh-eating marrow-wyrms. . . ."

"Then this must seem like a walk in the park," Janeway said. "Compared to your swashbuckling past."

"I suppose," the Talaxian said, sounding unconvinced. "So far."

Seven suspected that Neelix's tales of past adventures were intended to bolster his courage, but they seemed to be having the opposite effect. She blamed Tom Paris's absurd holo-adventures for filling the Talaxian's head with implausible scenarios and anxieties. Seven preferred her own diversions to be grounded in reality. The universe was hazardous enough without indulging in imaginary nightmares.

An archway at the end of the corridor led to what appeared to be a spacious burial chamber. A marble sarcophagus rested upon a tiered pedestal, which was singled out by an overhead spotlight, in contrast to the shadowy doorways or alcoves adjacent to the sarcophagus. Graceful pillars supported a vaulted ceiling. Seven noted that the tiled floor expanded on the motif from the corridor outside, with the circular floor divided into four interlocking wedges. It occurred to her that red and violet marked the ends of the visible spectrum for humanoid species, but she was uncertain if that was significant. Her own ocular implant extended her vision along a wider range.

"I knew it!" Neelix said unhappily. "I knew this was a tomb!"

"But whose?" Janeway asked. Her eyes searched the chamber, which was dimly lit aside from the sarcophagus and bier. "I don't see any inscriptions, in English or otherwise."

"Nor do I," Tuvok confirmed.

Seven scanned the sarcophagus with the tricorder. "I am detecting skeletal remains within the burial container—in an advanced state of deterioration."

"Human?" Janeway asked.

"Humanoid." Seven analyzed the readings. "The data is inconclusive."

"Naturally," Janeway said wryly. "What about that signal? Is it coming from the tomb?"

Seven switched to another display screen. "Negative. The energy readings are coming from farther within this complex." She nodded at the darkened doorways. "Possibly from an adjacent chamber."

For the moment, Janeway appeared more intrigued by the sarcophagus itself. She approached the bier cautiously. "I wonder . . . Could this actually be the final resting place of James T. Kirk himself?"

"Perhaps a closer inspection of the remains would resolve the matter," Seven suggested. "If necessary, we can exhume them and subject them to a full forensic examination aboard the ship."

"I don't know, Captain," Neelix protested. "Desecrating a tomb? That doesn't sit right with me. It sounds like sacrilege."

"You raise a valid point, Mister Neelix," Janeway said. "It's an old and thorny debate. When does archaeology—and the quest for knowledge—outweigh the right of the honored dead to rest in peace?"

"I fail to see the dilemma," Seven said. "The dead are past caring what happens to their remains. Their 'rights' are irrelevant."

"It's an issue of respect," Janeway attempted to explain. "To the deceased's posterity and culture, if nothing else. People tend to get touchy when their ancestors' bones are disturbed."

"That would not appear to be a factor here," Tuvok observed. "There is no indigenous culture at hand and every indication that this tomb has been long forgotten." He lowered his phaser. "It is uncertain who would take offense if we exhumed the remains."

Seven appreciated his logic. Her understanding was that Vulcan funeral practices placed greater emphasis on preserving the memories and knowledge of the deceased—what they termed the *katra*—than venerating the physical remains. This struck her as eminently sensible. The Borg attached no significance to the bodies of terminated drones, aside from recycling any salvageable components. It was the accumulated knowledge of the Collective that mattered, not lifeless organic matter.

"You told me once that a proper appreciation of history was essential to my development as an individual," she reminded Janeway, appealing to the captain's intellectual curiosity. "If this could indeed be the tomb of James Kirk, do we not owe it to history to determine his ultimate fate?"

"A persuasive argument," Janeway said. "I admit I can't help wondering if that signal was always intended to call us here, so that Starfleet could finally track down one of its own."

Seven suspected that, despite Janeway's ethical concerns, the captain was predisposed toward opening the tomb and simply looking for sufficient reason to do so. Janeway had been a science officer before she became a captain after all; her curiosity came close to rivaling her conscience. Seven hoped that science would win out over sentimentality.

"Let's poke around a bit more," Janeway suggested. "Perhaps we can find more evidence to help us decide, one way or another."

A reasonable course of action, Seven decided. Accumulating more data was always advisable. The tomb had gone undisturbed for a significant, if indeterminate, interval already. A brief delay would not affect the outcome of the investigation, and it might yield valuable results.

"Yes, Captain!" Neelix was visibly eager to exit the burial chamber. Giving the sarcophagus a wide berth, he hurried into one of the side corridors. Something dry and brittle crunched beneath his feet, even as the lights came on in the corridor to reveal the skeletal remains of a dead humanoid. Startled, Neelix let out an inarticulate yelp and stumbled backward in alarm. He tripped over a desiccated femur that had gone unnoticed in the dim lighting before. Losing his balance, he fell backward and slammed into the sarcophagus. His flailing body smacked against the bier with considerable force.

The results were immediate—and devastating.

A blinding white flash temporarily overloaded Seven's optical implants. She experienced a sense of disorientation and extreme discomfort. Her pulse and respiration ceased for what felt like a subjective eternity, only to abruptly resume. Her eyes rolled, exposing only the whites, and her legs lost their ability to support her. She collapsed onto the floor. Her last thought, before slipping into unconsciousness, was to reflect that perhaps Neelix's apprehensions had not been so irrelevant after all.

Was this what a "curse" felt like?

Seven stirred upon the floor of the burial chamber. Her eyes opened and she staggered to her feet. Nausea and lightheadedness threatened her balance, but the moment passed and she regained her equilibrium. Memories of Neelix's accidental collision with the sarcophagus, and the ensuing energy burst, rushed back to her. Her chronometric node informed her that only a few minutes had passed since the pulse. She stretched her limbs, reassured to find them in working order. She looked around urgently.

"Captain? Tuvok?"

She spotted the rest of the away team sprawled upon the floor. At first she feared that they had been killed, but then she spied evidence of respiration. She rushed to

Janeway's side and attempted unsuccessfully to revive the captain, who was pale and breathing shallowly. Radiation burns scarred Janeway's face and hands. Her pulse was weak and unsteady. She clearly required medical attention, as did Neelix and Tuvok.

"Seven of Nine to *Voyager*!" she hailed the ship. "We have a medical emergency. Request immediate beam-out."

Static greeted her hail.

"Seven to *Voyager*! Please acknowledge!"

Her hand came away from her combadge. The lack of response clearly indicated that her transmission was being blocked, perhaps by the dense stone walls of the monument. She glanced back the way they'd come. She hesitated, reluctant to leave her injured companions behind, but saw no other alternative. The sooner she could contact *Voyager*, the sooner Janeway and the others could receive the care they so urgently required.

"I'll be back," she said irrationally, knowing they were incapable of hearing her in the present condition. She felt compelled to do so anyway. "As soon as I summon assistance."

She dashed for the archway, only to bounce off a newly erected force field. Brilliant blue energy discharges marked her points of collision with the invisible field, which she assumed had also been triggered when Neelix forcefully came into contact with the sarcophagus. They had obviously run afoul of some automatic security mechanism. A booby trap, as the captain had put it.

Then why lure us in with a distress signal? she wondered, experiencing a flash of all-too-human anger at the tomb's unknown designers. *What purpose is there in drawing random travelers into danger?*

She cautiously tested the field with her hand and found it unyielding. Exerting any further pressure on the barrier would obviously be a waste of valuable time, so she turned back toward her unconscious comrades. She lacked the expertise of *Voyager*'s Emergency Medical Hologram, but her own first-aid skills would have to suffice until she found a way to deactivate the force field and restore contact with the ship. She suspected that it was the field that was blocking her emergency transmissions.

Her tricorder rested on the floor where she had fallen before. Retrieving it, she was dismayed to discover that the instrument had been damaged by the energy burst. She put the tricorder aside and examined Janeway directly, hoping to determine the extent of the captain's injuries. To her surprise, she found the symptoms consistent with the effects of a dangerous chroniton pulse, leading her to fear that temporal distortions at a cellular level had caused significant damage. Her ocular implant registered the distinctive aura of chroniton poisoning radiating from Janeway's body.

The diagnosis made sense—and explained why Seven was still standing. Her Borg physiology offered greater protection from chroniton pulses, while the nanoprobes in her cells and bloodstream were already repairing whatever damage she had suffered from the pulse. It was fortunate, Seven realized, that she had accompanied the away team on this mission, but that would do the captain and the others little good unless she managed to get them to sickbay in a timely fashion. Although Neelix had been equipped with a standard Starfleet medkit, this was insufficient to deal with injuries of this severity. The best she could do was stabilize them for a short period of time.

That was not acceptable.

Deactivating the force field became her top priority, which meant locating a control room or generator. She recalled detecting energy readings from an adjacent chamber, so she hurried toward it. This necessitated stepping over the skeletal remains that had so startled Neelix.

She spared a moment to inspect the remains. A distinctive skeleton, along with surviving fragments of clothing and other artifacts, identified the dead alien as an adult male of Species 8532, a spiny space-faring race once known as the Taaf. The Borg had assimilated the Taaf generations ago, but Taaf merchants and scavengers had traveled widely prior to their contact with the Borg. A quick scan of the bones revealed lingering traces of chroniton radiation. She deduced that the dead Taaf had fallen victim to the same booby trap that had waylaid the away team, which must have reset itself at some point afterward. She briefly wondered how the unlucky Taaf had made his way past the hidden doorway, but she decided that was irrelevant to her present concerns. For all she knew, he had simply risked beaming into the complex. Similarly, the absence of a Taaf vessel on the surface could be explained any number of ways, the most likely of which was that he had been abandoned by his comrades after being trapped in the tomb.

Seven doubted that *Voyager* would readily do the same.

Leaving the alien bones behind, Seven entered an antechamber that was notably smaller and less imposing than the burial chamber outside. Conduits and power grids of unfamiliar design, thrumming with azure energy, lined the walls of the chamber, while less-familiar apparatuses resisted easy interpretation. A string of linked generators, horizontally mounted to the floor, churned like turbines while occupying the center of the room. Each generator was twice the size of a photon torpedo and was equipped with automated backup systems and monitors. Heavy shielding insulated the power cores of the generators. The amount of visible redundancy in the equipment suggested to Seven that the system had been designed to function indefinitely without need of maintenance or organic operators. It was entirely automated and built to last.

Seven was encouraged by the technology on display, which suggested that she had found the complex's engineering center. She looked about for a control station and spied a glowing terminal located in a cylindrical booth roughly the size of her regeneration alcove back on *Voyager*. The control panel and monitor were installed at the back of the booth, while the floor of the booth featured the same divided disk motif she had observed before. Translucent red and violet wedges comprised the disk, which was about half the size of a standard transporter pad. The touch-activated interface on the control panel was unknown to her, but she had confidence in her ability to decipher it. The only question was whether she would be able to do so in time to save the rest of the away team. Her phaser, which remained affixed to her hip, was of little use in this instance.

The possibility of another booby trap gave her pause, but the urgency of the situation spurred her on. Janeway groaned pitifully in the burial chamber, and Seven quickened her step. Eschewing caution, she stepped into the control booth. The disk beneath her feet lit up abruptly.

All at once, a stardate flashed onto the monitor before her:

6122.5.

A second later, Seven was somewhere else.

Five

"And so I found myself on the planet designated Yusub, just in time to intervene in your conflict with the Orions."

The mysterious woman who called herself Annika Seven seemed quite at home in the briefing room of a Federation starship. The meeting aboard the *Enterprise,* which was still in orbit around Yusub, was closed to all but Kirk, Spock, McCoy, Scotty, and, at his insistence, Commissioner Santiago. Seven had argued, for reasons of temporal security, that the true nature of her arrival on Yusub be kept on a strictly need-to-know basis and that no record of this interview would be maintained. This struck Kirk as a reasonable precaution, assuming she was telling the truth.

"So you're a castaway from the future, who needs to be returned to her own time in order to avoid changing history?" He eyed the stranger skeptically, searching for the truth behind her composed, elegant features. He had changed into his standard duty uniform following their return from the planet. "Why do I feel like there's a lot more to this story than you're telling us?"

"Because that is precisely the case," she stated unapologetically. "I have deliberately edited my account to avoid revealing more of the future than absolutely necessary . . . as I expect you would do under similar circumstances."

"Would and have," Kirk admitted. He'd been stranded in the past himself on occasion. Painful memories from the Great Depression brought a pang to his heart; he shoved them out of his thoughts. "More than once, in fact."

"Then you understand the delicacy of my situation," she said, "and the urgency to return me to my proper coordinates in time and space."

Kirk considered their lovely guest, whose cool self-possession seemed almost Vulcan. According to her abbreviated account, she'd been exploring some vaguely described alien ruins at an unspecified time and place in the future when she had accidentally triggered an abandoned time machine of some sort, which had transported her across time and space to Yusub in the twenty-third century. His gut told him that she was being honest with him, as much as she could, but he still had plenty of questions.

"If you're so worried about changing the future," he asked, "why did you save my life down on the planet?"

"The *Enterprise* requires James T. Kirk, at least for the present. Put simply, it was not your time."

He refrained from asking her when exactly his time was. Frankly, he didn't want to know.

"I want to believe you," he said, "but I need to be sure." He glanced at Spock, who was sitting across from him. "Perhaps a mind-meld to verify her story?"

"That would not be advisable, Captain," she protested. "There is too great a risk of Commander Spock learning more than he should about future events and technology." She viewed Spock with a certain detached caution. The Yusubi idol, which she had refused to part with, rested on the table before her. "You may trust me on this, Captain. I have some experience of Vulcans and their gifts."

"She is quite correct," Spock stated. "A meld is not a surgical instrument. It is a profound union of minds that, by its very nature, transcends individual boundaries. There is no guarantee that I would extract only the relevant information . . . and nothing more."

"Would that be so bad?" Santiago asked. The diplomat had also changed into a fresh suit following their close call down on the planet, but he was obviously still on edge. His fingers drummed restlessly on the tabletop. "Advance warning of future crises and disasters could save countless lives in years to come."

Kirk could see how that could be tempting, especially to a man like Santiago, who had spent his entire career trying to bring peace and security to many worlds and civilizations. He hadn't witnessed firsthand the havoc time travel could wreak on reality.

"That would be a violation of the Temporal Prime Directive," Seven stated emphatically. "The consequences could be severe."

Santiago was unconvinced. "But the potential rewards . . ."

"That's a debate we can have in due time," Kirk interrupted, not wanting to get sidetracked into a discussion of alternate histories and temporal paradoxes. "Right now I'm more interested in verifying that our guest is indeed from the future. No offense, miss."

"None taken," she replied. "Your caution is prudent."

McCoy spoke up. "What about testing her story against an automated accuracy scan?" He attempted to explain his proposal to Seven. "We can program a computer to monitor your brainwaves, as well as other physiological signs, to determine whether you're telling the truth or not."

"I am familiar with the procedure," she said. "It is primitive and imperfect, but non-invasive." So far, she had not allowed McCoy to examine her, insisting that she had come through the firefight on the planet un-scathed. The prosthetics on her face and hands remained unexplained. "I will permit it . . . in the interest of gain-ing your trust."

"That's big of you," McCoy drawled, bemused by Seven's attitude. He looked her over. "So, no relation to Gary, I take it?"

"Who?" she asked.

"Never mind." McCoy let out an exasperated sigh. "Ordinarily, I'd have a medical technician assist me, but under the circumstances, I suppose Scotty and I will manage."

"Aye," Chief Engineer Montgomery Scott declared. A pronounced accent matched his surname. "Ye can count on me, although I confess I have no love for the infernal device."

Kirk couldn't blame him. The same procedure had been employed to cross-examine Scotty when he was accused of murdering those women on Argelius II. Al-though the engineer had ultimately been cleared of all wrongdoing, the whole experience was no doubt one that Scotty would prefer to forget.

"I appreciate that," Kirk said. "The fewer people who know about this, the better."

"Hell, I wish I didn't know about it," McCoy

grumbled. "Time travel's never been anything but trouble as far as I'm concerned."

Tell me about it, Kirk thought ruefully.

Seven observed McCoy with what appeared to be amusement. "Are all Starfleet physicians so opinionated? I had not realized until now that this was such a defining characteristic of the profession."

"What exactly do you mean by that?" McCoy asked.

"Nothing," she said. "Merely an observation."

"I'll have you know my bedside manner is impeccable," the doctor muttered. "All of my surviving patients say so."

Several minutes were required to set up the apparatus needed for the interview. Scotty installed a witness seat equipped with verification hardware, while Spock assisted McCoy in programming the computer to monitor Seven's physiological responses. She allowed a superficial scan of her person in order to establish a baseline for the computer. McCoy's eyes widened at the readings, and he frowned as he gave her a long second look. Something about the scan seemed to have given him cause for concern, but he kept any new worries to himself . . . at least for the time being.

"All right," Kirk said, after the preparations were complete. "Please take the stand."

"As you wish." She sat down in the chair. A sensor pad was located in an armrest. She placed her palm down on the pad without prompting. "You may proceed with the interview."

Kirk appreciated her cooperation. "Just to make sure the verifier is calibrated properly, please state an untruth."

"I was born in this century," she said without hesitation.

"*Inaccurate,*" the computer declared. The sensor pad flashed beneath her palm while indicator lights blinked on the box-sized computer terminal in front of McCoy, who carefully monitored the readouts as well.

"Looks like she's fibbing to me," the doctor said. "As nearly as I can tell given our 'primitive' technology, that is."

Kirk understood that the verifier was not one-hundred percent reliable, especially when dealing with an unknown entity like Seven, but it was better than nothing. A psychotricorder, which might be able to download Seven's memories of the last twenty-four hours, was not an option for the same reason the mind-meld wasn't. They had to confirm her story—without learning too much about her past in the future.

"Now state something true," he instructed.

"I do not belong here."

"*Accurate account,*" the computer verified. "*No physiological changes.*"

The verifier seemed to be working properly, so Kirk got down to business. "Is the account you just offered, of how you were transported into the past by a chance encounter with an alien time-travel device, what actually happened?"

"Will happen," Seven corrected him. "But, yes, that is correct."

"*Accurate,*" the computer declared. "*No physiological changes.*"

"And do you have any agenda beyond returning to your own time?" Kirk asked.

She weighed her words. "There is a situation in the future that urgently requires my attention, should I be able to return to precisely when and where I left, but I have no desire to change history or achieve any other objective in this era."

"*Accurate.*"

"So far, so good," Kirk said. He was reluctant to press her beyond yes-or-no questions for fear of eliciting revelations dangerous to the time line. He phrased his next query carefully. "And is there anything we should know that you're not telling us?"

She answered just as cautiously. "Not to my knowledge."

"*Accurate.*"

Kirk was grateful for the computer's watchfulness. Seven's aloof, confident manner made her difficult to read. He wouldn't want to play poker against her.

"What about the Orions?" Santiago interrupted. "Or the Klingons or Romulans? Do you know of any major attacks or historical tragedies in our future?"

"Naturally," Seven said. "But those events are part of history from my perspective. They have already occurred."

"*Accurate.*"

"How can you be so damnably cold-blooded about it?" Santiago lurched to his feet. The veins in his neck stood out. "We're not talking about abstract metaphysics here. We're talking about actual lives at stake . . . genuine, flesh-and-blood, sentient beings!"

"None of which outweighs the Temporal Prime Directive," Seven insisted.

"*Accurate.*"

"That's enough," Kirk ordered, before things went too far. "I think this interview has gone on long enough. We've learned what we needed to." He nodded at McCoy. "Shut down the verifier."

McCoy flipped a switch on the computer.

"Hold on there, Kirk," Santiago protested. "You can't just brush this issue aside. The potential implications for Federation security, for advances in science and medicine . . ."

"Are not my concern at the moment," Kirk said firmly.

"Maybe they should be," Santiago persisted. "We need to talk about this."

"In due time," Kirk repeated. He wasn't looking forward to that discussion, especially since he had his own mixed feelings on the subject. It wasn't as though he didn't realize how valuable and/or dangerous Seven's knowledge of the future was. She was Nostradamus and Pandora's Box all in one lovely package.

He got back to the matter at hand. "Well, Bones, what's your verdict?"

"Well," McCoy said, reviewing the data from the computer, "I can't be positive, given that our star witness seems to possess some . . . unusual . . . characteristics and enhancements." He regarded Seven with a somewhat troubled expression. "But all indications are that she's telling the truth."

Kirk wondered what about Seven's "enhancements" had spooked McCoy. He made a mental note to have the doctor scrub his recordings of Seven's baseline physiology just to be safe. Any future changes to humanity were not something that needed to be made public knowledge. Kirk wasn't sure he wanted to know about them himself.

"All right, Miss Seven," Kirk said. "You may step down. The computer and the good doctor both vouch for your honesty, so I'm inclined to give you the benefit of the doubt."

"Thank you, Captain." She returned to her original seat, by the idol she had brought back from Yusub. "And you may dispense with the honorific. 'Seven' will suffice."

Kirk gave her a winning smile. "Perhaps you'll allow me to call you Annika?"

"I prefer Seven," she replied coolly. "If that is acceptable."

McCoy chuckled in the background. It wasn't often that Kirk met a woman who was immune to his charm.

I'm glad you're amused, Doctor, Kirk thought.

"No problem. Seven it is, then." He took her rebuff in stride. "So how exactly do you propose that we get you back to your own time? I have to say I'm not keen on attempting to take the *Enterprise* on a voyage to the future . . . if that's even possible."

Jaunts to the past were tricky enough, Kirk knew. A trip to the future opened up a completely different can of worms—and possibly an even bigger one. Granted, there was always the Guardian of Forever, but Kirk wasn't about to reveal its existence to an enigmatic stranger or even Commissioner Santiago. As Kirk knew all too well, the Guardian was arguably more dangerous than Seven could ever be.

"I'll say," McCoy said. "Talk about the cure being worse than the disease."

Spock added his observation. "For once, I must agree

with the doctor. The future is an undiscovered country, and it should probably remain so."

"You are quite right, gentlemen," Seven said. "And there other considerations, which I am not at liberty to discuss, that render the *Enterprise* unsuitable for our purposes."

It dawned on Kirk that she had avoided mentioning where in the galaxy she had encountered the ancient mechanism that had sent her here. It was possible, he realized, that it was in a distant region of space as yet unexplored by Starfleet, perhaps even beyond the *Enterprise*'s reach.

"What's the alternative?" he asked.

"I have some ideas on that matter." She called their attention to the idol she had retrieved on Yusub. "Shortly upon my arrival on the planet below, I detected a distinctive chronal signature emanating from this artifact." She turned toward McCoy and held out her palm. "If I may trouble you for a laser scalpel, Doctor."

She had willingly surrendered her phaser upon boarding the *Enterprise*. It was currently locked away in the safe in Kirk's personal quarters. McCoy fished a scalpel from his ubiquitous medical kit and handed it to Seven.

"You planning to perform surgery on that idol?" he asked.

"Precisely."

Kirk and the other men leaned forward to get a better look as Seven expertly sliced through the glazed ceramic exterior of the idol to expose an object concealed within. The object was a translucent violet wedge, like a one-quarter slice of a larger disk, made of solid crystal. Kirk remembered how light the idol had felt before. He had to assume that the hidden item did not weigh very much.

"What the devil?" McCoy asked aloud.

Seven presented the wedge for the group's inspection. "This appears to be a fragment of the device that transported me across time and space to Yusub. I suspect that it has been hidden in the past . . . for reasons that remain obscure."

"Fascinating," Spock said, producing his tricorder. "Allow me."

He scanned the object, while Kirk waited impatiently for his report. Santiago, who had grudgingly returned to his seat, eyed the procedure intently. His fingers started drumming on the table again. It seemed to be a nervous habit.

"Well, Spock?" Kirk asked.

"I am indeed detecting unusual energies within this object," Spock said. "The nature of these energies, as well as the technology generating them, are unknown to me, and certainly not native to Yusub."

Kirk took his word for it. If Spock didn't recognize the technology, then it was undoubtedly unknown to Federation science, at least in this century. Kirk regarded the object warily.

"So where is the rest of the device?" he asked.

"That is what I propose we discover," Seven said. "Clues planted in my time and yours led us to this fragment. If I can find the remaining three components, I may be able to reassemble the device . . . and reverse the process that brought me here."

McCoy scoffed. "So what are we talking about? Some sort of interplanetary, cross-temporal scavenger hunt?"

"That's one way to look at it," Kirk conceded. Part of him was intrigued by the prospect, while another part balked at the idea of his ship being diverted onto a quest laid out by unknown parties from who knew where or when. He didn't like being manipulated—by Seven or anyone else. "What makes you think the *Enterprise* has nothing better to do than set off on what could be a wild goose chase?"

"I believe it is in both our interests," Seven said, "to work together on this endeavor. I have need of a starship to seek out the three remaining fragments, while you can surely see the necessity of protecting the time line by removing me from this era . . . and preventing my knowledge of the future from falling into careless hands."

She glanced pointedly at Santiago, who glared back at her. He huffed and crossed his arms across his chest. He was reputed to be a tough negotiator; Kirk didn't expect him to cave easily.

"But why the *Enterprise*? Why my crew?" Once again, Kirk felt certain that Seven wasn't telling him everything, albeit for good reason. "How do we fit into this treasure hunt of yours?"

"Let us just say that I have reason to believe that you and your ship have an important part to play in rectifying this situation."

"And that's all you're going to say about it?" McCoy challenged her.

"That is all I *can* say, safely." She addressed Kirk forcefully. "I assure you, Captain, that I do not make this request lightly. Trust me when I say that lives are at stake in my own time . . . and may be lost if I cannot get back to where I belong."

"But those lives belong to people who haven't even been born yet," Santiago said sarcastically, turning her own earlier argument against her. "And whatever future crisis you're worrying about might never happen. It's just a hypothetical possibility . . . from our perspective, that is."

Touché, Kirk thought. He could see how Santiago had earned his rep as a canny diplomat. The man could obviously hold his own in a debate.

"At the moment, I'm more concerned with the present," Kirk said, "and the effect a misplaced time traveler could have on it."

Santiago didn't back down. "Need I remind you, Captain Kirk, that you already have a mission?"

"Believe me, Commissioner, I haven't forgotten that slaughter down on the planet, but I have to wonder whether your mission is still salvageable after what happened at the conclave."

"Maybe not," Santiago admitted. The memory of the bloodshed took some of the wind out of his sails. He sighed ruefully. "I've already been in touch with some of the surviving chieftains, and I'm afraid that our negotiations went up in flames with that camp. It could take months, or even years, to bring all concerned back to the table again. . . ."

"In which case," Spock observed, "there is little to be lost by turning our attention to Seven's dilemma, which may pose an even more serious threat to reality as we know it."

Kirk couldn't fault Spock's logic—or his priorities. The ongoing problem of Orion piracy in this sector was a serious matter to be sure, but it paled before the potential danger to the time line. He and his crew knew better than most how much damage even a single dis- placed individual could do to the course of history and how much it could cost to restore the time line.

Edith . . .

"Jim," McCoy said, "you're not seriously considering this cockamamie quest?"

Kirk remembered a confused and disoriented doctor jumping through another abandoned time portal—with disastrous results. He made up his mind.

"I don't see where we have much choice, Bones." He looked squarely into Seven's striking pale blue eyes. "Do you really think you can lead us to the other fragments?"

She examined the wedged-shaped component. "If I am correct, and we are following a trail laid out for us in the future or the past, then I am hopeful that another clue can be found. Allow me time to find the key to this puzzle."

"Time is exactly what's at stake," Kirk reminded her. "Get to it."

"Hold on a second," McCoy said. "How are you going to explain this . . . and her . . . to the rest of the crew?"

Good question, Kirk thought. He disliked the idea of leaving his officers in the dark, but he couldn't risk con- taminating the present more than it already had been. He had learned his lesson since giving Captain John Christopher a tour of the *Enterprise* back in the twenti- eth century.

Spock came to the rescue. "Might I suggest, Captain, that the *Enterprise* has been directed to assist 'Doctor Annika Seven,' a distinguished Federation scientist, on an important archaeological mission that has been deemed of value by Starfleet."

"That could work," Kirk said. The *Enterprise*'s overall mission had always been broad enough to accommodate a wide range of objectives, from the diplomatic to the purely scientific. A deep-space archaeological expedition certainly fell under their purview. "A creative solution, Mister Spock."

"And so devious," McCoy added, unable to resist a chance to needle Spock. "Who knew you were so talented at fabrication? What would the folks back on Vulcan think?"

"Perhaps that I have spent too much time associating with humans," Spock replied. "I fear humanity's well-earned skill at mendacity may have rubbed off on me."

"To our advantage in this instance," Kirk said. "Your suggestion strikes me as a plausible cover story for our mission." He ran the idea by their guest. "What do you think, 'Doctor Seven'? Does that work for you?"

A hint of a frown marred her features. "I do not relish the prospect of 'flying under false colors,' as the saying goes, but I recognize the necessity of avoiding undue attention to our true objective." Her hand, with its odd cybernetic webbing, indicated the eye-catching metallic implants on her face. "Do you believe that your crew will accept me in this role? I do not entirely blend in with humans of your era."

"That's for sure," McCoy said.

Once again, Spock had the answer.

"Your unique prosthetics bear a superficial resemblance to the traditional cosmetic body art of the Phiema, a rather obscure culture in the Asogola system.

The Phiema are rarely encountered outside their remote homeworld, so few people will see through your story if you claim to have been raised among them as a child."

"I've got to admit, I've never heard of them," McCoy said.

"This does not surprise me, Doctor."

Seven ignored their banter. "That seems a workable alias. I can adapt."

"Then it's settled," Kirk said. Welcome to the *Enterprise,* Doctor Seven." He took it for granted that "Annika Seven" was not her real name. "I'll see to it that you're assigned guest quarters on the ship and perhaps a change of wardrobe." He rose from his seat and swept a stern gaze over all present, including Santiago. The commissioner maintained a brooding silence, clearly biding his time. "None of this leaves this room. Are all clear on that?"

"Clear as dilithium," Santiago said. "But don't think you can put off our talk much longer."

"I look forward to it," Kirk lied. "In the meantime, let's go find a time machine."

Six

"This is unconscionable!" Santiago ranted. He paced back and forth in his VIP stateroom aboard the *Enterprise*, getting more worked up by the moment. "Kirk is completely missing the big picture here!"

"So it appears," his aide agreed.

Cyril Hague, administrative assistant, second grade, was seated at a desk in the stateroom's work area. Microtapes containing the latest briefings and reports on Yusub and other diplomatic issues throughout the Federation were stacked neatly in front of the library computer terminal that was provided to the *Enterprise*'s high-ranking passengers. The stateroom was noticeably larger than the private guest quarters Hague had been assigned elsewhere on Deck D, but Hague didn't mind. At the moment, he was exactly where he wanted to be.

"Do you realize what an opportunity this is?" Santiago continued. "The knowledge in that young woman's head could leapfrog our technology generations ahead of the Klingons, the Romulans . . ."

"And the Orions, sir?"

"Don't get me started on the damned Orions!" Santiago raged. "Butchers and barbarians, that's what they are." His voice grew hoarse with emotion. "When I think about what they did to Denise and my beautiful nieces . . ."

"Please, sir. You can't keep dwelling on that."

"I know, I know." Santiago took a deep breath, reining in his emotions. "But this isn't just about protecting the Federation from the Orions and other hostiles. We could be talking about life-changing breakthroughs in science, medicine, even exploration. That woman is a strategic asset of unparalleled importance . . . and Kirk just wants to help her get home!"

Hague made a note on a data slate. "The captain's weakness for the fairer sex is well known. Perhaps he's simply being chivalrous."

"Chivalry be damned!" Santiago swore. "He's talking about throwing away a Rosetta stone to tomorrow . . . to protect a future that hasn't even happened yet. Hell, for all we know, this 'Annika Seven' has *already* changed history irreparably. The genie is out of the bottle, so we might as well get some miracles out of her."

Hague chuckled at the simile. "Nicely put, sir."

"If only I can get Kirk to understand," Santiago said. "Even if we *have* to return her to her own era eventually, for the sake of the time line, we ought to learn what we can from her while we have the chance." He stared out a port at the starry void outside the saucer. The *Enterprise* was warping away from the Yusub system with no clear destination as of yet. "The universe is a dangerous place, Cyril. Who knows what terrible menaces are waiting for us out there . . . or may already be heading our way?"

Hague egged him on, quite deliberately. "One shudders to think, sir."

"I do shudder, Cyril, because I fear for the safety of the Federation we both serve." He pounded his fist into his palm. "That woman has to warn us what's coming. She has to!"

"Please, sir! You're becoming overwrought." Hague rose from his desk. "You need to rest."

"Always looking out for me, aren't you?" Santiago cast a weary smile at his aide. "Don't think I don't appreciate it, Cyril. I don't know what I'd do without you." His shoulders slumped in exhaustion. "These last few years . . ."

"It's an honor, sir. I mean that."

"Thank you," the commissioner said. "For the record, by the way, you don't know about any of this. Kirk practically swore us all to secrecy."

For what little good that did, Hague thought. "My lips are sealed."

"Good," Santiago said. "I know I can count on your discretion . . . and loyalty."

"Always," Hague lied. "Now then, you really should try to get some rest." He crossed the stateroom to the food processor unit in the foyer. "Let me fix you your favorite nightcap."

He inserted a menu card into the appropriate slot. Seconds later, a dark burgundy beverage appeared in the dispenser bin. Hague took the drink, which came in an old-fashioned martini glass, and handed it to Santiago.

"One Centauri Stinger," the aide said. "To help you sleep."

Santiago accepted the drink gratefully. Hague knew the commissioner had developed a taste for the potent cocktail while serving as a cultural attaché on Rigel years ago. It was his only vice, aside from trusting the wrong people.

"Just what the doctor ordered." Santiago downed the drink in one gulp. He handed the empty glass back to Hague. "Have I ever mentioned that the Federation doesn't pay you enough?"

"Frequently, sir."

Hague glanced at the bottom of the glass. There was no residue of the powerful soporific he had discreetly added to the commissioner's cocktail. Granted, fatigue and the Stinger would have probably been enough to put Santiago out for the night, but why take chances? Hague had important business to get to—and he didn't want to be interrupted.

He steered Santiago toward the adjacent sleeping area. The commissioner yawned as the drug began to take effect. "You should turn in, too," Santiago said sleepily. "Head back to your quarters and get some rest."

"Soon," Hague promised. "If you don't mind, I'd like stay a bit longer and finish up some reports. You know how the bureaucracy is. There's no end to the paperwork . . ."

"Don't work too hard," Santiago said, already nodding off. Another yawn threatened to swallow his instructions. "That's an order."

"Understood."

A retractable partition separated the bedroom from the work area. Hague waited until he was sure Santiago was out cold before drawing shut the partition and sneaking over to the personal communication station at the opposite end of the work area. He sat down at the station and keyed in Santiago's classified prefix code, which the gullible commissioner had long ago trusted him with. He then established a secure link along a certain frequency. Full diplomatic protocols and encryption would ensure that this transmission remained confidential. Not even Santiago would know about it.

"Contacting *Navaar*," he whispered. "Top priority. Please respond."

The cloaked ship was not far away. Within moments, a woman's face appeared on the station's video screen. Lustrous purple hair tumbled past her bare green shoulders, which were the color of Vulcan blood. Shrewd jade eyes matched her elfin features. Plump emerald lips looked as inviting as ripe avocadoes. A scar on her cheek was a souvenir of battle.

"*What is it?*" K'Mara asked. The Orion woman did not waste time on pleasantries. "*Why have you broken silence?*"

"I have news," Hague said. "Valuable news."

K'Mara looked intrigued, but also concerned. "*This transmission is secure?*"

"As an old-fashioned diplomatic pouch," Hague assured her. He had used the same ruse to alert her Orion compatriots to the top-secret location of the conclave on Yusub. "We can talk freely."

She nodded. "*Speak.*"

"It's about the future," he began.

K'Mara stalked through the corridors of the *Navaar*, a knife on one hip and a disruptor pistol on the other. Her boots smacked briskly against the deck of the *Marauder*-class vessel. Sturdy black trousers and a matching halter top displayed less flesh than the typical Orion female, who flaunted her body to wield power over helpless males, but K'Mara had never been typical. Born without the higher level of pheromones her sisters used to enslave men, she had overcome this supposed handicap to become second-in-command of the *Navaar*. She had no regrets. Truth to tell, she preferred the life (and attire) of a pirate.

Electrum bangles graced her ears, neck, and wrists. A ruby stud in her navel matched the one at the end of her tongue. Her lithe form still drew appreciative leers from her crewmates, but she ignored their attentions. She had more important matters on her mind. Reaching the door to the captain's private chambers, she leaned on the buzzer.

"It's me!" she shouted through door. "You need to hear this."

"Enter," a gruff voice responded.

The captain's luxurious chambers were decked out with the spoils of previous raids. Rich tapestries, pillaged from dozens of unlucky ships and worlds, were draped over the bulkheads. A priceless Gabronese rug carpeted the deck. A plucked lizard-hawk roasted on a spit above a brazier of red-hot coals. The mouthwatering aroma almost distracted K'Mara from her mission.

Almost.

"Well?" Habroz demanded. "What couldn't wait for me to finish my dinner?"

The hulking pirate captain rose from his couch. Metal spikes jutted up from beneath his shaved green scalp, so that his bumpy cranium resembled the head of a mace. A black leather vest and trousers, similar to K'Mara's own attire, exposed his muscular chest, which was liberally adorned with ritualistic scarring. A latinum earring dangled from his one remaining ear; he had lost the other one in a raid on a Tholian mining colony.

Yellow teeth were filed to a point beneath a drooping black mustache. A disruptor pistol was thrust into his belt, balanced out by a serrated hatchet on his other hip. Heavy boots left deep impressions in the carpet. His prosthetic right hand glinted metallically. Servomotors hummed as he cracked his knuckles.

"I've received word from our sleeper agent aboard the *Enterprise*," K'Mara said. "He thought it worth breaking silence to inform us."

The Orion Syndicate had planted Hague in the Federation's diplomatic corps some time ago. Over the years, he had leaked much useful intel but never anything on the scale of what he had just divulged.

Habroz scowled. "Don't tell me those Federation meddlers still hope to turn the Yusubi against us? I thought we had put that ridiculous notion to the torch already."

K'Mara shook her head. "This is bigger than any of that. Remember that human female who showed up out of nowhere to interfere with our assault?"

"The tall female with the golden hair and impressive figure?" He nodded at the memory; the troublesome intruder had obviously made an impression on him. "What of her? I assumed she was another do-gooder from the *Enterprise*."

"Hardly," K'Mara said. "Turns out she's from the future."

Habroz's jaw dropped. It wasn't often the ruthless pirate was caught unawares, so K'Mara savored the moment while she could. She quickly filled him in on Hague's startling news, the implications of which were not lost on her. Whole new galaxies of profit were suddenly within reach.

"You realize what this means?" she asked.

"Easy credits," he grunted. "The Klingons will pay well for this intelligence."

She was appalled by his shortsightedness. *Typical male stupidity.*

"Forget mere intel," she said, leading him along. "Think of how much they would pay for this 'Annika Seven' herself. Imagine all the secrets locked up in that pretty blond head of hers." K'Mara's own imagination was racing at warp speed. "That human female is the most valuable prize in the quadrant!"

Understanding dawned in his bloodshot green eyes. "You think we should capture her."

Took you long enough, K'Mara thought impatiently. She often considered seizing command of the *Navaar* herself, but she was uncertain whether the crew would accept her as a captain. She was already defying Orion tradition by assuming the role of raider instead of seductress; she didn't want to carry this tricky dance too far, too fast. It was one thing for an Orion male to fight and die in the service of a beloved mistress. It was another thing altogether for the males to see a clothed female in the captain's chair. Better to let Habroz issue the orders . . . for now.

"The fates have dropped this bounty in our laps," she declared. "We would be fools not to seize it."

Habroz nodded. "Let it not be said that the captain of the *Navaar* is a fool."

"Never!" she said, flattering his ego. "Not while I live." She smiled in anticipation of the rich profits ahead.

Capturing Seven had just become their top priority.

Seven

"You have something for us, Seven?" Kirk asked.

"Yes, Captain," she replied.

All those knowledgeable of her true circumstances had reconvened in the briefing room, which was notably more primitive and utilitarian than the comparable facilities back on *Voyager*. Seven deemed the setting sufficient, however. Sealed doors and sturdy bulkheads guaranteed their privacy.

To better blend in aboard the *Enterprise*, she had donned twenty-third-century civilian garb over her usual dermaplastic attire. A pressed blue suit, tailored to her measurements, seemed appropriate to her role as a visiting scientist. Her *Voyager* combadge was discreetly concealed beneath the lapel of her jacket. She had felt oddly naked without it.

"I don't suppose you've reconsidered sharing some of your unique insights into the future," Commissioner Santiago said. "For the sake of the people of this era?"

By virtue of his rank, Santiago had claimed a place in this conference, but Seven privately wished that he could have been excluded. His persistent demands and confrontational tone were troubling, as were the thorny ethical questions they provoked. She exerted effort to conceal her discomfort.

"My position is unchanged, Commissioner."

Declining to take his seat at the table, he strode across the room to confront her. Probing eyes scrutinized her, as though attempting to peer past her veil of secrecy. Seven was grateful that most humans lacked telepathic gifts.

"You know something," he accused her. "I can tell. You're hiding something that we ought to know."

Seven winced internally. Guilt surged through her system like an EPS overload. Despite her apparent confidence in her convictions, she was acutely conscious of the date. By Terran reckoning, it was 2270. In less than a century, Starfleet would have its first recorded encounter with the Borg, leading to years of hard-fought battles and attempted invasions. Seven would be part of the Collective by then, taking part in the unwilling assimilation of thousands of unfortunate planets, species, and individuals. The conflict between the Federation and the Borg would extinguish billions of lives and cost many others their individuality. Guilt over her actions as a drone had long haunted Seven's human conscience. Could she atone for those crimes by warning the Federation in advance of the dire threat posed by the Borg . . . and perhaps even share some of the weapons and technologies that Starfleet had developed to combat the Collective?

It was even possible, Seven realized, that she could act to prevent her own assimilation as a child, nearly a century from now. She could see to it that little Annika Hansen never became Seven of Nine . . . but what would that mean to her own future?

"Well?" Santiago demanded. "Tell me I'm wrong."

Seven found herself at a loss for words, torn between her guilt and her responsibility to protect the time line.

Between the individual she had become and the fully human woman she might have been—or could still be.

"I . . . I am not certain what you mean," she said unconvincingly.

"Like hell you don't," Santiago said. "You're not nearly as inscrutable as you think you are." Stern eyes subjected her to a rigorous appraisal. "It's written all over your face."

"That's enough." Kirk stepped between Seven and Santiago. "This is my ship, Commissioner. I'll ask the questions here."

Seven appreciated his intervention. Santiago was far too perceptive for her liking. She preferred to keep her doubts and dilemmas private.

"Damn it, Kirk," Santiago protested. "You can't keep shielding her like this. Your duty is to your own time and people, not some possible future we know nothing about. You think the Orions would hesitate to take advantage of this opportunity? Or the Klingons or the Romulans or the Gorn? We have the chance here to jump-start our technology by who knows how many generations. We could leave the Federation's adversaries in the dust!"

It is not the Klingons you need to worry about, Seven thought. But the Borg were barely on Starfleet's radar yet, let alone the Dominion and other future threats to the Alpha Quadrant. "I repeat: That would be unadvisable."

"Why not?" Santiago demanded.

"To do as you suggest," she said, as much to herself as to the impassioned commissioner, "would upset the balance of power throughout the quadrant. You would risk destabilizing the entire galaxy for centuries to come."

"But think of all the lives you could save," Santiago

pleaded. "All the upcoming tragedies and disasters you can help us avert. All the pain you can spare us."

"Perhaps we need our pain," Kirk argued. "To help us learn and grow."

"Indeed," Spock said, joining the debate. "Like individuals, civilizations are shaped as much by their trials as by their victories." He contemplated Seven soberly. "It is possible that our guest would not be doing the Federation a favor if she helps us grow too quickly or too easily."

"Hell," McCoy chimed in. "Who's to say all that future knowledge, and superior technology, wouldn't change the Federation for the worse? You know what they say, power corrupts . . . and a little knowledge can be a dangerous thing, especially if we're nowhere near ready for it!"

Santiago appealed to Scotty. "Mister Scott, what do you think? You're a practical man. Don't tell me you don't see the opportunity here."

"Well, I admit the engineer in me would give my right arm to know what sort of future know-how we're talkin' about here," Scotty said, with an apologetic look at Seven. "It would be like gettin' a sneak peek at tomorrow's technical journals."

"Your scientific curiosity is understandable," Seven replied. "But consider your own Prime Directive. Just as Starfleet is forbidden to interfere in the affairs of less-developed civilizations, so should I avoid contaminating your era."

"I don't know," Scotty said. "Ye ask me, the Prime Directive can be a pain in the arse sometimes. Me, I'm an engineer. Never had much patience with philosophy or politics. I'm all about makin' things work better and faster. From that point of view, what's a wee bit of time travel between friends?"

"But even the most seemingly harmless innovations can be abused," Spock observed. "Galactic history is replete with cautionary examples of dangers posed by too-rapid technological development. Your own species nearly destroyed itself with nuclear weapons, while the premature discovery of antimatter led to the total extinction of the ancient Gabrallians over one million years ago. Many other such tragedies come to mind."

"Well, sure, there's always goin' to be an element of risk," Scotty argued. "But that comes with the territory. If we never took a chance on a new idea or two, we'd still be sittin' around in caves eatin' raw meat without so much as a fire to cook with. Ye know what they say, ye can't make a haggis without slaughterin' a sheep."

"Perhaps," Spock said, "but you would not want to kill the sheep before its grandparents were even conceived." He let the grotesque paradox sink in. "Timing is often everything."

Seven was impressed by the men's arguments. Although products of a more primitive era, they had an excellent grasp of the issues at hand. Their cogent reasoning helped to still the guilty voices undermining her resolve, as did her prior experiences with time travel.

Not long ago, relatively speaking, she had been recruited by the twenty-ninth-century timeship *Relativity* to assist them in unraveling a temporally convoluted conspiracy to destroy *Voyager*. Since finding herself stranded in the twenty-third century, she had dared to hope that *Relativity* might arrive to return her to her proper era, but since it had not already done so, within seconds of her displacement, she could only assume that no such convenient rescue was in the offing. Had her current predicament escaped their notice? Time was all but endless, after all, and *Relativity* could hardly be expected to police every temporal anomaly from the Big Bang to the heat death of the universe. Or was it that *Relativity* had some compelling reason *not* to intervene in this instance, perhaps to avoid some greater distortion to the time line? Seven had no idea, but it was clear that her future—and her return to same—was in her own hands.

For better or for worse.

"Timing is indeed crucial," she said. "Thus the importance of the Temporal Prime Directive."

Santiago was not swayed by such concerns. He appeared driven by other, more emotional considerations. His voice and manner grew ever more heated.

"So you intend to stay silent?" he pressed her. "Even if millions of innocent beings suffer the consequences?"

Billions, she amended. "Do not think I do so lightly."

"The Prime Directive can be a heavy burden," Kirk said, adopting a sympathetic tone. He seemed to speak from personal experience. "I'm sure the commissioner, of all people, can appreciate that."

Santiago snorted. "Don't lecture me about the Prime Directive, Kirk. I know your reputation."

"I may have *bent* the rules on occasion," Kirk said defiantly, not letting the other man put him on the defensive, "under extraordinary circumstances, but that doesn't mean I don't respect them . . . or understand why they exist." He held up his hand to forestall any further objections from Santiago. "Now then, I let this debate continue because I felt we needed to clear the air, but you're here as a courtesy, Commissioner. Don't make me regret that."

He stared down Santiago, who grudgingly turned away from Seven to take a seat at the table. "I hope you can live with yourself, Kirk, the next time Federation lives are lost to a planetary disaster *she* could have warned us about."

"Trust me, Commissioner," Kirk said solemnly. "They won't be the only lives on my conscience."

Or mine, Seven thought. "Shall I continue with my presentation, gentlemen?"

"Go ahead." Kirk sat down at the head of table. "You have the floor."

Seven held the lightweight crystal fragment up for their inspection. "I have conducted a thorough analysis of this component. Its means of operation eludes me, as does its exact composition, but a close examination reveals a small inscription on one side of the fragment." She indicated the location with her finger. "Here, to be precise."

Kirk reached for the wedge-shaped object. "If I may?"

She surrendered the fragment although she knew there was little point. He held it up to the light and squinted.

"I don't see anything," he confessed.

"The inscription is out of phase with time," she explained. Like the marker on the hidden door to the monument in the Delta Quadrant. "Your visual faculties are incapable of perceiving it . . . unlike mine."

"Why am I not surprised?" McCoy drawled. "Lucky for us you're here, then."

"Luck . . . or design?" Kirk pondered.

"That remains to be determined," she replied.

Spock inspected the fragment as well. His Vulcan eyes were no more equipped to detect temporal distortions than Kirk's. Only her optical implant could read the clue inscribed on the fragment.

"May I ask what the inscription is?" the science officer asked.

"It is a stardate," she revealed. "Thirty-Seven Fifteen Point Three."

Kirk processed the date. "That's about three years ago."

"Three years, four months, and sixteen days," Spock clarified. "That date corresponds exactly to the *Enterprise*'s visit to Gamma Trianguli VI."

"That is correct," Seven stated. She had already looked up the date herself and correlated it against the ship's logs. She noted the speed with which Spock had retrieved the data from his memory, without any need to consult the computer. Despite his half-human ancestry, his highly trained mind was clearly the equal of Tuvok's. No wonder he was held in such high regard even in the twenty-fourth century.

"Of course," Kirk said, remembering. "Vaal and his worshippers."

"Don't remind me," McCoy grumbled. "We nearly got our skulls crushed by those 'friendly' natives, as I recall . . . before you blew up their god and taught them about the birds and bees."

Santiago huffed. "What was that you were saying about the Prime Directive, Kirk?"

Kirk ignored the gibe. "Gamma Trianguli VI," he murmured, thinking aloud. "A coincidence?"

"Unlikely," Seven said. "A similar stardate, displayed on the control panel of the device that brought me here, coincided with your mission to Yusub . . . and the location of this fragment. I suggest that this new clue may point us in the direction of the next component."

"On Gamma Trianguli VI," Kirk said.

"Precisely."

She neglected to mention the towering monument to Kirk that had housed the hidden tomb complex. That particular detail seemed too provocative to share, but lent additional credence to her theory that Kirk was somehow key to the puzzle—or was perhaps being employed as *the* key to a code.

"I don't know," McCoy said dubiously. "That sounds like a stretch to me."

"Perhaps not," she allowed. "I have good reason to believe that we will find the second fragment on Gamma Trianguli VI."

Kirk read between the lines. "But you can't tell us why."

"No, but I believe my theory is sound."

Kirk smiled wryly. "In other words, you want us to set course for Gamma Trianguli VI, a planet light-years away, for reasons you can't divulge, based on an inscription only you can read."

"That is an accurate summation," she conceded.

"You're asking us to take a lot on faith, Seven . . . if that's even your real name."

"I would not ask were the stakes not so dire," she replied. "And need I remind you, Captain, that I *did* save your life down on the planet? I believe the expression is: You owe me."

McCoy chuckled. "Finally! An argument I can understand."

Kirk held his chin as he considered his decision. "Spock, how long to Gamma Trianguli VI?"

Seven had already performed the necessary calculations, allowing for the primitive nature of the *Enterprise*'s warp engines.

"Approximately four-point-nine days at warp seven," she informed him.

"Four-point-nine-two," Spock corrected her. "To be precise."

Kirk regarded the byplay with apparent amusement. He picked up the mysterious fragment and turned it over and over in his hands. "You've got this all figured out, haven't you?"

"I hope so, Captain. For all our sakes."

Kirk threw up his hands in defeat. "What the devil. In for a penny, in for a pound." He leaned forward and activated the ship's intercom. "Kirk to the bridge. Set a course for Gamma Trianguli VI."

"Aye, sir," a deep voice replied. Seven recognized the distinctive timbre of Lieutenant Hikaru Sulu, whom she had met shortly after arriving on the ship. The helmsman was doubtless puzzled by the ship's new destination, but he did not question the captain's orders. *"Setting course now."*

"Very good, Mister Sulu. Kirk out."

"Thank you, Captain," Seven said. "I appreciate your trust."

He shrugged. "The sooner we find the rest of that time machine, the sooner you can get back to where you belong. Not that we're in a hurry to get rid of you, of course."

Seven accepted his remark in the spirit in which it was intended.

"Of course."

Eight

Gamma Trianguli VI was a Class-M planet beyond the twenty-third-century boundaries of the Federation. Even in Seven's time, the primitive humanoids inhabiting the world had barely progressed beyond rudimentary agriculture and grass huts. They were still many millennia away from developing warp capacity, let alone time travel. The planet struck Seven as an unlikely place to find a component of a time machine, which might be a good reason to hide one there.

"I doubt you'll need this," Kirk said as he handed her back her phaser in the *Enterprise's* old-fashioned transporter room. "The natives are pretty friendly now that they're no longer under Vaal's influence."

Seven had studied the relevant mission logs, so she was aware that "Vaal" was the designation of an ancient super-computer that had once completely controlled the planet below. Kirk had liberated the planet's population, which was still designated Vaalian, from the machine's domination by draining its power reserves, not incidentally saving the *Enterprise* in the process. Subsequent investigations had suggested that the Vaalians were not native to the planet but had been transplanted there in a misguided social experiment designed to create an idyllic society that could not possibly advance to a level where it could destroy itself.

"Still, it never hurts to be prepared," he added.

"A wise precaution," she agreed, accepting the weapon. A primitive tricorder was slung over her shoulder, while the original lightweight fragment from Yusub was secured in a standard-issue Starfleet backpack. She had justified bringing the wedge along on the grounds that it might lead them to the next fragment, but if she was being honest with herself, she was simply not comfortable letting it out of her possession. The temporally displaced artifact held her best hope of returning to her own era in time (whatever that meant) to save Captain Janeway and the others.

"Can't say I'm looking forward to revisiting this place," McCoy grumbled. "As I recall, it's a lot more dangerous than it looks."

The away team—no, she corrected herself—*the landing party* consisted of herself, Kirk, McCoy, and a single security officer. Commissioner Santiago had wanted to join the expedition, if only to keep an eye on Seven, but Kirk had denied the man's request since this was a research mission, not a diplomatic one. Santiago had not taken the refusal well, but Seven was grateful for the captain's decision. She needed to concentrate on the task at hand, not waste energy deflecting the commissioner's persistent attempts to undermine her resolve. Days had passed since she had last regenerated, and the strain was wearing on her. It was imperative that she find the means to return to *Voyager* with all deliberate speed.

"You don't need to remind me, Bones." Kirk's voice and face grew grim. "I lost four good men on this planet. Everybody stay on their toes. Even without Vaal, there are still serious hazards down there. Poisonous plants. Explosive rocks."

McCoy shook his head. "You know, that never made sense to me. Who designs a planet-sized Garden of Eden, policed by a snake-headed computer god, and then stocks the place with venomous thorns and rocks that blow up if you bump them too hard? Kind of defeats the point of paradise."

"I can dispel your confusion, Doctor," Seven said. "I have reviewed the notes on Gamma Trianguli VI in the Starfleet database, including the studies conducted of Vaal's own memory circuits after you deactivated him, and am familiar with the prevailing theories."

"Of course you are." McCoy huffed. He cast an exasperated glance at Kirk. "I can see why you didn't bother including Spock on this little treasure hunt, Jim. Our friend here practically renders him redundant."

Seven was undisturbed by the doctor's irascible attitude. She was quite accustomed to prickly physicians. Indeed, she found herself wondering how much of McCoy's documented behavioral patterns and mannerisms had made it into the EMH's programming. Perhaps more than she had realized before?

"Do you desire explanations or not?" she asked.

"Go ahead," McCoy said with a sigh. "Shoot."

"To begin with, the venomous thorns are only harmful to non-Vaalians. It is speculated that they were a biological defense mechanism intended to protect the population of Gamma Trianguli VI from unwelcome visitors."

"Like us," Kirk said.

"Precisely." Seven took care to confine herself to only

those theories developed in Kirk's time. "Subsequent studies have also confirmed that the plants produce pollen that is beneficial to the Vaalian's immune system."

McCoy remained unsatisfied. "But what about those exploding rocks? I mean, even if the Vaalians knew enough to stay clear of them, accidents happen. Why litter paradise with natural land mines?"

"The answer to that is more complicated," Seven admitted. "The consensus is that the thermodynamically unstable rocks were not, in fact, part of the original design, but the result of a flaw in Vaal's programming that developed over the course of some ten thousand years. The terraforming process that maintained the planet's uniform ecosphere produced as byproducts various sediments and crystals that combined to form, via normal geological processes, the volatile compound that posed a threat to you and your crewmates." She frowned; this imperfection in the environment's design offended her sensibilities. "It remains unclear whether this was a result of a worsening malfunction . . . or simply an unanticipated consequence of the process."

Kirk nodded. "Maybe they just weren't looking ahead ten thousand years."

"Sounds like damned sloppy planning to me," McCoy groused.

"Small, seemingly insignificant changes can accumulate over time," Seven observed, "with potentially catastrophic results. The so-called 'Butterfly Effect.'" She stepped onto the transporter platform. "Hence the importance of returning me to my own time as promptly as possible."

"Point taken," Kirk said. "Let's get a move on."

The rest of the party took their places on the platform. Kirk addressed Chief Engineer Scott, who was manning the transporter controls.

"Beam us down, Scotty."

"Aye, sir," Scott replied with his distinctive burr. "Good luck to ye."

Seven clasped her hands behind her back. The whine of the transporter filled her ears as she braced herself for a routine transport, at least by the primitive standards of the time. Everything seemed normal at first, but then . . .

When the device on the nameless planetoid had transported her across time and space, she had briefly experienced an unsettling flux in her chronometric node, accompanied by a transient, almost subliminal distortion to her visual perceptions. For an instant, a photo-negative effect had reversed the shades and tones around her, before her vision returned to normal. The distortion was so fleeting that she suspected that a normal human, whose senses had not been enhanced by the Borg, might not have even registered the phenomenon. But Seven had been aware of it.

Just as she was aware of it now.

The peculiar sensation, and visual distortion, passed quickly. Seven found herself, as expected, on the surface of the planet, beneath a clear orange sky. The chronometric flux left her momentarily disoriented. She reeled unsteadily and blinked in confusion.

"Captain? Doctor?"

She wondered briefly if the rest of the landing party had experienced any unusual sensations, then she realized that she was standing alone in what appeared to be a lush tropical jungle. Dense green foliage, high humidity, and an overpowering floral aroma impressed themselves upon her senses.

"Captain Kirk? Doctor McCoy? Lieutenant?"

She looked in vain for her companions. Even the red-shirted security officer, Lieutenant Jadello, was nowhere to be seen. She reached instinctively for her combadge, then remembered to use one of the *Enterprise*'s primitive handheld communicators instead.

"Seven to *Enterprise*. Please respond."

But the communicator proved of no use in contacting either the ship or the other members of the landing party. She experienced an unhelpful flicker of anxiety. Clearly, something had gone wrong.

But what? And why?

She belatedly noticed a low humming noise coming from her backpack. She tugged it open in time to see that the crystalline fragment was emitting a violet glow, which gradually faded away before her eyes. Her ocular implant detected faint ripples of temporal distortion around the wedge-shaped artifact.

"Curiouser and curiouser," she murmured.

Had the fragment somehow "hijacked" the transporter beam to bring her here? And where and when was that precisely?

Drawing her phaser, she surveyed her surroundings. Blooming flowers and abundant greenery matched her expectations. The temperature registered a comfortable twenty-three degrees Celsius, while heavy floral bouquets perfumed the atmosphere. Prolific shrubs and ferns crowded her, limiting visibility beyond more than a few meters, but appeared consistent with the reported ecology of Gamma Trianguli VI. Ripe fruit weighed down the branches of leafy trees. A single main-sequence star burned in the sky, near enough to provide more than adequate light and warmth. Seven felt confident that she was on the right planet, despite being detoured by the fragment.

She was considerably less certain that she knew *when* she was.

Her survey of the environment offered no clues as to her current temporal coordinates. The planet's ecology had been in a state of stasis, artificially maintained by Vaal, for at least ten millennia. The fragrant tropical garden around her could and had existed at any time during that interval. These same varieties of flowers had blossomed continuously, and without change, for thousands of years.

Flowers . . .

Kirk's warnings came to mind, even as her Borg-enhanced senses alerted her to an ominous rustling behind her. She spun around in time to see a distinctive purple flower rotating toward her atop a tall, rigid stem. Sharp yellow thorns clustered at the center of the blossom. The flower tracked her as though drawn to her motion. Its thorns, she knew, were tipped with a powerful neurotoxin that was one thousand times more lethal than saponin, another plant-based poison. Identical thorns had once killed a crewman from the *Enterprise*— and nearly Spock as well.

Seven registered the danger immediately. She dived out of the way as the thorns fired explosively from the flower in a puff of vapor and pollen. The deadly thorns shot past her to disappear into the bushes and branches beyond. Seven exhaled sharply, acknowledging her narrow escape.

That had been closer than she would have preferred.

Although that particular blossom had discharged its venomous load without success, similar flowers were already turning their faces toward her. Seven found herself outnumbered by the homicidal foliage.

She did not hesitate to eliminate the threat. A sweep of phaser fire incinerated the flowers, thorns and all. She spied another clump of purple flowers nearby. Those particular blossoms had yet to take aggressive action against her, but Seven took no chances. She disposed of them with ruthless efficiency—as the Borg had taught her.

Not until her immediate surroundings had been sterilized, and the danger eliminated, did she pause to determine what other hazards might be at hand. A scattering of rough, reddish rocks caught her attention, and she approached them cautiously. According to her research, the planet's dangerously unstable rocks could be handled carefully but would detonate if jarred with sufficient force. Another of Kirk's men had been killed when he had accidentally trod upon an explosive stone.

Seven hoped to avoid that mistake.

Holding her breath, she gingerly lifted a rock from the ground and lobbed it at a seared flower bed several meters away. She braced herself for an explosion, but no such event occurred. The rock thudded harmlessly into the charred foliage.

Interesting, Seven noted. She recalled the theory that the explosive rocks had only developed over the passage of ages. Could it be that they did not yet exist at this point in time? Or were not yet sufficiently volatile?

Her discovery elicited profoundly mixed feelings.

On the one hand, it meant that her present environment might be less hazardous than she had initially feared. On the other hand, it meant that she was now even farther in the past and more distant from her own time—and *Voyager.*

Not to mention alone.

She wondered where Captain Kirk and the remainder of the landing party were. She surmised that, because they had not been carrying the troublesome fragment on their persons, they had beamed down to the planet without incident. Chances were, they were "now" on Gamma Triguli VI in the year 2270, wondering what had become of her.

It was highly possible that she would never see them again.

Perhaps it is just as well, she reflected. At least she would no longer be tempted to tamper with their history. Part of her wished that she had left the fragment back aboard the *Enterprise* before attempting to beam down with the others, but maybe she was precisely where—and when—she was supposed to be if she wanted to locate another component of the time-travel device.

Her circumstances had changed, she realized, but her objective remained the same. Using the borrowed tricorder, she scanned the area in hopes of determining which way to proceed. Subspace vibrations emanating from a vast climate-control apparatus deep beneath the planet's surface initially overwhelmed the sensors, forcing her to recalibrate the device to ignore the vibrations. The tricorder then picked up an antiquated Starfleet distress signal, identical to the one that had lured *Voyager* to the planetoid in the Delta Quadrant, coming from a location roughly half a kilometer away, on bearing two-three-two.

She set off in the indicated direction, while keeping one eye on the sky. Vaal had also been known to dispatch intruders with targeted bolts of lightning. At present, the orange sky was calm and cloudless, but Seven intended to seek shelter at the first sign of a thunderhead. It occurred to her that the Borg often ignored intruders until they proved themselves a legitimate threat. Perhaps that was why Vaal had yet to attack her directly. It was possible that she was still beneath his notice.

She hoped to keep it that way.

The dense vegetation impeded her progress until she stumbled onto a well-trodden footpath through the greenery. She took this as encouraging evidence that she was headed in the right direction. She gripped her phaser in one hand, ready to incinerate any hostile flora, while employing the tricorder with the other. The signal grew stronger as she made her way toward it.

So did something else.

It started as a faint whispering inside her skull, echoing dimly along her cranial implants. At first she thought it might be merely fatigue talking; her inability to regenerate continued to wear on her. Yet she soon identified the whispering as a genuine phenomenon, impinging on her consciousness via the interplexing beacon implanted within her brain. The beacon was a sophisticated transceiver designed to facilitate communication between Borg drones—and their queen.

A very human chill ran down Seven's spine. It was not too long ago that the Borg queen had invaded her thoughts in just this manner. The translink frequency carrying the whispers was unfamiliar to her, and it did not correspond precisely to those employed by the Borg, but the whispering unnerved her nonetheless. This was too close for comfort to what she had experienced before. The whispers seemed to be calling to her, urging her onward, even though she couldn't quite make out what they were saying.

Seven wasn't sure she wanted to.

The trail, the distress signal, and the whispering combined to lead her out of the jungle into an open clearing where she came face-to-face with an immense stone temple crafted to resemble the head of giant horned reptile. Polished green eyes with golden slits gazed out from beneath chiseled stone brows. A solitary horn, not unlike those sported by Species 4673, rose above the sculpture's gargantuan snout. Rough-hewn steps led up into the idol's gaping maw, which was lit up by an infernal red glow. Its stony exterior was rough and irregular in texture, like the leathery hide of some prehistoric saurian. Seven recognized the imposing creation at once.

This was Vaal.

The artificial god of Gamma Trianguli VI was nestled in the shadow of a rugged brown cliff and framed by flowering trees and bushes. The resemblance to the mammoth sculpture of Kirk back in the Delta Quadrant was not lost on Seven, although she was uncertain if this was a coincidence or not. She also noted a slight resemblance to a giant radioactive lizard who figured into some of Tom Paris's juvenile holodeck adventures.

She approached Vaal cautiously, not wanting to provoke the machine's wrath. That Vaal had obviously not yet been deactivated in this time frame confirmed that she had indeed traveled farther into the past, although it was still impossible to determine precisely how far she had gone, given the unchanging nature of this world prior to Kirk's intervention in 2267. For all she knew, she was ten thousand years before Kirk's time, shortly after the dawning of the Age of Vaal.

The whispers grew louder in her head, fraying at her nerves. She realized that her interplexing beacon was attempting to adapt to the alien signal, which was almost surely the voice of Vaal. She winced in discomfort. She could almost make out his words, if she wanted to. Instead she forced herself to focus on the readings from the tricorder, which indicated that the signal was coming from somewhere deep within Vaal.

Naturally, she thought.

Eager to locate the hidden fragment, and remove herself from Vaal's discomfiting presence, she approached the temple entrance, only to be repelled by a powerful force field before she came within ten meters of the stone steps. Frustration briefly drowned out the intrusive whispering in her head as she experienced an unwelcome flash of déjà vu. She was beginning to get very weary of force fields.

In fact, she was growing weary in general. Fatigue shortened her temper, making the incessant whispers even more irritatingly distracting. She lacked the mental energy to tune them out.

Seven scanned the force field, which registered as considerably stronger by several orders of magnitude than the one that had trapped her in the hidden tomb back in her own time. She knew that there was little chance that she could breach the field on her own; a sustained barrage from the *Enterprise*'s main phaser banks had been required to overcome the field in Kirk's time. A single hand phaser, albeit of superior twenty-fourth-century design, could not begin to disrupt the field. A direct assault was doomed to failure and might serve only to call down Vaal's lightning upon her. She slowly lowered her phaser to avoid presenting herself as a threat.

Now what? she wondered.

Startled gasps, coming from behind her, announced that she was no longer alone. Seven turned around to find a few dozen Vaalians staring at her with various combinations of wonder and confusion. The primitive humanoids were identical to those Captain Kirk would encounter sometime in the future. Copious amounts of burnished red skin were exposed by their scant attire, which was well-suited to the planet's balmy climate. The males wore only simple white linen skirts and bracelets of flowers wound around their wrists, while the females sported revealing two-piece outfits and adorned their snow-white tresses with colorful blossoms. Geometric patterns were painted on the awestruck faces of both sexes, and white eye makeup highlighted their bulging orbs. The men's cottony white hair was piled high atop their scalps, like the snowdrifts found only at the planet's extreme polar regions, many thousands of miles from this location. Bearing heavy bushels of fresh fruit and vegetables, the so-called "Feeders of Vaal" were understandably surprised by Seven's presence.

She noted, as Kirk and his crew had (or would), the total absence of children or geriatrics among the Vaalians. Eternally youthful, the tribe people neither aged nor reproduced, except on those rare occasions when an accidental death created a need for a "replacement." Caught in a state of cultural stasis, they lived only to serve Vaal endlessly and unthinkingly.

Like drones, she thought, *albeit somewhat less attired.*

Easily plucked from the planet's abundant trees and vines, the fruits and vegetables carried by the natives were intended for Vaal's consumption. That a sophisticated super-computer would be powered by raw organic matter had puzzled researchers; some anthropologists believed that the ritual was purely symbolic, intended to give purpose and structure to the Vaalians' lives, but this hypothesis failed to account for the fact that Kirk had weakened Vaal by depriving him of "food." A more convincing theory was that Vaal had been designed to run on an environmentally clean and self-sustaining energy system that involved no potentially hazardous technologies or materials, such as nuclear fusion or matter/antimatter reactions, which would be beyond the ability of the primitive Vaalians to maintain or replenish.

Seven saw merit in this approach. It was impossible to imagine the simple tribe people before her providing Vaal with fresh dilithium and antimatter. Fruits and vegetables were better suited to their limited abilities.

"Who are you? Where have you come from?"

A puzzled Vaalian stepped forward to address her. A pair of curved silver antennae, jutting from behind his ears, indicated that he was the leader of the tribe—and directly in contact with Vaal. He appeared to be about a decade older than the other Vaalians, although his actual age was impossible to determine. Seven wondered if this was the same village elder Kirk had/would encounter, or if there had been a replacement some-where over the ages.

"I am called Seven," she responded carefully. "I am a visitor from . . . far away."

"Far away?" The man was visibly baffled by the concept. "How far is far?"

"That is irrelevant," she answered. "And you are?"

"I am Akuta. I am the Eyes of Vaal." He examined her curiously. "What brings you here?"

His people held back, keeping their distance. They displayed no aggressive behavior, only a certain degree of apprehension. Seven recalled that the Vaalians had been completely ignorant of violence and killing prior to Kirk's arrival. She did not intend to given them occasion to learn.

"I am a friend," she stated. "I seek only an audience with Vaal."

Akuta grew even more confused. "But Vaal speaks only through me. I am his eyes and ears and mouth."

"So I understand, but perhaps Vaal can make an exception in my case."

"Exception?"

She peered more closely at the man's metal antennae. As she understood it, the implants served as a transceiver linking Akuta to Vaal, not unlike her own interplexing beacon. It was a case of similar technologies developed to serve uncomfortably similar functions. Akuta was akin to Locutus, she realized. A humanoid being modified to serve as the voice of a superior cybernetic intelligence.

A voice that grew ever louder and more insistent within Seven's own mind.

Feed me. I hunger.

Vaal's emerald eyes lit up from within. His voice could no longer be ignored.

Feed me.

Seven flinched. Her hand went instinctively to her temple in a futile attempt to block out the relentless commands. Vaal's "voice" was sterner and more mechanical than the Borg queen's, but almost as hard to resist.

"Quiet," she murmured. "Leave me alone."

Realization dawned in Akuta's eyes. He gaped at her in amazement.

"You too can hear the voice?"

Seven grimaced in discomfort. "Apparently."

"But how is this possible?" He seemed astounded, and perhaps a little alarmed as well. He backed away from her. "I do not understand."

Seven understood too well.

"I am of Vaal," she said. "Our thoughts are one."

The answer was intended to appease Akuta, but it was true to a worrying degree. As Vaal's voice echoed inside her brain, Seven saw both danger and opportunity in her unexpected connection to the machine. Was it possible that she could take advantage of the link to get past Vaal's defense force field, or was the risk of adapting fully to the Vaal's frequency too great? Memories of the Borg queen gave her pause. Seven had no desire to become a drone once more.

Feed me! I hunger!

Seven cautiously tried the force field again, only to find it still barring her way. Storm clouds began to form ominously overhead, blocking out the sun. A sudden wind whipped up the dirt and gravel around her feet.

The Vaalians trembled and murmured fearfully among themselves.

"Vaal is angered!" Akuta pointed an accusing finger at Seven. "He does not know you! You are not one!"

Not yet, Seven admitted. *Not fully.* She glanced about, searching for shelter from Vaal's thunderbolts, but saw nothing that might protect her. She needed to stop resisting Vaal's voice, she realized, and allow her own transceiver to adapt fully to the link, no matter the risk to her hard-won individuality. It was the only way she was going to convince Vaal to accept her—and allow her access to the temple.

"I am of Vaal," she repeated. "We are as one."

She opened herself completely to the voice, which was no longer a faint whisper but louder than thunder. As she stopped trying to block the signal, her interplexing beacon finished adapting to Vaal's translink frequency. His voice rang out as clearly as the Collective's once had.

Feed me! I hunger!

"Yes." She marched over to the Vaalians and claimed a basket of fresh fruit from a trembling native, who nervously surrendered it. She turned about sharply and headed back toward the towering stone snakehead, carrying her offering. "Vaal hungers. He must be fed."

She was not dissembling. She felt a need to be of use to Vaal, as well as a sense of union, of completeness, that she had not experienced since Captain Janeway had severed her from the Collective. At the time, she had found the sudden silence in her head alarming, accustomed as she'd been to constantly communing with the rest of the Collective. She had forgotten how much she had missed that. . . .

The force field parted before her. She climbed the stone steps leading to his crimson maw. Vaal's voice filled her mind and being, making it difficult to remember her original objective . . . which was what again?

Feed me!

A blazing pit awaited her offering. She could feel the heat of the furnace against her face as she dumped the basket of food down Vaal's adamantine gullet, where the organic matter was instantly converted to red-hot plasma. Seven experienced a sudden sense of gratification, although she was uncertain if it belonged to her or Vaal or if that distinction was even relevant anymore. Her offering fed Vaal's appetite.

I hunger!

She turned to seek out more food for Vaal, only to hesitate atop the steps. Despite Vaal's thunderous commands, she forced herself to focus on her actual objective, which was . . . ?

The fragment, she recalled. *I must find the fragment.*

Her eyes searched the interior of Vaal's mouth, which consisted of little more than a platform overlooking the superheated pit. Her gaze fell upon the seams of what might be a forgotten doorway located off to one side of the furnace. Squinting, she examined the possible service entrance. Her ocular implant registered a chroniton marker embedded in the stonework, in the shape of a familiar arrowhead insignia.

"Promising," she said.

Encouraged by the sign, she started toward it, but she was staggered by a forceful command from Vaal:

That is forbidden. Go no further!

Seven froze, caught between her own intentions and

the dictates from her cranial implants. She tried to block Vaal's commands, but she had already allowed him total access to her transceiver and, by extension, her cortical functions. His voice threatened to drown out her own thoughts and will. Resistance was futile . . .

You are of Vaal. Our thoughts are one.

She was on the verge of succumbing. It would be easy, too easy, to assimilate into this new Collective. There would be no more individual fears or guilt, no more tortuous moral dilemmas. Only the comforting certainty of a single shared purpose, a single voice. She started to turn away from the marker.

You are of Vaal. My voice, my eyes. Join my people.

Akuta and the other feeders remained gathered in the clearing, awaiting their turn to bestow their offerings upon Vaal, to serve only his will.

Like drones.

"No!" Seven blurted, overcome with revulsion. "I am not a drone. I will not comply!"

Another drone might have surrendered to the voice, as she might have only a few years ago, but she had grown and evolved since then. She was no longer merely Seven of Nine, Tertiary Adjunct of Unimatrix 01, and she had fought too long and too hard for her individuality to lose it to some imperfect substitute for the Collective. She rushed toward the concealed doorway, even as Vaal thundered in her brain.

Halt! Vaal commands you! Heed my voice!

"Your voice is irrelevant. Resistance is *not* futile."

Actual thunder shook the heavens. Lightning flashed outside the structure, but only as a warning. Seven doubted that Vaal would actually unleash his destructive thunderbolts on the temple itself. She was probably safe as long as she stayed within his mouth.

So Vaal resorted to a more desperate tactic.

"Stop her!" Akuta shouted frantically. "Vaal commands us!"

Faithful Vaalians stormed the steps of the temple. A muscular youth reached for Seven, but she impatiently elbowed him in the gut, sending him tumbling back into the charging tribe. The defensive strike momentarily halted the attackers, who were uncertain how to respond.

"She . . . struck him?" a female gasped in disbelief. "With her arm?"

"Do not be frightened!" Akuta exhorted his people. "Vaal will protect you. Feed her to Vaal!"

Seven evaluated her opponents. The Vaalians lacked combat skills and training, but their numbers and unquestioning loyalty to Vaal posed a significant threat. She could well imagine herself fed to the furnace as an offering to Vaal, bringing her mission through time to a singularly unproductive conclusion, unless she took immediate action.

She set her phaser on stun. "My apologies."

An azure blast, set for wide dispersal, dropped the Vaalians onto the grassy sward with welcome efficiency. Thunder boomed impotently overhead as Seven turned her back on the fallen natives and gave the concealed doorway her full attention. The proper Starfleet response code remained stored in her memory. The tricorder transmitted the code at the locking mechanism.

"Open Sesame."

As on the distant planetoid, a slab of stone descended

into the foundations, exposing a long-abandoned access tunnel. A steep flight of stairs led deep beneath the planet's surface, where massive machinery labored to maintain Gamma Trianguli VI's idyllic environment. Under other circumstances, Seven might have taken the time to thoroughly study the ancient equipment, with an eye to assimilating any exotic alien technology, but she was eager to complete her quest and locate another fragment of the time-travel device. Vaal's voice continued to bellow inside her brain, giving her a serious headache.

Turn back! You do not belong here!

"On that we agree," she said tartly. His imperious voice grated on her nerves, which were already frayed from lack of regeneration. She was sorely tempted to deactivate Vaal ahead of schedule, sparing his feeders from wasting untold millennia as drones, but no, that was Kirk's job, sometime in the future.

Vaal was doomed. He just didn't know it yet.

The tantalizing signal led her to an innocuous service panel deep in the bowels of the planet's environmental maintenance system. She pried open the panel to reveal another translucent crystal wedge, this one red in hue. By all indications, the signal was coming from the fragment itself, all but masked by the powerful subspace vibrations being generated by Vaal.

Seven removed the fragment from its hiding place and produced the original component from her backpack. The objects began to glow and hum in proximity to each other, as though eager to be reunited. Holding one in each hand, she hesitated briefly before connecting them, uncertain what the results would be.

Go, Vaal commanded. *Leave my world.*

Seven complied. "Our thoughts are one."

The interlocking fragments fit together perfectly. A sudden flux disrupted her chronometric node. Dark turned light and vice versa.

And then she was gone.

Nine

"Seven!" McCoy exclaimed. "She's gone!"

The landing party materialized on the planet's surface, minus their enigmatic guest of honor. McCoy saw only Kirk and Lieutenant Jadello standing beside him atop a wooded ridge thick with large tropical trees buttressed by spreading roots. The men looked about in confusion. Kirk flipped open his communicator.

"Kirk to *Enterprise*," he barked into the device. "We're missing Doctor Seven. Is she still with you?"

"*Nae, Captain*," Scotty's voice reported from the transporter room. "*I energized all four of ye . . . although my equipment registered an odd fluctuation in her pattern signal, like nothin' I've ever seen before.*"

"Understood," Kirk said grimly. "Send a copy of those readings to Mister Spock. Maybe he can make sense of them. Kirk out."

He tried to locate her via her own communicator next, with an equally frustrating lack of results. Lowering the communicator, he clipped it back onto his belt. "Scotty says she beamed down with us," he said, just in case the others hadn't heard. Frustration edged his voice as he glanced around, looking in vain for the absent woman. "So where the devil is she?"

McCoy didn't have a clue. "Or when?"

For all they knew, she had jumped through time

again, perhaps all the way back to whatever mysterious future she hailed from. Part of McCoy couldn't help thinking that maybe it was better that way. At least she wouldn't be contaminating their present anymore.

"Should we conduct a search, Captain?" Jadello asked.

The beefy security officer was a head taller than McCoy and the others. Waxy orange skin betrayed his Qubbezu roots and was more muted in tone than his cherry-red tunic. His deep voice held a lilting accent.

"Not a bad idea, Lieutenant," Kirk agreed, "but where to begin?"

Where indeed, McCoy thought.

The men occupied the crest of a forested hilltop overlooking fields of cultivated corn and wheat. The planet's soil was unusually rich, he recalled, and the Vaalians had obviously taken great strides in agriculture since the *Enterprise*'s last visit. Lush tropical foliage bordered the fields, although the climate was a bit hotter and more humid than McCoy remembered; he guessed that regional weather patterns, and the changing of the seasons, had asserted themselves now that Vaal was no longer controlling the environment. A wide river meandered sluggishly on the western side of the fields. Leafy trees provided shade from a hot yellow sun. Somewhere in the distance, a large animal honked for a mate. McCoy swatted away an annoying bug.

"You know, I don't recall any wildlife from before."

Kirk shrugged. "Well, we didn't have much of chance to check out the local fauna last time. We were too busy trying to save ourselves and the *Enterprise*." He craned his neck to get a better view. "Plus, I suppose it's possible that migratory patterns have changed since Vaal lost his grip on the planet's ecology."

"Since we deactivated him, you mean, and let nature run amok."

"Something like that," Kirk conceded. "The planet seems to be thriving, though."

McCoy couldn't disagree. They watched from the hill as, in the distance, a herd of agile ruminants grazed in a grassy meadow and watered along the riverbank. The shaggy beasts resembled a cross between a moose and a rhino, with a single large horn protruding from the forehead in lieu of antlers. *Rhinooses?* Matted white fur hung down their sides. Cloven hooves the size of snowshoes pawed the ground. Bovine eyes were supplemented by smaller orbs underneath. The beasts wallowed in the thick mud, blithely unaware of the alien visitors spying on them from the hills. A low wooden fence, guarded by a row of crude scarecrows, protected the Vaalians' crops from the beasts of the field. A flock of winged mammals flapped toward the jungle to the east. A fish splashed upstream. Pollen in the air aggravated McCoy's sinuses. He tried not to sneeze.

"Seems more like a real ecosystem," he observed, "and less like the Garden of Eden. That's progress, I guess."

"I like to think so," Kirk said. "Since we gave the Vaalians the apple."

McCoy turned away from the fields. On the other side of the ridge, smoke rose from the fires of the neighboring village. He glimpsed a rustic array of dirt roads and grass huts. Small red figures, including several children, could be seen going about their daily chores. A stray breeze brought the mouthwatering aroma of cooking fires. McCoy recalled that he hadn't had lunch yet.

"So where do you want to start looking for Seven?" he asked. "The village?"

They had deliberately beamed down a few klicks away from the village to avoid materializing directly into the Vaalians' midst. As curious as Kirk or McCoy might have been about the progress the natives had made in the last three years, there was also a desire to leave the Vaalians alone if possible. Why disrupt their lives unless they absolutely had to?

"Probably a good place to start," Kirk said. "If Seven did end up somewhere else on this planet and has just lost her communicator somehow, maybe Akuta and his people will have seen her. Or perhaps she'll seek out the closest thing to civilization in these parts."

"Who wouldn't?" McCoy said dryly. He contemplated the distant village. He wasn't looking forward to hiking all the way there. Maybe they could have the *Enterprise* beam them a little bit closer to their final destination?

He was about to suggest as much when, without warning, there was a blinding flash of light—and Seven stumbled out of empty air onto the ridge. She tottered uncertainly upon her feet, appearing disoriented and on the verge of collapsing. A glowing semicircle, composed of two linked wedges, was clutched against her chest.

The other fragment, McCoy realized. *She found it.*

But when?

"Seven!" Kirk rushed forward to catch her before she fell. He placed his arm around her shoulder to hold her up. His concerned eyes widened at the sight of the joined artifacts in her hands. "Where have you—? How—?"

She struggled to get her bearings. "Captain? I am back . . . in Twenty-two Seventy?"

"Looks like it," McCoy said. He scanned her with his medical tricorder, which detected high amounts of adrenaline and exhaustion, as much as he could tell from her . . . unusual . . . physiognomy. He scowled at the indications of widespread cybernetic implants throughout her body. Somebody had put a lot of time and effort into "improving" her biology.

If that was the future of humanity, McCoy wasn't sure he approved.

"How long was I gone?" she asked.

"Only a few minutes," Kirk said, "but you had us worried."

"Interesting," she mused. "There appears to have been a modest time lag in returning to these coordinates. Unsurprising given the intervals involved. A margin of error of only 'a few minutes' is essentially irrelevant at that scale . . . and quite impressive."

McCoy took her detached scientific tone as a good sign, medically speaking. She was sounding like herself again, for better or for worse.

"But where were you?" Kirk asked urgently. "What happened to you?"

"And where the heck did you find another piece of the puzzle?" McCoy added, nodding at the object in her grasp, whose eldritch glow was already dimming. "While we were just standing around here?"

"Rather more time passed for me," she divulged, "but perhaps a fuller explanation can wait until we are safely back aboard the *Enterprise*?" She gracefully extricated herself from Kirk's arm, clearly preferring to stand on her own two feet, but still appeared a bit unsteady. Her eyelids drooped as though she was having trouble keeping them open. "I confess to feeling somewhat . . . fatigued."

"That's not good enough," Kirk said, impatient for answers. "I need to know what just happened!"

"Jim." McCoy stepped forward and laid a restraining hand on his friend's shoulder. Compassion colored his voice. "Look at her, she's practically dead on her feet. Maybe it *would* be better to do this back on the ship, after she's had a chance to recuperate?"

Kirk frowned, unhappy with the situation, but willing to listen to reason and his chief medical officer.

"All right," he said grudgingly. "But you owe me answers, 'Doctor Seven.'" He plucked his communicator from his belt. "Kirk to *Enterprise*. Four to beam—"

"Captain," Seven interrupted, before he could complete the order. "Given what just transpired, I am reluctant to attempt another transport while in possession of these artifacts. It might be more prudent to return to the ship via a shuttle instead . . . in order to avoid another unexpected detour."

Kirk nodded. "I see your point." He spoke again into the communicator. "Belay that order. Please dispatch a shuttlecraft to our coordinates."

"*Acknowledged, Captain,*" Spock replied from the bridge. "*Mister Sulu will be on his way shortly.*"

"We'll keep our eyes out for him. Kirk out." He put away his communicator and turned his attention back to Seven. "I'm looking forward to hearing your story, once we're back aboard."

"I doubt you will be disappointed, Captain." She

leaned against a tree trunk, letting it support her weight. "I believe—" She stiffened abruptly and drew her phaser. "Listen. Do you hear that?"

Hear what? At first, McCoy had no idea what she was reacting to, but then the distinctive whine of a transporter beam reached his merely human ears. Not from the *Enterprise,* though; he'd had his atoms beamed up and down enough to know that irritating hum by heart. This didn't have the telltale ring of a Starfleet transporter. Somebody *else* was beaming down.

Maybe someone unfriendly.

"Good ears," Kirk complimented Seven. He drew his own phaser, as did Jadello. A pillar of dazzling emerald sparks manifested in front of the startled landing party, who assumed a defensive posture. McCoy reached for his own weapon. Within seconds, four phasers were directed at the alien transporter effect.

Better safe than sorry, McCoy thought.

He waited tensely for their mysterious visitor to finish materializing, but the process seemed to be taking unusually long. His mouth went dry. His pulse was racing. "What's keeping this party crasher?" he muttered under his breath. "Are they waiting for a holographic invitation?"

"I don't like this," Jadello said. "Something's not right...."

A third eye opened at the nape of his neck, scoping out their rear. "Captain!" he shouted in alarm. "Behind us!"

"What?" McCoy glanced back over his shoulder in time to see a gang of green Orion pirates creeping across the wooded hilltop toward them. Armed to the teeth, the men sported black leather gear and mean expressions.

Scars and metal piercing made them look like foul-tempered survivors of a shrapnel explosion. McCoy knew a band of bloodthirsty brigands when he saw them. His gaze darted in confusion between the glittering transporter beam, which now appeared to be dissipating, and the advancing pirates.

Where the hell had they come from?

Jadello's reflexes were faster than his. He shoved McCoy behind the thick trunk of a towering kapok tree, then spun around and fired at the intruders. A bright blue beam dropped one Orion, even as another raider, his surly features betraying his hostile intent, aimed a disruptor pistol at Kirk's exposed back. McCoy doubted that it was set on stun.

"Captain!" Jadello dived into the pirate's line of fire, firing back as he did so. A sizzling emerald blast struck the man head-on. A blinding green glow reduced him to atoms. Not even ashes remained of Jadello, whose final exclamation was cut off abruptly. "We're under att—!"

Attack, McCoy realized, completing Jadello's warning. Saved by the other man's sacrifice, Kirk grabbed Seven and joined McCoy behind the boulder. They fired back at the Orions from behind the substantial tree trunk, which was at least three meters in diameter. In turn, the alien cutthroats darted from tree to tree, dodging the phaser beams as they closed on what remained of the landing party. Emerald blasts chipped away at bark and wood. McCoy counted more than a dozen attackers, all out for blood. Pointy teeth gave them the look of cannibals, a cosmetic choice no doubt intended to make their enemies tremble in fear. It almost worked.

"Damnit," McCoy cursed. "They killed Jadello!"

"I know," Kirk said gravely. The valiant security officer had taken a disruptor blast for him. Kirk glared vengefully at the Orions. "That's another life those bastards owe me."

The apparent leader of the raiders—a hulking bruiser with a spiky skull and a missing ear—appeared equally upset by the killing. "Misbegotten slackwit!" he berated the pirate who had disintegrated Jadello. A prosthetic metal hand slapped the offending lackey across the face. "I told you! Stun only. We want the future-woman alive!"

Seven, McCoy thought. *They're after Seven!*

He suddenly realized that he'd forgotten all about the first transporter beam. Certain that he was about to be shot in the back, McCoy whirled around to discover that the sparkling column of energy had evaporated entirely, leaving not a soul behind. *A distraction,* he grasped. *That first beam was just to get us looking in the wrong direction.*

Good thing Jadello had literally had an eye at the back of his head.

He saved our bacon but good!

Kirk and Seven tried to hold off the attackers, but they were badly outnumbered. Seven remained cool as a cucumber, although her drawn face showed signs of strain. Her phaser blasts were precise and efficient, not wasting a shot. She took a moment to disassemble the captured fragments and secure them within her backpack.

"A prudent retreat is in order," she stated. "Before we suffer additional losses."

Kirk nodded in agreement.

"Contact the ship!" he ordered McCoy. "Get us out of here."

My prescription exactly, McCoy thought. Fragments or no fragments, an emergency beam-out was clearly the appropriate treatment for their condition. He flipped open his communicator, only to find the transmission blocked. Static assailed his ears. He dialed through every frequency without success.

"It's no good, Jim! They're blocking us!"

Ten

"Commander Spock!" Ensign Chekov blurted from his station on the bridge. A thick Russian accent betrayed his roots. "Another vessel has entered the system. It just dropped out of warp."

"Raise shields," Spock instructed. He was not aware of any other Federation ships in the sector, so it was best to take all reasonable precautions. He flipped a switch on the armrest of the captain's chair. "Yellow alert."

He rotated the chair toward the communications station. "Hail the unknown vessel. Request identification."

"I'm trying, sir," Lieutenant Uhura said. "They're not responding."

Curious, Spock thought. The unidentified ship's abrupt appearance, and ominous silence, were clearly cause for concern. In theory, the *Enterprise*'s current location and mission were known only to Starfleet.

"What's happening?" Commissioner Santiago demanded. He and his aide had insisted on taking residence upon the bridge, the better to monitor the status of the landing party's mission. The visiting diplomats stood just outside the recessed command circle, leaning against the reinforced red handrail. "Who is it?"

"That is what we are attempting to determine, Commissioner." Spock turned back toward Chekov. "Status of vessel?"

"Approaching Gamma Trianguli VI," the navigator reported. He shared the helm control station with Lieutenant Sharon Blackhorse, who was manning the helm while Sulu took a shuttle down to the planet to retrieve the landing party. She was an experienced pilot who often took the helm during the evening shift. Chekov kept a close eye on the sensor data. "Entering visual range."

"On-screen," Spock ordered.

The alien vessel resembled a cross between a shelled marine animal and a tank. Molded green plating, inscribed with alien hieroglyphics, armored the rounded contours of a squat, bulbous ship that was positively bristling with visible gunports. Its warp nacelles were tucked in dangerously close to the hull, so that they looked more like ribbing than the elegant extensions gracing the *Enterprise*. The vessel's configuration and energy signatures clearly marked it as an Orion marauder, of the sort employed by professional mercenaries, freebooters, and slavers. Squinting at the image, Spock thought he discerned a name emblazoned on the ship's green patina.

"Increase magnification," he instructed. "Factor three."

A closer view revealed cursive Orion script clearly printed on the beak-like prow of the ship. No serial number accompanied the name.

"*Navaar*," Uhura translated.

Chekov scowled at their unwelcome visitor. "Shall I ready weapons, sir?"

"Negative," Spock said. "The vessel's intentions are unknown. Arming torpedoes, or energizing the phaser banks, could be seen as provocative."

"Provocative?" Santiago sounded as though he could not believe his ears. "Are you out of your mind, Spock? Those are *Orions.* Probably the same ones who attacked the conclave at Yusub!"

"We do not know that, Commissioner, and I remind you that a state of war does not exist between the Federation and the Orion Syndicate."

"But they're pirates!" Santiago insisted. "Bloodthirsty raiders and barbarians."

"Quite often," Spock agreed. "But I am sure I don't need to remind you of the political complexities involved."

Although the Federation took a dim view of the Orions' more unsavory activities, prudence and the Prime Directive obliged Starfleet to more or less tolerate the Orions in areas of space that were not exclusively aligned with the Federation. If independent worlds, such as Yusub, wanted to do business with the Orions, Starfleet could not take unilateral action, provided no Federation ships, colonies, or citizens were victimized. Furthermore, many Orion privateers and mercenaries operated just within the boundaries of local laws, which tended to be enforced with various degrees of laxity throughout the quadrant. To Spock's knowledge, the Orions were currently supplying arms, soldiers, and slave labor to at least sixteen interplanetary conflicts and civil wars not involving the Federation. Orions sometimes clashed with Starfleet peacekeeping forces and were rumored to have frequent dealings with the Klingon Empire, but that hardly justified a preemptive attack. Gamma Trianguli VI was not an official Federation protectorate. Legally, the Orions had as much right to visit the planet as the

Enterprise—and Spock did not wish to initiate an armed conflict by reacting too hastily.

"Complexities be damned," Santiago snarled, taking the opposite view. "You should be opening fire, not clinging to legal niceties!"

"An unusual position for a diplomat," Spock replied. "Respectfully, I submit that your emotions are getting the better of you."

"At least I *have* emotions! And I know a threat when I see one!"

Spock found Santiago's presence increasingly distracting. "Do not force me to have you removed from the bridge, Commissioner."

"Please, sir," Cyril Hague pleaded, attempting to calm his superior. "I'm sure Commander Spock knows what he's doing."

"Like hell he does," the diplomat muttered. "This is on you, Spock, if we pay for your caution with our lives."

"I am quite aware of that, Commissioner." He focused on the task at hand. "Lieutenant Uhura, any word from the *Navaar*?"

"No, sir." She adjusted her earpiece. "They continue to ignore my hails."

Spock wondered what the Orions were after. Despite the variables involved, the possibility that the *Navaar's* arrival here, at the same time that the *Enterprise* was orbiting the planet, was a mere coincidence that defied probability. He calculated the odds at roughly 235.6 to one.

"The marauder has dropped its shields," Chekov reported. "It is beaming something—or someone—down to the planet."

"What is the current status of the shuttle?" Spock asked.

Chekov checked the shuttlecraft's flight telemetry. "Still several minutes away from rendezvousing with the landing party, sir."

Spock concluded that he could not wait for Sulu and the shuttle to reach Captain Kirk and the others, nor take the time to determine where precisely the Orions' transporter beam was targeted. Every moment counted.

"Contact the landing party," he ordered. "Prepare for emergency transport."

"Hold on!" Santiago protested. "You can't lower our shields to beam Kirk and the others back. Not with that Orion marauder out there!"

"The *Navaar*'s shields are currently lowered as well," Spock pointed out, although he privately acknowledged the significant risks involved. "And would you prefer to let the Orions capture the captain . . . and Doctor Seven?"

The dire implications of such an occurrence, and the possible repercussions with regards to Federation security, were not lost on the commissioner. "I . . . I hadn't thought of that."

"Then it is fortunate that I did," Spock said. "Please carry out my order, Lieutenant Uhura."

"Aye, sir." She immediately attempted to alert the captain. Her brisk efforts, however, swiftly gave way to a worried expression. "Commander! I can't get through to the landing party." She consulted her monitors. "We're being jammed."

"That should not be possible," Spock observed, "unless they know our secure frequencies and protocols."

Starfleet's encryption protocols were closely guarded. Multiple redundant systems were also in place to guarantee reliable communications capability. In theory, disrupting the *Enterprise*'s signals should have been beyond the Orions' abilities.

"I don't understand it, sir." Uhura worked her controls, trying to get past the interference. "It's as though they know just how to block us."

"Those crafty bastards!" Santiago fumed. "How the devil are they doing this?"

"I'm sure I don't know, sir," Hague replied.

"The Orions have completed *two* transports," Chekov announced. "The *Navaar* has raised its shields again."

Spock hoped that he had not missed an opportunity to disable the other ship, albeit without provocation. "Location of the transport?"

Chekov consulted his readings. "Somewhere on the southern continent, sir. Not far from the captain's last reported location."

Blackhorse glanced back at Spock, clearly worried about the landing party's safety. She maneuvered the *Enterprise* to present a smaller target to the marauder. "Now what, sir?"

"An excellent question, helmsman."

Spock found himself on the horns of a dilemma. In order to beam reinforcements down to the planet, or even to allow Sulu's shuttle to return to the ship, the *Enterprise* would indeed have to lower its shields, leaving it vulnerable to an attack. Spock doubted that the captain would approve. As daring as Kirk could sometimes be, he would surely hesitate to risk the entire ship for the sake of just four people. Even if one of those people possessed forbidden knowledge of the future.

"Make every effort to reach the captain," Spock instructed Uhura. "And continue hailing the *Navaar* as well." A lack of reliable data made anticipating the Orions' next move problematic. "What do we know of the *Navaar*?"

Ensign Rick Cozzone had taken Spock's usual post at the science station. He was a rangy, dark-haired youth who had recently served on Deep Space Station K-5, where he had shown an aptitude for sensor analysis.

"According to the computer, the ship is registered to a Captain Habroz. Beyond that, details are sketchy." Cozzone shrugged apologetically. "The Orions are not known for their compliance with interstellar navigation protocols."

Spock knew that to be a severe understatement. "So we have no idea why the *Navaar* is here . . . or what they are seeking on the planet's surface."

"Doesn't sound like it," Cyril Hague said.

Eleven

"Still no luck?" Kirk asked.

"Not so much as a four-leaf clover," McCoy grumbled. He smacked the uncooperative communicator with his palm, but to no avail. Nothing but static greeted his hails. "I can't reach the ship!"

Which meant they were stuck on Gamma Trianguli VI, at least until they could rendezvous with Sulu's shuttle. McCoy searched the sky but spotted no sign of their ride. Would Sulu even be able to land on the wooded hilltop—and in the middle of a firefight, no less?

An emerald stun blast zipped over McCoy's head, practically grazing his scalp. The charged atmosphere made his thick brown hair stand on end. The trigger-happy Orions were fanning out around them, attempting to block off the landing party's escape routes. Kirk and Seven tried to hold the bandits off with their phasers, but McCoy knew that the thick tree trunk wasn't going to protect them much longer. It was only a matter of time before the Orions got a clear shot at them.

Kirk saw that, too.

"Can you run?" he asked Seven, who had been showing definite signs of fatigue since her mysterious detour through time. McCoy wondered how much longer she could keep going.

"Self-preservation is a powerful motivator," she replied.

"All right, then," Kirk decided. He gestured toward the slope to their right. "We'll head downhill, away from the village, and make for the fields. With any luck, the crops will conceal us." He hefted his phaser. "I'll cover you."

McCoy glanced down the hill. The forested slope descended steeply to the waving rows of cornstalks below. The bluff looked worryingly precipitous, and far more intimidating than the rolling hills of his native Georgia. No gentle beds of honeysuckle or clover would cushion his fall if he missed a step. It was a long, bumpy way down.

Still, it beat being waylaid by a gang of bloody-minded thugs!

"Okay, Jim," he replied. "Ready when you are."

The leader of the Orions had another idea. "Just give us the woman from the future!" he bellowed from behind the shelter of another leafy kapok tree. Spreading buttress roots helped the tree cling to the side of the hill. The Orion's gravelly voice was deeper than the Altairian Abyss. "No one else needs to get hurt!"

Like the late Lieutenant Jadello.

"Go to hell," Kirk muttered. Obviously, he wasn't about to turn Seven over to the Orions, not with all the dangerous future knowledge she possessed. They might as well hand her over to the Klingons or the Romulans and be done with it. Kirk gave McCoy a shove to get him going. "Run for it. Now!"

The embattled trio took off down the hill. Disruptor blasts chased after them. They zigzagged from tree to tree, keeping their heads down to avoid being stunned. Bulging roots threatened to trip McCoy. His heart pounded in his chest. Sheer adrenaline gave his legs an extra boost, like a judicious dose of cordrazine. Kirk was right behind him, firing back at their foes as he bounded down the slope as nimbly as a wild stallion. Dazzling blue stun beams zipped past the Orions' wild green shots. Wary pirates fell back, preferring to unleash a blistering barrage from atop the hill. Angry shouts and curses gave voice to their frustration. Crude obscenities betrayed a lack of breeding.

"Faster, Bones!" Kirk urged him. "Full speed ahead!"

McCoy panted loudly. "I'm giving it all I can!"

"That's what Scotty always says! Get your own material!"

Seven refrained from comment but managed to keep up with the two men. McCoy was impressed by her stamina, given how exhausted she had appeared only minutes ago. The advantages of her "enhanced" physique and metabolism? Despite his reservations about such tinkering, he had to admit that she did seem to be physically superior to the average human.

Then again, they said that about Khan, too.

"After them!" the one-eared Orion leader shouted at his men. He gnashed his teeth. "Don't let them get away!"

Why not? McCoy thought sourly. *Sounds like a good idea to me.*

The rough terrain grew even steeper beneath their feet. It was all McCoy could do to keep from tumbling head over heels down the precarious incline. An energy beam missed him by a hair, shaking loose the leaves of an undeserving tree. He stumbled awkwardly over fallen branches, logs, and roots. The bottom of the hill seemed impossibly far away, yet came upon them with alarming speed. Miraculously reaching the bottom without breaking their necks, the trio plunged into the waiting cornfields. Tall, leafy stalks stretched above their heads. Stems and husks whipped McCoy's face, but he kept on running, trying to put as much distance as possible between himself and the green-skinned buccaneers on their trail. A stitch in his side reminded him that he was a doctor, not a track star.

"Stick together!" Kirk called out. "Keep your heads down!"

Disruptor blasts seared the air above them. For a second, McCoy feared that their foes might set the fields ablaze, but no, the Orions wouldn't want to risk burning up Seven by mistake. *Even if Jim and I are expendable.*

"Where to now?" he asked Kirk, who was lagging behind them.

"Just keep going." Kirk caught up with McCoy and Seven. The physician in McCoy noted that the fit young captain wasn't even breathing hard. A close encounter with a jagged branch had torn Kirk's yellow tunic, baring one shoulder. Scratch marks gouged the exposed skin. "We just need to find someplace where Sulu can pick us up."

Pushing through the densely packed stalks was more tiring than McCoy had anticipated. Unlike Kirk, he was soon gasping for breath. Sweat dripped down his face and glued his black undershirt to his back. Weary, his muscles ached, while the stitch in his side felt like a laser scalpel burning into his flesh. Random scratches stung like paper cuts. Fatigue threatened to overcome adrenaline. The oppressive heat and humidity added to his discomfort; McCoy found himself pining for the planet's once-controlled climate. At least things hadn't been quite so blasted muggy under Vaal. . . .

A row of stalks parted before him, and he suddenly found himself confronted with a wide-eyed Vaalian child, who appeared to be no more than three years old. McCoy froze in his tracks, less than a meter way from the pint-sized orange humanoid, who was proof positive that the formerly chaste natives were no longer anything of the sort. The child, who had apparently wandered away from the village, froze as well, looking just as startled as the bizarre pink-skinned apparition before her. Painted white eyes widened in fright. Tiny fingers let go of a crude doll fashioned from corn husks. She shrieked in terror.

"Hush!" McCoy pleaded, worried that the child's cries would attract their enemies. His skills as a pediatrician were a bit rusty, but he hastily adopted his most soothing manner. "It's all right. I'm not going to hurt you."

His words did nothing to calm the child, who turned and fled madly away from him, squeezing between the stalks in her panicky flight. McCoy was relieved to see her running away from the direction of the pirates. He could hope that she would make it back to her village safely.

"Congratulations, Bones," Kirk commented. "You've just become the boogeyman."

"Wouldn't be the first time," McCoy muttered. He would have thought that his heart couldn't race any faster, but apparently he was mistaken. He clutched his chest. "Gave me a bit of a jolt, I admit!"

Seven eyed the path taken by the retreating toddler. "I suspect she was more alarmed by you than you were by her."

"Who said I was alarmed?" McCoy protested. "I was just startled, that's all!"

"If you say so, Doctor," Seven replied.

"Enough chatter." Kirk glanced back over his shoulder. Egged on by their determined commander, the Orions were making their way down the slope after the outnumbered landing party. The most eager among the raiders slid upon their leather-clad rears, the faster to reach the bottom. Dislodged leaves and ground cover raced them to the base of the hill. Kirk looked ahead, unwilling to lose their lead. "Keep moving."

The chance encounter with the Vaalian child had cost them precious moments. They angled east toward the jungle to avoid leading the pirates the way the frightened toddler had gone. An irrigation ditch, connecting the fields to the river, crossed their path. They ran down into the shallow ditch and waded into the water, which was no more than ankle-deep. McCoy's heels sank into the slippery mud. Hot and sweaty, he was tempted to scoop up a handful of trickling brown water to wet his parched throat but thought better of it. The last thing he needed right now was a gut full of nasty intestinal parasites.

Water was never his favorite beverage, anyway.

The trio was halfway across the ditch when Seven cried out in pain. She collapsed into McCoy's arms, a cluster of yellow thorns embedded in her back. Too late he spotted a stand of bright purple flowers sprouting from the loamy side of the ditch. Another blossom rotated toward him.

"Jim!" he shouted. "Watch out! It's those blasted flowers!"

Kirk was already on it. A crimson beam shot from his phaser, incinerating the flowers, which glowed incarnadine for an instant before disintegrating. McCoy was grateful for his friend's swift reflexes.

But was it already too late for Seven?

Kirk took a second to make sure there were no more lethal blossoms in the vicinity before rushing over to McCoy, who gently rested Seven against the sloping wall of the ditch. The doctor plucked the thorns from her back and angrily flung them into the water, where they were washed away by the current. Kirk looked on anxiously.

"Can you help her, Bones?"

The last time they had visited this planet, McCoy had managed to save Spock from the thorn's poison, but a human crewman had died instantly. At the time, McCoy had credited Spock's green blood as much as any immediate treatment he'd received. Now McCoy prayed that you didn't need to be Vulcan to survive the neurotoxin. . . .

"I don't know," McCoy confessed. He yanked open his medkit and extracted a hypospray preloaded with masiform-D. A powerful dose of the drug had helped save Spock before, so McCoy had prepared the hypospray in advance, just in case. The hypospray hissed as he pressed it against her shoulder, administering the powerful stimulant directly through her suit. "Her constitution is . . . unusual, but she's still human, basically. I can't promise this will work."

The injection roused Seven, who sat up slightly. Against all odds, she somehow managed to speak.

"I was . . . inattentive," she said weakly. "My apologies."

She sagged against McCoy, who struggled to support her weight. That she was still alive at all was a promising sign, but the doctor knew they were not out of the woods yet. Her elegant face took on a sickly pallor, and her eyes dilated. Her smooth skin turned cold and clammy to the touch. She seemed groggy and only semi-conscious. "Must . . . regenerate," she murmured.

"How is she?" Kirk asked.

"Well, she's not dead, Jim, but I need to get her to sickbay, stat!"

They could hear the Orions crashing noisily through the corn rows behind him. From the sound of it, they were less than a quarter of a kilometer away. Kirk gave the racket a dirty look. "Somehow I doubt that's what our boisterous friends have in mind."

Abandoning Seven was not an option. She was arguably more valuable than the *Enterprise* itself. The Orions could not be allowed to get their greedy mitts on her.

No matter what.

"Yeah, I'm getting that impression, too," McCoy agreed. He wondered how he was going to fight off the pirates and take care of Seven at the same time. He glanced up at the sky. "Where the hell is Sulu?"

"Probably trying to find us in this chaos." He reached for his communicator. "Kirk to shuttle. Can you read me?"

"*Captain!*" Sulu's voice crackled over the communicator. "*What's going on down there? I'm registering weapons fire!*"

McCoy briefly wondered how they could contact the shuttle when their communications to the ship were jammed. Maybe the problem was in space, at the *Enterprise*'s end of things? That was the only explanation that made sense.

"We've run into some unwanted company," Kirk informed Sulu, "and Doctor Seven has been hurt. What's your position?"

"*Approaching your coordinates,*" Sulu reported. "*And looking for a suitable landing spot. I can see open meadows ahead, inhabited by a large herd of the local wildlife.*"

"Yes, we spied them before." Kirk's eyes lit up with a crafty look that McCoy knew too well. A smirk lifted the corners of the captain's lips. He glanced to the west. "Over by the river . . ."

He's up to something, McCoy realized, with a mixture of hope and alarm. That look usually meant that life was about to get even more interesting. "Er, what exactly do you have in mind, Jim?"

"Just look out for Seven," Kirk said tersely. He splashed out of the water and up onto the lip of the ditch. Scoping out the terrain, he kept in touch with the shuttle. "Listen closely, Mister Sulu. Here's what I need you to do . . ."

The shouting of impatient Orions kept McCoy from hearing the rest of the captain's instructions. Drawing nearer by the moment, the pirates called out harshly to each other as they spread out through the fields in search of their quarry. McCoy felt like a fox being hunted by a pack of baying hounds. Only these hounds had disruptors.

I don't know what you're planning, Jim, he thought. *But you'd better do it soon!*

Seven went limp, making McCoy the only thing holding her up. Blood trickled down her back where the thorns had pierced her skin, making her harder to hold on to. He shifted his grip while trying to keep the small wounds away from the mud and the possibility of infection. He considered dragging her out of the ditch and laying her down on dry land, if only to free up his hands to fight the Orions when the raiders finally caught up with them, which was going to be any moment now. *Probably not a bad idea,* he thought. *Maybe I can try hiding her among the stalks. . . .*

Before he could try moving her, however, there was a loud whooshing noise overhead. A shadow fell over the creek. Startled, McCoy tilted his head back in time to see a Starfleet shuttlecraft soar over the ditch. The boxy spacecraft cruised past at an altitude of approximately ninety meters. Twin thrusters, mounted to its undercarriage, glowed like cobalt pontoons. The speed of its passage rustled the tops of the corn stalks, causing a leafy green wave to ripple across the fields. Sulu was flying the shuttle like an old-fashioned barnstormer, coming in fast.

But to what end? The Orions were already firing at the shuttle, trying to bring it down. At the moment, it was flying too high for their disruptor pistols, but as soon as Sulu tried to bring it in for a landing, the raiders would be targeting the shuttle with everything they had. Even if Sulu managed to get the shuttle to the ground in one piece, he wouldn't be able to lower its shields long enough for McCoy and Kirk to haul Seven into the shuttle and take off again. At the moment, the airborne shuttle remained maddeningly out of reach. McCoy wondered what Kirk thought he was up to.

If we can't get to the shuttle, what's the point?

The answer came moments later as the shuttle reached the far end of the grassy meadow beyond the fields, then executed a smooth loop and an inverted roll that brought it swooping down over the teeming hordes of rhinooses. The shuttle came in low over the animals, throwing the herd into a panic. Booming honks issued from their throats. The thunder of heavy hooves rocked the ground as the frenzied rhinooses stampeded away from the shuttle, straight toward McCoy and the others. Kirk dove into the ditch, even as the panicked beasts crashed through the wooden fence defending the fields. Pounding hooves trampled over scarecrows.

"Down!" he hollered to McCoy and Seven. "Flat as you can!"

The quaking ground was all the prompting McCoy needed. "Hold tight!" he warned Seven as he threw the two of them down into the shallow water. The abrupt movement tore an anguished gasp from Seven, but the poisoned time traveler was conscious enough to grasp what needed to be done. They lay flat against the muddy floor of the ditch, turning their heads to one side, as a veritable tidal wave of galloping ruminants jumped the ditch, their flying hooves passing only centimeters above the humans' heads. McCoy hugged the ground, while shielding Seven with one arm. The roar of the stampede was deafening. Dislodged soil and rocks tumbled into the ditch, splashing into the water. McCoy hoped to God that the Vaalians had indeed cleared the field of any explosive stones—and that none of the agile beasts missed a step. A single hoof would punch through his skull or spine like a high-g press.

Flying mud and earth pelted his head and shoulders. The rank odor of the rhinooses nearly suffocated him. Cold, muddy water soaked him to the skin and shocked Seven into alertness. She stirred beside him.

"Are all your landing parties so tumultuous?" she asked.

"You have no idea," McCoy muttered.

A clumsy fawn didn't quite make the jump. Its rear hooves splashed down in the water, missing McCoy's head by a hand's breadth. It scrambled up the opposite side of the ditch, but not before kicking a clod of mud right into McCoy's face. Sputtering, he spit a mouthful of muck into the water. It tasted worse than a Denebian slime devil.

Remind me why I joined Starfleet again. . . .

Not for the first time, he hoped Kirk knew what he was doing.

Twelve

"Get them, you motherless curs!" Habroz cursed his men. "I want that time traveler!"

He led the charge down the hill after Seven and her miserable Starfleet guardians. Stumbling against an unyielding tree, he scraped his shoulder before bouncing off it angrily. Frustration churned in his gut as he hastily descended the slope. This whole raid was taking too long; it should have been just a quick snatch-and-grab, not a goddess-damned chase! Every minute they wasted pursuing Seven left the *Navaar* in the *Enterprise*'s sights. What if K'Mara turned tail and ordered the marauder to depart?

He suspected that she would abandon him if necessary. Orion females often considered males expendable. She had ambitions of her own and was unlikely to risk the *Navaar* for his sake. Captains could be replaced easier than ships.

The raiding party reached the bottom of the hill. Waving curtains of crops hid his prize from him. Drawing his hatchet from his belt, he hacked at the irritating corn stalks, carving his way through the field. He wished it was a human he was slashing instead.

"Fan out!" he ordered his crew. "The man who finds Seven will win a greater share of the rewards! And you will all suffer my wrath if she gets away!"

Habroz had already put out feelers to the Klingons, who had made it clear that they would pay a queen's ransom for the woman from the future, although K'Mara had suggested auctioning Seven to the highest bidder instead. Habroz was not sure that was wise. It did not pay to anger the Klingons. . . .

None of which mattered, of course, if Seven was not theirs to barter with.

"Faster, you vermin!" he roared. "Search every acre of this wretched compost heap. Find me that woman!"

"Yes, Captain!" answered Pommu, his bosun. He was a pot-bellied old scoundrel with a scraggly chartreuse beard. A metal skullcap was screwed into his cranium, while a necklace of humanoid teeth hung around his neck. His belt was stuffed with more knives than one raider should ever need. "And the Starfleet swine?"

Habroz spat in disgust. He slashed his way through the stalks.

"Kill them!"

A shadow fell over them. Craning back his head, Habroz was dismayed to spy a Starfleet shuttlecraft zipping by overhead. "Cesspools!" he swore. Had the humans already sent reinforcements to the aid of their landing party? He had not been expecting that; K'Mara was supposed to be keeping the *Enterprise* busy.

This entire operation was going to hell!

Unlike his men, he didn't bother shooting at the shuttle. He knew better than to waste his disruptor blasts on the high-flying craft, whose deflectors could easily repel mere sidearm fire. Raising his metal hand to shield his eyes from the sun, he watched as the shuttle made its way to the far end of the grassy plains beyond the fields, then reversed course. Moments later, a cacophonous roar came thundering across the meadows, sounding like a mounted cavalry staging a charge. Racing hooves churned up the fertile soil, raising a huge cloud of dust. The ground trembled beneath his boots.

A memory flashed through his mind of many large-horned herbivores grazing at a river. He had glimpsed them before while sneaking up on the Starfleet landing party. The shaggy beasts resembled the megayaks of his native Rigarus. In his youth, he had enjoyed hunting them from levitating blinds, but even then he'd known better than to get in the way of a terrified herd. He instantly recognized the sound racing toward them.

"Stampede!"

His warning came too late for some of his men. The herd crashed into the raiders like a marauder at ramming speed. One man was gored upon a bony horn, while another was trampled beneath an onslaught of heavy hooves. The pirates fired at the stampede, cutting animals down right and left, but it was like trying to repel a meteor storm with a disruptor cannon; for every panicked beast they killed or stunned, dozens more galloped into the fields. An agitated megayak tossed an impaled raider into the air, honking loudly as it did so. He landed smack in the path of yet another oncoming beast. His gutted corpse vanished beneath an unstoppable tide of wildlife.

Habroz did not waste time mourning the fallen. The life of a raider was often a short one; that came with the job. Along with what was left of his men, he turned and ran from the stampede. "Climb the trees!" he hollered. "Get out of their way!"

Racing back up the hill, he clambered up the side of

the nearest leafy sanctuary. Prosthetic steel fingers found purchase in the living bark and wood as he ascended to the upper branches of the tree. Just as he'd hoped, the stampede parted to go around the obstacle. Speeding megayaks streamed past him on either side of the tree trunk. Another pirate scrambled to climb up after Habroz, but not quickly enough. The herd slammed into him, sweeping him away. Habroz mentally added him to the death list. The man's weapons and property would be auctioned off to pay for his funeral expenses, after the captain got first pick of his effects, as was his due.

The shuttle circled overhead, further agitating the herd. Habroz realized belatedly that the stampede had been no accident. He shook his metal fist at the flying shuttle.

Starfleet scum! You will pay for your trickery!

Climbing to his feet atop a sturdy branch, he saw that maybe half of his men had made it to safety. Pommu waved at him from a nearby tree, even as a never-ending flood of horned megayaks continued to rush past them. The bosun appeared to have lost his pistol in the chaos but looked otherwise intact. Who knew the fat old bastard could move so fast?

"Captain!" Pommu shouted to be heard over the thundering hooves. Choking clouds of dust coarsened his voice. "The time traveler! What about—"

A wooden spear slammed into his back, reducing his words to a bloody gurgle. Clutching his back, he tumbled out of the tree and into the path of the stampede. Pounding hooves drowned out his final breaths.

"Pommu!" The unexpected attack caught Habroz by surprise. "What in perdition?"

Since when did Starfleet resort to spears?

More missiles came whistling through the air. Spinning around, Habroz spied a party of red-skinned humanoids targeting them from the crest of the hill. The white-haired natives took shelter from the stampede behind the widest tree trunks, while continuing to take arms against the Orion invaders. A spear sped toward Habroz's face, and he snatched it out of the air only a heartbeat before it took out his eye. His metal grip crushed the shaft of the arrow, reducing it to splinters. He glared furiously at the offending natives.

They should mind their own business!

He drew his pistol, intending to teach the ignorant hunters a lesson. Crude spears were no match for disruptors. He laughed scornfully at the natives' primitive weaponry. *Next they'll be throwing rocks at us!*

Then a flying stone slammed into the ground nearby, exploding with tremendous force. The concussive impact nearly knocked Habroz from his arboreal perch. Smoke rose from a newborn crater, only a few meters away. The explosion left Habroz dazed, his ears ringing.

"What—?"

He saw a native pluck another stone from a bag. The red-skinned hunter drew back as though to throw the rock at the Orions. More spears took flight.

"Enough," Habroz muttered. A wise captain knew when a battle was turning against him. Firing back at the cursed natives, he shouted into his wrist-communicator. "Habroz to *Navaar*! We're under attack! Beam us up now!"

They would have to snatch Annika Seven another day.

Alarmed by the spears and explosion, the panicked megayaks tried to change course. Their enormous weight crashed into the tree trunk below, almost spilling Habroz once more. Sparking emerald transporter beams flared across the hillside, grabbing the surviving raiders. Habroz managed to regain his balance even as he dissolved into atoms. A final blast from his disruptor killed one of the spear-tossing natives, avenging Pommu's death.

It wasn't enough.

"Commander Spock!" Chekov exclaimed. "The *Navaar* has lowered its shields again. They're beaming a party aboard."

The silent marauder maintained its inexplicable orbit around Gamma Trianguli VI. The *Enterprise*'s main viewer kept watch over the *Navaar,* which had yet to reveal its purpose here. Spock processed this latest development as he occupied the captain's chair. Had the marauder's landing party completed its unknown mission? And what did that mean for Captain Kirk and the others?

He had too many questions—and too little reliable data.

Chekov's fingers were poised above the weapons controls. "Shall I target their engines, sir, before they restore their shields?"

"Hold your fire," Spock instructed the impetuous ensign. "The *Navaar* has taken no hostile action against us. It would be premature to initiate a military engagement."

"But they are Orions!" Commissioner Santiago blurted predictably. "How long are you going to cling to this ridiculous, and frankly irresponsible, insistence on giving them the benefit of the doubt? For all we know, they've already butchered your captain . . . and taken possession of Seven!"

"That possibility cannot be ruled out," Spock conceded, "but we know nothing for certain. I will not open fire on a vessel on the basis of sheer speculation. To do so would be in clear defiance of Starfleet's rules of engagement . . . and basic diplomacy."

"Don't talk to me about diplomacy!" Santiago snapped. "I've ended wars!"

"And I am hoping to avert one, Commissioner. Not all Orions are criminals and slavers." Spock could think of at least one noted Orion astrophysicist. "If the Orions attempt to enslave or exploit the Vaalians, then we *may* have to consider taking action to protect the native population on Gamma Trianguli VI, but not before carefully weighing the facts as we know them."

"But why won't they talk to us?" Chekov asked. "What are they hiding?"

"A pertinent question," Spock replied, "but mere silence does not constitute grounds for an attack. Only judicious caution on our part." He gave the *Navaar* his full attention. "Your apprehensions are not unwarranted, however. Stand by to defend the ship if necessary."

Spock was not naïve. Although the Orions had done nothing to provoke them so far, he knew that Chekov—and the commissioner—had good reason to be suspicious of their motives. History indicated that Starfleet and the Orions frequently had conflicting agendas, and the ruthless aliens were not known for their pacifism.

As the captain and the others may have already discovered.

"Lieutenant Uhura." He addressed the communications officer. "How go your efforts to reestablish contact with the landing party?"

"Negative so far, sir." She diligently worked her controls. "This interference is posing a challenge, but maybe if I stagger the phase variance and scan on all frequencies . . ." Her expert fingers kept up with her improvisations. "Yes! I'm getting through to them!"

Spock admired her creative thinking. "Well done, Lieutenant."

But her jubilation was quickly supplanted by alarm. "Mister Spock! I'm receiving a distress call from the planet. Doctor Seven has been hurt!"

Hurt? Spock was immediately concerned, not just for Seven's well-being but for the possible effects on the time line of her perishing long before her birth. Logically, this news was preferable to discovering that Seven had fallen into the hands of the Orions, but it was hardly a development to be welcomed. "What is the extent of her injuries?"

"Commander!" Chekov interrupted. "The *Navaar* has raised its shields again. It's pulling away from the planet!"

"They're still on impulse power," Blackhorse confirmed. "Shall I set course to pursue them? We'll have to move quickly if we want to catch up with them before they warp out of the system."

"Negative, Lieutenant," Spock said. While he remained curious as to why the Orions had set foot on Gamma Trianguli VI, now was not the time to investigate; the distress call took priority. "Beam the landing party aboard. And alert sickbay to expect casualties."

"Aye, sir," Chekov responded.

On the main viewer, the *Navaar* warped out of sight. Moments later, the long-range sensors lost track of it as well.

"The Orion ship has left the system," Chekov reported.

The marauder had vanished as it had appeared: without explanation. Spock wondered where it had gone—and whether the *Enterprise* would encounter it again. Although he had little data on which to make such a prediction, he suspected that they had not seen the last of the *Navaar* and its crew. Captain Kirk might call such an expectation a hunch; Spock preferred to think of it as an educated guess.

"Damn it," Santiago said. "They got away . . . again!"

"Good riddance," his aide said. "If you ask me."

Spock had more pressing matters to attend to. "The landing party?"

Uhura received confirmation from the transporter room. "Doctors McCoy and Seven are back aboard, sir, but the captain chose to return via the shuttle instead. A full trauma team is currently conveying Doctor Seven to sickbay."

"Thank you, Lieutenant," Spock said, curious as to why Kirk had decided not to beam back with the others. "Keep me apprised of her condition."

Chekov stared at the vacated space on the viewscreen. "I hope we didn't just let the people who hurt Doctor Seven escape."

Spock's stoic expression never faltered. "I share your concern, Ensign."

Thirteen

Kirk rushed into sickbay, muddy and out of breath. He had run straight from the shuttlebay after arriving back on the *Enterprise*. The backpack containing the captured fragments was strapped to his shoulders. After rapid deliberation, he had taken the pack from Seven so that they could beam her directly back to the ship without risking her disappearing again. Just to play it safe, he had ridden back in the shuttle with Sulu instead.

He found McCoy tending to Seven, who was stretched out on a bio-bed, beneath an insulating gold blanket. A sterilization field protected her from further infection, while the overhead sensor cluster monitored her vital signs, which were reported on the wall monitor above the bed. Kirk saw at a glance that her pulse and respiration were weak but climbing. To his relief, she was able to speak.

"The components?" she said anxiously.

He patted the pack. "Safe," he assured her. "Don't worry about it."

His words seemed to calm her. Her eyes closed as she drifted off. Kirk eyed the monitor tensely.

"How is she, Bones?" he asked.

"She'll live," McCoy said. The doctor had changed into a clean and presumably more antiseptic uniform, but he still had traces of mud in his hair. Both men looked as though they'd been through the wars. "It was touch and go for a while there, and she's going to need plenty of rest, but I'm pretty sure she'll pull through."

Kirk was glad to hear it. "Good work, Doctor."

"I wish I could take all the credit, but her . . . unique . . . recuperative abilities did most of the heavy lifting." McCoy glanced around to see if any of his staff was listening and lowered his voice. "I've never seen anything like it, Jim. As nearly as I can tell, there are microscopic machines in her bloodstream that are already filtering out the toxins and repairing the damage to her cells. It's uncanny."

Kirk caught a note of unease in the doctor's voice. "You sound like you don't entirely approve."

"Maybe," McCoy admitted. "As far as I'm concerned, some people—and technologies—should stay in their own eras. What's been done to her body seems to go beyond medicine . . . and maybe even humanity."

"Commissioner Santiago would disagree," Kirk pointed out, "at least about the future technology part. And who knows? Maybe he has a point. From what you're saying, there's a lot we could learn from her."

Kirk was curious to get McCoy's take on the dilemma. Knowing Bones, the doctor was bound to have an opinion.

McCoy did not disappoint.

"I don't know, Jim." He shook his head thoughtfully. "Maybe we're not meant to know the future. How do we know we're ready for whatever Seven is hiding?"

Kirk was inclined to agree, but he felt obliged to play devil's advocate, if only to address his own doubts. "But what about the potential medical breakthroughs?

Suppose she's holding back a cure for Anchilles Fever? Or Irumodic Syndrome?"

McCoy wavered. "You've got me there," he admitted. "I'd give up my miserable excuse for a pension to crack just one of those plagues. All the same, something about this business doesn't sit right with me. Even seemingly harmless new medical advances can be abused if they fall into the wrong hands. Life-saving new drugs can lead to addiction and social collapse. Revolutionary surgical techniques can be used to lobotomize, mutilate, and torture. Cybernetics can transform people into machines. Expanding lifespans and fertility can lead to overpopulation, like on Malthus Prime." His voice grew heated as he warmed to his theme. "Look at Earth's own history. Genetic engineering held the promise of eradicating birth defects and hereditary disease. Instead we ended up with the Eugenics Wars . . . and Khan Noonien Singh."

"Good point," Kirk said. "But like it or not, Seven *is* part of our time line now. Perhaps we can't just ignore that?"

"Why not?" McCoy argued. "I swore an oath enjoining me to 'First do no harm.' Maybe Commissioner Santiago should take a hint from Hippocrates." He glanced down at his sleeping patient. "I don't know about you, but I'm planning to scrub all records of those micromachines in her blood . . . and everything else that's not of this era. I'll sleep better that way."

Kirk nodded. "You make a persuasive case, Doctor."

"Damn straight I do." McCoy looked the disheveled captain over. "Now then, let's get you checked out as well."

"That's not necessary, Bones." Kirk started toward the exit. "I'm needed on the bridge."

McCoy moved to block him. "Not until you get some of those cuts and scrapes looked at." Kirk started to protest, but McCoy cut him off. "Don't even try arguing with me. Have you glanced in a mirror, Jim? You look like hell."

Kirk peered down at himself. His tunic was torn and muddy. His soggy uniform dripped onto the sterile white floor. Water sloshed in his boots. Various nicks and scratches barely seemed worth bothering with, but it probably wasn't a bad idea to have them cleaned out and disinfected. Who knew what sort of alien microbes had been lurking in Gamma Trianguli VI's air and water?

"All right, Bones. You win."

Confident that Seven was out of immediate danger, and that Spock could hold down the fort a while longer, Kirk let McCoy lead him away to an adjacent examination room. Stripping to the waist, he sat down on the edge of a spare bed while McCoy tended to various small cuts and bruises. Nurse Ufgya, a petite blue-skinned Andorian, fetched the captain a towel, which he used to wipe away most of the mud caking his face. Kirk tugged off one boot and tipped it over. Dirty brown water spilled onto the floor.

"A shame about Jadello," McCoy said. "He was a good man."

"That he was," Kirk agreed. He made a mental note to recommend him for a posthumous commendation. Like Bergstrom back on Yusub, the martyred lieutenant was hardly the first crew member to perish under his command, and he would surely not be the last, but

Kirk hoped that he would never take such sacrifices for granted. He was not looking forward to notifying Jadello's family of his demise. Was he married? Did he have any children? Siblings? Kirk hoped not. He knew what it was like to lose a brother . . . and a child.

Somebody was going to miss Jadello. That was for sure.

And all because some cutthroat tried to kidnap Seven.

Anger flared inside him as he recalled the ambush. A rapid-fire briefing, conducted en route back to the *Enterprise,* had brought him up to speed on the ship's inconclusive encounter with the *Navaar.* His fists clenched at his sides as he committed Captain Habroz's name and face to his memory. As he'd promised McCoy back on the planet, he wasn't going to forget about the Orions' vicious attack.

Nobody kills my people and gets away with it.

"Please lift your arms, Captain," Ufgya requested as she supplemented McCoy's efforts by waving a glowing wand over Kirk's battered torso. The sterilizing radiation raised goose bumps on his skin. Minor lacerations itched all over. Her twin antennae studied him professionally. "This won't hurt a bit."

"I'll bet you get tired of saying that."

Ordinarily, Kirk might enjoy being fussed over by an attractive nurse, but right now he had more serious matters on his mind. As he submitted to Ufgya's ministrations, he considered the full implications of what had transpired down on Gamma Trianguli VI. Hostile forces were after Seven, either the Orions themselves or whomever they were working for.

"How did they know how to find us?" he asked aloud, after the nurse had wandered off. "Could there be a leak at Starfleet . . . or maybe even a spy on the ship? I don't want to think that a member of my own crew might sell us out, but not even Starfleet's screening processes are perfect. Look at Ben Finney or Marla McIvers."

"Heck, they let you into the Academy," McCoy cracked. "And Spock."

Kirk appreciated his friend's attempt to lighten the atmosphere, but he wasn't in the mood. "I'm serious, Bones. How did the Orions manage to jam our comm systems? They would need to know classified Federation codes and frequencies to pull that off. Are we dealing with a snake in the grass, or am I just being paranoid?"

"I wish I knew, Jim." Worry creased the doctor's brow. "Maybe the Orions are just more technologically adept than we knew? And they cracked our codes somehow?"

"Maybe," Kirk said. "And yet—"

"Excuse me, Doctor," Nurse Ufgya interrupted. "Doctor Seven is awake. She's asking for you . . . and Mister Spock."

Kirk hopped off the bed. "See to your patient, Bones. I'll relieve Spock on the bridge."

After he scrounged up a clean shirt, of course.

"How are you feeling?" McCoy asked.

"Uncomfortable," Seven admitted, lying awkwardly on a primitive bio-bed. Her back stung where the thorns had pierced her skin. "I am not accustomed to resting supine in this manner."

McCoy gave her a puzzled look. "And how exactly do you usually sleep?"

"That is what I need to discuss with both you and Commander Spock." She tried to rise to a sitting position, only to experience a moment of lightheadedness. The lingering aftereffects of the neurotoxin, no doubt, along with her ongoing fatigue. A dull headache interfered with her cortical processing. "Excuse me, I require a moment."

McCoy elevated the head of the bed. "Is that better?"

"Yes. Thank you, Doctor." She glanced at the entrance to the recovery ward, waiting for Spock to arrive. A degree of anxiety attended her anticipation. She eyed with concern the diagnostic monitor positioned over the bed. She disliked seeing her vital signs so readily on display. It made her wonder what else the doctor's examination had uncovered.

McCoy followed her gaze. "Something bothering you?"

"Do not think me ungrateful, Doctor, but I am troubled by what you might have discovered while treating me for my injuries . . . and by what I may have to divulge to you and Commander Spock."

"I'll bet," McCoy said, as though he was already well aware of her modifications. He gestured for his staff to give them some privacy and waited until they had the ward to themselves. "As far as that goes, your singular anatomy—and anything else you care to disclose—is fully covered by doctor-patient confidentiality." He checked her pulse in a distinctly archaic fashion, while comparing the results to the display on the monitor. "They do still have that in your time, I assume?"

She was familiar with the principle. "That depends on the species."

"Well, I'm an old-fashioned, red-blooded country doctor, so your 'medical history' is safe with me."

Spock entered the ward in time to overhear McCoy's remark.

"You must forgive the good doctor," he said dryly. "He is excessively and illogically proud of his iron-based blood, but you may rely on his professional integrity."

McCoy huffed. "And Spock can be annoyingly tight-lipped when he wants to be. The time he went into *pon farr*, he almost died before admitting it."

"You are hardly doing your reputation for discretion any favors," Spock observed. "That is a private matter which most Vulcans prefer to keep to themselves."

"I assure you," she interrupted, hoping to head off another round of inefficient banter, "that the concept of *pon farr* was already known to me. But there is another medical issue that I fear I can no longer avoid sharing with you."

McCoy regarded her attentively. "If this is about the poison, I think I can promise you a full recovery. . . ."

"This is another matter," she stated. "Unrelated to the incident on Gamma Trianguli VI, except perhaps as it contributed to my failure to detect the threat in time." She attempted, cautiously, to explain. "In my own time and place, where I belong, I do not sleep as you do. I require regular periods of regeneration in an apparatus compatible with my cybernetic implants. Without such rest cycles, my ability to function is impaired, and I am subject to the fatigue you witnessed on the planet's surface, Doctor. This condition can and will worsen with time."

Indeed, she was already finding it difficult to focus.

Her eyelids drooped as though weighed down by heavy gravity. Her limbs felt inert.

"I had hoped to return to my own time before this issue became significant, but our quest has proven too time-consuming. The distances to be traversed are too great to expect that we will locate the remaining components before lack of regeneration impairs my motor functions—or worse."

As a drone, connected to the Collective, she had been capable of going without regeneration for approximately two hundred hours before suffering ill effects, but since becoming an individual, she had found it advisable to regenerate at least three hours a day. In an emergency, she could remain active for longer periods, much as baseline humans could sometimes do without sleep when required, but she was by now badly in need of regeneration. It was only a matter of time before her cognitive and motor functions began to break down, perhaps irreparably.

"Dear Lord," McCoy whispered. "Whose bright idea was it to 'improve' upon sleep?"

"That is irrelevant, Doctor. The fact remains that I require your assistance to remain functioning until I can return to a time and place where I can regenerate as I am configured to do."

"Of course," McCoy said. "We'll do whatever we can to help you. Perhaps drugs or neuro-electric stimulation to induce deep sleep, maybe even suspended animation while we're traveling between planets. And stimulants to keep you on your feet when you need to be."

Seven nodded, having already considered those approaches. "Such measures will surely be required, and they may help buy me the time I need."

"It's going to be a tricky balancing act," McCoy said, "but I suppose we have no choice, if what you say is true."

"You need not rely on my word, Doctor. A thorough study of my vital signs will confirm my growing need for rest and regeneration."

McCoy ran a medical scanner over her. "Hmm. I see what you mean. Your electrolyte levels are lower than I'd like, you have elevated levels of cortisol, and other stress factors associated with significant sleep deprivation."

"Or, in my case, lack of regeneration."

McCoy nodded and put away the scanner.

"But why did you ask for Spock as well? What can he do to help you?" the doctor asked, glancing at his Vulcan colleague. "No offense, Spock."

"None taken, Doctor," Spock said. "I suspect that Seven requires my scientific expertise as well as your medical prowess."

"That is correct," she stated. "My difficulty is as much technological as biological. My cybernetic implants are a factor here. It is my hope that, working together, Commander Spock and I can address that aspect of my condition."

"An intriguing challenge," Spock declared. A pensive look suggested that his formidable mind was already at work on the problem. "You mentioned a specialized regeneration apparatus before. Would it be possible to re-create such an apparatus aboard *Enterprise*?"

She recalled, rather longingly, her alcove back on *Voyager*. That apparatus had been salvaged from a Borg cube destroyed by Species 8472. At this point in history, the nearest cube was likely in the Delta Quadrant.

"That is unlikely . . . and inadvisable," she replied. "The necessary materials and components are not readily obtainable in this era. Furthermore, even if such a project was feasible, I would hesitate to install such advanced technology aboard your ship. The potential for temporal contamination would be . . . extreme."

She was not exaggerating. Integrating Borg hardware and programming into *Enterprise* could be catastrophic in ways she could only begin to imagine. If there was even a remote chance of a Federation starship being assimilated, and perhaps attracting the attention of the Borg almost a century ahead of history, she had to find another way.

"It may be possible, however, to modify a twenty-third-century power transfer conduit to reenergize my implants as needed. With your assistance."

According to Starfleet records, which Seven had reviewed back in her own time, the crew of a later *Starship Enterprise* had once done the same to sustain a captured Borg drone for a time. The power system aboard Kirk's ship was a generation more primitive, of course, but she had hopes that it could be adapted to serve the same purpose, at least for the time being.

"My familiarity with the *Enterprise*'s systems is at your disposal," Spock said. "In addition, there is another, less technological resource I can offer. Certain Vulcan meditation techniques can be used to combat mental and physical fatigue. In my experience, they can be highly effective in maintaining mental acuity despite extreme sleep deprivation." He cast a sideways glance at McCoy. "Perhaps even more so than the good doctor's stimulants."

McCoy scowled. "Well, I don't know about that. Meditation is all very well and good, but—"

"I said *Vulcan* meditation, Doctor. Not the rudimentary version practiced by most humans."

"The utility of Vulcan mental exercises is not in dispute," Seven stated, having discussed the topic with Tuvok on occasion. He had shared a few basic techniques with her following their mind-meld a year ago. They had indeed helped to restore her mental equilibrium following a harrowing case of multiple-personality disorder. "A colleague of mine is well-versed in such matters . . . or will be."

Spock arched an eyebrow. "Fascinating. I am gratified to hear that my people's teachings still find favor in the future."

She could tell that he was curious to learn more, but he knew better than to pursue that line of inquiry. The future of the Vulcan people and philosophy was best left unspoken.

"Of course you are," McCoy muttered.

"If you wish, I can instruct and guide you in these techniques," Spock volunteered.

"That would be beneficial," she agreed. "In conjunction with a suitable power source . . . and Doctor McCoy's medicinal efforts."

"Don't you worry," the doctor said, putting aside his rivalry with Spock. "One way or another, we'll get you through this."

She wished she shared his optimism. While all the strategies they had discussed might alleviate her symptoms and delay her inevitable decline, she was under no illusion that they were anything more than stopgap measures. She needed to return to her own time—and alcove—while she still could.

Her eyelids began to droop again. She felt chilled despite the foil blanket and found herself trembling. Her left hand began to shake. Its exoskeleton chafed against her skin, which felt dry and raw.

McCoy noted her distress. "First off, you need some serious rest." He prepared a hypospray. "This is a sedative to help you sleep . . . the old-fashioned way."

"An admirable suggestion, Doctor, but . . . not yet." She held up her hand to deter him. "I require the fragment I obtained on Gamma Trianguli VI. I have not yet had the opportunity to examine it closely, and I am eager to continue our quest for the remaining components . . . while I am still able."

Then, and only then, she might be able to rest.

Fourteen

Cheron was a dead world.

The planet on the viewscreen was gray and ashen, its funereal pallor broken up only by rusty red seas and rivers. Although Cheron had once been inhabited by a thriving civilization that had, in many ways, been more technologically advanced than the Federation, no artificial lights could be seen on the night side of the planet. Nor were there any spacefaring vessels in orbit around Cheron, only a handful of dead satellites in decaying orbits.

"Not exactly the hot spot of the galaxy," Chekov commented from his post.

"More like a graveyard," Sulu agreed. "Never thought we'd come back here again."

Chekov shook his head. "If we have to revisit old stops, couldn't we have swung by that Shore Leave planet instead?"

"I am afraid that is not currently on our itinerary, Ensign," Spock announced from the captain's chair. He contemplated the bleak sphere on the viewer. "I would prefer to hear a report on the planet below us."

"Aye, sir," Cozzone reported from the science station. A viewing scope cast a gentle blue glow on his aquiline features. "Long-range sensors indicate abandoned cities and traffic systems, devoid of activity or power sources. Urban structures crumbling and gradually being reclaimed by encroaching wastelands. Bio-scanners pick up only lower life-forms, although there are numerous humanoid remains, in various states of decay and mummification, lying unburied in the ruins of the cities." Cozzone grimaced in distaste. "They're all dead, sir. Everyone on the planet."

"As was to be expected, Ensign," Spock said. The readings were consistent with what the *Enterprise* had discovered on Cheron during its first visit to the planet, approximately 1.364 years ago. The warring peoples of Cheron had destroyed themselves in senseless, fratricidal conflict at some unknown point in the last fifty thousand years, rendering their entire species extinct, save for two long-time adversaries.

It was those individuals who concerned Spock now. He removed a microtape from the armrest of his chair and walked it over to Cozzone at the science station.

"This tape contains the specific bio-signatures of Bele and Lokai, the Cheronian survivors who took control of the ship on a previous occasion," he explained to Cozzone, who had joined the crew after that incident. "Both men were capable of generating unusual energies. Please calibrate the sensors to determine their present locations."

When last encountered, the feuding Cheronians had been left to continue their ageless conflict in the blighted ruins of their world. Given the bellicose nature of the two aliens, and their extraordinary abilities, Spock hoped to avoid engaging with them on this particular mission. Ordinarily, locating two specific individuals on an entire planet would be a daunting task, but the fact that Bele and Lokai were now the *only* surviving humanoids on Cheron improved the odds of success by a significant margin. "Scan also for any signs of habitation, no matter how small."

"Aye, sir." Cozzone fed the microtape into the data input slot.

Spock waited for the results of the scan. He was tempted to reclaim his usual post at the science station and perform the sensor sweep himself, but Cozzone was a qualified officer; Spock trusted him to do his job.

"Got them, sir!" Cozzone said triumphantly. "I'm picking up two humanoid life-forms matching those signatures. They're holed up in what appear to be armed bunkers at opposite ends of the planet. In the remote polar regions, to be exact."

"Figures," Uhura commented with obvious disgust. "Even after seeing what prejudice did to their world, they've still managed to get as far away from each other as they possibly could. I don't know whether to find that funny . . . or unbearably sad."

Spock shared her revulsion. "Blind hatred knows no logic, Lieutenant. But let us hope that Bele and Lokai remain barricaded in their bunkers for the duration of our mission here. That would surely be advantageous for all concerned."

"*Why* are we back here, Mister Spock?" she asked. "Can you tell us anything?"

Spock considered his answer carefully. Contrary to myth, Vulcans were perfectly capable of lying when there were logical reasons to do so, but out of respect for the crew, he attempted to adhere to the truth as closely as possible.

"An artifact uncovered by Doctor Seven on Gamma Trianguli VI indicated that an exploratory mission to Cheron was the next logical stage in her studies. Captain Kirk and I concurred with her findings and set course for the planet accordingly."

To be more precise, Seven had detected another stardate inscribed on the crystalline component she had located within Vaal: 5730.8, which corresponded to the *Enterprise*'s first and only visit to Cheron. As the previous inscription had successfully led them to the fragment hidden on Gamma Trianguli VI, albeit many years in the past, it had seemed only logical to seek out the next piece on Cheron. Spock could only hope, however, that this expedition would prove less hazardous.

"And the Orions, sir?" Chekov asked. "Where do they fit in?"

Spock felt he owed the crew at least a partial explanation. He was grateful that Commissioner Santiago was not on hand to interject his own intemperate views on the subject. The commissioner and his aide were presently in their quarters, occupied with their own diplomatic duties. Spock was in no hurry for them to return to the bridge.

"Doctor Seven's research could lead us to lost alien technology of unknown potential and application. The Orions apparently wish to claim that technology, as well as Doctor Seven's specialized knowledge of such matters."

Crew members nodded, accepting Spock's explanation at face value. This was a logical response, he realized, considering how often the *Enterprise* had dealt with ancient technology left behind by vanished civilizations on forgotten worlds. Billions of years of galactic history had left the quadrant seemingly littered with exotic, often dangerous relics on planets such Exo III, Camus II, Mudd's planet, Arret, Amerind, and many others; it was hardly unprecedented for the *Enterprise*—and the Orions—to be in search of more of the same.

"So what exactly are we dealing with here, Mister Spock?" Chekov asked impetuously. "More androids? Artificial intelligence? Another time portal?"

The young Russian had no idea how close he was to the truth.

"That, I am not at liberty to disclose, Ensign." Spock chose to shut down any further speculation by redirecting the bridge crew to their duties. "Is there any sign of the *Navaar* or any other potentially hostile vessels?"

Chekov consulted his navigations sensors. "No, sir. We appear to have the system to ourselves."

Cheron was located in a remote region in the southernmost part of the quadrant, near the desolate Coalsack Nebula. This sector remained largely unexplored; it was highly unlikely that any other vessel would be in the vicinity unless it was deliberately tailing the *Enterprise*.

"Thank you, Ensign." Spock took this report as a positive development although he could not help wondering where the *Navaar* was at this moment. He activated the intercom built into the armrest of the chair. "Spock to transporter room. You are all clear, Captain."

"Acknowledged," Kirk replied, pressing the speaker button on the intercom. "We're preparing to beam down . . . to whenever. Kirk out."

He stepped away from the transporter console, which, in the interests of secrecy, had been cleared except for Seven, Scotty, and McCoy. He presented a striking appearance, with makeup applied to paint his face white on the left side and black on the right. Instead of his customary Starfleet uniform, he wore a fabricated gray tunic and trousers. Matching gloves eliminated the need to tint his hands as well. A metallic silver chain circled his neck.

He eyed Seven skeptically. "You sure you're up for this?"

"Yes, Captain," she replied. "I appreciate your concern, but I believe I am fully capable of taking part in this expedition."

Seven had spent most of the journey to Cheron in an artificially induced state of deep, delta-wave sleep, while a power conduit adapter, devised by her and Spock, had allowed her to recharge her implants by plugging her hand's assimilation tubules directly into the adapter. Neither provided a fully satisfactory substitute for a normal regeneration cycle, but they would have to suffice. At least her hand was no longer shaking . . . at present.

"All right," Kirk said. "What do you say, Bones?"

The doctor was on hand to keep an eye on his patient. He scanned Seven with his medical tricorder. "Well, her electrolyte levels are still pretty low, but I suppose she's cleared for duty." He handed her a hypospray pre-loaded with a powerful stimulant. "To be used as needed," he instructed. "Just try to avoid getting poisoned this time."

"I will do my best," she assured him.

Kirk stepped back to inspect her. "I must say, 'Doctor Seven,' you make an attractive Cheronian."

Like the captain, Seven was disguised to resemble the largely extinct denizens of the planet below. She wore identical makeup and gray attire, although her hair had been tinted a light brown, since it was apparently unknown whether blondes had been a rarity on Cheron or not. The bisected pigmentation of the planet's inhabitants was unique in her experience; the Borg had never assimilated a species with such improbable coloring.

"I will take that as a compliment," she remarked dryly. "I can only hope the effort to camouflage ourselves proves worthwhile."

"It ought to," he said, "if you really think we're going to beam down into sometime in Cheron's past."

"That is my hypothesis," she confirmed. Beaming down to Gamma Trianguli VI with the first fragment had indeed diverted her to the planet's past, where she'd located the second component—and a clue pointing to the third. It seemed reasonable to suppose that beaming down to Cheron with the first two fragments might well result in another trip through time. "It only remains to test it."

"I still don't understand," McCoy complained. "Why bother hijacking the transporter beam to send you into the past? Wouldn't the hidden puzzle piece still be waiting in the present as well?"

"Not necessarily, Doctor," she reminded him. "Time, wars, natural disasters, climate change, and other variables might conspire to damage, destroy, or relocate the artifact. If the intent is to guide us to a prize hidden in deep time, it makes sense to provide a route to the designated location in space *and* time."

"I can see that," Kirk said. "Come to think of it,

research teams from the *Enterprise* looked Vaal over pretty thoroughly after we deactivated him last year. I don't recall us stumbling onto a hidden alien artifact at the time."

"Perhaps because I had already removed it in the past," Seven said, "long before your first visit to Gamma Triranguli VI. That would also serve to explain why you never detected a Starfleet distress signal emanating from the planet."

"Because you took care of that days ago, ages in the past, millennia before you first arrived in our time, but after you beamed down from the *Enterprise* . . . depending on how you look at it." McCoy groaned and rolled his eyes. "Maybe this makes sense to you two, but time paradoxes just give me a headache."

Seven recalled Captain Janeway expressing similar sentiments. "Trust me, Doctor, you are not alone in that respect."

The components Seven had already acquired rested atop the transporter control console. Currently inert, they had been detached from each other so that she and Kirk could each have a fragment in their possession during transport. Seven had reservations about this strategy.

"I remain unconvinced," she said, not for the first time, "that splitting the recovered half of the device is advisable. Perhaps it would be better if I carried both components, linked together as one, and conducted this expedition on my own."

"Not a chance," Kirk said firmly, his mind made up. "By your own admission, you ran into trouble on your solo mission before and almost didn't succeed in reaching the fragment. You have better odds of success if you bring someone along to watch your back." He walked across the room to claim one of the fragments and placed it in a fabricated gray carryall. "More importantly, I don't like being left in the dark. I'm going with you this time . . . if I can."

She continued to argue her case. "But what if the fragments must be linked to initiate the next transport?"

"Then we'll cross that bridge when we come to it," he said. "But first we're going to try this my way."

His stubbornness reminded her of Janeway as well. Perhaps it was a distinguishing characteristic of starship captains, who ultimately had to rely on their own decisions and judgments. Seven found this vexing, but she conceded that it was probably inevitable. She had learned from experience that there was often little point in attempting to dissuade a captain once he or she had settled on a course of action.

"Very well." She claimed the remaining fragment and secured it in her backpack. "Let us proceed."

Scotty programmed the chosen landing coordinates into the transporter console. In the absence of any other data, they had targeted an area near the planet's equator, as distant as possible from both Cheronian survivors. A location in the western hemisphere allowed for sufficient daylight in which to carry out the search. Beyond that, the landing party would have to hope that the captured fragments would steer them in the right direction—as they had on Gamma Trianguli VI.

"Ready when you are," the engineer announced.

Kirk and Seven took their places on the transporter platform, each of them carrying a bundle containing a fragment. Seven noted again how light the enclosed fragment felt. Neither she nor Spock had yet succeeded in deciphering its composition. It was fashioned from a substance unknown to even the Borg.

McCoy placed his hand on the lever. "Be careful, both of you. Cheron's ugly past is no paradise, and race hatred can be a lot more dangerous than poison thorns."

"Consider us warned, Doctor," Kirk said. A confident air belied the possible dangers ahead. "With any luck, we'll be back in no time at all . . . literally."

He nodded at Scotty.

"Energize."

Fifteen

Along with Kirk, Seven beamed down into a city in flames.

They found themselves on an upper floor of what appeared to be a large building or complex in the heart of an embattled metropolis. Anxious Cheronians, all of the dominant black-right race, hurried briskly through the corridors, while others huddled together in front of a large transparent window overlooking the apocalyptic spectacle outside. A sizable urban population center composed of towering skyscrapers and spacious plazas had become one of Cheron's last battlefields. Smoke and flames billowed from torched structures and abandoned vehicles. Periodic explosions rocked the war-torn streets and causeways, which were littered with fallen bodies. Stealth aircraft, evident only from the discharge of their weapons, strafed outlying districts in an apparent attempt to suppress a violent insurrection. Rioters clashed with civil authorities just outside the besieged complex. Personal force fields flashed crimson as the opposing forces engaged in vicious hand-to-hand combat. The unmistakable din of warfare penetrated the walls and windows of the building, alarming its inhabitants, which now included two visitors from the future. Understandably distracted by the tumult outside, no one appeared to notice the strangers' arrival.

"Please remain calm!" a public-address system announced. *"The authorities are bringing the disturbance
under control. Please remain indoors until the situation is
resolved."*

This struck Seven as an overly optimistic assessment
of the situation. The assembled Cheronians appeared unconvinced as well. Angry curses punctuated frightened
sobs and whimpers.

"I knew it!" a furious Cheronian exclaimed. Anger
flushed the white side of her face. "I knew those half-
white savages would burn everything down one day. We
should have exterminated their entire miserable breed
years ago. We were fools to even try to civilize them!"

"But why are they doing this?" a distraught companion asked. "Why couldn't they just stay in their own
districts and tend to their own problems? Why all this
destruction and bloodshed? What do they hope to accomplish by rioting?"

"Because that's all they know, all they're capable of,"
the first woman spat. "It's written all over their ugly half-
white faces!"

Seven found both the strife outside and the attitudes
within distasteful, but it was consistent with what she
had read of Cheron's self-destructive racial divisions.
Due to the danger posed by the planet's two remaining
inhabitants, whose lifespans were believed to extend for
millennia, Cheron remained largely off-limits even in
the twenty-fourth century, but as with Gamma Trianguli
VI, theories abounded about the planet and its tragic
history, as well as about the root causes of the animosity
that eventually destroyed their starkly divided society.

A plausible theory held that the Cheronians'

distinctive duotone pigmentation was the result of millions of years of selective breeding driven by ancient religious and/or cultural dictates and reinforced by an inviolable taboo against interbreeding that eventually led to the sharp distinction between the black-rights and the white-rights. Indeed, some xeno-biologists speculated that the two "races" had actually evolved into separate species that had diverged at some unknown point in the planet's prehistory. In any event, it was clear that uncounted generations of prejudice, exploitation, retaliation, and hostility had long ago dissolved whatever common ground might have once united the two peoples.

Seven frowned. Segregation was an inefficient use of biological and cultural diversity. The Borg favored assimilation, albeit of a forced variety. That seemed almost preferable to perpetual conflict over irrelevant variations in skin pigmentation.

"Please remain calm!" the PA system repeated. *"Everything is under control."*

"Not from where I'm standing," Kirk said in a low voice. "We seem to have beamed into a full-scale race war."

Outside, in a courtyard in front of the building, gray-suited guards formed a defensive line just inside the complex's outer walls. An explosion blew a reinforced steel gate off its hinges, and a flood of white-right rioters stormed the courtyard. Crackling force fields strobed as the fields smashed against each other. Neither side was armed in the conventional sense, Seven observed; instead, the combatants pitted their own bodily energies against their opponents—in a battle of wills as much as physical prowess. For the moment, the wall of guards appeared to be holding, but Seven doubted that they could long withstand the forces arrayed against them. Even as she watched, more rioters were pouring into the courtyard, shouting loudly. A muffled chant reached her ears:

"NO MORE CHAINS! NO MORE POISON!"

Seven wondered at its meaning. *Poison?*

"I can't believe this," a trembling Cheronian said nearby. "They're coming for us. They're going to kill us all!"

"Believe it!" her companion snarled. "They're nothing but filthy, bloodthirsty animals. Killing is in their blood." He turned to Kirk to confirm his bias. "Am I right, brother?"

"Absolutely," Kirk said, playing along. "They can't be trusted. Any of them." He took Seven by the arm and started to guide her away from the worried bystanders. "Excuse me, we're needed elsewhere."

The outraged Cheronian wasn't done venting his ire. "Just let me wring a few half-white throats before they get me! That's all I ask!"

"You and me both," Kirk said, mimicking the mood of the crowd. "That's the spirit. Make the savages pay!"

Seven felt obliged to express similar sentiments in order to blend in. "They are too imperfect to be allowed to continue."

The outspoken Cheronian gave Seven a baffled look, and Kirk quickened their pace. "Perhaps you should leave the invective to me from now on," he whispered, before raising his voice again. "Half-white scum!"

Seven was relieved to put the emotional crowd behind them. "I dislike assuming the guise of a racist," she admitted.

"Tell me about it," he agreed.

Prior to beaming down, it had been decided that adopting the coloration of the planet's ruling class would permit them greater freedom and mobility. Seven wondered now if that had been a mistake.

"DEATH TO THE OPPRESSORS!" the mob shouted outside, taking up a new chant. "BLOOD AND JUSTICE!"

"The situation here is unstable," she concluded. "I suggest we carry out our mission with all due haste."

Kirk nodded. "Lead the way."

She discreetly removed a tricorder from her pack and began to scan for a certain Starfleet distress signal. The energies emitted by the clashing combatants outside provided unwanted interference, forcing her to compensate accordingly. Kirk kept watch as she adjusted the sensor controls. This took longer than she would have preferred, but it yielded the desired result.

"I have located the signal," she informed Kirk. "It is coming from several levels below us, possibly an underground bunker or sub-basement."

"Sounds like a safe place to hide the next fragment," Kirk said. "Relatively speaking. Let's get a move on."

Seven and Kirk followed the signal through a maze of corridors and stairwells, past open doors and archways that revealed a variety of laboratories and offices, most of which appeared to have been abandoned by fearful workers. Visual evidence suggested that the building was some manner of biological research facility, possibly government-sponsored. Large flags and posters frequently adorned the walls, no doubt for propaganda purposes. She noticed that the inspirational figures depicted

on the posters—leaders, scientists, soldiers, teachers—
were invariably black on the right side. Cheronians of the
right-white variety appeared only on "Wanted" posters.

Of course, she thought.

Panic and disarray spread through the complex.
Agitated Cheronians rushed past them, often clutching research materials or personal possessions. Sobbing
citizens huddled in corners. Others desperately tried to
contact friends and loved ones through handheld communication devices. Explosions without continued to
shake the building. Seven counted on the confusion to
cover their own covert activities.

This proved insufficient.

"You there!" a harsh voice rang out. "What are you
doing here?"

A squad of stern-looking Cheronians confronted
them. Seven assumed they were guards or security forces
of some variety, although they sported the same unisex
gray attire that every other Cheronian seemed to wear. She
noted that the aliens each wore a metal necklace of varied
design. Perhaps to indicate rank or assigned function?

"Excuse me," Kirk said, adopting an amiable tone. "Is
there a problem?"

"This is a secure area," the leader of the guards declared. "Identify your names and purpose here."

Seven let Kirk talk to the guards. He seemed to have
a talent for improvisation.

"I'm sorry," he said. "We must have gotten lost. We're
just looking for someplace safe." He feigned fear and
confusion. "Have you seen what it's like out there? We
didn't know where to go, what to do . . ."

The guards were unmoved. They surrounded Seven

and Kirk, crowding them in a manner clearly designed to intimidate. They appeared unarmed, but Seven suspected that was deceptive. From what she had seen and read, Cheronians relied on their own psychic and/or biological energies for self-defense. She regretted that she lacked the personal force field of a true Cheronian.

"Let me see your authorization," the head guard demanded.

Seven had no idea what sort of documents or tokens the guard wanted. She doubted Kirk did either.

"Look," the captain pleaded. "We barely escaped with our lives, let alone our authorizations. We're just looking for shelter, that's all." He tried to slip past the guards. "We can move on if you like."

The guards blocked his attempted departure. Their stony expressions did not melt. Seven began to doubt that Kirk would be able to talk them out of this situation. Her phaser was tucked beneath the waistband of her gray trousers. She casually moved her hand toward it in what she hoped was an unobtrusive fashion. It might be that a more efficient response was required.

The head guard regarded them suspiciously. "How do I know you're not a spy or a saboteur?"

"Are you blind?" Kirk replied with mock indignation. "Look at me! Do I look like a bloodthirsty half-white?"

"Maybe not, but you could be some bleeding-heart, liberal sympathizer." The guard nodded at their respective bundles. "Let me see what's in your packs."

Seven decided that the time for dissembling was over. She had no intention of turning the precious fragments over to the guards. Moving swiftly, she drew her phaser, which was set on stun.

"I cannot allow that," she stated firmly.

"Is that a weapon?" the guard growled. "Surrender it at once!"

"I am sorry. I cannot comply."

She fired at the head guard, hoping to give Kirk time to draw his own weapon, but an incandescent force field manifested around the guard, absorbing the phaser blast. She switched to a higher setting, but this proved equally ineffective. A guard grabbed her wrist, and a sudden energy discharge jolted her nervous system and temporarily disrupted her hand's exoskeleton. The shock caused her to drop her phaser, which clattered onto the floor.

"Seize them!" the guard ordered. "Overpower their shields!"

"What shields?" a puzzled officer asked aloud. He was the same one who had shocked her hand. "I didn't feel anything when I grabbed her."

The security team closed in on them. Kirk threw a punch at another guard, but his clenched fist bounced off the man's force field. Kirk yanked back his hand as though it had been shocked. No such obstacles prevented the guards from subduing the intruders. Their gloved hands delivered jolts of discharged energy that quickly eliminated any possibility of resistance. Prying fingers wrested Kirk's phaser from his grip, then relieved him and Seven of their tricorder and gear. The head guard tore open Kirk's carryall and removed one of the crystal wedges.

"What's this?" he demanded. "Some kind of explosive?"

"Trust me," Kirk said. "You wouldn't believe it if I told you."

"You think this is funny?" The guard slapped Kirk across the face with the back of his hand—and looked surprised when his hand actually connected with Kirk's face instead of a force field. "What's wrong with you? Why aren't you defending yourself?"

"Chief Sergeant!" one of his subordinates cried out. "Look at your hand . . . and his face!"

Black makeup was smeared on the sergeant's glove. Pink skin showed through Kirk's half-and-half makeup. Seven realized that their situation had just taken a significant turn for the worse.

"What—?" the sergeant gasped in surprise. He reached forward and wiped a streak of makeup off Kirk's face, then did the same for Seven. His eyes widened in shock and he stepped back from them. "You're aliens! Both of you!"

Seven saw no point in denying it. "That is correct, but we have no stake in your present conflict. We mean you no harm."

"She's telling the truth," Kirk insisted. "We're not here to cause trouble, for either side."

But the sergeant wasn't listening to them anymore. He paced back and forth, trying to decide on an appropriate course of action. Seven assumed that dealing with alien spies was outside his usual duties.

"The major needs to know about this," he decided. "Take them to Command Operations!"

A rough hand shoved Seven in the back, pushing her forward. The guards marched Seven and Kirk down the corridor, keeping a close eye on both prisoners. Seven noted, with a degree of satisfaction, that they seemed to be proceeding in more or less the direction that she and

Kirk had been heading before they had been detained by
the guards. A secure elevator carried them down to the
lower levels of the complex, which Seven also chose to
take as an encouraging development. She attempted to
keep the confiscated fragments in view. Recovering them
was essential; without the components, they had no hope
of leaving this era, let alone completing their mission.

"What is this place?" she asked, now that there was
no longer any point in pretending that they belonged
here.

The sergeant snorted. "The Center for Biological Security, of course. Like you didn't know that!"

"Never hurts to ask," Kirk said.

Sixteen

The elevator discharged them into an underground bunker occupied primarily by security forces and technicians. A small chapel, which appeared to be built into the original foundations, offered comfort and sanctuary to several of the latter, who sheltered together in hopes of deliverance. The sergeant and his troops escorted Kirk and Seven past the chapel, which was apparently not their final destination. The party passed through several increasingly stringent levels of security before being admitted into a central control center dominated by a large wall of monitors depicting images of conflict and carnage. Tense analysts, under obvious stress, sat at rows of terminals, struggling to keep up with a flood of information pouring into the war room. The air reeked of perspiration and anxiety. A heated argument was under way.

"We can't wait any longer!" a middle-aged black-right female declared. Cropped brown hair had silvered at the temples. Her military bearing and authoritative tone told Seven more about the woman's position than the necklace she wore. "We're losing control all over the planet. Just look at what's going on out there!"

She gestured at a wall of monitors, which depicted numerous fronts being waged in a variety of time zones. Streets and cities had become infernos. Hordes of rioters overran military bases and government installations.

Captured aircraft and armored vehicles joined the insurrection. An illuminated map of the world was lit up with blinking indicators of battles and bombings. The violence appeared to be taking place on every corner of Cheron and in the sky and seas as well.

"Major Rathis!" an analyst called out from his station. "New Alaspus has gone dark! We've lost the capital!"

"You hear that, Doctor Lael?" the female commander asked. "All hell is breaking loose out there. The half-whites can't be contained anymore. We have to unleash the virus now before they tear down our entire civilization!"

The target of her remarks was an older male who stood out from the others by wearing a rumpled gray lab coat over his conventional attire. His lean face was drawn and haggard, as though he hadn't slept in days. A balding pate revealed that his bisected coloring extended to his scalp.

"But I keep telling you, Major," he said. "The virus isn't specific enough yet. It can't differentiate between us and them. If we release it now, it will infect everyone, not just the enemy!"

That was not what Rathis wanted to hear. "You've been saying that for months now," she snarled in frustration. "What's the big holdup? How hard can it be to whip up a bug that can tell us from those animals? They're nothing like us. Hell, we can't even interbreed. They're a completely different inferior breed!"

"I know, I know," Lael said wearily, as though he had already tried to explain this many times before. "But we share a common ancestor and biology. Indeed, some studies indicate that the differences between us are primarily cultural and educational . . ."

"Spare me your radical theories, Doctor!" the major snapped. "Growing up, I was always taught that the Anti-Maker created the half-whites as a perverse mockery of the true Creation and, frankly, that's good enough for me. Now I'm sure that sounds very quaint and old-fashioned to an intellectual such as yourself, but—"

"Excuse me, Major," the sergeant interrupted. "But we caught these monotone aliens snooping around . . ."

That instantly caught the attention of both Rathis and Lael.

"Aliens!" The major stormed over to inspect the prisoners. Bloodshot eyes bulged from their sockets, while Lael appeared both intrigued and dumbfounded. Rathis reached out to test Kirk's makeup with her own fingers. Black and white paint smeared together as more pink flesh was exposed. "Who are you?" she demanded. "What are you doing here?"

"That's rather hard to explain," Kirk said, "but we want no part of your conflict here. We aren't taking sides."

"Of course!" Rathis said sarcastically. "You just happened to drop by our planet and attempted to infiltrate a vital government facility because you had nothing better to do with your time." A sneer twisted her lips. "Let me guess. Some rabble-rousing malcontent made it off-planet and spun you a heart-rending sob story about how his poor, oppressed people were being treated oh-so-cruelly here on Cheron, while neglecting to mention their relentless attempts to topple our society. Well, we know how to deal with outside agitators like you!"

Seven disputed the accusation. "My companion is

correct. Your civil strife is irrelevant to us. We are here merely as . . . observers."

"So you can report back to your people, and every neighboring system, what tyrannical monsters we are?" She flung the charge at the strangers like a photon grenade. "How would you like it if we trespassed on your planet and interfered in your own internal affairs? The Styxxians tried that once, generations ago, but they learned better. A retaliatory attack on their homeworld taught them to mind their own business."

Seven recalled that, according the *Enterprise*'s mission logs, the Cheronian fugitive Lokai had claimed that his people had been forcibly conscripted to fight in interplanetary wars against Cheron's enemies. She suspected that this was what he had been referring to. It seemed that the black-right rulers of Cheron had little patience with "outside agitators," which did not bode well for her and Kirk.

"Where are you from?" Rathis demanded. "Tartarus? Sheol?" She jabbed her finger into Kirk's chest. "How many others of your kind are on this planet?"

"Just us," Kirk said. "I promise."

The sergeant stepped forward and presented the captured gear and weapons to Rathis. "The aliens had these in their possession, Major." He handed over Seven's phaser. "This is an energy weapon of some sort."

"Is that so?" Rathis said, accepting the weapon.

"Let me see those personal effects," Lael said, eager to examine the otherworldly equipment. He immediately zeroed in on the colored fragments contained in the packs. He held a wedge up to the light, his scientific curiosity aroused. "What is this? What is it made of?"

"That is unknown," Seven said. "Please take care with that artifact. It is of considerable importance to my work."

"Why?" Rathis peered at her suspiciously. She toyed with Seven's phaser, playing worryingly with the settings. "What are you up to?"

Before Seven could attempt an answer, sirens blared throughout the bunker. Annunciator lights blinked furiously. Exhausted technicians sat up straight, while the guards went on high alert.

"Major!" an analyst at a terminal cried out. "The rioters have breached our defenses. They're inside the building!"

A monitor screen confirmed his report. White-right intruders rampaged through the upper floors of the complex, attacking terrified black-right citizens. Individual force fields were overwhelmed by the crackling energy discharges of multiple assailants. Labs and offices were ransacked and torched. A white-right face, contorted with fury, glared directly into the camera on one screen. He mouthed inaudible obscenities before a sudden green flash lit up the screen, which then dissolved into visual static. Muffled screams, shouts, and explosions filtered down from the floors above. The violence sounded disturbingly nearby and getting closer.

"No," Lael whispered. The white half of his face went paler still. "The virus. If they get to the biohazard facilities, violate the sterile fields, or just blow up the entire complex, they could unleash a plague that would wipe out everyone, no matter what side they're black on!"

Rathis half-blanched as well. "But those labs are locked up tight!"

"So was this building . . . in theory." Now it was Lael's turn to point to the unfolding chaos on the monitors. "They're already setting fire to the facilities above. If they reach the secure areas . . . We have to destroy the virus now, before it's too late!"

Rathis hesitated. "You can't be serious. We've sunk too much time and resources into this project. It's our best hope of solving the half-white problem once and for all."

"If we don't destroy that virus now," Lael insisted, "a world-wide insurrection will be the least of our problems!" She raced to the nearest computer terminal and shoved a technician out of the way. She spoke into an attached microphone. "Activate emergency sterilization procedure. Security code: three-zero-S-Q—*Vali*—double-X-five. Repeat: Activate emergency sterilization procedure."

Seven shared a concerned look with Kirk. She was uncertain what the center's "sterilization procedure" entailed, but she feared that it would not be conducive to completing their mission. It was more than possible that Lael intended to incinerate the entire complex—and everyone in it.

The distraught scientist called out anxiously to Rathis. "Major, I need your authorization, too!"

"Damn it," Rathis cursed under her breath, before reluctantly joining Lael at the terminal. "Emergency sterilization authorized. Security code: eight-seven-V-K—*Farfin*—double-X-five. Repeat: Emergency ster—"

An angry crackle from the computer terminal cut off her command. The overhead lights flickered and went out, as did the wall monitors. For a second, the bunker was thrown into darkness before the emergency lights kicked in. Analysts stared in dismay at dead screens. They stabbed frantically at control panels. The smell of burning circuitry filled the command center.

"No, no, no," Lael blurted, panic tingeing his voice. He tried and failed to reactive the terminal. "They've burnt out the control circuits! I can't reinitiate the sterilization sequence!"

"That's not possible," Rathis protested. "Their inferior minds are simply not capable of that kind of concentrated willpower. It takes centuries of specialized training to achieve that degree of skill. The half-whites don't have the discipline to master the power of their minds!"

Lael laughed bitterly. "It seems we underestimated them . . . again."

"No!" Rathis refused to believe it. "They must have had help! Misguided liberal collaborators and race traitors." She wheeled about to glare at Seven and Kirk. "Or alien accomplices like these two!"

"We had nothing to do with this!" Kirk insisted.

"Liar! You meddling monotone do-gooder!" Rathis aimed Seven's confiscated phaser at the prisoners. "Tell me how you did this or—"

An explosion went off in the corridor outside, followed by the din of pitched combat. Hoarse voices shouted a familiar slogan, which now seemed much more relevant to the present situation:

"NO CHAINS! NO POISON!"

Seventeen

A cadre of white-right revolutionaries burst into the command center, hurling crude explosive devices. Seven and Kirk hit the floor, throwing their hands over their ears, even as the center's staff was thrown into disarray by the attack. Crackling force fields protected Rathis and Lael and the others from flying shrapnel, but the bombs wreaked havoc on the furnishings and equipment. Seven watched in dismay as their personal effects, including the two fragments, spilled onto the floor in the chaos. Doctor McCoy's hypospray rolled within reach and she snatched it while she could. Kirk scrambled across the floor to rescue his phaser. His gray suit was torn. Soot joined the smeared makeup on his face.

"Stop them!" the Cheronian sergeant shouted at his officers. "Repel the invaders!"

A handful of black-right security forces tried to mount a last-ditch defense, but they were rapidly overrun by superior numbers of rioters. The sergeant's force field succumbed to the flashing energies of more than a dozen attackers. Along with the rest of the guards, he was beaten to the ground by glowing fists and boots. Within minutes, the rebels had seized control of the bunker.

"Stay sharp," Kirk advised Seven as they cautiously

rose to their feet amid smoke and debris. He held on to his phaser. "I think we may have just gone from the frying pan to the fire."

"I was not aware the Cheronians were cannibals," Seven replied.

Her auditory implants attempted to compensate for the ringing in her ears, with mixed results. She glanced about for her own phaser and spotted Rathis groping on the floor for it. A rebel boot came down on her hand, and she yelped in pain. Blood-stained white fingers reached down and claimed the phaser instead. A sardonic voice mocked the fallen soldier.

"Looking for something, Major?"

The voice belonged to a smirking right-white male. His ripped gray suit was spattered with red. An old scar stretched diagonally across his face from white to black. Mussed blond hair suggested that tinting Seven's own tresses had been unnecessary. He lifted his boot from the major's hand.

Rathis glared up at the rebel with sheer, undisguised hatred. Spittle sprayed from her lips.

"Udik! You half-white maniac!"

"Nice to see you again, too," the rebel replied. "Bet you wish you'd listened to me now, when I demanded justice for my people!"

"I only wish we'd executed you and the rest of your murdering kind!"

"Too late for that," Udik gloated. "You and your half-black comrades won't deprive us of our dignity any longer or poison us with your obscene experiments." He glanced around with contempt at the trashed command center. "That *is* what you were doing here, correct?

Plotting to sterilize us, sicken us, turn us into addicts, perhaps even exterminate us?"

Seven knew that his charges were not unfounded, but she held her tongue. She saw little to be gained in fanning the flames.

"And why not?" Rathis snarled, unrepentant. "You're vermin, all of you! Nothing but trash and parasites!"

"No! That's what you want us to be, what you tried to make us!" Udik viciously kicked Rathis in the ribs. "But not anymore! You're going to pay now, every one of you!" He raised his voice to exhort his comrades. "Tear this place apart!"

"Wait!" Lael cried out frantically. Scrambling to his feet, he pleaded with Udik and Rathis. "You can't do this, not here. There are dangerous biological materials in this center. You have to call off this madness . . . for everyone's sake! It's not safe!"

"Oh, *now* you're worried about safety?" Udik said scornfully. "What do you call this place again? 'The Center for Biological Security'?" He spit upon the floor. "More like the Center for Attempted Genocide!"

Lael flinched at the accusation but kept trying to get through to the rebel leader. "It doesn't matter what you think we've done in the past. You have to believe me. Everyone on this planet is in danger!"

"I'd listen to him," Kirk advised, stepping forward.

His intervention surprised Seven, who wondered what Kirk hoped to accomplish by speaking up. Cheron's fate was already engraved in history, its population destined for extinction. Was Kirk attempting to change history, or merely to ensure their own survival for the time being? She trusted that he was simply trying to gain control of the situation long enough for them to complete their mission.

"Who?" Udik finally got around to noticing Kirk and Seven. Pocketing her phaser, he took a closer look at the aliens, whose "disguises" now barely qualified as such. Only traces of their facial makeup remained. Torn gray fabric exposed pink, monotone flesh. Udik gaped in surprise, taken aback by this unexpected development. "Who . . . no, *what* are you?"

"As though you don't know!" Rathis seemed to regard Udik's startled reaction as just an act. "As though you haven't plotted together to destroy everything good and decent on this planet!"

"Quiet!" Udik punctuated his order with another kick. "I'm not talking to you now." He advanced on Kirk and Seven. "Again, who are you . . . and whose side are you on?"

Kirk kept his phaser at his side. "We're just visitors, accidentally caught in the middle of your war. We're on nobody's side."

"Your paint job says otherwise," Udik noted. "At least what's left of it. Why choose to pattern yourselves after our oppressors?"

"What can I say?" Kirk shrugged. "It seemed like a good idea at the time. From what little we knew of your world, it was obvious that there were . . . disadvantages . . . to looking like one of your people. We were simply hoping to avoid being persecuted during our stay here. Surely you can understand that?"

As Kirk spoke, Seven attempted to slowly edge her way toward the fallen fragments, which had been forgotten during this dramatic sequence of events. Ultimately,

Cheron's bygone race wars were just a distraction. She needed to remain focused on their sole objective: finding the next component and continuing their quest.

"Perhaps," Udik said warily. "But you'll forgive me if I question your motives, given that I find you in the company of our enemies, at the very nerve center of an insidious plot to poison us!"

A white-right female, with long brown hair and a murderous expression, accosted Udik. She reeked of smoke and chemical explosives. "I don't like this! We should kill them, just to be safe!"

"Not so fast, Fissa," he replied. "We could need allies in the days to come. Our battle is not yet won."

Rathis chuckled humorlessly. "I knew it. I knew you were in league with these aliens. You bestial savages could have never pulled an uprising on this scale without help. You're not disciplined enough!"

"One more word out of you, Major," Udik snarled, "and I'll show you just how 'bestial' I can get!"

An explosion upstairs rattled the bunker. Dust and debris rained down from the ceiling. The smell of smoke grew stronger and more oppressive. Seven coughed hoarsely. The strain of these events was beginning to tell on her. She felt herself succumbing to fatigue once more.

"Stop this, all of you!" Lael shouted, growing increasingly agitated. "You don't understand. None of this matters if the virus gets loose! We have to call off the fighting, secure this facility, or we're all doomed!"

He got too close to Udik and was brutally knocked aside by Fissa. The scientist's force field was no match for the rebel's; it flickered weakly but absorbed only a fraction of the blow. Seven deduced that Lael had little experience in using his field in combat. That didn't stop the desperate scientist from trying to avert a disaster.

"Please! This is insane! You have to listen to me. . . ."

"No!" Udik shouted. "The time for listening to your kind, to your empty promises and excuses, is over. No more decrees from the master race, no more threats and lies! Starting today, all that changes! We don't have to listen to you any—"

A thunderous roar, coming from above, cut off his oratory. It sounded like a maglev train going off its track, or perhaps a starship plunging into a dense atmosphere. All eyes turned upward in alarm.

"Too late," Lael whispered. "We're too late. . . ."

Fissa closed her eyes and concentrated, as though tapping into some unknown source of data. A second later, her eyes snapped open. Naked fear showed on both sides of her face.

"It's a stealth bomber, losing altitude. It's coming down, right on top of us!"

"What?" Udik exclaimed. "I don't understand. How—?"

Numerous explanations quickly presented themselves to Seven. A suicide attack. Aerial combat. Anti-aircraft fire from one faction or another. With an entire planet at war, there was no shortage of reasons why an aircraft might be crashing.

"Whose bomber is it?" Udik demanded, fixating on the only question that ever mattered to him. "Is it one of ours . . . or one of theirs?"

"That is irrelevant," Seven said. "Seek cover . . . now!"

She threw herself on top of the precious fragments, shielding them with her body, even as Kirk and the others dived for safety. Only Lael made no effort to seek shelter. He simply dropped to his knees and buried his face in his hands.

"There's no hope," he murmured. "No hope for any of—"

An earth-shaking crash, exceeding all the previous explosions, rocked the bunker. The ceiling buckled, and mangled support beams were driven into the floor, flattening workstations and terminals. Viewscreens shattered, spraying the room with jagged shards. The emergency lights went black, so that only the erratic glow of individual force fields provided any illumination. Sparks flared from damaged equipment. Seven feared that the entire ceiling might collapse, burying them all alive, but, to give credit where it was due, the bunker proved more solidly constructed than that. The walls held even as dust and ash rained on her. She held her breath in a singularly human fashion.

The past, she concluded, left much to be desired.

Eighteen

Long moments passed and the deafening impact of the crash gradually gave way to scattered moans and coughs, as well as the crackle and hiss of various small fires. The ceiling groaned alarmingly, suggesting that its structural integrity could not be relied upon for long. Sparks fell from severed cables and conduits. A smoky haze added to the confusion. Trapped individuals, buried beneath rubble, whimpered or pleaded for help. Dazed rebels and guards, their personal energies exhausted, lay strewn about the ruined command center. Seven suspected that little of the building above had survived.

She hoped the worst was over, but she knew better than to count on it.

Priorities asserted themselves. Rising from the floor, Seven inspected herself for damage. Her gray suit was shredded, and numerous bruises and lacerations hurt to a degree disproportionate to their severity, but she appeared largely intact. Wincing, she extracted a chip-sized shard from her shoulder and brushed off a thick layer of ash and dust before checking on the vital fragments.

Scattered flames and sparks provided erratic lighting, but her ocular implant soon adjusted to the murky haze. To her relief, the wedges had survived the crash; she had discovered aboard the *Enterprise* that a great deal of energy was required just to cleave a sample from them for analysis. Their stubborn durability, which had frustrated her earlier, was now cause for celebration.

But what of Kirk?

"Captain?" she called out.

A pained grunt answered her from a few yards away. "Over here."

She found Kirk pinned beneath a fallen steel beam, unable to extricate himself. The beam lay across his chest, wedging him against a crushed workstation and trapping both his arms. He had been fortunate; the beam could have easily crushed his skull had it landed at a slightly different angle. She strained to lift it high enough for him to slide out from beneath it, but the mass of the beam was more than even her Borg strength could overcome. The effort exhausted her, yet failed to budge the twisted length of metal. She paused to catch her breath, feeling more than ever the need to regenerate, and a more efficient solution came to mind.

"Your phaser?" she inquired. "Do you still have it?"

He nodded. "Held on to it for dear life."

"A wise decision. Can you pass it to me?"

"I think so, maybe." He squirmed awkwardly beneath the beam that stretched diagonally across his chest. The task required considerable grunting and exertion, but he succeeded in stretching his arm far enough to bring a portion of the phaser within her reach. "Here. Take it."

The weapon was crude compared to the advanced models she was accustomed to, but she judged that it would serve her needs. Setting the phaser to its highest setting, she proceeded to slice through the beam to free Kirk. The crimson beam shone brightly in the darkened bunker. She could feel its heat as it slowly burned through the metal.

"Careful with that," Kirk said unnecessarily. Perspiration beaded on his brow, causing what was left of his makeup to run. "Don't cut through anything I might need later."

"My measurements are precise," she assured him. "Provided you remain still and make no unexpected movements."

Despite her words, she was not entirely as confident as she sounded. Her hand was beginning to shake again, despite her best efforts to keep it steady, and her carpal exoskeleton was cramping. She switched the phaser to her other hand, taking advantage of the fact that she was ambidextrous, yet found her ability to concentrate flagging. Her vision blurred.

"Seven?" Kirk asked with understandable concern. "Are you all right?"

Her implants obviously needed energizing, yet she could do little about that here. Instead she switched off the phaser and retrieved Doctor McCoy's hypospray from the remains of her suit. Thankfully, it had also come through the crash intact. Starfleet equipment was rugged and durable, even in the twenty-third century.

"Allow me a moment, Captain."

The hypospray hissed as it delivered a powerful stimulant into her bloodstream. Within moments, her vision cleared and her hands stopped shaking. She was grateful for the doctor's foresight and prescription.

"Seven?" Kirk asked.

"Remain still," she reminded him as reactivated the phaser. "And quiet."

With her fatigue momentarily at bay, she cut through the steel beam until it broke apart into two smaller pieces. Working together, she and Kirk succeeded in sliding him out from beneath them. Kirk rose stiffly to his feet. He winced in discomfort.

"Are you functional, Captain?"

"Nothing a few hours in a sickbay and a good massage won't cure," he insisted. He glanced around the smoky ruins. "Which way out?"

She handed him back his phaser and rescued their tricorder from beneath a crumpled workstation. Placing the fragments in her pack, she guided Kirk toward the nearest emergency exit, which was partially blocked with rubble. She hoped Kirk's phaser had enough charge to disintegrate the debris.

"Going somewhere?" a voice intruded. "Drop your weapon before I give you a taste of your own medicine!"

Udik stumbled out of the wreckage, clutching Seven's stolen phaser. Blood dripped from a scalp wound, turning his white side red. He limped toward them, favoring one leg. His hair and clothing was singed. A torn tunic revealed patches of black-and-white flesh. Purple bruises blurred the distinction between them.

"Just let us go." Kirk lowered his phaser, but did not let go of it. "You have no quarrel with us. See to your people, tend to your injured, fight your senseless war if you have to, but leave us out of it!"

Udik shook his head. "Not until I know whose side you're on!"

"I keep telling you," Kirk said, losing his temper. "We're not on either side. You have nothing left but hate, and no future either. You've doomed yourselves, and you don't even know it!"

"Shut up!" Udik shouted, waving the phaser wildly. "You don't know us! You don't know our struggles, the pain and humiliations we've endured!" He tottered unsteadily on his feet, grimacing in discomfort. "We're fighting for justice, for freedom, for—"

A painful convulsion gripped him, and he clutched his gut with his free hand. A violent cough racked his body, and he spit up a mouthful of greenish bile. Viscous tears streamed from his eyes. Black pustules formed on the white side of his face, while white pustules swelled on the black side. He stared in horror at his white hand, which was similarly afflicted.

"What is this?" he screeched. "What have you done to us?"

The virus, Seven realized. It was loose and spreading swiftly. Agonized groans, broken up by the sounds of coughing and vomiting, could be heard throughout the wrecked command center. Sprawled bodies went into convulsions. Force fields flickered impotently before burning out.

"You did this to yourselves," she stated. "Both of you."

"No! This is your fault!" Udik swung the phaser back and forth between Kirk and Seven, who was unable to tell if it was still set on stun or not. "Monotone monsters! You don't belong here!"

Seven tensed, calculating her odds of disarming the diseased revolutionary before he could fire at both her and Kirk. She exchanged a look with Kirk, who appeared poised for action as well. They awaited their moment, should Udik give them one.

"Fissa was right," Udik snarled. "You both need to die!"

He wavered, as though uncertain whom to shoot first. Seven got ready to jump him if he aimed at Kirk, but before any of them could make their move, a ragged figure lunged from atop a heap of rubble, tackling Udik and knocking him to the floor. They crashed against the scattered debris, only a few meters from Kirk and Seven, who were caught by surprise by the attack.

"You lunatic! You half-white animal! Why didn't you listen to me?"

Doctor Lael had his hands around Udik's throat, trying to throttle the life out of the other man. No trace of the civilized scientist remained, only a hate-crazed racist. Black-and-white pustules disfigured his face, as did his contorted expression. Veins bulged on his forehead. Failing force fields sputtered and died.

"You killed us all, you filthy radical!"

Udik spit in his face. "No! You did! This is all your fault!"

They thrashed upon the floor of the ruined bunker, trying to kill each other with their last choking breaths. Udik lost his grip on Seven's phaser, and she darted forward to reclaim it. She wondered for a moment if there was any point in stunning the two men before they murdered each other.

Kirk tugged on her arm. "There's nothing we can do here," he said, visibly disgusted. "Let's get the hell out of this place."

Seven was inclined to agree.

Twin phaser blasts cleared away the debris blocking the exit, and they escaped into the smoky hallways beyond. The ceiling continued to buckle ominously. Flames spread through the corridors, where white-rights and black-rights were locked in frenzied hand-to-hand combat, even as the infectious virus consumed them. Choking and coughing on the smoke, Seven and Kirk made their way through corridors strewn with rubble and bodies. To her dismay, Seven felt the stimulant already beginning to wear off. Her legs grew limp and rubbery, like overcooked Talaxian pasta.

"We need to hurry," Kirk said. "This whole place is coming apart, in more ways than one."

"You need not state the obvious," she said irritably, then regretted it. Fatigue was taking its toll on her temper as well, making her snappish. "My apologies, Captain. My nerves are . . . on edge." She consulted the tricorder. "The signal is coming from this direction."

To her surprise, the signal led her to the small chapel she had noted before. Only a handful of worshippers remained, many of them already succumbing to the disease. They prayed hopelessly to be spared.

Seven did not have time to pity them. "Out!" she ordered, firing a warning shot above their heads. "Vacate this location immediately!"

The sight of two ragged, soot-stained aliens bearing weapons was enough to ignite a frantic exodus that rapidly cleared the chapel area, surrendering it to the invaders. Kirk waited until the last straggler was gone, then he slammed the door shut. A phaser blast fused the locking mechanism.

"That should give us a few minutes of privacy at least," he said. "Now, where's that fragment?"

Seven took a moment to inspect their surroundings.

Compared to the modern look of the bunker and command center, the stone walls and mosaic tiles of the chapel suggested that it predated the rest of the complex, which she theorized had been built on top of and around an older structure. She speculated that the chapel had been preserved in its original state, perhaps in deference to religious tradition or historical significance. A series of murals running along the tops of the walls depicted scenes of presumably theological importance. Seven noticed at once that the black-rights were invariably portrayed as virtuous, as opposed to the vile white-rights, who were consistently shown leering from the wilderness, despoiling unwilling black-right virgins, being driven back into the shadows, cast into darkness, and so on. It was obvious that the animosity between the two tribes was deeply entrenched in the planet's myths and culture and had been for a very long time.

The same point was made, rather unsubtly, by the imposing stone statue dominating the far end of the chapel, above and behind the altar. The sculpture, which was carved from fused black-and-white marble, depicted a heroic black-right champion of noble proportions standing astride a defeated white-right ogre. Sculpted shackles chained the subdued savage to the pedestal beneath. The craftsmanship was exquisite, the message repugnant.

A shudder rocked the chapel, shaking loose some of the murals, which crashed onto the tile floor. Acrid black smoke seeped through the sealed entrance. The fires outside went from crackling to roaring. Ceiling tiles fell from above. Screams of rage and despair penetrated the chapel walls.

"The fragment?" Kirk prompted her.

The tricorder pointed her toward the sculpture. As she stumbled forward, her ocular implant faltered, blurring her vision once more, but she managed to make out a fuzzy Starfleet insignia inscribed invisibly on the pedestal.

"It's here!" she said urgently. "Beneath the statue."

"Good." Kirk eyed the crumbling ceiling with concern. "Let's get it and go, before what's left of this place comes down on our heads."

"Understood."

The response code was already keyed into the tricorder, but Seven's shaky hands still struggled to operate the device, and she found herself wishing that she had another hypospray. It took her two tries before she successfully transmitted the code—and a hidden panel slid open on the pedestal.

"Open Sesame," she said hoarsely.

The third wedge-shaped fragment was waiting. With trembling hands, she plucked the prize from its hiding place. The crystalline component was violet-colored, matching the one she had claimed on Yusub.

"Take it," she told Kirk, as she retrieved the first two components. "We need to assemble it together, so neither of us gets left behind!"

Kirk accepted the fragment. "Yes, I think I'd just as soon avoid that!"

Working together, keeping their hands in contact with the pieces at all times, they linked the first two components together and prepared to add the third. Kirk held on tightly to the original half-circle. Seven prepared to connect the next fragment. Chips of stone and plaster pelted her head and shoulders as the ceiling began to cave in. Billowing smoke invaded her lungs. Vibrations began to tear apart the two-toned sculpture, right down the middle. Black marble tore loose from white, or maybe it was the other way around.

If nothing else, she reflected, there was little chance of them changing history, one way or another. Flames, explosions, plague, and war would likely eliminate any evidence of their visit, while the mysterious disappearance of two nameless aliens would be lost in the violent death throes of a doomed civilization.

"Here goes nothing," Kirk said.

"Or everything," she amended. "On the count of three."

Kirk nodded. "One, two . . . three!"

They put the pieces together. Seven's vision turned inside out. She sagged against Kirk as they blinked away from Cheron.

Fire and stone crashed down onto an empty chapel.

Nineteen

"Feeling better?" Kirk asked.

He found Seven back in sickbay, reclining upon an elevated bio-bed that had been converted to serve her unique requirements. Flexible tubules, extending from the exoskeleton on her left hand, interfaced with an exposed power conduit equipped with an adapter of specialized design. A cable connected the adapter to the conduit, which had been accessed via a panel in the adjacent wall. Kirk saw that Seven had also apparently been making use of the computer library access terminal on the other side of the bed. Spock was keeping her company.

"To a degree," she stated, although her face was still drawn and pale. Like Kirk, she was no longer made up to resemble a Cheronian and had changed back into more customary attire. Even her hair was blond again. "Commander Spock has been guiding me through certain meditation techniques. They are proving of use in preserving my cortical functions and ability to concentrate."

"I am pleased that I can be of assistance," Spock said. "You may find that the exercises will also allow you to better regulate your autonomic bodily functions, so that they can better rest . . . if not regenerate."

Kirk could believe it. He had known Spock to remain sharp for days at time during a crisis and to be able to refresh himself with only short periods of focused meditation. Kirk had often envied his friend's ability to go without sleep for long periods at a time without noticeable effect.

"Glad to hear it," he said. "You had me worried a few times back on Cheron."

After linking the three fragments together, he and Seven had found themselves in the burned-out ruins of a dead city, at the precise coordinates that they had originally attempted to beam down to. It had been impossible to tell how long ago the city had died, but weeds, vines, and gritty gray sand already had overrun the crumbling buildings and pavement. Mummified corpses, preserved by the arid environment, lay exposed to the elements, while startled lizards and insects had scurried away at the arrival of the strangers. Kirk had glanced around briefly to see if he could locate the remains of the Center for Biological Security, but one heap of weathered, carbonized rubble looked much the same as any other. For all he'd known, they weren't even in the same city anymore, nor had he been inclined to linger and investigate further. Better to put Cheron behind them . . . for good.

"I regret that I gave you cause for concern," Seven said. "I will require an extended period of induced hibernation soon, but I wish to brief you on our next destination before I let Doctor McCoy put me under again."

Kirk nodded. Seven had been too exhausted to inspect their prize immediately upon their return to the *Enterprise*. Truth to tell, he had been pretty worn out by their experiences on Cheron, too, but now that he'd had a chance to get patched up and recover a bit, he was eager to discover what new clue Seven might have found inscribed on their latest acquisition. In theory, they only needed one more component to complete the device—and perhaps send Seven back where she belonged.

The ship had already left Cheron's system and was warping away from the Coalsack. Beyond his natural desire to get as far as he could from the graveyard Cheron had become, Kirk thought it wiser to move on before the *Navaar* caught up with them again. He couldn't imagine that the Orions had given up on capturing Seven and her priceless knowledge of the future, which was all the more reason to complete her quest as expeditiously as possible.

"Did you find anything on the third fragment?" he asked. "Another stardate?"

"Indeed," Spock replied. "Stardate Five-nine-four-three-point-seven, to be precise, which presents a notable complication."

Unlike his first officer, Kirk could not immediately place the date, although the first few digits put it sometime last year, by terrestrial reckoning.

"Refresh my memory."

Spock readily obliged. "The date in question corresponds exactly to our mission to Sarpeidon, which I am certain you recall."

"Very well," Kirk said as the details of that harrowing visit came back to him. He immediately grasped the "complication" Spock had mentioned. "But Sarpeidon was destroyed when its sun went nova. The planet doesn't exist anymore."

"Not in the present," Seven observed, "but it still exists in the past."

"That's true," Kirk realized. His heart sank as he saw another temporal paradox coming on. "I see your point."

"I remind you, Captain," Spock said, "that the people of Sarpeidon practiced time travel on a massive scale."

Kirk didn't need reminding. Faced with the imminent demise of their world, the entire population of the planet had escaped into the past, taking refuge throughout their own history. He and Spock and McCoy had come damn close to getting stranded in Sarpeidon's past as well, barely making it back to the present in time to escape the planet's destructions.

"You think we're dealing with the same technology here?" he asked.

"Possibly," Spock said cautiously. "As you recall, time traveling on Sarpeidon could be as easy as stepping through a doorway. Its people possessed a mastery of temporal mechanics that far surpassed anything currently possessed by the Federation. They even employed it to exile political prisoners and dissidents to the past." A slight, almost imperceptible hint of bitterness entered his voice. "Often unjustly."

A pained expression briefly disturbed his Vulcan reserve. It was subtle enough that most people would not have caught it, but Kirk knew his friend, and he knew what Spock had left behind on Sarpeidon . . . five thousand years ago. This discussion was doubtless stirring up poignant memories, even if Spock would never admit it.

Seven, on the other hand, remained focused on the present.

"I have been reviewing the mission logs on your previous visit to Sarpeidon," she said, indicating the computer library terminal attached to her bed. "The process that transported me here does bear a certain superficial resemblance to what you both experienced on Sarpeidon, but there is no indication that the 'atavachron' was capable of transporting individuals across space as well as time, as was done to me."

Seven had never divulged where exactly her involuntary journey had begun, but Kirk had gotten the impression that it wasn't from anywhere nearby, cosmically speaking. Certainly, she didn't seem to have beamed in from some future version of Yusub.

"The full capacities of the atavachron remain unknown," Spock said, "since the technology was lost along with Sarpeidon. It is possible that it could be used to travel through space as well."

Kirk didn't buy it. "But if they had a way of getting off their own planet, why didn't they use it when their sun went into its death spiral? Why retreat into their past instead?"

"Perhaps they simply preferred their own world to any other," Spock suggested. "Despite their obvious mastery of time travel, there is no indication that they ever ventured into space. This may be attributable to the fact that Sarpeidon was the only planet orbiting its sun, which meant its people had no attainable worlds within reach. The stars were too far away to tempt them."

"No baby steps," Kirk realized. "No neighboring planets to explore, like the early Mars or Saturn missions. They would have had to go straight to interstellar travel to get anywhere at all. No wonder they never bothered looking up."

Spock nodded thoughtfully. "Instead they looked backward, exploring the fourth dimension rather than the third . . . with just as much innovation and success as other species devoted to reaching the stars."

Boldly going, Kirk thought, *through time, not space.*

He was intrigued by the notion of a species that developed time travel before attempting space exploration. That wasn't exactly the usual pattern; to his knowledge, most of the major spacefaring civilizations were still just tentatively sticking their toes into the murky waters of trans-temporal exploration—or steering clear of it altogether.

"It is also possible that we are dealing with a variation on the same technology, with additional capabilities," Seven pointed out. "Or some mechanism of an entirely different origin."

"True enough," Kirk said. "But all this is just speculation. Perhaps we can get some answers once we get where the planet *used* to be." Kirk headed for the nearest intercom in order to instruct Sulu to set a course for Sarpeidon's former location out along the borderlands. "In the meantime," he told Seven, "get some sleep."

"Thank you, Captain," she replied. "I will attempt to comply."

"How far to the Beta Niobe system?" Kirk asked. "What's left of it, I mean."

The supernova that destroyed Sarpeidon would have left behind a stellar remnant in the form of an ultra-dense neutron star. Kirk intended to maintain a safe distance from the remnant while occupying the orbit formerly held by Sarpeidon.

"We are sixteen-point-three-two-two hours from the system," Spock reported from the science station. "We can expect to encounter various waves of expelled radiation and gases en route."

Kirk understood. Only two years after the supernova

explosion, its residue would still be expanding outward through space in all directions. "Do these shock waves pose any danger to the ship?"

"Not that I anticipate," Spock assured him. "There may be some minor turbulence, but nothing that our deflectors cannot cope with."

Kirk was glad to hear it. "Mister Sulu, full speed ahead."

"Actually, Captain, I would advise a more cautious approach," Commissioner Santiago stated. After spending several days holed up in his quarters, dealing with matters diplomatic, he had returned to the bridge to observe the ongoing mission. "It might be best to be more circumspect, given our proximity to the Klingon Neutral Zone . . . and our previous run-ins with the Orions."

Their course from Cheron to the Beta Niobe system took them through the borderlands along the southwestern edge of Klingon Space. Across the Neutral Zone, the Klingon Empire held dominion, and they tended to react aggressively to unwanted incursions. Starfleet Intelligence was aware of imperial listening posts all along the border. It was possible the *Enterprise* was already on their radar.

"The Commissioner's logic is sound," Spock said. "Despite the urgency of our mission, we would not want to encounter another ambush."

Kirk weighed Seven's deteriorating physical condition against the danger of her falling into the wrong hands. Considerations of speed warred with caution. It was a thorny dilemma, but the captain made his decision.

"Mister Sulu, lower speed to warp five . . . and take the scenic route." He didn't want to telegraph their destination by aiming straight at the Beta Niobe system. "Mister Chekov, keep an eye out for our Klingon neighbors."

"Absolutely, Keptin!" the young ensign said. "Although their cloaking devices make that easier said than done."

"Acknowledged, Ensign," Kirk said. *We could be surrounded by enemy warbirds before we even knew they were there.*

All the more reason to keep clear of the Neutral Zone.

Kirk glanced at Santiago. Given a choice, he'd prefer not to provoke a diplomatic incident with a high-ranking Federation official aboard. He had been looking for a chance to drop Santiago and his aide off at the nearest convenient starbase, but so far such an opportunity had not presented itself. And would Santiago even agree to leave the ship, given his intense interest in finding out what Seven knew of the future? The commissioner had not pressed the issue recently, but Kirk was certain that the older man still regarded Seven as a strategic asset of incalculable value. Maybe they needed to get a few things settled before the *Enterprise* reached its destination—and before Seven tracked down the fourth and final component of the time machine.

"Commissioner," Kirk began. "Perhaps you can join me in—"

"Captain," Uhura interrupted. "I'm receiving an emergency distress signal." She double-checked the coordinates. Her worried tone conveyed the promise of more bad news. "From the Neutral Zone."

Kirk did a double take. *You can't be serious?*

It was the Kobyashi Maru scenario all over again.

Kirk had taken the infamous "no-win" simulation three times before he'd finally beaten it by hacking into the program and changing its parameters. The episode had nearly gotten him kicked out of Starfleet before the Academy decided to give him a commendation for "original thinking" instead. But he never had expected to run into the same scenario in real life, after all these years.

"Wow," Sulu murmured. "Déjà vu."

Obviously, Kirk wasn't the only person who found the situation disturbingly familiar. Any Starfleet cadet on the command track had been through the exercise in one capacity or another.

"I assure you, Helmsman," Spock declared, "this is no simulation."

That's for sure, Kirk thought. "Put it on-screen."

"Aye, sir," Uhura said.

An alien visage appeared upon the main viewer. Bristling silver whiskers sprouted from the sagging jowls of an unfamiliar humanoid whose droopy features reminded Kirk of a mastiff . . . or maybe a walrus. Fleshy pouches shadowed the alien's wide pink eyes. Floppy ears hung past his jowls. Stubby yellow tusks protruded from his lower lip. A disheveled orange turban sat askew atop his head. A voluminous crimson robe, embroidered with elaborate astrological symbols, clothed a stout torso. A polished bronze medallion, studded with a constellation of glittering gemstones, hung on a chain around his neck. Numerous small tentacles wriggled from his sleeves. Coiled metal springs were stretched over the tentacles like jewelry. Soot powdered his robe and leathery, blue-gray hide. Blood and mucus dripped from a moist black snout. His eyebrows were singed.

Kirk didn't recognize the species.

At least it wasn't a Klingon . . . or an Orion.

"Deliver us!" the canine alien blubbered. He had a rotund, sonorous voice. *"For the love of the star-spirits, let us not perish in the cold and dark!"*

A smoky haze suffused the cabin behind the alien. Sparking cables dangled in the background. Alarms beeped and buzzed. Offscreen voices cursed and shouted in alarm. Kirk got the impression that there was plenty of commotion going on. Static and video tiling distorted the image.

"This is Captain James T. Kirk of the Federation *Starship Enterprise*," he hailed the other ship. "Please identify yourself."

"I am Papa Yela," the alien responded. *"We are the Mavela. Our vessel, the O'Spakya, is in dire jeopardy! We beseech your aid!"*

"We'll see what we can do," Kirk promised. "What is the nature of your emergency?"

"A warp imbalance in our engines threw us violently out of subspace into the gravity well of a voracious gas giant. We barely escaped with our lives, praise the star-spirits, but the O'Spakya was badly wounded. Plasma fires are spreading through the ship. Our hull is buckling. We have lost propulsion. Life-support is ebbing." He wrung his tentacles in agitation. *"Our fate is in your hands!"*

"Understood." Kirk muted the sound in order to confer with his crew. "Assessment?"

"The Mavela are a nomadic species," Spock supplied, "who are more or less tolerated by the Klingons as long as they pay regular tribute to the Empire. They make their living as traders and entertainers, while occasionally indulging in low-level smuggling and the odd confidence scheme, not unlike our old acquaintance Harry Mudd. They claim to have precognitive abilities, although this has never been scientifically verified. The Vulcan Science Academy currently regards that as a hyperbole."

Chekov nodded in understanding. "Space gypsies."

"A reasonably accurate description," Spock confirmed. "In any event, they are not known to be hostile and should, in theory, pose little threat to a *Constitution*-class starship."

Kirk wondered if Spock had pulled this information from the ship's computer or his own formidable memory. "Thank you, Mister Spock. Always useful to know who we're dealing with."

He signaled Uhura to restore the audio.

"Please hurry!" Papa Yela pleaded. *"Our ship is falling apart . . . and my mate is about to give birth to our litter! Our babies are in danger,"* Papa Yela insisted. *"They may not live to take their first breaths!"*

"That's not going to happen," Kirk said forcefully. "Trust me." His face hardened into a portrait of resolve. *"Enterprise* out."

The alien's bewhiskered countenance vanished from the viewer, replaced by the starry void ahead. Kirk couldn't see the border of the Neutral Zone nearby, but he knew it was there—beyond the point of no return.

"A word of caution, Captain." Santiago leaned over the rail surrounding the command circle. "I've learned from hard experience that alien races cannot always be trusted, especially those in bed with Klingons. We can't rule out that this is a deliberate attempt to manipulate us."

"I am well aware of that, Commissioner," Kirk assured him. "This isn't my first distress call."

He regretted that Santiago's aide was not around to keep his boss in line, but Cyril Hague was apparently back in his quarters, buried under in administrative work. Kirk couldn't help wishing that Santiago also was pushing paper at the moment, instead of second-guessing him in the middle of an emergency. In general, Kirk had little patience with pushy bureaucrats who interfered with the running of his ship.

"Captain?" Uhura said. "The Mavela are getting more anxious. What shall I tell them?"

Kirk didn't need long to think about it. "Mister Sulu, plot a course for the *O'Spakya.*"

"In the Neutral Zone?" Santiago asked. "Do you really want to do that?"

Kirk crossed over to the science station to consult with his first officer. "Spock, your thoughts?"

"The risk of provoking a confrontation with the Klingons is undeniable," the Vulcan said. "But, as a certain starship captain once said, risk is our business."

Kirk chuckled. "I like the way you think." Treaty or no treaty, he wasn't about to abandon a ship in distress just because it *might* be a trap. There were too many lives at stake to play it safe. "Lieutenant Uhura, inform the Mavela that we're on our way. Mister Chekov, raise shields." He nodded at Sulu. "Warp factor six."

"Aye, aye, sir," Sulu said dubiously. "Into the Neutral Zone we go."

"This is on your head, Kirk," Santiago said, "if something goes wrong. And if Seven falls into the hands of the Klingons."

Tell me something I don't know, Kirk thought.

Twenty

Stars zipped past at warp speed.

"Crossing into the Neutral Zone," Sulu announced. He glanced back at Kirk, as though giving the captain one last chance to change his mind. This was a risky move, of the sort that could cost an officer his career. Everybody knew Sulu hoped to command his own ship someday. Breaking major treaties wasn't generally considered a plus on one's resume.

"Hold her steady, Lieutenant," Kirk said. Having made up his mind, he wasn't going to waste time second-guessing himself. Nearly two hours had passed since they had first received the *O'Spakya*'s distress signal, and he was eager to reach the endangered ship. The icy vacuum of space could be cruelly unforgiving for a damaged vessel. Every minute counted. "Yellow alert."

Caution lights lit up the helm and navigation stations. Throughout the ship, emergency systems were placed on standby. Routine sensor sweeps increased in frequency. Additional personnel reported to their posts.

"Wouldn't know this was the Neutral Zone," McCoy drawled. The doctor had hurried up from sickbay to check out the situation. He contemplated the starry gulf upon the viewer. "Looks just like ordinary space to me. Cold, black, and empty."

"What were ye expectin'?" Scotty asked him. He

was manning the engineering station, while his protégé, Lieutenant Charlene Masters, held down the fort in engineering. "A picket fence with a grand big 'KEEP OUT!' sign posted on it?"

"Couldn't hurt," McCoy said. "Back home, where I grew up, we used to say that good fences made good neighbors."

Chekov's alert eyes scoured the screen. "I think the Klingons prefer *dead* neighbors."

"The Klingons are rather more complicated than that," Seven commented as she stepped from the turbolift onto the bridge. "But it is true that they are not known for taking prisoners."

Her arrival caught Kirk by surprise. "Shouldn't you be resting?"

"In light of the present crisis, Doctor McCoy thought it best to wake me," she explained. One hand held on to the pack containing the fragments, which she was understandably reluctant to part with. She placed herself at the auxiliary science station, next to Spock. "And I confess that I have grown weary of sickbay. No offense, Doctor."

"None taken," McCoy said. He lowered his voice to confide in Kirk. "Figured she ought to be up and about in case things go south in a hurry. Stuck in artificial hibernation, she'd be a sitting duck if we had company . . . and something happened to the rest of us."

"Understood," Kirk said, approving of the doctor's decision. He wouldn't want to be out cold during an unauthorized jaunt into the Neutral Zone either. "Lieutenant Uhura, any signs that the Klingons have noticed our incursion?"

"Not yet," she reported. "I'm not picking up any unusual activity or alerts. Of course, they could be communicating on an encrypted channel. Or maintaining audio silence."

"True enough," Kirk agreed. The absence of any obvious alarms was no guarantee that the Klingons were unaware of their arrival. "Keep your ears open, Lieutenant."

"I always do, sir."

Kirk knew he could count on Uhura to keep him posted on what the Klingons were up to. He reminded himself that the Neutral Zone extended for light-years across the quadrant; not even the Klingons could patrol every centimeter of it every second of the day, or get an armada to this sector at a moment's notice.

If we're lucky, he thought, *we can get in and out without a fight.*

When had things ever been that easy?

"Never mind the Klingons," Scotty said. "Personally, I'm more worried about the Orions. My gut tells me we have not seen the last of those brigands."

"Gut feelings are rarely scientific," Spock observed.

Scotty shrugged. "Would ye care to make a wee wager on the subject? Fifty credits say we run into the ruffians again."

McCoy stared at the doughty engineer incredulously. "Good God, man. Are you seriously taking bets on whether we'll be attacked by pirates?"

"And why not?" Scotty asked. "Might as well make things interestin'."

"The question is academic," Spock said. "Vulcans do not gamble."

Besides, Kirk thought, *it's a sucker bet.* Captain Habroz and his crew weren't going to give up after one failure. Annika Seven, and the knowledge she possessed, were too valuable a prize, as Commissioner Santiago surely agreed. Kirk noted that Seven was maintaining a polite distance from Santiago, who was watching her like a hawk. She chose to focus on the auxiliary science displays instead.

"I suppose that figures," Scotty said. "Can't blame a fellow for tryin', though."

Kirk chuckled at Scotty's audacity. If nothing else, the exchange had helped lighten the atmosphere on the bridge, despite (or perhaps because of) McCoy's indignant reaction. Kirk caught Sulu and Chekov exchanging amused grins.

If ever we need a morale officer, Kirk thought, *I think I know the right man for the job.*

"What about you, Doctor?" Scotty asked, pressing his luck, as he often did his engines. "Are ye a bettin' man?"

Before McCoy could reply, Spock got back to business. "The *O'Spakya* is within visual range, Captain."

"On-screen," Kirk ordered. "Full magnification."

Half-expecting to see a Klingon warbird, or perhaps the hostile Orion marauder from before, he was relieved to discover a much less intimidating vessel up ahead. As it turned out, the *O'Spakya* was more gaudy than imposing. A gilded masthead, in the semblance of a noble bloodhound, adorned the tapered prow of the merchant ship, whose hull was liberally decked out with garish neon-colored tiles and an excess of shiny gold filigree and trim. Rows of bright yellow running lights lit up every angle of the ship. The gaudy trappings might have been intended to distract the casual viewer from the generally ramshackle appearance of the ship, which Kirk judged to be at least a generation old. Its outdated configuration consisted of a long tapered cylinder with a bulging sphere halfway down its length, so that it looked as though the ship was trying to digest an oversized melon. A pair of dormant nacelles, jutting out at angles from the tail of the cylinder, appeared purely decorative at the moment. The merchanter was drifting rudderless through space, just as Papa Yela had described. Vapor vented from a crumpled Bussard collector. Kirk noted that the *O'Spakya* was only a third the size of the *Enterprise*. In theory, they would be able to evacuate the smaller ship's entire crew if necessary.

"Tactical status?" Kirk asked.

Chekov scanned the becalmed vessel. "Shields down. Phaser banks inactive. Not much in the way of weapons, actually. Just some rudimentary phasers for self-defense and blasting away obstacles." His tone was dismissive. "It's a circus wagon, not a fighter."

That fit with Spock's description of the Mavela, yet Kirk wasn't taking anything for granted. "Appearances can be deceiving. Update your firing solutions."

"Aye, Keptin."

Kirk inspected the battered merchanter, which looked as though it had been dragged through an asteroid field or two. Many of its running lights were shattered, while a lateral sensor array was a mangled wreck. Color ceramic tiles had flaked off across its hull. He recalled the Mavela's supposed powers of clairvoyance. *Guess they didn't see this one coming.*

Just as well. He already had one reluctant oracle on his hands. Seven refrained from comment as she silently observed the image on the viewer. Her inscrutable expression offered no clue as to what she knew—or didn't know—about this incident . . . if it had even happened in the time line she came from. Having a tight-lipped time traveler aboard, he reflected, could drive you nuts if you thought about it too hard.

He turned toward Santiago instead. "Tell me, Commissioner. In your travels, have you ever encountered the Mavela before?"

"I'm afraid not, Captain. We're in murky territory here . . . in more ways than one."

"Best not to waste any time, then," Kirk said. "Mister Scott, what do you make of the damage to the *O'Spakya*?"

The engineer squinted at the screen. "Hard to say without gettin' up close and personal, but it looks genuine to me. Ye can see traces of scorched duranium through the rips in the outer plating. Sensors confirm they're venting deuterium. That sorry lassie's definitely seen better days." He scratched his chin. "Then again, it's still in one piece. That's something, at least."

"Fixable?" Kirk asked.

"Everything's fixable, Captain," Scotty boasted, "if ye know what ye're doin'. Give me a little time, and I ought to be able to get the poor girl patched up again. If the engines aren't bollixed enough, I might even fix it so they can limp to the nearest starbase on their own power." He tinkered with the visual display to examine the *O'Spakya* from another angle. "From the looks of things, they're goin' to need plenty of repairs in spacedock once they make it to a safe harbor."

"Time is at a premium," Kirk reminded him. "I don't want to linger here any longer than absolutely necessary."

Scotty nodded. "I hear ye, Captain. We wouldn't want to outstay our welcome."

"Maybe we can lock onto the *O'Spakya* with a tractor beam," Chekov suggested, "and tow it back across the border?"

Scotty shot down that idea. "I can't recommend that, Captain, not until I've had a chance to check out the structural integrity of their hull. A tractor beam could exert undue stress on any compromised bulkheads."

"And let's not forget about the passengers," McCoy said. "Never mind the bulkheads. Are we picking up any life signs?"

"Yes, Doctor," Chekov answered. "Multiple life-forms. A full crew's worth."

The report did little to placate McCoy. "They could need medical assistance now, not ninety minutes from now. If their life-support is failing, they might not last until we're safely clear of the Neutral Zone."

Kirk agreed. It had taken the *Enterprise* too long to get here already. They couldn't afford another long trek back to Federation space.

"Excuse me, Captain," Uhura interrupted. "Papa Yela is hailing you again."

Kirk wasn't surprised. No doubt the *Enterprise*'s arrival had registered on the *O'Spakya*'s sensors.

Papa Yela's face appeared on the main viewer. Although the bridge behind him looked somewhat less smoky than before, the alien skipper was, if anything, even more agitated. Sweat drenched his face. Pink eyes rolled wildly in their sockets. Panting hard, he waved his tentacles in the air.

"*Enterprise! Praise the star-spirits you are here at last!*

Our air is growing thinner! My mate gasps for breath even as our unborn offspring near their nativity!"

Concerned for his patient, McCoy took charge. "How far along is her labor?"

"I . . . I'm not certain," Papa Yela stammered. *"The litter may drop at any minute."*

Kirk didn't like the sound of that. He looked at McCoy. "Maybe we should have her beamed directly to the *Enterprise*?"

"Beamed? No!" Papa Yela was visibly appalled by the suggestion. *"Forgive me, Captain, but my people reject the dangerous temptation of transporting living beings. The body can be broken apart and reassembled, yes, but the soul is forever lost!"*

"Even in an emergency?" Kirk asked. He didn't wish to disparage the man's beliefs, but did Papa Yela really want to risk his family over some abstruse philosophical dilemma? "Your mate—and the babies—might be safer in our sickbay."

Papa Yela shook his head. *"Not at the cost of their irreplaceable souls. What materialized aboard your ship would not be my cherished ones, but only false copies. Mere soulless simulacra. They would be my family in matter only."*

"I see," Kirk said tightly. This was a complication he had not anticipated. He looked to McCoy to back him up. "Perhaps our ship's doctor can convince you of the urgency of the situation."

"Actually, Jim," McCoy said, "he may have a point."

Come again? Kirk was surprised to hear McCoy agreeing with Papa Yela. He knew the doctor wasn't exactly a fan of having his atoms beamed from place to place, but he'd never thought of him as a total Luddite where transporters were concerned, especially when an expectant mother's life was at stake.

"Bones?"

"To be honest, Jim, I'm reluctant to transport a woman in mid-labor, particularly without knowing more about how her species copes with the physiological demands of beaming. Most humanoids can be transported safely, but there *are* exceptions. The Bixoxi need to be placed in an induced coma first, while the HoSo tend to split into their male and female halves without warning. And the Solem implode if transported during their larval stage." He sounded like he could easily rattle off a dozen more cautionary examples if necessary. "We have no idea what the side effects of transporting a pregnant Mavelan female might be."

Kirk got the message. "Point taken, Doctor. Looks as though you're going to have to make a house call." He addressed Papa Yela. "Very well. Please transmit the precise coordinates of your bridge. Help will be on its way shortly."

"*Bless you, Captain!*" The alien fluttered his tentacles in benediction. "*May the star-spirits reward your compassion and generosity!*"

"Your safety is the only reward we require. Kirk out."

At his signal, Uhura cut off the transmission, restoring their view of the *O'Spakya*. He rose from his chair, his mind made up on how to proceed. "All right, I'll lead a small scouting party over first, just to get the lay of the land, before we mount a full rescue-and-repair operation." He marched briskly toward the turbolift. "Bones, you're with me."

He expected Spock to take the captain's chair in his place, but the Vulcan had other ideas. "Perhaps you should reconsider, Captain. I understand that it goes against your instincts to stay behind, but these are special circumstances. Given our present location, and the recent engagement with the Orion raiders, prudence dictates that the captain remains on the bridge for as long as we are in the Neutral Zone." He stood to accompany McCoy. "Permit me to lead the scouting party instead."

Kirk thought it over. As much as he preferred to take a hands-on approach to most missions, Spock was right; now was not the time for him to leave the ship—or for Seven to leave. He needed to keep a close watch on both.

Besides, he thought, *what's the point of having the best first officer in the fleet if I don't take his advice once in a while?*

"A very logical argument, Mister Spock." Kirk reluctantly returned to his chair. "The mission is yours. Take a security officer with you, just in case the Mavela are less harmless than they appear."

"Captain, shouldn't I tag along to inspect the damage to the ship?" Scotty asked.

"Not just yet," Kirk said. "I'm certain Mister Spock can make an initial assessment of what repairs are needed. In the meantime, Scotty, I want you personally manning the transporters. We need to be ready to beam the entire scouting party back to the *Enterprise* the minute the Mavela even look at them funny."

"Aye, sir," Scotty replied. Worry furrowed his brow. "And if the *O'Spakya* isn't really as damaged as she appears and she should warp away with our people first?"

That possibility had already crossed Kirk's mind.

"In that case," Kirk said, "I want my resident miracle worker here . . . and not abducted as well."

Twenty-one

McCoy hated beaming.

Even though he was well-versed in the literature on the subject, and he knew that the process had been approved for human subjects for more than a century now, the very concept still made his skin crawl. Being dismantled on an atomic level, then reassembled like some sort of molecular jigsaw puzzle? The prospect was about as appealing as going through another nasty divorce. *If I wanted to be taken apart bit by bit,* he thought, *I would have stayed married.*

Maybe the Mavela had the right idea after all.

The three-man scouting party materialized deep within the *O'Spakya,* where the ship's bridge was apparently located. McCoy exhaled a sigh of relief; once again, his atoms had not been strewn across the galaxy. As usual, he resisted an urge to pat himself down to make sure all his parts were still there . . . and in the right places. A quick glance confirmed that Spock and Lieutenant Tang had arrived intact as well. The short, compact security officer had one hand on the grip of his phaser, just in case. A medkit was slung over McCoy's shoulder.

"Welcome!" Papa Yela greeted them. The Mavelan patriarch was taller than McCoy expected, standing more than a head above his visitors. A fresh robe and turban rendered him somewhat more presentable than before. His tentacles nervously fondled a showy jeweled medallion. "Would that we poor, unlucky souls could bestow upon you the lavish hospitality you deserve!"

McCoy glanced around. The dimly lit control room of the *O'Spakya* looked more like a temple or a fortune teller's lair than the bridge of a starship. Instead of a forward viewscreen, a large crystal orb floated at the center of the star-shaped chamber. The luminous orb held a three-dimensional display of the surrounding space. Mavelan crew members, their backs turned away from the scouting party, squatted before blinking control panels tucked away at the points of the star. Their loose-fitting beige robes were less elaborate than their leader's. Plush cushions served in lieu of seats. Gilded filigree adorned the bridge's railings and decorative molding. Glittering constellations, composed of glowing crystals, sparkled across the high-domed ceiling. The same celestial patterns were reflected upon the ornate tile floor. Burning incense failed to exorcize a smoky odor left behind by the fires earlier. Scorched bulkheads and cracked tiles also testified to the beating the ship had apparently taken. Damaged conduits and cables showed evidence of having been hastily patched together. A charred crystal gemstone, which had presumably fallen from one of the ersatz constellations overhead, crunched beneath McCoy's boot.

"That is not necessary," Spock stated. "We are here to render assistance."

Papa Yela eyed the scouting party quizzically. "Captain Kirk is not joining us?"

"Perhaps later," Spock said, before introducing himself and the rest of the party. "Our captain instructed us to conduct a preliminary inspection of your situation.

Additional *Enterprise* personnel will be beamed aboard as necessary."

"Of course! Whatever your noble captain deems best." Papa Yela looked askance at Tang's phaser. "But, please, there is no need for weapons. We are a peaceful people who wish only to live in harmony with the all-seeing spirits of the stars."

"A precaution only." Spock's own Type-1 phaser remained hidden beneath his uniform. "The Neutral Zone is not without its hazards."

Papa Yela nodded somberly. "As we have had the misfortune to learn. A pity our ship's own defenses could not avert the calamity that befell us."

The man's flowery patter reminded McCoy of a politician or snake oil salesman. "Speaking of which," he interrupted, eager to cut through the chit-chat, "where is my patient?" He looked around the bridge, his eyes gradually adjusting to the gloom. Although a handful of other Mavela could be seen at their posts, chanting softly to themselves, there was no sign of a woman in labor. Was she elsewhere on the ship? McCoy was surprised that Papa Yela was not at his spouse's side. Then again, perhaps their culture required fathers to keep their distance from the actual birth. McCoy had run into similarly squeamish males before. "I understood that your mate requires my attention."

"The midwives are attending to her in the infirmary," the alien explained. "Let me inform them that you have arrived."

A bejeweled tentacle pressed a stud on his amulet. McCoy figured Papa Yela was simply contacting their version of sickbay.

He was wrong.

An agonizing sonic attack assaulted McCoy's ear-drums, dropping him to his knees. He clapped his hands over his ears, trying to block the piercing siren, but it was no use. Blood dripped from his ears; he lost all sense of balance. A scream tore itself from his lungs but was drowned out by a high-frequency whistle shrill enough to make his teeth hurt. Out of the corner of his eye, he glimpsed Spock and Tang reeling from the attack as well. Spock teetered, but he amazingly managed to stay on his feet. Tang struggled to hold on to his phaser. Through the pain, McCoy guessed that the brutal noise was no accident.

It was a trap . . . and they had beamed right into it!

The Mavela, on the other hand, appeared completely unaffected. Papa Yela backed away from the flailing scouting party. Waving tentacles made a protective gesture.

Then, all at once, they were not alone. Green-skinned Orion raiders sprang from hidden trapdoors in the floor, propelled upward like a stage ghost or demon making a spectacular entrance. All that was missing was flash pots, smoke, and a theatrical clap of thunder. Like the Mavela, the Orions seemed immune to the sonic barrage. Olive-colored fists gripped bludgeons and disruptor pistols.

They fell upon the stricken Starfleet officers. Tang, a squat fireplug of a man, tried to fight back, despite the debilitating siren. He succeeded in getting off a wild shot with his phaser, but with Tang unable to concentrate on his aim, the beam went astray, zipping past Papa Yela's turban to harmlessly "stun" an embossed bulkhead. The

Orions didn't give him a chance to shoot again; before he could fire another beam, a snarling pirate smacked him across the back of his head with the butt of a disruptor pistol. The cold-cocked security officer collapsed onto the floor. His phaser flew from his grip to land at Papa Yela's feet. The treacherous alien recoiled from the weapon as though it were unclean. A nearby Orion claimed the phaser instead, tucking it into a black leather bandoleer.

Like the bandits didn't already have enough weapons!

Another Orion snatched Spock's own phaser from his belt. His sensitive hearing overwhelmed by the blaring siren, Spock was unable to stop the Orions from disarming both him and McCoy. Weapons drawn, the raiders surrounded the rescue party. McCoy counted at least five Orions, all unfazed by the excruciating noise.

Did they have eardrums of steel or something?

The apparent leader of the raiders was, surprisingly, an Orion woman who hardly resembled the seductive "animal women" of salacious legend. Instead of being barely clad in diaphanous silks, she was dressed for action in heavy-duty boots, trousers, and a black leather vest that exposed only her verdant midriff. Shimmering purple hair tumbled past her shoulders.

The woman signaled Papa Yela by drawing a finger across her throat. McCoy hoped she was referring to the sonic assault and not the scouting party. As a doctor, he knew how quickly a slashed throat could bleed out, especially when a heart was beating as fast as his was.

A nervous-looking Papa Yela fumbled with the control gems on his amulet. Merciful silence replaced the blaring siren. McCoy gasped in relief, despite their dire predicament. At least his brains didn't feel like they were leaking out of his ears anymore. He briefly worried that he might have been rendered deaf by the attack, but then he heard the pirates celebrating their victory.

"Success, First Mate!" an Orion gloated. He waved his pistol triumphantly at the prisoners. "The Starfleeters are ours!"

"Not so fast," the woman cautioned her underling. She removed a pair of miniature filters from her ears. "These are only pawns in a larger game. We have yet to capture our prize."

Spock lowered his hands from his ears. Green blood trickled from the pointed organs. Regaining his equilibrium, he assumed his usual dignified posture, appearing neither perturbed nor intimidated by the Orions. He subjected Papa Yela to his austere scrutiny.

"It seems your hospitality leaves something to be desired."

"Forgive me, my ill-starred guests," Papa Yela whinged. Deft tentacles extracted his own ear filters. "But Captain Habroz and his crew gave me no choice. Take my word for it, they are not individuals you can safely refuse." He looked sheepishly at the Orion woman. "Pardon me, Mistress K'Mara, I get the credits you promised me, yes?"

McCoy's blood pressure spiked. "Damnit, man! We offered you our help. And you sold us out for filthy lucre?"

The alien Judas shrugged beneath his robes. "Destruction or profit. What other choice was there?" He rubbed his tentacles together in anticipation of the payoff to come. "A small charitable donation should be sufficient to lift the stain from my soul."

"And your mate?" McCoy challenged him. "The one who's supposed to be giving birth any moment now?"

"Alas, I am a widower at present," Papa Yela admitted. "But with the bounty the Orions have promised me, I shall be able to afford several new wives."

McCoy's face soured. "Well, bully for you."

Now that his ears were no longer ringing, he noted that the trick doors in the floor had closed up again. Were they ordinarily used for smuggling, he speculated, or for staging phony séances? Either fit with what Spock had said about the Mavela.

"The more intriguing question is," Spock added, "who is paying the Orions?"

"Mind your own business, Vulcan!" K'Mara thrust her own disruptor into her belt. She raised a wrist-communicator to her lips. "We have them, Captain!"

McCoy realized that he and the others had just gone from rescuers to hostages.

Remind me to think twice about making any more house calls!

Twenty-two

"Keptin!" Chekov announced in alarm. "The *O'Spakya* has raised its shields!"

Kirk sat up straight. His pulse quickened. "What? I thought they were supposed to be damaged?"

"Apparently not, sir." The young ensign looked mortified at being caught unawares. "They just snapped into place . . . without any warning."

Kirk punched open a line to the transporter room. He leaned into the audio pickup in his armrest. "Scotty, beam them back, pronto!"

"*I cannae do it, Captain!*" Frustration exaggerated the engineer's familiar brogue. Kirk visualized him frantically working the transporter controls. "*It's too late!*"

Uhura gazed anxiously at the main viewer. "What's happening to them?"

Kirk wished he knew. "Any word from the scouting party?"

"No, sir," she reported. "I'm trying every frequency, but I can't get through to them."

Anger ignited inside Kirk. "Hail the *O'Spakya*!"

"Already tried, sir," Uhura stated. Her fingers stabbed her control panel. "They're not responding."

Kirk mentally blasted Papa Yela with an imaginary phaser. He knew a double cross when he saw one. The unctuous Mavelan patriarch had clearly played them for suckers, right down to that whole business about his wife going into labor. Kirk kicked himself for not seeing through such a transparent attempt to manipulate his emotions.

And now three of his men were in jeopardy.

"You see, Kirk," Santiago said. "I told you this was a mistake!"

Kirk figured the commissioner was entitled to an "I told you so," but he didn't have time to acknowledge it. "Mister Sulu, be ready to pursue the *O'Spakya* if it tries to get away. I wouldn't be surprised if their engines are suddenly in working order, too."

Spock obviously had been on target about the Mavela being con artists. No doubt all that eye-catching "damage" to the *O'Spakya*'s exterior was just fancy window dressing. Nothing but smoke and mirrors.

"Yes, sir!" Sulu responded. "No way am I letting that ugly ship abscond with our people."

Good man, Kirk thought. "Mister Chekov, power phaser banks and arm photon torpedoes."

"Aye, Keptin!"

Kirk was reluctant to fire upon the *O'Spakya* while his crew was still aboard, but he might have to take out the other ship's warp nacelles to keep them from escaping. And maybe a few warning shots across their bow would get Papa Yela's attention.

"Lieutenant Uhura, inform the Mavela that continued silence on their part will have serious consequences." His fist pounded the armrest. "I want answers and I want them now."

Santiago wheeled about to confront Seven. "Did you know about this? Could you have warned us?"

"No," she stated flatly. "I had no prior knowledge of this incident."

Kirk believed her. "Uhura?"

Before the communications officer could respond, Chekov spoke up urgently. "Keptin, another ship is de-cloaking . . . directly ahead!"

What the devil? Kirk glared at the screen, where a ripple effect distorted the empty space beyond the *O'Spakya*. He recognized the telltale signature of a Klingon or Romulan vessel deactivating its cloaking field, most likely in preparation for an attack. Given their proximity to the Klingon border, he wasn't worried about Romulans.

"Red alert!" he barked. "Shields at maximum."

They had lowered their shields in order to beam the scouting party over to the *O'Spakya,* but now the missing men were doubly cut off from the *Enterprise.* In response to Kirk's command, mounted annunciator lights flashed crimson. All over the ship, every crew member and department assumed a heightened state of readiness. Level 4 diagnostics were run on all crucial systems. Phaser banks, photon torpedo launchers, and shuttle-craft were energized to standby mode. Deflectors were raised to tactical levels, far beyond that needed simply to repel random space dust. Non-essential scientific and recreational pursuits were suspended for the duration of the alert.

Damn, Kirk thought. *Of all times for the Klingons to show up!*

But instead of the warbird he was expecting, an Orion marauder shifted into view, looking transparent at first, like a badly rendered hologram, but rapidly taking on mass and opacity. Kirk immediately recognized the *Navaar* from recordings of the *Enterprise*'s earlier encounter with the ship, when it had beamed down those murderous pirates to Gamma Trianguli VI. The captain didn't need to call for a sensor report to see that the marauder was easily within firing range. It faced the *Enterprise* across the void, assuming the same vertical orientation as the two other vessels.

"Huh?" Sulu blurted. "Since when do the Orions have cloaking devices?"

"I was wondering that myself," Kirk said.

"Keptin," Chekov reported. "The Orion vessel is arming its weapons."

Naturally, Kirk thought. *Why else would it decloak?* Thankfully, nobody yet had figured out a way to safely fire disruptors or photon torpedoes while cloaked. At least not in this century; he wondered if things were different whenever Seven came from.

All the more reason not to let the Orions—or anybody else—get their hands on the castaway from the future.

"Now do you see, Kirk?" Santiago said. He was gripping the handrail hard enough to turn his knuckles white. "The Orions are a menace. We should have delivered Seven to a secure location when we had the chance!"

Seven bristled. "Even against my will, Commissioner?"

"See how much your will matters when the Orions get hold of you!"

That's not going to happen, Kirk vowed. "Stand by to open fire if necessary." Throughout the ship, he knew, his crew was rushing to battle stations. Too bad the

Enterprise now found itself outnumbered and far from home. It truly was the Kobyashi Maru all over again.

Uhura adjusted her earpiece. "The *Navaar* is hailing us."

This should be interesting, Kirk thought. "Put it through."

Captain Habroz appeared upon the viewer. Kirk remembered the pirate commander from the conflict on Gamma Trianguli VI. Metal spikes jutted from his scalp. A prosthetic hand gripped a silver goblet. The burly Orion sat atop a sumptuously upholstered throne. The skull of a horned animal was mounted on the bulkhead behind him. The lighting on his bridge had a greenish tint.

"*Greetings, Kirk,*" he said gruffly. "*We meet again.*"

Kirk maintained a steely expression. "Captain Habroz, I take it."

"*Commander and owner of this fine vessel,*" the pirate boasted. "*I confess I am very proud of it. Not quite a Federation starship, but it's won me a fair share of plunder over the years . . . and defeated many an enemy.*"

Kirk was in no mood to trade war stories. "What are you doing here?"

"*I could ask you the same question, Kirk. This is the Neutral Zone, after all. You're the one who doesn't belong here.*"

"We're here on a rescue mission," Kirk stated. "An errand of mercy."

Habroz laughed harshly. "*Or so you thought!*"

Kirk didn't like being made fun of, especially when his crew's lives were at stake. "No more games. What do you want?"

"*The woman from the future,*" Habroz said. "*The one you call Annika Seven.*"

Startled gasps escaped several of the bridge crew, who

had been unaware of Seven's true origins. Curious eyes turned toward the time traveler, who appeared unruffled by the attention. She sat stiffly at the auxiliary science station. Kirk resisted an urge to glance in her direction.

"The future? I don't know what you mean." Kirk scratched his head in mock confusion, stalling for time while he tried to figure out how to deal with the Orions *and* the Mavela. He wondered if he was dealing with two separate adversaries or if the hostile ships were in cahoots. He strongly suspected the latter. "Perhaps there's been some kind of misunderstanding?"

"*Don't insult my intelligence, Kirk.*" Habroz scowled beneath his drooping black mustache. "*We both know that Seven fell into your lap from sometime in the future and that you have been foolishly searching for a way to return her to her own time.*" He put down his goblet and snarled across space at Kirk. "*Trust me when I say that I am not known for my patience. I propose a simple trade: the hostages for Seven.*"

Forget it, Kirk thought. As concerned as he was for the scouting party, he knew he could not allow Seven to be spirited away by the Federation's enemies. "I take it the Mavela are working for you?"

"Of course they are," Santiago muttered.

"*We have an arrangement,*" Habroz disclosed. "*Which means you have to deal with me if you want your men back.*"

"And if I refuse?" Kirk asked.

A cruel smile bared pointed teeth. "*Let me demonstrate how far I am willing to go to claim my prize.*" He lifted a communicator his lips. "*K'Mara, you know what to do.*"

Twenty-three

"Yes, Captain."

Aboard the *O'Spakya,* K'Mara drew a serrated dagger from her belt. The exotic Orion pirate stalked toward McCoy, who waited for his life to pass before his eyes. He hoped it would skip over the more annoying parts.

"Don't I at least get an anesthetic first?"

She smirked at the doctor's defiance. Papa Yela averted his eyes. "Please, for the love of the star-spirits, be swift about it!"

"Oh, it will be quick, all right," she promised. She nodded at her men, who took hold of the hostage's arms to keep them still. McCoy strained against his captor's grasp while a burly pirate twisted his arm behind his back. The doctor's throat felt painfully exposed; he suddenly flashed on Khan Noonien Singh holding a scalpel to his neck a few years earlier. K'Mara tested the edge of the blade against an olive-colored thumb. "I keep my knives sharp."

McCoy swallowed hard, possibly for the last time.

"You are about to commit a serious error," Spock warned K'Mara. "The murder of a Starfleet officer carries irrevocable consequences. The entire fleet will devote itself to your capture. You will be hunted across the galaxy."

K'Mara spit upon the tiles. "That's what I think of

Starfleet." The muzzle of a disruptor pistol was pressed against the back of Spock's skull. "Be thankful that you are *slightly* more valuable than these weakling humans."

"Says who?" McCoy protested. "I resent that remark."

"Not for much longer," she promised. "It has been too long since this blade tasted pink skin."

McCoy decided he liked the green dancing girls better. He braced himself for the fatal incision. "It would be most effective if you cut the carotid artery, just under the right ear."

K'Mara came closer. A predatory grin betrayed a sadistic nature. She licked her lips, providing a glimpse of a glittering ruby stud in her tongue. "As you desire."

"Don't!" Tang shouted. "He's a doctor!"

Born and raised on a heavy-gravity mining planet, Tang's strength belied his compact frame. The power of his muscles took the Orions by surprise as he threw off his captors and lunged at K'Mara. He grabbed the pirate's wrist, and they grappled for control of the dagger. McCoy and Spock moved to join the fight, but the other Orions tightened their grips on the two men. McCoy felt another blade pressed against his jugular. A nameless raider growled into his ear. His breath smelled of Orion whiskey.

"Stay where you are, human!"

Unable to intervene, McCoy could only watch impotently as Tang tussled with K'Mara, who clearly knew her way around a brawl. The other Orions circled about, knives, bludgeons, and disruptors drawn, aiming to get a clear shot at Tang. Papa Yela retreated fearfully to one of the pointed control nooks, frantically waving his tentacles, while the other Mavela scrambled for safety.

The majority fled the bridge altogether, diving through hidden trapdoors and exits. The cowardly nomads were clearly tricksters, not warriors.

"Enough, please!" Papa Yela wailed. "I beg of you, no more violence!"

No one listened to him.

"You want to die instead, Red Shirt?" K'Mara snarled. "Be my guest."

She tried to butt Tang with her skull, but he yanked his head out of the way in time. Locked in combat, they slammed against the navigation globe floating at the center of the bridge. Knocked from its stasis, the massive sphere crashed to the floor, inflicting yet more damage on the already cracked tiles. It rolled across the deck like a transparent moon kicked from its orbit, the image inside it spinning wildly so that the *Enterprise* and the *Navaar* appeared to be tumbling head over heels.

"The orb!" Papa Yela squealed. "Somebody rescue the orb!"

The globe bowled over a slow-moving raider before ricocheting off a bulkhead toward Papa Yela himself. The treacherous Mavela dived under a control console instants before the orb bounced up against it. The sphere came to rest against the workstation, trapping him inside his cramped, makeshift hidey-hole. He looked to be in no hurry to extricate himself, at least not until the battle stopped raging.

Like a rat in its hole, McCoy thought. *Figures.*

The odds were against Tang, but so far he was holding his own against K'Mara. "You picked the wrong crew to mess with," he grunted as he took on the knife-wielding Orion female. His thumb applied pressure to a nerve cluster on K'Mara's wrist, causing her to let go of her dagger. The blade clattered to the floor. Tang shoved K'Mara up against a bulkhead. "Starfleet trained me to deal with lawless scum like you!"

"But did they prepare you for this?"

Her tongue flicked from her lips, pressing its ruby stud against his jugular. There was a vicious hiss like the sound of a striking serpent.

Or a hypospray.

He staggered backward, clutching his neck. He gasped for breath, stumbling across the bridge as though poisoned. His eyes bulged from their sockets. Swollen black veins spread from where the stud had kissed him.

"D-doctor," he said hoarsely. "Help me—"

The Orions didn't give the venom a chance to kill him. A crimson beam struck Tang. He flared brightly before disintegrating.

"No!" McCoy exclaimed. Tang was gone in a heartbeat. "You didn't have to do that!"

K'Mara seemed to agree. "Perdition!" she swore. "What greedy bilge rat stole my prey from me?"

A sheepish Orion, still clutching Tang's own phaser, was quickly abandoned by his comrades, who slunk away from him, leaving the hapless raider to face K'Mara's wrath alone. "But . . . I had a clear shot!"

"Did I look like I needed your help?" She reclaimed her fallen dagger and thrust the unbloodied blade back into her belt. "His worthless life was mine to take!"

"My mistake, First Mate," the trigger-happy raider said hurriedly. He could not put the stolen phaser away fast enough. "It won't happen again!"

Once was enough as far as McCoy was concerned.

He stared in horror at the empty space Tang had occupied only moments before. The man was gone . . . just like Jadello and Bergstrom. Another life lost to this gang of murderous thugs. Despite the knife at his throat, McCoy could not keep silent.

"You green-skinned witch!"

K'Mara wheeled about and smacked McCoy across the face with her hand. Despite her slender frame, the blow was strong enough to rattle his teeth. Deprived of her kill, she grabbed McCoy's collar and hurled him across the room. Spittle sprayed from her plump green lips. Pearly teeth gnashed furiously.

"Watch how you speak to an Orion woman!"

"Talk to me, Habroz!" Kirk said. "There's no need for bloodshed."

The pirate captain laughed. *"On the contrary, Kirk. There's always cause for a little healthy bloodletting, as long as it's not Orion blood that's spilt."* He raised his wrist-communicator to his one remaining ear. A shark-like smile stretched across his face. *"I've just received word from my second-in-command aboard the* O'Spakya. *I'm afraid you've lost a security officer, Kirk. But don't worry, I'm told he put up a good fight before being blasted to atoms!"*

Daniel Tang, Kirk realized. A surge of relief that neither Spock nor McCoy had been sacrificed yet was immediately followed by guilt over valuing his friends' lives above any other member of his crew. That guilt over an understandable human reaction fed his fury about the Orions' callous disregard for sentient life.

"That's three lives you and your people have taken,"

he accused Habroz. "Don't think you're getting away with that."

"*Spare me the empty threats, Kirk,*" the pirate captain said, betraying not a hint of remorse. "*I still have two more hostages . . . and I want my prize.*"

"Not to mention a sizable bounty from the Klingons?" Kirk guessed. How else could the marauder have acquired a cloaking device, not to mention the freedom to operate so openly within the Neutral Zone? "That *is* who you're working for, isn't it?"

"*That's my business, Kirk. You'd be wise to keep your nose out of it.*" Habroz leaned forward on his throne as though trying to invade Kirk's personal space from four hundred kilometers away. He clenched his prosthetic fist. "*I want Seven. What I choose to do with her is none of your concern.*"

Not where the Klingons are involved, Kirk thought. He could not risk Habroz handing Seven over to the Federation's rivals. But how could he hang on to her without losing Spock and McCoy?

He was racking his brains when Scotty raced back onto the bridge. "I knew that bloody marauder would be back to trouble us again," he muttered. The engineer must have assumed, correctly, that he'd be of more use on the bridge than in the transporter room now that the Orions had joined the party. He gave Habroz a dirty look. "So that's the sneaky cutthroat behind all this deviltry. He looks the part all right."

Habroz ignored the interruption. "*No more stalling, Kirk. My deal remains the same: Seven for the two remaining hostages. Give me your visitor from the future . . . or your Vulcan dies.*"

"I wouldn't do that if I were you," Kirk warned. "Seven has confided in me, privately, that it was the future Spock who invented the device that sent her back to our time in the first place. If you kill him now, he will never do so . . . and Seven will vanish instantly from our time."

Chekov leaned over to whisper to Sulu, too low to be heard by an audio pickup. "Is that for real?"

Not in the least, Kirk thought. But that didn't matter; he just needed Habroz to believe it.

"Er, how is that again?" Habroz's arrogant attitude faltered and his scarred brow wrinkled in confusion. Uncertain how to process this new complication, he shifted awkwardly upon his throne. Puzzled jade eyes glanced offscreen, perhaps searching for confirmation from one of his crew.

Good luck, Kirk thought. He doubted that there were many experts on temporal mechanics among the raiders. Habroz was on his own.

"You're bluffing," he said without conviction.

"Am I?" Kirk shot back. "Think about it. If you kill Spock today, he'll never create the time machine that brought Seven here. You'll be erasing that entire future." He called upon his star witness. "Isn't that so, Doctor Seven?"

She stepped confidently into the recessed command well so that Habroz could see and hear her. Kirk hoped she'd be able to play along convincingly.

"That is correct," she stated. "My very presence in this era would be negated due to the crucial alteration of the time line." She spoke with the absolute assurance of a stern schoolmistress lecturing her pupils. "No doubt you are familiar with Janeway's Fundamental Principle of Trans-Dimensional Causality?"

Habroz's blank look spoke volumes.

Janeway who? Kirk thought. *Did she just make that up?*

"If you wish," Seven volunteered, "I can provide you with the relevant equations."

"That won't be necessary," Habroz snarled, visibly frustrated. He slammed his metal fist into his palm. *"Don't forget, Kirk. I still have another hostage. Hand over Seven or the doctor dies!"*

"Kill McCoy and you have no more bargaining chips," Kirk pointed out, doing his best to sound much more cold-blooded than he felt. Aside from possibly Spock, McCoy was closer to Kirk than anyone else aboard the *Enterprise*. "Besides, it would be a pointless gesture anyway. We both know there's no way I can let you have Seven, no matter how many hostages you threaten. This is a matter of Federation security, as I'm certain Commissioner Santiago would agree."

The diplomat stepped forward to play his part as well. "That's right, Kirk. By the authority vested in me by the United Federation of Planets, I expressly forbid you to turn over the time traveler known as Annika Seven to a known ally of the Klingon Empire." His stony face and stern tone brooked no dissent. "That's an order, Captain."

"You see what I mean?" Kirk threw up his hands. "I couldn't trade Seven for my own mother."

Habroz's face hardened. *"Then we'll have to take her."*

He gestured at an unseen lackey. A moment later, enemy fire buffeted the *Enterprise*. The bridge rocked back and forth, throwing Kirk against the side of his chair. A loose data slate crashed to the floor. The inertial buffers strained to compensate. Seven grabbed the back of Kirk's chair to keep from falling. Santiago stumbled against the handrail.

"Both the *Navaar* and the *O'Spakya* have opened fire on us," Chekov announced redundantly. Real-time images of the attacking ships appeared on the main viewer, relegating Habroz to an insert window in the upper-right-hand corner of the screen. Green and purple beams targeted the *Enterprise*. "Phasers and disruptors only!"

"Do not think of retaliating!" Habroz bellowed. *"Or you will never see your ship's doctor again!"*

Chekov looked at Kirk, clearly eager to return fire. "Keptin?"

"Hold your fire," Kirk said, the words leaving a bad taste in his mouth. He wanted to strike back at the Orions just as much as the impetuous Russian, if not more so, but he hadn't given up on Spock and McCoy yet. As long as Habroz thought McCoy still had some value as a hostage, he had no incentive to kill Bones, except purely for spite . . . which, unfortunately, Kirk wouldn't put past him. "And shut up that son of a slime devil before I say something I regret."

"You and me both," Uhura said, muting the transmission. Habroz blustered silently in his corner of the screen. The enemy ships fanned out to pummel the *Enterprise* from above and below. Tactical displays, employing the latest Starfleet software, offered Kirk multiple views of the conflict from a variety of angles. Status reports flashed across the bottom of the screen.

"No major damage so far," Chekov reported. "Shields are holding."

But for how much longer?

"Evasive maneuvers, Mister Sulu," Kirk ordered. "Be creative."

"Aye, sir!"

The *Enterprise* tilted at an angle, presenting a narrower target to the Orion marauder, which was obviously the greater threat. It threaded between the hostile ships, trying to get them to fire upon each other. Kirk winced as an emerald disruptor beam bounced off the *O'Spakya*'s shields; he was all too aware that Spock and McCoy were still trapped aboard the Mavelan merchanter. He didn't want the *O'Spakya* to take any fatal blows from either the *Navaar* or the *Enterprise*. The ongoing hostage crisis tied his hands, making a bad situation worse.

Serves me right for letting Papa Yela play me like that, he thought. *Want to bet there's actually no baby Mavela about to be whelped?*

Seven made her way to the Science station, where she took it upon herself to relieve Cozzone. "Allow me, Lieutenant. I believe I may be of assistance."

Cozzone glanced at Kirk, who nodded in confirmation. With Spock away from his post and in jeopardy aboard the *O'Spakya,* Kirk welcomed Seven's expertise and trusted her judgment. If she thought she could help out in this crisis, he wasn't about to say no. Perhaps her future knowledge could give them an edge over their adversaries?

She certainly seemed to know her way around a science station. "Shields at eighty-three percent," she reported. "But dropping."

No surprise there. The *Enterprise*'s deflector array

was state of the art, but even it couldn't withstand a nonstop barrage from two enemy vessels for long, which was surely what Habroz had in mind. Destructive beams slammed against the ship's shields like space-age battering rams.

"Divert more power to the deflectors," Kirk ordered. "And concentrate the shields over the most vital compartments."

Scotty took over at the engineering station. "I don't understand. Why only disruptors? Don't they have any photon torpedoes?"

Habroz's strategy made perfect sense to Kirk. "They don't want to risk killing Seven by blowing us up. They want to knock out our shields so they can board the *Enterprise* and take her by force."

"Aye, that makes sense." Scotty glanced over at Seven. "She's a profitable prize, to be sure. Why, it wasn't too long ago that I was covetin' her future know-how myself."

"Precisely, Mister Scott," Kirk said, "which is why it is imperative that we keep the Orions from getting their hands on her."

"Understood, Captain." Scotty didn't need to have the potential consequences spelled out to him. He grimaced at the thought. "I hate to say it, sir, but maybe a judicious retreat is in order?"

Kirk shook his head. "I'm not ready to abandon Spock and McCoy yet." He still didn't believe in no-win scenarios; there had to be a way to rescue the hostages without surrendering Seven. "Besides, I doubt that Habroz and his raiders will let us make it all the way back to the border."

"That is unlikely," Seven agreed. "Our shields are weakening at a geometric rate. I estimate that the Orions will be able to beam through our defenses in approximately twelve minutes."

Kirk realized that they had to be ready for company. He opened a channel for a shipwide broadcast. "Attention, all hands. This is the captain. We are likely to be boarded by armed intruders. All crew members are instructed to secure their posts and assist in any efforts to repel the invaders. Let's make them regret that they ever set foot on our ship. Kirk out."

He turned his attention back to the bridge. "Dispatch security teams to defend the bridge, engineering, the warp nacelles, and other high-value locations. Lock down the crew quarters and sickbay."

Ensigns and lieutenants scrambled to carry out his orders.

"Kirk!"

Habroz found his voice again, despite Uhura muting the audio moments ago. She shrugged apologetically; apparently the Orions had managed to override the blockage somehow. Once again, as when they'd jammed the *Enterprise*'s ship-to-planet signals at Gamma Trianguli VI, they seemed to know more about Starfleet comm protocols than Kirk would have liked. More proof that they had a mole aboard?

"That was rude of you, Kirk, cutting me off like that." Habroz smirked. He obviously enjoyed having the upper hand. *"It's not too late to avoid any further bloodshed. Just give me Seven . . . and I won't be forced to slaughter everyone aboard your ship."*

"No deal." Kirk was already fed up with Habroz's

threats and bullying. Times like this, he wished the universal translator wasn't quite so reliable.

The translator . . .

Inspiration struck him. He threw a pointed look at Uhura and tapped out a message on the armrest of his chair, employing old-fashioned Morse Code. He had every confidence that the savvy communications expert would pick up on his signal.

She smiled slyly back at him.

"Captain!" she exclaimed so convincingly that Kirk was impressed by her acting skills. "That last blast was too much for the translator. It's crashing . . . !"

"*What was that?*" Habroz glared suspiciously in Uhura's direction. "*Is this some kind of vexaly pwaformee sug?*"

His indignant queries devolved into what sounded like gibberish.

"*Ren! Mujo kopsa geb?*"

"I'm sorry. What are you saying?" Kirk didn't need to feign confusion. As instructed, Uhura had disabled the universal translator, just to make this stunt more convincing. She threw her hands up in the air, acting uncharacteristically helpless. Kirk stared in bewilderment at the viewer. "Can you repeat that?"

"*Cuomm fids sug?*" Habroz looked equally baffled by what Kirk was saying. He turned angrily toward a subordinate. "*Veet kow nial yedraf?*"

Uhura, who spoke Orion like a native, typed quietly at her control panel. Subtitles appeared below Habroz's face, translating the agitated pirate's words for all to see:

"*Is this a trick? What the [EXPLETIVE] is he saying?*"

His flunky shrugged. "*Efderae gom likt.*"

"I don't speak Standard."

Habroz looked like he wanted to tear the hapless Orion's tongue out with his metal hand. Letting out an inarticulate howl of frustration, which Uhura didn't even try to interpret, he slammed his fist down on the armrest of his throne. His irate face vanished from view as he gave up trying to communicate with the *Enterprise.*

"Good riddance," Kirk muttered. "So much for trying to negotiate the terms of our surrender."

Additional security personnel poured onto the bridge, staking out defensive posts at every entrance and strategic position. The bridge itself, Kirk recalled, could be sealed off with force fields in order to defend it from hostile forces, fires, hull breaches, and other emergencies. In theory, the bridge could withstand a full-scale siege, and the saucer itself could separate from the rest of the ship, not that Kirk had any intention of abandoning any part of his ship or crew. Habroz didn't dare risk destroying the *Enterprise* as long as Seven was aboard. His hands were also tied to a degree, even the metal one.

"Notify Starfleet of our situation," Kirk ordered.

"I'm already trying to do so," Uhura said, "although they've attempted to jam our signals again." She attacked the controls with fierce determination. "Uh-uh. Not this time."

Another salvo rocked the bridge.

"Yes!" she exulted a moment later. Judging from her triumphant tone, she had succeeded in getting through whatever interference the Orions had thrown up against her. "Emergency message transmitted, sir."

"Well done, Lieutenant," Kirk congratulated her. It

was important to keep Starfleet informed, even if there was little the brass could do for them this far out on the frontier. Not only were the nearest reinforcements light-years away, but Starfleet could hardly send in the cavalry while the *Enterprise* was smack-dab in the middle of the Neutral Zone, not without provoking an open conflict with the Klingons. Still, at least the folks back home would have the full story if something happened to *Enterprise.* "Make sure Command is provided with regular updates."

"Shields at eighteen percent," Seven reported. "Defensive integrity is nearly compromised."

"Then we need to get you out of here," Kirk decided. The bridge was the first place that Habroz's foot soldiers were going to look for Seven, and there was no guarantee that even its defenses could hold off the Orions forever. "Scotty! Get Seven to the shuttlebay. The *Enterprise* can try to hold off the *Navaar* long enough for you to get away."

With Spock out of the picture, there was nobody Kirk trusted more than Scotty to keep Seven safe and out of the grasp of the Orions. Sulu was probably the better pilot, but Kirk needed his best helmsman on the bridge during this three-way battle. And Chekov, although brave and enthusiastic, was simply too green to be trusted with such a vital responsibility, not when the time line itself might be in jeopardy.

That left Scotty.

"If you say so, Captain," he responded readily, "although I don't like leaving you in the lurch."

"Seven's safety is our top priority now," Kirk said. "The future may depend on it."

"Understood, Captain." Scotty nodded grimly and gestured toward the turbolift. "After you, lass."

Seven turned away from the science station but did not immediately head for the exit. She approached Kirk's chair instead, deftly managing to keep her balance despite the blasts jolting the bridge. Kirk got the distinct impression this wasn't her first space battle.

"While I appreciate your determination to keep me away from our enemies, perhaps there is another way." She leaned in toward Kirk, lowering her voice so that only he could hear. "Allow me to suggest an alternative strategy."

Kirk remembered how she had handled herself on Yusub, Gamma Trianguli VI, and Cheron. He was more than willing to take advantage of her obvious smarts and resourcefulness.

"I'm listening."

Twenty-four

"Our shields have been breached, Keptin! The Orions are beaming aboard!"

Damn, Kirk thought, even though he'd been expecting this ever since the *Navaar* and the *O'Spakya* opened fire on them. He braced himself for the siege to come, glad that Scotty and Seven were already en route to the shuttlebay. Now if only Seven's audacious plan went off as planned. . . .

In the meantime, he had a starship to defend.

"All right, people," he said firmly. "Just because our drawbridge is down, doesn't mean we have to turn the *Enterprise* over to the invaders. This is our ship, and no one is going to take it from us."

He was pleased to see Chekov, Sulu, and the rest nodding in agreement. He knew he could count on every member of his crew to stand fast against the Orions—except maybe the traitor he still feared was lurking somewhere aboard.

There was no time to worry about that now, though. Pillars of coruscating emerald energy manifested all around him, indicating that the Orions had launched a direct assault upon the bridge. It was a brazenly reckless move, as multiple phaser pistols zapped the invaders as soon as they fully materialized. Azure beams, expertly aimed by the alert security forces, stunned the Orion boarders without hitting a single *Enterprise* crew member or workstation. Kirk was impressed by—and grateful for—the guards' marksmanship.

Looks like all that Academy target practice paid off.

A single Orion, notably faster than his comrades, managed to deflect a phaser beam with an ablative steel wristband. He lunged at Sulu, no doubt hoping to seize control of the helm, but Sulu's reflexes were too fast; leaping to his feet, he met the charging raider with a sideways kick to the gut. The Orion was propelled backward into the sturdy red handrail around the command circle. He grunted with pain as his back slammed into the rail. A second phaser blast from another guard dropped the raider onto the deck and ensured that he wouldn't be getting up again anytime soon.

"Well, that was different," Sulu remarked before resuming his place at the helm. Chekov, who had instantly taken over steering the *Enterprise* from his own console, returned control of the ship to his comrade. Sulu took a moment to catch his breath. "I don't often get my hands dirty on the bridge like that."

Chekov grinned at him. "What hands? Looked to me like you used your boot."

"Nicely done, Mister Sulu," Kirk said, unsurprised by the helmsman's talent for hand-to-hand combat; he and Sulu had fought side by side on numerous occasions. "Too bad you didn't have a sword at hand."

Sulu shrugged. Fencing was his sport of choice. "Lucky for him I didn't."

Six Orions had beamed onto the bridge, only to be dispatched with admirable efficiency. Kirk waited for the second wave of the assault, but the Orions seemed to abandon any direct attack on the bridge. The battle for the ship was hardly over, however, as every moment brought more reports of deck-to-deck fighting throughout the *Enterprise*. Multiple windows opened up on the main viewer, picking up images from the ship's internal sensors. A computer algorithm of Spock's design filtered out any irrelevant images and selected the views Kirk needed. He frowned at what he saw.

Hordes of raucous Orions rampaged through the ship's gleaming corridors. The pirates whooped and hollered with savage glee. Starfleet intel had it that Orion raiders ingested massive quantities of ultra-testosterone before going into battle. A squat buccaneer, making his way toward the bridge, spotted a security scanner in the ceiling and opened fire with his disruptor pistol. A blinding green flash masked the image before that window went black and vanished from the viewer. Moments later, Kirk heard disruptor blasts slam against the reinforced blast doors protecting the gangway to the bridge. A security window caught the Orions trying to force their way past the barricade. Although the turbolift was shut down, the gangway on the starboard side of the main viewer provided alternative access to the bridge in the event of an emergency. Alas, this was the wrong sort of emergency.

"Security protocol Delta-Six," he ordered. "Flood all access corridors and turbolifts to the bridge with anesthezine gas."

The potent knock-out gas was expressly intended for scenarios like this when dangerous individuals needed to be subdued quickly; Kirk had used the same gas to reclaim the *Enterprise* from Khan and his followers. He watched intently as billowing white fumes vented into the corridor directly outside. For a second, he thought the anesthezine was just what the doctor ordered, as the Orions started coughing and choking on the vapors, but then the experienced boarders extracted collapsible air filters from their belts and clamped them over their mouths and nostrils. Adhesive edges held the filters, which resembled transparent surgical masks, in place. Within minutes, the pirates resumed their attack upon the blast doors, even as the swirling fumes gradually dispersed.

Kirk scowled at the pirates' countermeasures. *I should have known it wouldn't be that easy.*

"Funny," Chekov said. "It's almost like those Cossacks know our standard security procedures."

Kirk remembered the possibility of a mole. "Let's assume they do. We can't afford to underestimate our foes for an instant."

"What about gassing the rest of the ship?" Chekov suggested. He stared at the viewscreen, where Orion boarding parties could be seen swarming all over the ship. "We still have plenty of anesthezine left."

"Don't bother." Kirk figured that the other pirates were equipped with filter masks as well. At worst, gassing the rest of the *Enterprise* might just knock out the ship's embattled personnel, leaving them unable to defend themselves. "Seems we're going to have to do this the hard way."

Uhura contemplated the stunned Orions littering the bridge. Security teams were busy placing restraints upon the unconscious prisoners even as their fellow officers stayed on guard against further beam-ins. The downed raiders were dragged into an out-of-the-way corner of the bridge.

"You know," she observed, "we have hostages of our own now." Kirk knew she had to be worrying about Spock and McCoy. "Maybe we can propose an exchange?"

"I appreciate the thought, Lieutenant, but that's probably wishful thinking." He hated crushing her hopes, but he had to be realistic. "Habroz strikes me as the type who is perfectly willing to sacrifice his own people to get what he wants, especially when there's a sizable bounty at stake."

He could only imagine how much the Klingons would pay for Seven and her untapped knowledge of the future. Everything Kirk knew about the Orions suggested that Habroz wasn't going to quit until he had Seven.

"Kirk to engineering," he ordered via the intercom in his chair. "I need our shields up and running again, no matter what it takes."

"*Yes, sir,*" Charlene Masters replied from the engine room. Was it just his imagination or had the able young officer picked up a trace of her mentor's Highland brogue? "*I'm doin' all I can.*"

Kirk had faith in Masters's abilities, but he found himself wishing that he had two Montgomery Scotts: one to work on restoring the shields and another to see Seven to safety. And he wouldn't have minded having Spock and McCoy back at their posts as well. He felt like he was fighting for his ship without his right and left hands, and worrying about their safety at the same time.

He needed Spock and Bones. The *Enterprise* needed them.

The fighting throughout the ship filled up the viewer. From the look of things, the invaders were meeting stiff resistance from ship's security forces, but they showed no sign of retreating back to the *Navaar*. Kirk looked for Habroz, but he did not spot the pirate captain among the intruders. *Probably still aboard the* Navaar, he guessed, *waiting for his prize.*

That was fine with Kirk. They had more than their hands full with the Orions already aboard the *Enterprise*. Kirk watched tensely as phaser fire and disruptor blasts scarred the ship's pristine corridors. The conflict spread from deck to deck, turning his ship into a battlefield. A schematic on the viewer charted the intruders' progress through the ship. Like the bridge, engineering was under siege, but it had not yet fallen to the invaders. Blast doors guarded the warp core and impulse engines. Emergency power reserves had been diverted to electrify the doors in order to shock the pirates into insensibility. To Kirk's frustration, engineering teams were forced to turn away from crucial repair efforts to fortify the key propulsion units. On a separate viewer window, Masters directed the efforts from atop a metal catwalk, shouting orders to the workers below. Sweat drenched her attractive, dark-skinned features. Kirk wished her luck. He didn't want any more of his people to fall victim to the pirates.

Now if Scotty and Seven could just make it to the shuttlebay in time!

"Hurry along, lass," Scotty said. "We haven't a moment to lose."

Their heels pounded against the floor of P Deck. For the first time ever, he wished that the *Enterprise* was not so grand in proportions. The long blue-steel corridors seem to go on forever, and they still had a ways to go.

"I aware of the need for haste, Mister Scott," Seven replied. "And I believe I am keeping pace with you sufficiently."

"Aye, that ye are."

Accompanied by a pair of heavily armed security officers, they raced for the shuttlebay at the rear of the engineering hull. Red-alert lights and blaring klaxons spurred them on, along with the unmistakable din of battle coming from adjacent decks, halls, and compartments. It was obvious that the Orions had well and truly boarded the *Enterprise,* making it all the more crucial that he get Seven off the ship as fast as humanly possible. Their entire plan depended on it.

"This way, lads!" Scott said urgently, gesturing with his phaser pistol. As the turbolifts were shut down for emergency purposes, they had no choice but to make their way by foot, while trying to steer clear of the worst of the fighting. Despite her recent stay in sickbay and her close encounter with a poison plant, Seven easily kept up with her three-man escort. Scotty was impressed by her stamina.

Guess they grow them hearty in the future, he surmised. *Good to know.*

Compared to the usual hustle and bustle of the *Enterprise,* the corridor was strangely empty; Scotty assumed that his crewmates were either engaged in combat elsewhere or else holed up tight at their designated emergency posts. It felt strange to have the hallway to themselves; if not for the klaxons and shouts and energy blasts echoing through the corridors, he would have thought he was aboard a derelict ship, haunted by the Ghost of Lasses Yet to Come.

"It appears we vacated the bridge just in time," Seven observed, still very much corporeal for the time being. A tricorder was slung over her shoulder, while a Starfleet pack was strapped to her back. Her right hand gripped a phaser. "I suspect that Captain Kirk has the bridge thoroughly sealed off by now."

Scotty recalled the numerous measures designed to secure the bridge against unwelcome guests. "Aye, these pirates won't be crackin' that nut anytime soon." Still, it pained him to think of gangs of ill-mannered ruffians stomping uninvited through the finest ship in the fleet. "This sort of fracas ever happen in your time?"

"On occasion," she admitted.

An intersection lay before them. The way appeared clear, so Scotty started to hurry forward, only to be called back by one of the security officers. "Hold on, sir." Ensign James Pierce gripped a phaser rifle with both hands. He wore a Starfleet flak jacket over his red tunic for extra protection. His bright red hair was mussed. "Let me take point."

Leading the way, while his partner, Ensign Michelle Robbins, guarded the party's rear, he fired a blue stun beam into the crossways just to provoke a response from any lurking Orions. When nobody fired back, he glanced back over his shoulder and nodded at Scotty and the others. "All right. After me."

But before he could step all the way into the intersection, an entire cadre of Orions beamed into existence right in front of them, blocking their path. The newly arrived raiders began firing their disruptors even as they

materialized, shooting wildly in every direction just to
be safe. An emerald beam sizzled past Scotty's head; he
knew better than to think that the pirates' firearms were
set on stun. Chances were, the pistols would reduce them
to atoms.

That was too close for comfort, he thought.

Bloodshot green eyes spotted the humans. *"Feoje!"* a
nameless raider barked in Orion, making Scotty wonder
what had become of the universal translator. The armed
intruder, who smelled as though he hadn't bathed since
the first Romulan War, pointed energetically at the
Starfleet quartet. *"Sycun zi!"*

Pierce dropped the observant pirate with a blast
from his rifle, but not before the stunned Orion alerted
his partners in plunder. The other raiders spun around
to confront Seven and her escorts. Thinking fast, Scotty
dashed over to a control panel mounted on the wall right
before the intersection. He jabbed a blinking red button with one hand, while hauling Pierce backward with
the other. A shimmering energy field buzzed into place,
almost slicing off the security officer's toes. Cut off from
their targets, the Orions swore furiously on the other
side of the barrier. Disruptor beams ricocheted off the
force field, producing bright actinic flashes. A foolhardy
raider threw himself against the wall. A high-voltage
shock taught him the error of his ways. The other pirates
contented themselves with blasting away at the field, trying to disrupt it through sheer firepower. Visible distortions in the energy lattice testified to the effectiveness of
the barrage. *"Niog velf pekkaly!"*

Scotty thought it best not to stick around. "All right.
Not that way, then."

Unintelligible curses, no doubt defaming the humans' ancestry, evolution, and reproductive propensities, chased after Scotty and the others as they retreated back in the direction they had come. Robbins found herself leading the way. She glanced back at Scotty.

"Which way now, sir?"

Scotty knew the ship's nooks and crannies as well as the back alleys of Glasgow. Alas, he couldn't think of a quick route to the shuttlebay that didn't lead them right back toward the Orions, which left them with only one other option. "Seems we need to take a wee detour."

Seven seemed to read his mind. "The transporters?"

"Where else?" he replied. Intraship beaming was a risky business, not to be undertaken lightly, but they had run out of viable alternatives. "I'll get ye to that shuttle even if I have to beam ye directly into the driver's seat!"

He quickly charted the best route in his mind. The ship's primary transporter room was several decks above them, where the bulk of the fighting seemed to be concentrated, but maybe the cargo transporters on Level 19 would be easier to get to? They were generally used to beam large loads directly into the cargo storage facility, but there was no reason they couldn't transport a couple of items of human baggage in a pinch. Circling back the way they'd come, they headed toward an emergency stairwell that was too many meters away for Scotty's peace of mind. He wanted to slow down and get his bearings, but that wasn't a good idea; raucous whoops, coming from the blocked intersection, made it clear that the Orions had finally blasted their way through the force field and were right behind them. Scotty exhaled a sigh of relief as he finally spotted the sealed entrance to the stairwell about halfway down the corridor before them. Thinking ahead, he tried to figure out the best way to bar the door behind them.

Maybe by wielding it shut with the phaser rifles?

A command authorization keycode unsealed the door guarding the stairwell, which was intended for use when the turbolifts were inoperative. It slid open to reveal a spiral stairway leading down to lower decks. "All clear!" Robbins announced after poking her head and the muzzle of her rifle past the entrance. Scotty shoved Seven in after her and was just about to follow when a blistering crossfire erupted in the corridor. He and Pierce abruptly found themselves caught between the Orions at one end of the hall and Starfleet defenders at the others. Crisscrossing beams shot up and down the corridor like a First Contact Day fireworks display. Scotty ducked his head to keep from being scalped by the sizzling energy discharges.

"In, laddie!" he prodded Pierce. "Step lively!"

The other man moved quickly, but not fast enough. An azure bolt of friendly fire grazed his leg, numbing it from the hip down. He collapsed at the foot of the door, unable to support his own weight. A pained grimace hinted at his discomfort, but nary a groan slipped past his gritted teeth. He kept a tight grip on his phaser rifle.

Blast it all, Scotty thought. *We cannae catch a break.*

Attaching his own phaser to his belt, he grabbed Pierce beneath the shoulders and dragged him out of the crossfire into the stairwell. Deflected energy beams, both blue and green, bounced off the doorframe, bright enough and close enough to make Scotty's eyes hurt. Sparks sprayed off the metal frame.

"Pierce!" his crewmate exclaimed. "You're hit!"

"Nothing serious," he grunted. Cradling his rifle in his lap, he took hold of his stunned leg and yanked it out of the way of the door, which slid back into place behind them. Scotty hastily sealed it from the inside, changing the security code for good measure. Robbins tried to help Pierce to his feet, but he shrugged her off. "Leave me. I'll just slow you down." Bracing his legs against the opposite side of the tube, he aimed his rifle at the door. "I'll hold them off for as long as I can."

Robbins tugged on his arm. "Forget it, Pierce. We're not leaving you."

"Come now, laddie," Scotty said. "Don't be a hero."

Pierce didn't budge. "It's not about being a hero. It's about looking out for the future." He glanced down over at Seven. "Isn't that right?"

"You are correct," she stated, "although I wish you were not. Speed *is* of the essence."

Scotty faced reality. He didn't want to abandon the wounded crewman, but getting Seven off the *Enterprise* took priority. "That it is," he conceded. "You do what you need to do, Ensign." He took a moment to communicate Pierce's location and status to the bridge; with luck, an *Enterprise* security team could get to Pierce before the Orions did. "I owe ye a drink when this is all over."

"I'll hold you to that," Pierce promised. He patted his inert leg. "Figure this is worth some bootleg Romulan ale at least."

Scotty rolled his eyes at the youth's taste in spirits. To his mind, no unearthly blue concoction could compare to a good Scotch, but he held his tongue. Robbins reluctantly stepped away from her fellow officer. "You had better not get yourself killed, Pierce, because I am so not working your shifts if you do."

He waved her away. "Go on, get out of here."

Scotty could still hear the firefight raging on the other side of the door as he, Seven, and Robbins clambered down to Level 19. They cautiously emerged from the stairwell into a hallway, only to hear yet another band of Orions raising havoc just around the corner. "Bloody hell," Scotty muttered. The noxious cutthroats seemed to be infesting the entire ship. "They're spreading like tribbles."

And between them and the cargo transporters. Of course.

Twenty-five

"*Osphai!*" an Orion shouted as he rounded the corner and caught sight of Scotty and the others. He hollered sharply to his compatriots. "*Yrhan chark ayalo!*"

Scotty was forced to improvise again. "Back down the stairs! Keep on going!"

The fugitive trio rushed back into the stairwell. Scotty slammed the door shut behind them, but he doubted that it would hold back the raiders for long. He had no way of knowing if the pirates had spotted Seven, but he had to assume the worst. They scrambled down the steps to the next available exit, which just happened to lead to the ship's sprawling gymnasium.

Intended to keep the crew fit on long treks through space, the gym was two decks high and large enough to accommodate a variety of strenuous activities. Separate compartments boasted weight-lifting apparatus, stationary bikes, spas, saunas, padded exercise mats, adjustable climbing walls, obstacle courses, trampolines, fencing equipment, racketball courts, circular zero-g treadmills, and just about anything else Starfleet figured would keep the crew in fighting trim. Scotty couldn't remember the last time he'd set foot in the place. Curling up with a stiff drink and a stack of engineering manuals was sufficient recreation to his way of thinking.

I get enough exercise climbing Jefferies tubes, dodging

disruptor blasts, and holding this ship together, thank ye very much!

Scotty figured that they could try to cut through the gym to ditch their pursuers, while searching for another route to the transporters. "Any port in a storm," he muttered. "Just as long as nobody expects me to do any bloody chin-ups."

"I doubt that will be necessary," Seven said dryly.

Needless to say, the gym was empty at the moment. No guards had been deployed to defend the exercise equipment, which wasn't exactly essential to control of the ship. Nevertheless, Scotty heard the rambunctious Orions heading their way. Angry fists pounded at the sealed entrance to the gym. They would be blasting away at the lock next.

"The Orions are persistent," Seven observed.

That's one way to put it, Scotty thought. "Or just plain greedy."

Looking about for a convenient escape route, Scotty wished that he was a wee bit more familiar with the layout of the gym. Had they remodeled the place since the last time he'd wandered in by mistake? He scowled in frustration. If this had been the engine room, he could've found his way around blindfolded.

"Er, give me a moment to reconnoiter."

Ensign Robbins came to his rescue. "I have an idea. Follow me."

She was a trim, energetic lass with freckles and short brown hair. She led them past an array of balance beams and gymnastic horses to the last place Scotty would have ever thought of: the women's locker room. He couldn't resist glancing around as they hurried past the empty dressing rooms and shower stalls. Open lockers and discarded towels hinted at the speed with which assorted female crew members had reported to their posts once the red alert sounded. Scott felt as though he was exploring an undiscovered country.

Moving stealthily, they exited the locker room, which opened up onto the ship's Olympic-sized swimming pool. Clear blue water reflected the overhead lights, casting rippling shadows on the walls of the spacious chamber. A high ceiling provided plenty of room for diving boards of various altitudes. The bottom of the deep end boasted a furnished lounge area for the ship's more amphibious crew members and guests. Smaller, satellite pools had adjustable temperature and salinity controls. The pool could also be frozen to allow for ice sports.

Scotty heard Orions converging on the pool area from opposite ends. The bright lights left him feeling uncomfortably exposed. He ran over to the nearest control panel. "Computer, dim lights!"

The voice-activated system responded instantly, throwing the pool into murky shadows. Harsh voices and pounding boots blocked their escape in every direction. Scotty gazed into the pellucid depths of the pool. Water lapped against its tiled sides. He sighed in resignation.

"Over the side," he whispered. "Into the water."

Seven and Robbins descended into the pool, disappearing beneath the surface. Scotty waited until they were fully submerged before taking a deep breath and sliding into the water himself, being careful not to make too much of a splash. Cool water chilled his sweaty skin and soaked his uniform. Sodden fabric and heavy boots weighed him down as he sank deeper and deeper. He grabbed a rung on a metal ladder to keep from bobbing to the surface. Looking around beneath the water, he spotted his companions holding their breaths nearby. Robbins's brown hair rustled like a sea anemone atop her head, while Seven's tight blond 'do remained more or less in place, as did her cool, focused expression. Tiny bubbles escaped their lips and nostrils. He hoped that wouldn't be enough to give them away.

How good were Orion eyes anyway?

They had gotten into the pool just in the nick of time. Three meters of water muffled but did not eliminate the sound of two packs of Orions meeting alongside the pool. The raiders greeted each other raucously, while boasting of their exploits. Scotty couldn't make out a word, but he'd run into enough barroom braggarts to recognize the tone. They were probably each claiming to have singlehandedly licked an entire deck of *Enterprise* crew members—and with their bare hands, no less!

With luck, the Orions would be too busy trading tall tales to look closely into the pool. After all, who would expect a time traveler from the future to be hiding out in a gym of all places, let alone at the bottom of a pool? Chances were, the pirates would soon move on to more promising hunting grounds. Where was the profit and glory in plundering a swimming pool? And as far as Scotty knew, Orions were not aquatic.

But will they leave 'fore we run out of air?

Scotty's cheeks were already bulging like a Drofoxian blowfish. Bubbles slipped past his lips no matter how hard he tried to hold on to his last breath. He gazed longingly upward, vaguely glimpsing the shadowy figures of the Orions. His lungs ached. White knuckles clung to the underwater rung as he fought an increasingly insistent urge to kick toward the surface. This was like being trapped on a Class-N planet without a proper environment suit. He was on the verge of drowning.

Get going, ye loud-mouth renegades, he silently railed at the Orions, who seemed in no hurry to vacate the premises. *Share your inglorious war stories elsewhere!*

A finger tapped him on the chest. Robbins got his attention as she fished a compact plastic rebreather from a pouch on her flak jacket. She cupped the translucent mask over her own mouth, took a deep breath, then passed it on to Scotty. He took hold of it eagerly, grateful for her foresight. He pressed it to his lips. Molecular processors instantly converted exhaled carbon dioxide back into oxygen, which he sucked down hungrily. The recycled air was perhaps the sweetest he'd ever breathed.

He couldn't be greedy, however. Since Robbins apparently only had one rebreather on her person, he quickly passed it over to Seven, who waited for it patiently, almost as though her lungs were more efficient than an ordinary human's of the twenty-third century. Still, she did not refuse the lifesaving breathing apparatus.

The fresh oxygen quieted Scotty's lungs, allowing him to bide his time until the rebreather came his way again. By the time Robbins took another breath, however, he was already running out of air once more. Hanging on to the ladder with one hand, he reached for the portable device a little too hastily. The rebreather slipped from his fingers, sinking to the bottom of the pool.

Bollocks, Scotty thought. Mortified, he looked sheepishly at Robbins and Seven before diving after the lost
gadget. He had to kick softly to avoid disturbing the
placid surface of the pool. The deeper he swam, the more
he craved the precious breath he had literally let slip between his fingers. Why the hell couldn't he have dropped
the bloody thing *after* he'd sucked down some more air?

His frantic eyes searched the deep end of the pool.
Inflatable lounge furniture, filled with heavier-than-
water gases, was anchored to the floor for the convenience of water-breathing passengers and crew. Scotty
didn't see the missing rebreather lying on the bottom
anywhere. Could it have fallen on or under the submerged furniture? Sinking to the bottom, he groped
beneath an underwater coffee table, his desperate
fingers finding nothing, even as, nearby, Robbins over-
turned a comfy bean bag chair and Seven methodically
inspected the corners of the pool. The well-furnished
lounge didn't make finding the rebreather any easier.

Blast it, he thought. *Where are ye, you slippery doo-
hickey?*

Lack of air made it hard to concentrate on what he
was doing. Bulging cheeks filled with stale carbon dioxide. The surface of the pool and the blessed air above it
seemed as far away as the Galactic Barrier. He glanced
over at Robbins, hoping against hope that she was having
better luck than he was, but she shook her head in defeat.
Her bulging cheeks looked like a chipmunk's. Seven appeared in a bad way, too.

Abandoning the coffee table, he rummaged amidst
the cushions of a waterproof couch. It was worth a shot;
in his experience, seat cushions exerted a gravitational

pull directly proportional to the value of the object being sought. He sometimes joked about submitting a paper on the subject to the *Interplanetary Journal of Theoretical Physics*. Now his life and that of his imperiled comrades depended on a practical test of that hypothesis.

It has to be there, he thought. *It's got to be.*

Soggy fingers fished between the cushions. At first, they found nothing but water, but then they closed on a piece of flexible plastic.

Yes!

He would've gasped in joy if that wouldn't have entailed drowning. Instead he yanked the rebreather from its devilish hiding place and waved it before his companions' eyes. Holding the device to his lips, he helped himself to a couple lungfuls of recycled oxygen.

Maybe I should submit that article after all. . . .

The air gave him the means to swim over to Robbins and Seven and share the rebreather with them. Minutes passed as they discreetly handed the device back and forth while waiting for the Orions to depart. The coolness of the pool seeped into Scotty's bones, causing him to shiver. His boots filled up with water, dragging him down. Seven adjusted her backpack, while Robbins hung on to her phaser rifle. Scotty prayed the Orions weren't in the mood for a quick dip.

Finally, just when he was starting to feel like the Loch Ness Monster, whose deep-water breeding grounds had been discovered late in the twenty-first century, the sound of marching boots charging away from the pool penetrated its depths. Noisy echoes receded into the distance before fading away entirely.

Had the Orions finally moved on?

Scotty counted to a hundred, just to be safe, before signaling Seven to scan the area above with her tricorder. A waterproof casing protected the sturdy instrument from contamination as she probed for life-forms. She reviewed the readouts before gesturing that it was safe to get out of the water. Phaser in hand, Robbins insisted on confirming the results with her own eyes. She handed Scotty the rebreather and peeked above the surface, keeping low in the water like a crocodile on the prowl. A thumbs-up signal gave Scotty and Seven the go-ahead. Robbins extended her hand to help them out of the pool.

Despite her assurances, Scotty searched the shifting shadows, half-expecting a lurking Orion to lunge from hiding. But there was no trace of the raiders, who must have gone in search of greener pastures, no pun intended. Scotty wondered briefly how the bridge and engineering were faring before focusing again on his own mission.

First things first, he thought.

His uniform was drenched; his boots sloshed as he walked. Water dripped from his hair into his eyes. Seven and Robbins were equally soaked. Seven removed her backpack long enough to briskly strip off her soggy suit to reveal a skintight blue outfit complete with a metallic Starfleet emblem pinned to her chest. Robbins placed the rebreather back in the pocket of her flak jacket.

"Good thing ye had that on ye, lassie," Scotty said. "Or we would've had to choose between drownin' and throwin' ourselves on the mercy of those barkin' ruffians."

"Just good tactics." Robbins patted her well-supplied jackets. "Always be prepared." She winked at Scotty.

"Remind me to tell you about the time I had to evac some kidnapped Za'Huli scientists from an undersea terrorist base on Ricou Four."

"It's a date," Scott promised. "But first we need to dry off."

Time was running out, but their water-logged uniforms were just going to slow them down, not to mention leave a trail of puddles behind them. Scotty crossed the floor to the nearest high-speed drying booth. He stepped into the humanoid-size alcove, which was built into the side of the wall. A toasty red glow dried him out to a passable degree. His hair and socks were still a wee damp, but he no longer felt as though he'd just swum across the Firth of Forth.

"That's more like it," he declared, emerging from the booth. He wrung a few stubborn drops of moisture from his sleeve, even as Seven and Robbins followed his lead. Within minutes, the trio was ready to resume their interrupted dash for the transporters. Exiting through the men's locker rooms this time, they crept steadily toward the gym and the hall. A fallen door, blasted off its track by enemy disruptors, lay on the floor before a breached doorway. "Here's hoping the lot of them moved on a few decks. . . ."

No such luck.

Robbins cautiously poked the muzzle of her rifle out the door. An emerald beam nearly zapped it out of her hands. She darted back inside. Phaser fire from farther down the corridor greeted the Orions' blast. The ensign shook her head. "It's still a battle zone out there. There's no way we're going to get to the transporters that way."

"What about the Jefferies tubes," Seven suggested,

referring to the network of service tunnels crisscrossing the ship. The narrow crawlways ran above, below, and between the various decks and bulkheads.

"No," Scotty said. "The tubes are automatically sealed off if a ship is overrun by hostiles, to prevent access to vital areas. Like the transporters, say."

"A sensible, if inconvenient, precaution," Seven acknowledged, "which I had hoped had not yet been instituted in your era." She contemplated her left hand, which was graced by a sophisticated exoskeleton. Despite her aloof manner and expression, you could practically see the wheels turning beneath her bonny blond locks. "It may be, however, that I can remedy this situation."

Scotty heard the melee outside growing nearer. "I'm not sure you'll get the chance." He glanced back toward the pool, hoping they wouldn't have to take refuge beneath the water again. That ploy may have worked once, but they could hardly spend the rest of the invasion hiding in the pool; that wasn't going to get Seven where she needed to be. "Sounds like we're about to have some more company."

"Leave that to me," Robbins said. Hefting her rifle, she raced out the door and opened fire on the approaching Orions. She was out in the open before Scotty even realized what she was up to. "Heads up, greenies!" She fired another beam and took off down the hall. "Tag, you're it!"

She is luring them away, he grasped, *to give us a chance to get into the tubes.*

It was too late to stop her. Scotty and Seven could only hide alongside the open doorway as a mob of shouting raiders stampeded past the gym, hot on Robbins's trail. Scotty held his breath and prayed that the intrepid young ensign was as fast as she looked and could link up with the Starfleet forces before the Orions caught up with her. The pirates didn't sound like they were in the mood to take prisoners.

"Godspeed, lassie," he whispered. "And thank ye."

He was not about to let her daring go to waste. "Come with me, Doctor Seven."

She waved away the honorific. " 'Seven' will suffice, Mister Scott."

"If ye say so."

That this remarkable lass was from the future had not escaped his memory. He wondered what time and place she came from and how much she truly knew about the shape of things to come. Part of him still wanted to pry a few hints about the future of starship engineering out of her, perhaps over a bottle or two, but he knew the captain wouldn't approve of it, what with the bloody "Temporal Prime Directive" and all.

Instead Scotty focused on the task ahead: getting into the Jefferies tubes. The nearest access panel was in the ceiling, directly above the climbing wall. An unobtrusive metal ladder, mounted to an adjacent wall, offered an easier route up, but it wobbled in an unsettling fashion when he took hold of it. He figured that it had been shaken loose when the ship had been fired on earlier. No doubt the *Enterprise* was going to require a thorough inspection, and plenty of repairs and maintenance, when they got out of the Neutral Zone.

He let go of the unstable ladder. A weary sigh escaped him; things were not exactly going their way. Craning his head back, he gazed up at the daunting face of the mock-granite climbing wall, which stretched several meters above their heads. Its rugged face was constructed of pliable pseudo-concrete that could be adjusted to various levels of difficulty. He glanced over at Seven. "Ye up for a climb?"

"I can adapt," she informed him, although she looked as though she'd just come off a five-day bender at Wrigley's Pleasure Planet. Swaying slightly, she approached the wall. "After you, Commander."

"Call me Scotty."

More intent on speed than exercise, he dialed the wall's difficulty level down to beginner's level. Its rough, uneven surface reconfigured itself. New holds, more generously distributed, bulged outward, while deepened hollows offered more purchase for their fingers and feet. It still looked like a strenuous climb, fit for Starfleet personnel, but he saw no need to make it harder than it had to be. Their mission was tricky enough as is.

Centimeter by centimeter, hold by hold, he scaled the wall. *Don't look down,* he thought as, huffing and puffing, he left the floor of the gym behind. In theory, an emergency anti-grav field would catch him if he fell from too high up, but he didn't feel like testing the safety protocols at the moment. Just his luck, the anti-grav plates had been knocked out by the *Navaar*'s attack.

His left boot, which was still a bit wet from the pool, slipped off an annoyingly small bulge in the wall. Gravity ambushed him and he found himself dangling precariously over a deck above the mat-covered floor. Only five remaining fingers held him in place, so that his arm felt as though it was being tugged from its socket as his hanging feet searched for purchase. The foothold he'd been using before seemed to have vanished. He grunted through gritted teeth. His fingers ached horrendously. He couldn't hold on much longer. . . .

"To your left," Seven advised him from below. If he fell, he would surely hit her on the way down, which may have contributed to the emphasis with which she delivered her instructions. "At approximately seven o'clock."

Doing his best to stay cool and listen to her directions, he swung to the left. At first he couldn't find the promised foothold, but then . . . eureka! Gasping in relief, he planted his slippery boot squarely on a narrow outcropping, barely more than four centimeters across. The bulge supported his weight, taking the pressure off his fingers. Exhausted, he sagged against the pebbly surface of the wall, catching his breath. Sweat dripped down his face.

"Are you secure, Mister Scott?" Seven inquired.

"Aye." He wiped his brow with his free hand. It struck him that they were in an unenviably vulnerable position should the Orions happen upon them again. Short of flying, there was no way they could avoid being blasted off the wall. That dismal prospect was all the motivation he needed to get to the access panel as soon as possible. Taking a deep breath, he started climbing again. "Don't ye worry about me."

A few grueling moments later, they reached the access panel in the ceiling. He attempted to open it, but, as feared, it was sealed shut for security reasons. Not even the override code worked; it was locked up tighter than a Quefian pilgrim's chastity belt.

He made the mistake of glancing down at Seven, who was clinging to the wall about half a meter below, and caught a glimpse of the vertiginous drop awaiting them if they lost their grip. He gulped and turned his attention back to the stubborn access panel.

"I don't suppose you have a crowbar on ye, or maybe a plasma torch?" He fingered the phaser pistol on his belt. He hated the idea of vandalizing his own ship, but he supposed he could melt a hole through the hatchway eventually. Scraped knuckles rapped the unyielding metal, producing a hollow sound. He set his phaser on full power. "Excuse me while I make some more work for my repair crews."

"That might not be necessary," Seven said. "Permit me."

Climbing higher, she squeezed past him to lay her augmented left hand on the uncooperative locking mechanism. He gaped in surprise as flexible steel tubules extended from her exoskeleton to penetrate the mechanism and interface directly with the circuitry beneath. The lock hummed softly, as though cycling through multiple settings, until Scotty heard a distinctive click on the other side of the hatch. He tested the doorway, and it slid open manually with only a little pressure.

"Well, I'll be a mugato's uncle," he exclaimed. "How the devil did ye do that?"

"As I said earlier, I can adapt."

"A handy talent," he marveled, wishing he had the specs for her various implants and attachments. He suspected that the gewgaws on her face were more than decorative as well. "Ye could have a whole new career as a safecracker."

"Not one of my aspirations," she said, "but I will take it under advisement." She nodded at the now-open hatchway. "Shall we proceed?"

"Absolutely!"

Twenty-six

They wasted no time climbing into the Jefferies tube, which stretched diagonally toward the decks above. The service tunnel was so narrow that they had to crawl forward on their hands and knees, keeping their heads down to avoid banging them on the low ceiling. Thankfully, claustrophobia was not among Scotty's weaknesses; one could hardly be a ship's engineer unless you were comfortable squeezing into tight spaces. Cables and conduits, color-coded by function, lined the curved walls of the tube, which lacked the glossy sheen of the other walls. These crawlways weren't supposed to be pretty, just convenient. Track lighting provided enough illumination to see by. Blinking subprocessors guided their way. Cables hummed in their ears. Scotty spotted some burnt-out circuitry that would need to be replaced later, fortune willing. Redundant backup systems kept things running, more or less. Warning labels identified potential hazards. Sparks drizzled down from a severed conduit.

"Watch yourself," Scotty advised, his voice echoing off the tunnel walls. "Seems we're not exactly shipshape."

"Duly noted," Seven said, somewhat irritably.

Single file, with Scotty in the lead, they headed in what he judged to be the right direction. Blueprints and schematics scrolled before his mind's eye as he navigated the tubes. Numbered panels and directional signs made his task easier. They had only gone about ten meters, however, before their progress was blocked by a sturdy steel barrier, supplemented by a charged energy field. For the first time ever, Scotty found himself annoyed by the thoroughness of the ship's security measures. Unlike that clueless Orion earlier, he knew better than to touch the crackling field. His much-abused fingers didn't need a painful zap.

One again, his command codes proved ineffective.

Figures, he thought. *When it rains, it pours.*

He scooted to one side to give Seven access to the port. "If ye don't mind . . ."

Her cybernetic extensions once again came to their rescue, picking the lock with alarming ease. Prying open the panel, Scotty allowed himself a smidgen of hope. Maybe this hare-brained scheme was going to work after all. Certainly they were overdue for a lucky break or two.

Ultimately, Seven had to override at least five security seals on their way to the cargo transporters. They crept through the tubes as quietly as Lermossian voles, keeping chatter to a minimum and their voices low to avoid being detected by the raiders overrunning the ship. More than once, they heard the Orions rushing through the decks above and below them. At such times, Scotty held his breath and froze until the pirates moved on. The keening of energy blasts and the cries of the wounded made it clear that the battle for control of the *Enterprise* was far from over. Scotty wished the ship's defenders luck, taking pride in the fact that his valiant crewmates weren't making it easy for the invaders. Even still, it seemed like forever before he and Seven got where they were going. His knees, back, and neck ached from crawling through the cramped tunnels. He couldn't wait to stretch his legs again.

Seven was breathing hard, too.

"End of the line." He halted before a sealed hatchway in the floor of the tube, then paused to double-check his bearings. "By my reckonin', we ought to be right on top of the cargo transporters." He pressed his ear to the hatch door, praying that he wouldn't hear any inconvenient Orions below. After all their obstacles and detours, the last thing he wanted to discover was that the raiders had already captured the cargo bay. "Sounds clear to me, but I wouldn't want to stake my life on it."

Seven employed her tricorder. "I am detecting a solitary life-form." She gave Scotty a reassuring nod. "Human."

Saints be praised, Scotty thought. Just the same, he slid the panel open only a hair at first and peered down furtively into what was indeed the main cargo transporter complex. Twin platforms, each large enough to accommodate a standard Starfleet cargo module, were operated from a central control room. Three humanoid-sized transporter pads were installed on each platform for use by personnel overseeing the transport of sensitive items. Scott was pleased to see that the complex appeared undamaged by the commotion elsewhere on the ship. In theory, he could use the personnel transporters to attempt to beam Seven directly to the shuttlebay, although that was going to be a tricky business to be sure. One miscalculation, and she could easily end up beamed into a bulkhead instead!

As Seven had foretold, a single humanoid figure could be seen pacing restlessly between the platforms, his phaser pistol raised and ready. His gaze fixed on the entrance to the facility, the man failed to notice Scotty peering down at him from above. A dark business suit, as opposed to a Starfleet uniform, instantly pegged him as Commissioner Santiago's aide. What was his name again?

Hague, Scotty recalled. *Cyril Hague.*

"Ye were right," he said, grinning at Seven. "He's one of ours."

Convinced that their luck was finally turning, Scotty tried to slide the panel all the way open. Warped metal resisted his efforts. "Bloody thing's stuck," he grumbled. Putting his full weight into it, he gave the stubborn panel a hefty shove, and the whole hatch came loose beneath him. He tumbled headfirst through the opening. "Oh, hell . . ."

He landed on his rump in the middle of the central control room. His clumsy entrance did not go unnoticed by Hague, who spun toward the thudding noise. Scotty found himself staring into the muzzle of the man's phaser. Wincing, he threw up his hands before the startled diplomat did something rash.

"At ease, lad! It's just me."

Hague blinked in surprise. He stepped toward the fallen engineer. "Mister Scott?"

"In the bruised flesh, lad." Scotty clambered to his feet, his posterior still smarting from his crash landing. The treacherous hatch rested on the floor less than a meter away. Lowering his hands, he greeted Hague.

"Well, you're a sight for sore eyes, I must say. Holding down the fort, are ye? Good man."

Truth to tell, he suspected that the civilian aide merely had been hiding in the cargo bay, but he chose to give the man the benefit of the doubt as well as a chance to save face. He noted that Hague had yet to lower his weapon, while Scotty's own phaser was still hitched to his belt. "Er, ye mind pointin' that phaser elsewhere, lad?"

Hague smirked. "I'm afraid I can't do that, Mister Scott."

Without warning, he squeezed the finger of the trigger. A scarlet bolt shot from the weapon at short range, striking Scotty's phaser. The engineer yelped in surprise as he felt a sudden burning sensation against his hip. The phaser turned red-hot for an instant, then dissolved into atoms.

"What the—!" Scotty reached for his weapon, only to find himself unarmed. He gaped at Hague. "Have ye lost your senses?"

"Hardly." Hague aimed his phaser at Scotty's head. "I see we both had the same idea about using the cargo transporters, although I suspect we had different destinations in mind. My own plan was to escape via the *Navaar* should events turn against us. I fear a full investigation of this incident might turn up certain communications that would be difficult to explain down the road."

"Communications?" Scotty realized that Hague had been working against them all this time, conspiring with the enemy at every turn. "Is that what you've done? Kept the Orions posted on our plans? Told them when and where we were goin' to be, like at Gamma Trianguli VI?" As the aide of a high-ranking Federation commissioner, and apparently an accomplished spy in his right, it would have been easy enough for Hague to hide coded messages in what appeared to be routine diplomatic transmissions—and to cover his tracks afterward. "Instructed them how to jam our communicators? Informed on us for a bunch of murderous thugs?" Scotty found it hard to believe that any Federation official could be capable of such perfidy. "How could ye do it, man?"

"Just doing my job . . . as an Orion, that is." He savored Scotty's shocked expression. "Don't be fooled by this pallid pink disguise. I'm pure Orion green where it counts." He patted his chest with his free hand. "Right here."

Scotty found himself in a nasty fix. A furtive glance at the exit revealed that the emergency blast doors had been locked from the inside. He was trapped in the cargo transporter complex with an armed traitor who was clearly up to no good.

So much for my luck taking a turn for the better!

"This is quite fortuitous, running into you like this," Hague gloated. "My people are having trouble locating Seven, although there are scattered reports of a woman matching her description at large in the ship. Where is Kirk hiding her? On the bridge? Somewhere else?" He kept his phaser aimed at Scotty. "Give me a reason not to slice you apart, piece by piece."

It dawned on Scotty that Hague didn't realize that Seven was still hiding in the Jefferies tube directly above them, and she was doubtless eavesdropping on this entire exchange. Scotty realized that he had to keep Hague distracted so that Seven could remain undetected.

"What about Santiago?" he challenged Hague. "How can you betray his trust like this?"

"The commissioner is a fool," Hague said, snickering at his boss's gullibility, "and all the more so since he let his kin's death unman him. I've been practically running his office since his sow of a sister and her brats were massacred; killing Santiago's family turned out to be a goddess-send for the syndicate." He chuckled cruelly. "I just wish I could say we did it on purpose."

Scotty couldn't contain his disgust. "You cold-hearted, two-faced—"

"Spare me the righteous indignation," Hague said, cutting him off. "Just tell me where Seven is . . . before things get messy."

"Do your worst," Scotty said. "A good engineer doesn't mind a little mess."

Hague eyed him suspiciously. "You're hiding something." A question occurred to him. "What did you want with these transporters, anyway? I can't imagine a good Starfleet officer like you would be trying to save himself over his ship. What's this all about?"

Scotty shrugged. "That would be telling, lad."

"Typical Starfleet. Arrogant to the last."

Scotty braced himself for a red-hot phaser beam even as bagpipes played a mournful dirge at the back of his mind. He hoped Captain Kirk and the others would drink a toast to his memory.

"Don't try my patience, Mister Scott."

"Why? Are ye going somewhere?"

Hague sneered. "You certainly aren't."

Scotty thought his number was up, but then Hague shifted his aim. A crimson beam shot past Scotty to strike the transporter control station instead. Sparks and smoke erupted from the console. The acrid odor of burning circuitry polluted the air. Blinking display panels went dark.

"There," Hague said smugly, perversely proud of his vandalism. "No one is beaming anywhere now. Whatever you were up to is not going to happen, and we have time for a nice long chat."

For a moment, his phaser was not pointed at Scotty. The engineer considered tackling Hague and maybe wrestling the weapon away from him, but Seven took even more efficient use of the opportunity. She dropped from the open hatchway overhead, landing nimbly behind Hague. A burst from her phaser stunned the traitor, who crumpled to the floor of the control room. Limp fingers released his weapon.

"My apologies for the delay," Seven said, "but I was reluctant to intervene while you were in harm's way."

"I'm not complaining." Scotty sighed in relief. "For a few moments there, I thought I was as good as vaporized." He confiscated Hague's phaser, then gazed down on the unconscious aide, shaking his head. "Can ye believe it? Who would've thought there'd be a traitor in our midst?"

"Individuals have been known to switch loyalties," Seven said soberly. Something about her tone suggested that she spoke from bitter experience. She examined the door to confirm that it was securely barred, then she inspected the damaged control station. Tendrils of white smoke rose from the blasted console. "But his motives are irrelevant at the present moment. What matters is that our task has become significantly more difficult."

Scotty saw her point. Leaving Hague sprawled upon the platform, not far from the fallen metal hatch, he joined Seven at the control station and whistled at the damage. The phaser blast had done more than just knock the system off-line; the control panel was a charred ruin. "I see what ye mean. That two-faced villain made a real mess of things."

"Can you fix it?" she asked.

Scotty stepped back and considered the challenge. "I don't suppose your handy finger-tube thingies can help us out again?"

She shook her head. "Not if I wish to beam myself to the shuttle as planned. I cannot interface with the console and occupy the pad at the same time."

"Aye, that's a problem." He stroked his chin as he hit upon another possible solution. "Let me have that tricorder, if ye don't mind. In theory, I might be able to reroute the command signals through the tricorder. We lucked out that Hague chose to shoot the controls and not the transporter pads themselves. Thank heaven for small favors. If he'd thought to trash the actual platform, we'd be bollixed but good!"

"His tactics were flawed," she agreed. "I suspect he was acting on impulse." She handed over the tricorder as requested. "Do you require any assistance?"

"No. Ye've done enough already." Scotty figured he knew more about twenty-third-century transporter technology than anybody else in the quadrant; the day he needed help fixing a busted console was the day he'd book a rocking chair at the home for washed-up old relics. "But I'd welcome your assistance calculating the precise coordinates for beaming into the shuttlebay. That's going to be a tricky operation, and I'm not too proud to admit it."

Seven nodded. "I will comply."

He got to work. Ignoring the charred control panel, he pried open the insulated casing of the column beneath it, exposing the central processing unit. He nodded in satisfaction at the sight of the station's innards; despite their dire situation, it felt good to be doing some hands-on engineering again, as opposed to rock climbing or scuba diving.

This is more like it, he thought.

From the looks of things, the phaser blast had overloaded the subprocessors, shutting them down, but it took only a few tweaks to get the core systems up and humming again. He directed the tricorder at the naked CPU. It took a wee bit of fine-tuning, but he soon established a remote link to what was left of the transporter controls. So far, so good; now he just needed to clone the interface software onto the tricorder.

Seven accidentally stumbled against him.

Scotty looked up from his work. "Are ye all right, lass?"

"A moment of fatigue," she confessed. "It will pass." She straightened her posture, doing her best to disguise any weakness or infirmity. She shook her head to clear away any cobwebs. "The transporter?"

Scotty got the impression she was going on pure

willpower and cussedness alone. He wondered how much longer she could keep running on fumes—and whether she still had strength enough to do what needed to be done.

"Almost ready," he said. "The autosequencing program was corrupted by the energy surge, but not fatally. I just need to patch up the code some. It won't take but a moment or two."

Stampeding boots, coming from the corridor outside, interrupted his report. An angry fist pounded against the door. *"Lormus ardeo!"* a guttural voice demanded. Scotty couldn't speak a word of Orion, but he knew when he was being threatened. *"Eypholmir hojot skyopu!"*

Seven faced the clamor with her phaser drawn. "I suggest you hasten the repairs, Mister Scott."

"Aye." Scotty got back to work. Lines of broken code scrolled across the tricorder's display screen, demanding his attention. He started keying in the missing links. "Probably a good idea."

Disruptor blasts slammed into the sturdy steel doors protecting them from the intruders. The bellicose Orions seemed more than willing to tear the entire ship apart to find Seven and claim her knowledge of tomorrow. Scotty saw now why the captain had worked so hard to hide her true origins. Seven's secrets were just too tempting a target should word spread of her existence.

"I have completed the necessary calculations," she informed him. "Now we require only a working transporter."

"Just another moment."

Scotty tried to focus on slaving the transporter

controls to the tricorder. It was hard to concentrate with the Orions blasting away at the door, but the damaged code wasn't going to patch itself. Despite the distracting gunfire, the tricorder's miniature display screen soon resembled the transporter's standard control panel.

"Done!" he announced. A hasty diagnostic confirmed that everything checked out, although he would have preferred a few trial runs. "It's fast and dirty, but it should do the trick . . . assuming you've got the right coordinates."

"My calculations are correct." She borrowed the tricorder long enough to load the coordinates into a cloned copy of the targeting controls. He couldn't help noticing that her hands were shaking as though palsied. "Certain adjustments will be purged from the tricorder's memory upon completion of the transport, to avoid temporal contamination, but you may rely on these coordinates."

"Ye sure about that?" he asked. "It's not as though ye are beamin' from one transporter room to another, which would be tricky enough. A wrong calculation, and ye could end up somewhere you don't want to be. Like inside the warp core, maybe, or out in the vacuum of space."

"In which case," she observed, "I will indeed be beyond the Orions' reach." She took her place upon the starboard transporter platform. "But I believe those coordinates will suffice."

Her obvious confidence in her own abilities eased Scotty's worries almost as effectively as a restorative shot of whiskey. Still, he felt obliged to make certain she understood the risk she was taking. "I'm serious, lass," he insisted. "Ye could be beamin' to your death."

"A calculated risk," she acknowledged. "Proceed."

"Very well." He aimed the reconfigured tricorder at the transporter. He hit the command key. "Godspeed."

A transporter beam flared to life. Seven dissolved into a dazzling cascade of energy.

Scotty sighed wearily. He had done his part. The rest was up to Seven.

And the Orions.

Twenty-seven

"Keptin!" Chekov called out. "A shuttle has left the *Enterprise*!"

About time, Kirk thought. He wondered what had taken Scotty and Seven so long. *Must have run into some trouble on the way to the shuttlebay.*

The main viewer picked up the shuttlecraft. Registry numbers emblazed on its hull identified it as the *Galileo II*. With the *Enterprise*'s shields down, nothing prevented the shuttle from exiting the starship. It pulled away from the ship as its ion engine engaged.

"I am receiving a transmission from the shuttle," Uhura reported. "It's Doctor Seven."

Kirk had figured as much, but it was good to have that confirmed. He signaled Uhura to turn the translator back on. Habroz would surely be monitoring their communications. Kirk wanted the pirate captain to hear this. "Put her through."

Seven's elegant visage appeared upon the viewscreen. The cramped cockpit of an F-Class shuttlecraft served as a backdrop. Kirk was glad to see that Seven appeared none the worse for her protracted trek through the besieged ship, although she was showing obvious signs of fatigue. Scenes of heated conflict between Starfleet forces and invading Orions continued to fill multiple windows upon the viewer. Closer at hand, an Orion boarding party was still trying to blast their way onto the bridge. The persistent racket scraped on everyone's nerves, adding to the tense atmosphere. Security and engineering teams worked overtime to reinforce the blast doors. Plasma torches welded fresh crossbeams across potential entrances. Portable deflector units, aimed at the doors, bolstered their defenses.

"Greetings, Captain," Seven addressed him. "My apologies for my sudden departure, but, in my estimation, the Enterprise is no longer a secure location." On the primary screen, the shuttle pulled away from the starship and sped back toward the Federation's side of the Neutral Zone. "I would appreciate it if you would guard my retreat."

Kirk feigned outrage. "Damnit, Seven, get back here! You'll never make it!"

"That remains to be seen, Captain," she replied, unfazed by his outburst. "And a slim chance is better than none at all."

Even as the shuttle accelerated toward the border, however, the Navaar went into pursuit. Turning away from the Enterprise, the marauder set off after Seven. Just as expected.

Good, Kirk thought. He took the bait.

The shuttle's impulse engine was no match for the Navaar, which swiftly caught up with the fleeing craft. An aquamarine tractor beam latched onto the Galileo II, halting its progress. The shuttle's boosters fought to break free from the beam's relentless pull, but to no avail. Like the prehensile tongue of some space-faring alien predator, the marauder began to reel the shuttle in. Kirk saw Seven being shaken violently by the titanic stresses exerted on the shuttle. Only a safety strap kept her from being hurled from her seat. It was obvious that the shuttle would soon be sucked into the bowels of the *Navaar,* terminating her seemingly desperate flight for freedom. Habroz was about to claim his prize.

Kirk knew what he had to do next.

"Mister Chekov, open fire on the shuttle."

Shocked gasps greeted the captain's order. Commissioner Santiago stared at him in disbelief. "Kirk!" he blurted. "You can't! Seven will be killed. There *must* be another way!"

"I wish there was, Commissioner." Kirk's tone was grave. "But as you've often reminded me, this is a matter of Federation security. Habroz cannot be allowed to turn Seven over to the Klingons . . . or anyone else." He faced her without apology, his face as hard as solid duranium. "I'm sure Seven understands."

"Indeed." She maintained a stoic expression, although her teeth rattled as she spoke. *"The Temporal Prime Directive must be maintained. The needs of the future outweigh the needs of the present."*

"Or the past," Kirk agreed. He glared at the navigation station, where Chekov appeared reluctant to carry out his orders. The young Russian looked like he was hoping that the captain would change his mind. "You heard me, Ensign. Open fire!"

Every moment they delayed, Seven and the shuttle came closer to vanishing into the *Navaar.* Overworked boosters, unable to withstand the marauder's tractor beam, burnt out one by one, leaving the shuttle without propulsion. The *Galileo II* wasn't going anywhere but backward.

"Aye, Keptin." His face pale, Chekov hit the firing controls. "Phasers on full."

Brilliant red beams shot from the underside of the *Enterprise*'s saucer. They sliced through space at the speed of light but missed the shuttle by less than a meter. The off-kilter shots flew off into the vacuum. A subsequent blast barely grazed the shuttle's deflectors, resulting in nothing more than a harmless flash of blue radiation, before passing through the *Navaar*'s tractor beam.

Kirk scowled. "Something wrong with your aim, Ensign?"

"I'm sorry, Keptin." Chekov blushed with embarrassment. "The targeting sensors appear to have been knocked out of alignment during the earlier attack." He fiddled anxiously with the controls. "I'm attempting to compensate. . . ."

"Make it fast," Kirk barked. "The future depends on it."

Habroz's black heart missed a beat as the *Enterprise*'s phasers flew toward the shuttle. For a split-second, he feared that his much-sought-after prize was about to be blown to atoms before his eyes. He cursed himself for not anticipating this tactic and blasting the *Enterprise*'s phaser banks when he'd had the chance; Kirk was obviously more ruthless than the typical Starfleet weakling. Habroz could respect that, but not when it looked to cost him a fortune.

Damn you, Kirk! If you've stolen Seven from me . . . !

His silent threat went unfinished as, miraculously, the crimson phaser bolts missed their target, sparing Seven's life for at least a few more moments. Cheers and mockery from the crew greeted the humans' poor marksmanship.

"Hah!" one of the pirates jeered. Daol manned the helm at the front of the bridge. A silver ring dangled from his nose. Close-cropped blond hair met in a widow's peak above his brow. "A blind mud louse could shoot better than that! They couldn't hit a gas giant from inside its atmosphere!"

Habroz perched on the edge of his throne, which rested on a pedestal overlooking the marauder's delta-shaped bridge, which Habroz had customized to his own specifications, so that it resembled a small auditorium facing an oval viewscreen. The throne had the upper, rearmost tier to itself, allowing him to look down on the descending rows of control stations beneath him. The throne was flush against the rear wall; a smart commander never turned his back on his own men. On the screen, Seven survived another minute. Habroz let out a relieved breath.

The dice are rolling in my favor, he thought. For the moment, his dreams of a princely ransom—from the Klingons, or the Romulans, or whoever else might meet his price—had been preserved, but he did not intend to give Kirk a second chance to dash his hopes by eliminating Seven. Too much time and trouble had been invested in this endeavor; no smug, pink-skinned human was going to deprive him of his profits. He was already envisioning an auction the likes of which the quadrant had never seen—with the elusive time traveler going to the highest bidder. The Klingons wouldn't be happy if they lost, but their own cloaking device would help the

Navaar evade their wrath. He'd just have to avoid the wrong side of the Neutral Zone for a time. . . .

"More power to the tractor beam!" he ordered. "Get that shuttle into our cargo bay now!"

"Are you sure, Captain?" Daol asked. Undue caution stayed his hand. "It will be necessary to lower our own shields to bring the Federation craft aboard."

The man's recalcitrance infuriated Habroz. Now was no time for timidity.

"I know that, you faint-hearted gelding! Do as I say!" He raised his communicator to his lips. "Habroz to K'Mara! Defend that shuttle. Keep the *Enterprise* busy. Block their phasers if you have to. Whatever it takes to keep them from killing Seven!"

Her husky voice answered him. *"Understood, Captain! Consider it done."*

"See that it is!"

Despite his impatience, he could not fault the speed with which K'Mara carried out his commands. On-screen, the *O'Spakya* maneuvered to place itself between the *Enterprise* and the endangered shuttle. Enemy phaser beams bounced off the *O'Spakya*'s shields, even as the ludicrous Mavelan vessel fired back at Kirk's ship with its own meager phasers. Per his earlier orders, K'Mara deliberately held off from targeting the *Enterprise*'s most vulnerable areas. Not that it really mattered; Habroz doubted that the lowly merchanter had enough fire-power to annihilate the *Enterprise*, even with Kirk's shields down.

Unless the *Navaar* opened fire as well?

He toyed with the possibility. Now that Seven was

no longer aboard the *Enterprise,* he was sorely tempted to destroy the Federation starship once and for all, but then he recalled that more than seventy of his own men were still aboard Kirk's vessel. It would be a waste to sacrifice so many loyal raiders—unless it was absolutely necessary.

Better to give his men a chance to capture the *Enterprise* instead. A *Constitution*-class starship would fetch plenty at auction as well, and it might even appease the Klingons should they fail to win the bidding on Seven. Starfleet's most celebrated ship, the vessel that defeated the Doomsday Machine and foiled the Klingons on numerous occasions, would make an excellent consolation prize.

But he was getting ahead of himself. First, he needed to make sure that Seven was truly his. Habroz glared at the screen where, with what seemed like agonizing slowness, the captured shuttle was being drawn inexorably backward toward the *Navaar.* He knew he would not truly rest easy until the precious cargo was safely secured within his brig.

"Faster!" he bellowed. "Get me that shuttle!"

Twenty-eight

Phaser beams rocked the *O'Spakya*.

The tiled floor of the bridge lurched beneath Spock's feet, but it did not prevent him from paying careful attention to the unfolding crisis. Although he and McCoy remained captives of the Orions, his analytical gaze took in every detail of the space battle being waged in the Neutral Zone, as well as all that transpired aboard the Mavelan ship. Chance favored the prepared mind, a sagacious human had once said, and Spock agreed. The more data he accumulated about their enemies and environment, the better his odds of turning the situation to his advantage. That was the Vulcan way—and good Starfleet tactics.

Watch and wait, he counseled himself. *The right opportunity will arise.*

The central navigation orb had been wrestled back into place by Mavelan technicians. A trio of Orion guards stood watch over Spock and McCoy, twisting the hostages' arms behind their backs, while K'Mara and her helmsman commanded the *O'Spakya,* guiding it directly into the path of the *Enterprise*'s phasers. The levitating globe revealed that the *Navaar* was in the process of capturing the *Galileo II.* Spock gathered that Seven was aboard the ensnared shuttlecraft. Small wonder that the

Enterprise appeared intent on destroying the shuttle before the Orions could take custody of it.

Spock would have done the same in the captain's place.

"What are you doing?" Papa Yela squealed as another volley of phasers shook the merchanter. The lights flickered, and warning annunciators flashed around the star-shaped bridge. Emergency klaxons wailed. Decorative molding rained down from the ceiling. Dismayed by the damage being inflicted on his ship, he crawled out from beneath the console where he'd taken refuge before. He staggered across the quaking bridge toward K'Mara, flapping his tentacles anxiously. A crumpled turban sat askew atop his head. His canine jowls quivered. "By the star-spirits, cease this madness! You're wrecking my ship!"

K'Mara batted him away impatiently. "Hold your tongue! Who cares what happens to this broken-down scow? The secrets of tomorrow are nearly within our grasp!"

A handful of Mavelan crew members watched the confrontation uneasily, torn between their fear of the Orions and their loyalty to Papa Yela. K'Mara glared ferociously at them. Her saw-toothed dagger reflected the flashing warning lights. "Stay at your posts, you miserable dogs, or I'll toss your wormy guts out an airlock!"

Cowed, the Mavela remained at their stations, leaving the helm to one of K'Mara's men. Papa Yela whimpered in protest. "Please, we've done all you asked. We are a peaceful people. This is not our fight!"

"It is now!" She yanked Papa Yela's medallion off his chest, breaking the chain. She hurled it to the floor and ground it beneath her heel. Sparks flared as the inner circuitry shattered. She shoved the alien patriarch away from her, sending him flying into a scorched steel bulkhead. Moaning, he slumped to the floor. His turban unraveled, adding to his pathetic appearance. K'Mara gave him an extra kick for good measure. "Now keep out of my sight!"

Spock observed the encounter with interest.

"Why is that shuttle still in one piece?" Kirk demanded. A scowl betrayed his frustration as the *O'Spakya* blocked his view of the *Galileo II*. Enemy phasers scarred the *Enterprise*'s durable outer plating, but he couldn't worry about that now. His eyes were fixed on the shuttle on the screen. The gap between Seven and the *Navaar* was shrinking by the second. "We need to take it out . . . now!"

"I'm trying, Keptin!" Chekov said. "I can't get a phaser lock on the shuttle. The Mavelan ship is intercepting our shots!"

"So get past them!" Kirk looked to the helm for assistance. "Mister Sulu?"

"Aye, sir." Sulu executed a sudden turn, trying to get Chekov a clean shot at the shuttle, but the *O'Spakya* was smaller and more maneuverable than the *Enterprise*; whoever was piloting the merchanter matched them move for move. Evasive tactics spared the *Enterprise* from the worst of the Mavelan phaser barrage, yet it brought them no closer to nailing the shuttle.

"The *Navaar* has lowered its shields," Chekov reported. "It's opening its cargo bay doors."

On-screen, an open maw appeared at the base of the *Navaar*'s prow. A hatchway lowered like the jaw of some enormous deep-space behemoth, offering a view of a dark, cavernous cargo more than large enough to hold the captured shuttle. Peering past the intrusive Mavelan ship, Kirk caught a glimpse of the *Galileo II* being pulled into the open cavity. Within moments, Seven would be Habroz's prisoner.

"Arm photon torpedoes!" Kirk ordered. "Fire them right through the *O'Spakya* if you have to."

Uhura gasped in alarm. "Captain! Mister Spock and Doctor McCoy are aboard that ship!"

"I know that, Lieutenant," Kirk said grimly. "And I know what I have to do."

The shuttle disappeared into the *Navaar*'s voracious maw. Scalloped steel doors began to shut, trapping the *Galileo II* in the bowels of the marauder.

"It's too late, Keptin!" Chekov held his fire. "We'd be killing Spock and the doctor for no reason!"

The ensign's logic was irrefutable. "Damn," Kirk swore. "We lost her." He looked at Seven's visage on the screen. Who knew what unspeakable tortures Habroz and his Klingon sponsors had in store for Seven? A mind-sifter could extract all her secrets, while damaging her brain irreparably. "I'm so sorry, Annika."

"*Seven,*" she corrected him. "*Thank you for your hospitality . . . and your efforts on my behalf. You have done all you were able. The future is in my hands now.*"

Uhura looked away. "That poor woman."

"*Bozhe moi,*" Chekov whispered.

"You were right, Kirk," Santiago said glumly. "She didn't belong in our time. All this bloodshed in pursuit of her secrets . . . and now the Orions have her. Heaven help the Federation!"

The cargo hatch closed on the shuttle. Seven's window blinked out.

"The *Navaar*'s shields are back up, Keptin."

Wait for it, Kirk thought.

A heartbeat later, just as planned, the shuttle exploded inside the marauder.

"No! Furies damn it!"

K'Mara cried out as an exploding ion engine tore open the *Navaar*'s cargo hold. She stared in horror at the violent cataclysm visible within the observation globe. A blazing orange fireball briefly lit up the interior of the hold before being snuffed out by the vacuum of space. The spectacular detonation threw the marauder for a loop, sending it spinning uncontrollably on its axis. Fused steel debris, including a charred segment of a nacelle, erupted from the breached hull. A flickering force field struggled to patch the gap. Billowing black smoke slipped through cracks in the field. Stuck aboard the *O'Spakya*, the other Orions could only watch as the wounded marauder tumbled through space, even as Spock registered the fact of Seven's apparent self-destruction.

Had she truly just blown herself up?

"Habroz!" K'Mara shouted into her wrist-communicator. "Captain!"

Concern for her captain or their prize was quickly driven from her thoughts by the fact that the huge marauder was hurtling straight toward the *O'Spakya*. Her jade eyes widened in alarm. "Evasive action!" she shouted at the Orion helmsman. "All hands, brace for impact!"

The helmsman threw the merchanter hard to starboard, while simultaneously giving the ship a sudden burst of acceleration that sent everyone on the bridge stumbling to one side. The guard assigned to Spock let go of his captive, grabbing a nearby pylon for support, while McCoy's watchdog staggered backward, away from the doctor. A third Orion, the one who had killed Lieutenant Tang, smacked his head into a bulkhead. He collapsed to the deck, his skull bleeding profusely. Papa Yela prayed feverishly for deliverance. The other Mavela, cowering at their stations, did likewise.

Interesting, Spock thought. *And promising.*

The helmsman's frantic maneuver was only partially successful. Before any of the pirates or prisoners could regain their balance, the *Navaar* portside nacelle scraped against the *O'Spakya*'s shields as the marauder careened past them, barely avoiding a more catastrophic collision. But even a glancing blow was enough to throw the bridge into chaos. Grinding metal echoed like thunder. Clashing deflector grids produced a bright actinic flash that briefly whited out the image inside the floating orb. A tremendous jolt reminded Spock of an avalanche he had once experienced on Vulcan's rugged Mount Seleya.

He did not let that distract him.

Thrown off-balance by the impact, K'Mara came within reach of Spock. Seizing the moment, he administered a nerve pinch to her neck. Her eyes rolled upward until only the whites could be seen, and she sagged backward against Spock, who grabbed the unconscious pirate to keep her from falling. His Vulcan ancestry gave him sufficient strength to easily hold her up with one arm even as he reached for her disruptor pistol with his free hand. The weapon was right where he had noted earlier: on K'Mara's hip.

"Excuse me, madam. I need to borrow your side-arm."

In the confusion, the other Orions did not immediately grasp what was happening. Showing admirable presence of mind, Doctor McCoy extracted a loaded hypospray from his medkit, and before his captor could recover from the crash, the doctor spun around and pressed it to the pirate's tattooed shoulder. A powerful anesthetic knocked the Orion out *almost* as effectively as a nerve pinch. Spock was impressed by McCoy's resourcefulness.

"Ably done, Doctor. You never cease to surprise me."

"Hell, man," McCoy drawled. "You don't need green blood to keep cool in a crisis. Any trauma doc can tell you that!"

Spock's own captor, seeing his comrades going down, lunged at the former hostages. "Stinking pink offal!" he snarled. "Release K'Mara!"

"If you insist."

Spock pivoted on his heel and flung K'Mara's limp form at the oncoming raider. The woman hit the other Orion like a life-size green rag doll. They crashed to the floor in a tangle of limbs and leather. Spock followed up by blasting the male raider with K'Mara's disruptor pistol, after setting it on stun, of course. Despite the brutal murder of Lieutenant Tang, Spock was not intent on vengeance, only the safety of McCoy and the *Enterprise*. Orion deaths would not restore Daniel Tang to life.

That left only the Orion helmsman, who was too busy trying to keep the *O'Spakya* under control to take part in the brawl. Papa Yela gulped at the sight of the pistol in Spock's grip.

"Mercy, wronged ones!" A tentacle reached for his medallion, perhaps hoping to trigger another sonic attack, but the jeweled control mechanism lay in pieces on the floor, where K'Mara had stamped on it earlier. His blubbery jowls quivered. Pink eyes leaked yellow tears. "We are not to blame. In their wickedness, the Orions compelled us!"

McCoy shook his head in disgust. "Can you believe this character?" His face fell as he recalled what they had witnessed in the orb only minutes ago. "Good Lord, Spock! Seven . . . She was in that shuttlecraft when it exploded. She sacrificed herself for all of us!"

"So it appears," Spock concurred. More immediate concerns presented themselves. He scanned the nearby workstations. During his captivity, he had taken advantage of his forced inactivity to thoroughly observe the bridge's instrumentation and operations. He raised the stolen disruptor, knowing precisely where to aim it. "Farewell, Papa Yela. You will forgive me if I refrain from wishing you either long life or prosperity."

"No! Mercy, I beg of you!"

Thinking Spock was about to shoot him, Papa Yela dived for cover, but he was never the intended target. Instead a brilliant green disruptor beam leapt from the muzzle of the pistol to strike a specific control panel. A geyser of sparks erupted from the console as it burst into flame. A malfunction alarm beeped loudly.

"Now then, Doctor. I believe we have overstayed our welcome."

McCoy scoffed. "You think?"

Twenty-nine

Despite the ongoing battles, both within and without the *Enterprise,* the explosive demise of the *Galileo II* cast a hush over the bridge. Kirk, who had been anticipating the blast ever since Seven first suggested the ploy to him, was nonetheless impressed by the force of the explosion. When Seven had rigged the shuttle's ion engine to overload, she hadn't messed around. Kirk smiled grimly at the thought of Habroz's reaction. Apparently Orion mythology did not include any Trojan horses.

Going off inside the *Navaar's* shielded hull, the self-destructing shuttlecraft had caught the Orions totally by surprise. Kirk briefly had thought that maybe the blast would destroy the *Navaar* completely, but the damaged marauder merely had spun out of control instead. Seven had just hurt the enemy ship, not killed it.

Kirk couldn't complain. *Under the circumstances, I'll take what I can get.*

"It worked, Keptin!" Chekov exclaimed finally. His faulty marksmanship had all been part of the ruse, as had been Sulu's seeming inability to get past the *O'Spakya;* the entire bridge crew had put on a master class in acting. "The Cossacks fell for it!"

"But Doctor Seven . . ." Uhura's somber tone was

unfeigned. "I can't believe she's really gone. It seems like we barely got a chance to know her."

"But she lived long enough to see a future we'll probably never know," Kirk reminded her, offering his crew what consolation he could. "This was never her time. Perhaps she wasn't meant to live among us . . . or find her way home."

"Maybe it's better this way," Santiago mused. "Look at all the carnage her very presence spawned. There could be no peace in the galaxy as long as she existed in this era."

Now *he gets it,* Kirk thought, refraining from saying "I told you so." He had more important things to worry about.

What about Spock, he wondered, *and McCoy?*

Kirk watched tensely as the *Navaar* almost collided with the *O'Spakya,* practically scraping the paint off its hull. The nerve-racking near miss had not been part of Seven's plan; her kamikaze strike against the Orions had almost claimed Spock and McCoy as well. "My," Sulu said, "that was a close one."

You can say that again, Kirk thought.

He was trying to figure out how to rescue the hostages when Chekov piped up with a surprising announcement. "Keptin! The *O'Spakya*'s shields are down!"

What? Kirk thought. *How did that happen?*

The answer came to him at once.

"Spock." A grin crossed Kirk's face. "He knocked out their shields somehow." Kirk immediately hailed the transporter room via the intership, hoping it wasn't currently overrun with Orions. "Kirk to transporter room. Report."

"Aye, Captain." A familiar voice answered his hail. "Scott here."

Kirk was confused. As far as he knew, Scotty had somehow managed to escort Seven to the shuttlebay.

"How did you end up in the transporter room?"

"By way of the cargo transporters, sir, from one transport platform to another . . . it's a long story that I can share with ye later." Disruptor blasts sizzled in the background, forcing Scotty to raise his voice to be heard. "Pardon the ruckus. I'm afraid we've got some unwelcome guests banging at the door. We're holding them off as best we can, but they're raising quite a racket. . . ."

Kirk signaled Uhura to dispatch reinforcements to the transporter room. "Never mind that right now. The O'Spakya has dropped its shields. Beam our people back!"

The besieged engineer instantly grasped the urgency of the situation. For all they knew, the Mavela might restore their shields at any time. Kirk wasn't going to waste this window of opportunity. Spock and McCoy were depending on them.

"Aye, aye, sir!" Scotty answered. "I'm right on it!"

Kirk held his breath while he waited for the news from the transporter room. What if this was just another Orion trick? On the viewer, the Navaar was already beginning to right itself; Kirk doubted that Habroz was through with them yet. He leaned into the intercom receiver on his chair. Was that the faint hum of a transporter beam he heard in the background? "Are they there, Scotty? Did you get them?"

Another voice replaced Scotty's. "Doctor McCoy and I are both safely aboard, Captain," Spock reported with his customary lack of drama, although a hint of regret could be heard over the intercom. *"I am sorry that I cannot say the same for Lieutenant Tang."*

"Understood, Mister Spock." Kirk checked to make sure reinforcements had been deployed to drive the Orions away from the transporter room. "Hold tight. Security forces are en route to your position."

"Thank you, Captain," Spock said. "I look forward to resuming my post on the bridge."

"It hasn't been the same without you." Kirk felt a load slip off his shoulders. With the surviving hostages back aboard the *Enterprise*, there was no further reason for them to stick around in the Neutral Zone. "Mister Sulu, get us the hell out of here."

The helmsman didn't need to be asked twice. "Music to my ears, sir." Sulu backed away from the enemy ships. "Fasten your seatbelts, everybody."

Not wasting any time, the *Enterprise* executed an old-fashioned Immelmann loop that sent it zooming back toward the border. A barrel roll tested the limits of the bridge's inertial dampers. Kirk's stomach turned and part of his breakfast came up again. An unsecured first-aid kit slid to the floor. One of the bound Orion prisoners lost his lunch. Apparently he was fond of raw lizard.

"Ugh." Uhura wrinkled her nose. "That's disgusting."

Nobody objected to the roller-coaster ride. Everyone on the bridge was eager to put the Neutral Zone behind them.

Granted, they still had a mob of homicidal raiders swarming the ship, but maybe the Orion boarding parties would surrender once they found themselves back in Federation space. In any event, Kirk knew he'd rather fight them on his own ground than here in the Neutral Zone, where he had no allies and plenty of enemies.

"Full speed ahead, Mister Sulu. Warp factor eight."

"Yes, sir!"

Stars streaked past on the viewscreen as the *Enterprise* slipped the bounds of Einsteinian space-time, achieving superluminal velocity. Kirk settled back into his chair, nursing the hope that maybe Habroz would call it quits now that capturing Seven was no longer an option. With the marauder needing serious repairs, Kirk could see the pirate captain deciding to cut his losses. Or was that just wishful thinking?

Apparently so.

"The *Navaar* is pursuing us, Keptin! Aft sensors show her closing fast."

So much for a clean getaway, Kirk thought. "Show me."

A rear view appeared on the screen, verifying Chekov's report. The battle-scarred marauder was swooping through subspace after them like a bat out of hell. Disruptor beams shot from the *Navaar*'s cannons, forcing Sulu to resort to increasingly wild evasive maneuvers. Kirk tried to discern Habroz's motives for taking up the chase. Did he want his boarding parties back or simply revenge? Kirk leaned toward the latter. Space had no fury like an Orion raider cheated out of his plunder.

But Habroz had lost his hostages as well, which made this a whole new ballgame. Kirk didn't have to hold back anymore.

"Discourage him, Mister Chekov. Fire at will."

"Aye, sir," the Russian blurted. He jabbed his firing controls. "Photon torpedoes away."

A salvo of missiles shot from the rear of the *Enterprise,* targeting the *Navaar.* Moving too fast to evade them, the marauder met the torpedoes at warp speed. Blinding photonic discharges blossomed against the *Navaar*'s forward deflectors. Kirk grinned wolfishly. He hadn't liked having his hands tied before.

"Don't let up," Kirk instructed Chekov. "Show them who they're messing with."

Chekov looked like a kid who had just been allowed to open his Christmas presents early. "Absolutely, sir!"

He followed up the torpedoes with a blistering phaser assault. Crimson beams slammed into what was left of the *Navaar*'s shield. Phasers and disruptors collided with each other in the shrinking gap between the ships. A second wave of torpedoes tested the marauder's deflectors and plating. Brilliant detonations lit up subspace, causing minute ripples in the continuum. Shock waves buffeted the *Enterprise.*

"She's backing off, Keptin!" Chekov gloated. A second glance at his readouts muted his enthusiasm to a degree. "But she's not giving up. They're still coming after us."

Kirk could see that for himself. The *Navaar* remained on their tail, only farther back, just out of firing range. *At least we taught them not to tailgate,* he thought. "Estimated time to border?"

He was used to Spock providing such information at once. It took a little longer for Chekov to calculate the answer. "Approximately eighty-five minutes, Keptin."

Kirk assessed their strategic situation. The *Galileo II* had knocked the wind out of the *Navaar* and probably weakened its offensive capabilities as well, but with her own shields still down, the *Enterprise* could not outfight even a damaged marauder. They would have to rely on speed, not strength.

"That's not good enough," Kirk said. "Mister Sulu, increase warp speed, beyond recommended safety limits."

The helmsman nodded. "Yes, Captain. Going to maximum warp."

A sudden burst of acceleration shoved Kirk against the back of his chair. The streaking stars on the viewer grew even more energetic. An unsettling vibration shook the bridge, rising up from the floor in the very marrow of his bones. A coffee mug rattled atop one of the aft consoles. Chekov cast a nervous look at the throbbing bulkheads.

He wasn't the only one.

Scotty's not going to be happy about this, Kirk thought. He could readily imagine the engineer fretting over the unfair demands being placed on his beloved warp engines, but there was no point in sparing the engines if they ended up losing the ship. He just hoped the *Navaar* was the *only* ship after them.

"What about the *O'Spakya*?" he asked. The last thing they needed was a second hostile vessel at their heels. One angry bloodhound was bad enough. "Any sign of them?"

"Negative, Keptin." Chekov looked away from the viewer to check on the Mavelan merchanter. The bone-shaking vibration added a warble to his voice. "Long-range sensors show the *O'Spakya* accelerating in the opposite direction. They're heading deeper into the Neutral Zone."

Thank heaven for small favors, Kirk thought. It seemed Papa Yela had chosen the better part of valor; apparently he was more interested in preserving his own ship than in assisting the Orions. Habroz was on his own.

Kirk could live with that.

"The *Navaar* is closing again," Chekov alerted him. "Coming within firing range."

Kirk had to applaud Habroz's persistence. The pirate wasn't giving up.

"Mister Sulu, you know what to do." He opened an all-ship bulletin. "All hands, brace for evasive maneuvers."

"Yes, sir," Sulu respond. "Everybody hold on."

Working the helm like a virtuoso, Sulu put the *Enterprise* through a high-speed stress test. He banked from side to side to side, zigzagging in three dimensions in order to baffle the *Navaar's* targeting scanners. Abrupt, unpredictable changes in pitch and yaw tossed captain and crew back and forth. The port armrest smacked into Kirk's side, bruising his ribs. Uhura held on to her console for dear life, while upright security officers and engineers grabbed safety rails, chair backs, and consoles. A portable deflector unit toppled over. The bound Orions swore obscenely as they bounced against each other. Kirk regretted not having them gagged.

"Having fun, Mister Sulu?"

"A bit, sir," the helmsman confessed. "My flight instructor would be having a heart attack right now."

"Good," Kirk said. "Keep it up."

Sulu's barnstorming tactics did what they had to:

keep the *Enterprise* one hairpin turn after another away from the *Navaar*'s disruptors, but at a cost. The ship's circuitous flight path prolonged their escape from the Neutral Zone, with every random zig and zag resulting in another momentary detour. Kirk judged that they were still heading in roughly the right direction, but they were hardly making a beeline for the border. Then again, considering Sulu's enthusiastic efforts to keep them out of the marauder's sights, it was impressive that the overworked helmsman was still managing to steer toward their destination at all.

But how much longer could Sulu pull this off?

Emerald beams shot from the *Navaar*'s gunports. Kirk didn't need any sensor readings to know that the disruptors were getting way too close.

"Keptin!" Chekov shouted. "They're targeting our nacelles. That last beam missed us by only forty-six meters!"

He's just trying to disable us, Kirk realized, *not destroy us.* Habroz apparently wanted his men back, or maybe just the *Enterprise.* Capturing a Federation starship would go a long way toward recouping his losses, but that was going to take some tricky shooting on the Orions' part. *No wonder they haven't nailed us yet.*

Kirk knew he was pushing his luck, though. Not even Sulu could duck those disruptors forever, and they were still several light-years from the border. They couldn't risk being crippled by a lucky shot.

The captain pounded the intraship. "Engineering. Where the devil are my shields?"

As if on cue, a trio of transporter beams manifested on the bridge. Attentive security officers, anticipating another sneak attack, drew their phasers on the shimmering columns of energy, only to relax slightly as the energized silhouettes resolved in the familiar figures of Spock, Scotty, and McCoy.

The Vulcan first officer apparently had heard Kirk's intemperate query.

"Allow Mister Scott and me to remedy that situation, Captain."

Thirty

Spock had returned to the bridge just in time.

He walked briskly to the science station. A few dried green bloodstains on his collar hinted at what he had endured aboard the *O'Spakya*. Cozzone stepped aside to surrender the post to Spock. The captain estimated that the ship's odds of making it out of the Neutral Zone had just improved significantly.

"Can you get the shields up, Mister Spock?"

"That is my priority, Captain." Spock analyzed the relevant data, his remarkable mind instantly bringing him up to speed on the current status of the repair operations. "The primary deflector grids remain inoperative, but it may be possible to simulate their effect, at least temporarily, by heightening the polarity of the structural integrity field by a factor of approximately forty-eight-point-six-five." His fingers moved across the controls without hesitation. "I am attempting to augment the graviton flow through a tertiary relay."

Kirk assumed Spock knew what he was doing. "Concentrate your efforts on the aft and upper lateral shields. The Orions are gunning for our warp nacelles."

"I anticipated as much," Spock said, "and will prioritize accordingly." Without lifting his gaze from his work, he called out to one of the other new arrivals. "Mister

Scott, I am encountering a severed field conduit at Deck Sixteen, wave junction two-one-zero-eight-beta."

"Leave that to me," Scotty declared. Hurrying across the bridge, he bounced a hapless ensign from the main engineering station, then opened a channel to the lower decks. "Palmer, Scott here. I know ye and your crew have your hands full fightin' off a great muckle load of pirates, but I've got one more task that ye need to see to, pronto." He forwarded the specs to his besieged assistant. "Get that SIF conduit fixed in a jiffy!"

Kirk trusted his crew to get the job done. He turned to McCoy for an update on another situation. "The transporter room?"

"You mean that battleground we beamed into?" McCoy sounded like his usual exasperated self, despite the flecks of dried blood visible on his ears. With no designated post on the bridge, he joined Kirk in the command well. "For a second there, I thought we'd jumped into the proverbial skillet, but then those reinforcements of yours turned up, loaded for bear. They sent the Orions running." He snorted in disdain. "Those green-skinned carpetbaggers are probably pillaging the mess hall by now."

"Better that than the armory," Kirk said. "Or sickbay."

A glance at various shipboard monitors suggested that the *Enterprise*'s crack security teams were finally managing to confine the roving Orion boarding parties to less essential decks of the ship. Starfleet training and precision was winning out over the raider's undisciplined ferocity. At least onboard, the tide of battle seemed to be turning in their favor. Kirk hoped they hadn't taken too many casualties.

This had been a costly wild goose chase.

Spock looked up from the controls. "I believe we have partial shielding, Captain. Thanks to Mister Scott's timely assistance."

Chekov confirmed Spock's report. "Shields at thirty-four percent, sir!"

"Thirty-four-point-four-seven-nine, to be exact," Spock clarified. "With a half-percent margin of error."

Kirk chuckled to himself. "Good to have you back, Mister Spock."

"And what am I?" McCoy grumbled. "Chopped liver?"

"You, too, Bones."

Kirk welcomed the status update. Even at only thirty-four percent (plus or minus a half point margin of error), the improvised shields gave them a fighting chance to make it back out of the Neutral Zone. There was less likelihood that a single well-aimed disruptor beam would leave them dead in the water.

"Enough with the fancy flying, Mister Sulu," he ordered. "Straight for home . . . as the crow flies."

"Thank goodness," the helmsman said, wiping his brow. He looked understandably relieved not to have to singlehandedly keep the *Enterprise* out of harm's way anymore. "Setting a direct course for the border. Estimated arrival time: six minutes."

The screech of ruptured metal violated the bridge. A security chief, Luz Hernandez, shouted at Kirk from the sealed gangway doors. "Captain! The Orions are breaking through. We can't hold them back anymore."

Kirk had been expecting as much. The bridge had been designed to be impregnable, but no security measures were perfect, especially when dealing with an assault force that really wanted in; he always had assumed that the relentless pirates would bust through the barricades eventually. "Are we ready for them?"

"Yes, sir!" Hernandez reported. Under her supervision, a squad of field techs was hastily finishing up some creative adjustments to the floor paneling in front of the embattled emergency entrance. The bridge's built-in barricades had bought its defenders time to rig a little surprise for the stubborn Orions, one that wasn't in the standard Starfleet playbook. A perspiring tech, his sleeves rolled up, laid down one last plate and snapped it into place. Hernandez gave the tech's work a quick once-over, then she granted it a thumbs-up. "All right. Fall back, everybody."

The techs retreated behind a line of armed security officers. Noncombatants cleared out of the area, leaving behind empty consoles. Hernandez gave Kirk a worried look. "You might want to take cover, Captain."

"Forget it," Kirk said. No way was a band of would-be hijackers going to send him into hiding on his own bridge. He confidently occupied his chair. "I'm not going anywhere."

"Easy for you to say," McCoy muttered. "I'm the one who has to keep patching you up."

Kirk shrugged. "Think of it as career security."

"More like a textbook case of terminal pigheadedness."

An explosion at the gangway interrupted their banter. Reinforced steel buttresses snapped in two. Mangled blast doors caved in, crashing to the floor only a few meters away from the viewscreen. Multiple disruptor blasts shredded the defensive force fields. The supplementary deflectors shorted out; fiery orange sparks erupted from the portable field generators. Flying shrapnel scarred the walls and ceiling. A glowing blue screen shattered.

"Hold your fire!" Kirk shouted over the clamor. One last force field, held in reserve, shielded the security team. Their phaser rifles were set on stun. "Wait till you seen the greens of their eyes!"

The force field collapsed. Whooping boisterously, like a mob of J'smorru dervishes hyped up on godweed, more than a dozen Orions stormed the bridge, their disruptors blazing. "Seize the ship!" a scar-faced raider exhorted his comrades. A bandolier across his chest held multiple pistols, knives, and photon grenades. Gripping a disruptor pistol in each hand, he fired wildly at the defenders. "No mercy!"

Kirk delayed until the first wave of invaders was all the way through the breached doorway. Disruptor blasts ricocheted off the flickering force field, generating bursts of bright blue Cerenkov radiation. Kirk didn't even flinch at the flashes.

"Now!" he ordered.

A switch was flicked, and the Orions crashed to the floor as though stomped on by a giant invisible boot. Augmented gravity plating under the deck yanked them down with irresistible force, holding them fast even as they strained against the unbearable pull. Heavy gs tugged on their flesh and bones, distorting their faces. Their bodies piled on each other, the unlucky pirates on the bottom flattened against the hard, unyielding deck. Teeth cracked under pressure. Metal piercings tore themselves free.

"C-cowards!" the leader of the boarding party snarled. He struggled to raise his pistol from the floor, but it might as well have been fused to the deck. His speech was slurred since he could barely lift his tongue to form the words. "R-r-release and f-fight like men!"

Not a chance, Kirk thought. Knowing that the mole had possibly warned the Orions of the bridge's usual defenses, he had been forced to think outside of the box. Kirk once had been on the receiving end of a similar gravitational snare; memories of that mission had inspired this brainstorm, which had worked even better than he'd anticipated. *Just be grateful we didn't dial up the gravity even higher,* he silently admonished the outraged Orion. The pull was almost, but not quite, strong enough to shatter bones. *We could have turned you into pancakes.*

Pinned to the floor, the helpless Orions were sitting ducks for the security forces. "Lower shield!" Hernandez barked. The crackling force field evaporated, and her team opened fire on the heaped raiders. A volley of azure stun beams silenced the Orions' furious oaths.

Unfortunately, the defeated pirates were not alone. A second wave of raiders assaulted the bridge from the starboard gangway, exchanging fire with Hernandez's forces. Disruptor blasts targeted the booby-trapped floor, knocking out the gravity generators. The Orions appeared perfectly willing to risk shooting their own comrades to gain access to the bridge. Kirk didn't know whether to be impressed or horrified by the raiders' relentless ways.

"Watch out!" Hernandez shouted.

A photon grenade was flung with sufficient force to clear the damaged gravity snare. It arced above the line of defenders to land in front of the communications station, right at Uhura's feet. Without missing a beat, she scooped it up and flung it back at the Orions.

From the gangway, a raspy voice swore in surprise. "Hell's balls!"

A blinding flash, followed by a concussive blast, wreaked havoc on the remaining Orions. Hernandez led her team into the chaos, taking the fight to what was left of the invaders. Phaser beams chased after the injured pirates, who fled in disarray. Limping footsteps retreated from the bridge, followed by the rapid tread of the pursuing Starfleet security detail. A backup team remained behind to guard the bridge.

"Nice throw, Lieutenant," Kirk praised Uhura. He didn't want to think about what would have happened had her reflexes been just a heartbeat slower. A photon grenade could inflict a lot of damage, as the battered Orions had just experienced firsthand.

"Thank you, sir." Uhura was unshaken by her close call. "You should see my curve ball."

"Federation border dead ahead," Sulu reported, bringing Kirk's attention back to the *Enterprise*'s headlong retreat from the Neutral Zone. On the viewer, the line of demarcation was denoted by a brilliant red graphic. A digital display counted down the time and distance. The Federation was so close that Kirk could practically taste it.

Which only increased Habroz's determination to blast apart their nacelles first. "*Navaar* closing fast!" Chekov reported, as though Kirk couldn't see that for himself in the main viewer. "They're gaining on us!"

Kirk was reminded of an old-time drag race. No way

in hell was he going to fall short this close to the finish line. "Scotty! Any way we can boost our engines one more time?"

"Are ye jokin', Captain?" Scotty looked chagrined at the very suggestion. "We're already breakin' me poor bairns' backs as it is!"

Kirk sympathized, but he needed every edge he could muster right now. "You're the miracle worker, remember? Tell me you have one more trick up your sleeve."

"Well," Scotty conceded, "there is a wee idea I've been toyin' with in me meager spare time. Not sure I'd call it a miracle, exactly. More like a doodle . . ."

"No false modesty, Scotty." Kirk gambled that Scotty's doodles were more reliable than most engineers' fifty-page feasibility studies. "It doesn't become you." He nodded at Scotty. "Just do it . . . before we end up as eunuchs in an Orion harem!"

"Right ye are, sir!" Scotty got back on the horn to Palmer in engineering. "Listen to me close, lass. I want you to fire up the impulse *and* the warp engines simultaneously. Crosslink the fusion generators to the matter/antimatter plasma stream if ye have to, and be sure to synchronize the relative thrust ratios." A horrified protest greeted Scotty's instructions. "Don't tell me it can't be done, Lieutenant. Just make it so!"

Kirk knew Scotty was breaking every rule in the book, but he didn't stop him. What did they have to lose, except maybe their hull integrity? Given a choice, he'd rather tear the *Enterprise* apart than surrender his ship to Habroz. He knew his crew felt the same.

Here goes nothing.

The overhead lights flickered alarmingly. Annunciators and safety monitors had a collective nervous breakdown. Worrisome black ripples streaked the warp effect on the viewer. A tortured grinding noise emanated up from engineering, many decks below. Scotty looked as though he was in actual physical distress from the abuse his poor engines were taking. He wiped sweaty palms on his trousers.

But the *Enterprise* kicked it up another notch, rocketing ahead like it had just acquired a third warp nacelle. Supercharged acceleration practically gave Kirk whiplash.

"Not bad, Mister Scott!"

All eyes were fixed on the flashing red line on the viewer. The digital countdown hit zero. Spontaneous cheers erupted across the bridge as the *Enterprise* swept across the border, leaving the Neutral Zone behind. Chekov and Sulu high-fived each other. Uhura beamed at Kirk, figuratively speaking. Even McCoy cracked a smile.

"Okay, it's still cold, airless space," the doctor muttered, "but at least it's *our* space."

Kirk wasn't ready to break out the Saurian brandy just yet. Sure, they were out of the Neutral Zone, but was that going to stop Habroz? He wouldn't put it past the determined corsair to follow them out of the Neutral Zone. *We're still out on the far frontier,* he thought. *It's not like there's a Starfleet space station just up ahead.*

"Chekov, what about the *Navaar*? Is she turning back?"

The ensign shook his head. "Negative, Keptin. She's still coming, faster than ever." On the viewer, the marauder tore through the glowing red graphic. "She's crossed the border after us."

"And I thought my ex couldn't take a hint," McCoy drawled. "Where's a good restraining order when you need one?"

A violent shudder rattled the *Enterprise*. Bulkheads groaned in agony. Cracks spiderwebbed across display screens and monitors. The vibration throbbing through Kirk's chair went up several notches, until he felt like he was sitting on top of an unstable pulsar. Damage reports and emergency alerts filled up the margins of the main viewer, practically overlapping each other. The screen itself seemed to be caving inward, the images upon it warping like reflections in a funhouse mirror. The marauder turned into a distorted nightmare version of itself.

"Captain!" Scotty blurted. "We've got to slow down. The engines can't take it anymore." A temporary imbalance between the warp nacelles sent the *Enterprise* lurching to port before Sulu leveled the ship out again. Subspace turbulence rocked the bridge. Another jarring tremor backed up Scotty's agitated outburst. "I'm serious. I mean it this time!"

Kirk believed him. The *Enterprise* sounded like it was on the verge of shaking itself apart. His ship had performed heroically, beyond all reasonable expectations, but even Kirk recognized that there were limits. He'd pushed the ship as far as it could go.

All right, he decided. *No more running.*

"Reduce speed, Mister Sulu. Slow to impulse." He gripped the armrest of his chair. "Habroz wants a fight? Let's give him one."

"Hoo boy," McCoy said. "Here we go again."

The inky blackness of ordinary space-time replaced the light-speed effect on the viewer. The distant stars were just pinpricks in a vast stygian expanse. Kirk hoped Spock's improvised shields were up to the demands of a full-fledged space battle. To survive, the *Enterprise* would have to score a quick and decisive knockout. They were in no shape to go twelve rounds.

"Mister Chekov, arm all phasers and torpedoes."

Before they could fire a single salvo, however, Uhura called out. "Captain! We're being hailed. There's another ship approaching!"

Kirk looked up at the screen. Sure enough, a moving dot denoted the presence of a third vessel approaching them at warp speed. Within moments, it would be within firing range.

What the devil? he thought. *Now who are we dealing with?* The Klingons? The Mavela? Had the *O'Spakya* circled around to intercept them somehow? Kirk feared he was once again outnumbered two to one.

"Identify," he demanded.

Uhura flashed a dazzling smile. "It's the *Bellingham,* sir! Responding to our distress call."

Kirk recalled Uhura sending out the message at the onset of the crisis, despite the Orions' best efforts to jam the transmission. It seemed her efforts had paid off now that they were back in Federation space. The *Bellingham,* another *Constitution*-class starship, warped into view. Cheers greeted her appearance on the viewer. Kirk guessed that, aboard the *Navaar,* the reaction was considerably less enthused. He smirked at the screen.

Now who was outnumbered?

Thirty-one

Kirk was impressed and relieved by the *Bellingham*'s timely arrival. Her captain, Sam Greer, must have pulled out all the stops to get to the outskirts of the Neutral Zone this quickly. Kirk watched with satisfaction as the other starship took up a defensive position alongside the *Enterprise*.

"Tell Captain Greer I owe him dinner."

Uhura cheerfully carried out his order. "He says he likes Italian, sir."

"And the *Navaar*?" Kirk asked.

"Retreating back toward the border," Chekov reported. He sounded disappointed at being cheated out of another heated military engagement. "Looks like Captain Habroz doesn't want to take us both on."

"Especially now that Doctor Seven is dead," Sulu observed. Catching himself, he gave Kirk a sheepish look. "No disrespect to the deceased intended, sir."

"None taken," Kirk assured him. "Your assessment is right on target. With Seven out of the picture, Habroz has much less incentive to risk an armed encounter with two Federation starships."

"And on our side of the border, no less," McCoy commented.

"Exactly," Kirk said. He counted his lucky stars that they'd made it out of the Neutral Zone in time to rendezvous with the *Bellingham*; Captain Greer might have been reluctant to risk interstellar war by venturing into the Zone. One errant starship on a supposed rescue mission was bad enough. The Klingons would not have taken kindly to *two* Starfleet vessels waging battle against the Orions so close to their empire. Kirk wouldn't have blamed Greer if he'd chosen to stay out of the restricted territory. And neither would have Starfleet. As is, Kirk suspected that he already had given the brass a few ulcers.

Tough, he thought. Even though the Mavela's distress signal had turned out to be a trap, Kirk didn't regret his decision to go to their rescue. The *Enterprise* wasn't about to turn her back on ships in trouble, not while he was captain. If he had to do it again, he'd make the same choice—just perhaps a little more warily next time.

At least one diplomat seemed to agree with him. "For what it's worth, Captain Kirk," Santiago said, "I'll vouch for you if there's any question regarding your choice to enter the Neutral Zone. I can see now why Starfleet places so much faith in you and your crew. To be honest, I'm not so worried about the Federation's security, now that I've seen the caliber of the people protecting us out here on the frontier."

"Thank you, Commissioner," Kirk said graciously. "I appreciate the vote of confidence."

"How tragic what happened to Seven, though." He gave Kirk an odd look, as though he had something else on his mind. "A painful, if sadly necessary, sacrifice."

"Yes," Kirk said tersely, not wanting to talk about it. "We owe her our future."

"Captain," Uhura said. "We're being hailed."

"Captain Greer?" Kirk looked forward to thanking him personally.

"No, sir," Uhura said sourly, as though she just had bitten down on a piece of rotten fruit. "It's Captain Habroz."

McCoy snorted. "Let him eat static."

"Not so fast, Bones." Kirk appreciated the sentiment, but he was curious, too. "Let's hear what he has to say."

Scotty made his opinion known. "Nothing worth hearing, I'll wager. A bloody-handed scoundrel, that's what he is."

"You'll get no argument here," Kirk said. "Just the same, put him through."

"Yes, Captain," Uhura said without enthusiasm. "On-screen."

Habroz's piratical visage appeared on the viewscreen. *"Congratulations, Kirk. It seems your translator is working again."* The seething resentment in his tone and expression belied any attempt at civility. *"Convenient, that."*

"Yes," Kirk said. "Very."

The Orion captain scowled. *"I confess: This is not how I hoped to resume our conversation. I was looking forward to better making your acquaintance . . . in my brig. But it appears the Fates have outsmarted us all,"* he said in a transparent attempt to save face. He obviously wanted to declare the match a stalemate. *"Neither of us will benefit from the precious secrets Seven took with her to oblivion."*

"Perhaps that's just as well," Kirk suggested. "To my mind, tomorrow belongs in the future, not here and now."

"There may be something to what you say, human.

How boring it would be to know everything in advance." Habroz sat solidly atop his throne, which looked a little worse for wear after the battle. Scratches and scorch marks defaced its formerly polished surface. The plush upholstery was torn. The mounted skull hung askew upon a wall, now missing its lower jaw. *"In the meantime, I desire the return of my men . . . in the interests of preventing any further bloodshed."*

"Don't hold your breath." Kirk had the upper hand now. The Orion boarding parties were already losing ground aboard the *Enterprise*. Now that the *Bellingham* had arrived to provide additional reinforcements, he had no doubt that they would be able to subdue the remaining invaders. "Your men will face charges for assault, piracy, terrorism, assassination, and the callous murder of Starfleet personnel."

He had not forgotten Bergstrom, Jadello, Tang, and every other member of his crew that had fallen victim to the Orions' ruthlessness. Nor was he going to overlook the sneak attack on the oasis back on Yusub. Justice demanded that the raiders not be allowed to go their own way without retribution.

"Easier said than done," Habroz growled. *"You will find that Orions do not surrender meekly in the face of unbeatable odds. They are proud of their manhood . . . and even prouder of their women. We would sooner die than shame ourselves in their eyes."*

Kirk was not intimidated by his boasts. "And how are the Klingons going to feel about *you* disappointing them? Especially after they provided you with a cloaking device and free passage through the Neutral Zone?"

The memory of Lieutenant Jadello disintegrating before his eyes burned in Kirk's memory as he twisted the knife with his words. "Last I heard, the Klingons weren't exactly forgiving of failure. . . ."

Habroz's green skin turned a shade paler. An involuntary shudder shook his beefy frame as he grasped how bleak his prospects had become. If nothing else, Habroz was going to be looking over his shoulder for what was likely to be a very short and uneasy life.

"Now who has a price on his head?" Kirk gloated. "I wouldn't be surprised if one of your fellow pirates turns you in for the bounty. If the Klingons don't get to you first."

"*Goddess curse you, Kirk!*" Habroz raged. "*May you and your crew fly into the path of a black star!*"

Kirk shrugged. "Been there, done that."

His furious visage vanished abruptly from the screen. An instant later, the *Navaar* dropped completely off the *Enterprise*'s sensors.

"Well, that was rude," McCoy commented. "Not so much as a proper good-bye."

"If I was him, I wouldn't stick around either," Chekov said. "Not this close to the Klingon border."

"He won't get far," Kirk predicted. "Want to bet that the Klingons built a tracking mechanism into that cloaking device they loaned Habroz?"

"That would be a prudent precaution," Spock agreed. "And the Klingons are not known for their trusting natures."

Kirk was counting on that. "Couldn't happen to a nicer fellow." He dismissed the fugitive Orion from his mind, confident that Habroz's days of unrestricted piracy were over. "Now then, who wants to tell his men that their glorious leader has left them in the lurch?"

The Orions made their last stand in the lower reaches of the ship. Driven away from the bridge and engineering by Starfleet security forces, the remaining pirates holed up in the huge cavernous space. Grunting raiders shoved massive cargo containers across the bay to construct a makeshift fort. The durable steel drums scraped loudly against the floor. At the rear of the hold, a wall-sized duranium space door protected them from the killing vacuum outside.

"Step lively, you mulish lummoxes!" Chotto shouted. The unlucky raider found himself in command of the stragglers, now that Master Chief Vaen had been blown apart by his own grenade. An improvised sling supported Chotto's crippled right arm. A blood-stained bandage wrapped his skull like a bandana. He shook his only working fist at the laboring men. "Put your backs into it!"

Less than a fraction of the original boarding parties had found refuge in the inhospitable cargo bay, and even fewer were still combat-worthy. Wounded raiders, too weak to aid in bolstering their defenses, huddled on the floor behind a wall of containers. A single medic, himself sporting a tourniquet on one arm, struggled to tend to a surfeit of injuries. Bandages and anesthetics were already in short supply. Painful cuts and burns elicited equal quantities of groans and curses from the casualties. An anguished gunner bit down on the ivory hilt of his dagger as the medic roughly reset a broken limb. The sound of splintered bones grinding against each other set Chotto's pointed teeth on edge.

Perdition! Chotto despaired. This was not how this raid was supposed to go. Captain Habroz had promised them easy pickings and rich rewards if only they captured the female from the future. Chotto and his fellow boarders had expected only feeble resistance from the oh-so-civilized Federation weaklings. Who knew these Starfleeters would put up such a fight?

The last container was hauled into place. Plasma torches welded the front entrance of the cargo bay shut, buying them a bit more time. Chotto was a realist, however. He had no illusions that such impromptu fortifications would keep out the Starfleeters for long. He and his men were sorely in need of rescue and reinforcements.

"Famrac?" he barked at a signalman. "Any word from the *Navaar*?"

"Not a whisper, Mister Chotto." Famrac fumbled with his wrist-communicator. His front teeth had been knocked out by the butt of a Starfleet phaser rifle. "I can't get through to the ship. The damn humans are jamming the signal!"

Turnabout is fair play, Chotto conceded grudgingly. Kirk's crew members were fast learners, he'd give them that. "Keep trying!"

He slumped against a looming cargo container. The ultratestosterone was wearing off; adrenaline and artificial stimulants could only keep one going for so long. Exhaustion and blood loss sapped his vitality. If the Starfleeters were to burst in right now, he wasn't sure he still had the strength to fight them.

The cold metal drum propped him up. The damn storage container didn't even contain any useful arms, food, or medicine. Cracking one open, the men had been disappointed to find only several cartloads of self-sealing stem bolts. Nothing they could use to defend themselves.

Unless they wanted to throw the worthless trash at their foes' heads!

"*Orion boarding parties!*" A stern voice blared from the ship's intraship system. A pink face appeared on a large screen mounted over the space doors; Chotto guessed that it was usually employed for docking operations. "*This is Captain Kirk, the commander of the ship you have failed to seize for your own.*" The human captain, whose youthful face lacked any proper scars or piercings, also flashed onto smaller communications screens throughout the cargo bay, so that it felt as though he was surrounding them singlehandedly. "*Listen to me carefully. Captain Habroz has abandoned you. The* Navaar *has activated its cloaking device and fled back to the Neutral Zone. Your first mate, K'Mara, is a captive aboard the* O'Spakya, *which has also abandoned this sector. Your fellow boarders are either dead or in custody. The battle is over. You've lost.*"

"Rubbish!" Famrac jeered. "He's bluffing. The captain would never desert us."

Chotto knew better. Any good captain knew when to retreat to fight another day and that rank-and-file crewmen were expendable. Such were the fortunes of war and piracy. If the *Navaar* had truly departed, then Captain Habroz must have had sound reasons to do so.

"*I repeat,*" Kirk said, "*your attack on the ship is over. Our sister ship, the* Bellingham, *is prepared to transport you to the nearest Federation starbase, where you will face justice for your crimes. If you lay down your arms and offer no further resistance, I promise you a fair trial under Federation law.*"

"A plague on Federation law!" Famrac spat upon the deck; a piece of broken enamel clattered onto the floor. He looked to his superior for direction. "What now, Chotto? What do we tell that lying pus-rag?"

Famrac wasn't the only raider expecting answers from Chotto. Confused eyes, full of fury and frustration, turned to the reluctant leader, who wished wholeheartedly that Vaen hadn't been fool enough to get himself blown up. Conscious of the men's scrutiny, Chotto stopped leaning against the drum. He forced himself to stand up straight, like a commander should. His head swam dizzyingly. His broken arm ached like plasma fire.

"No word from the *Navaar*?"

Famrac shook his head. "Nay, sir. The jamming's gone, but I can't reach the ship. It's as though she's long gone."

Chotto feared that was the case. In his heart, he knew Kirk had spoken the truth. The campaign was lost, and the *Navaar* had sought out safer harbors. They had been left behind.

Which left only one acceptable course of action.

"What shall we do?" Famrac repeated.

"Do?" Chotto sneered at the foolish gunner. Drawing his disruptor pistol with his good hand, he took aim at Kirk's vile countenance. An emerald blast reduced the intrusive monitor to a smoking ruin. Blackened shards rained down onto the floor. *If only,* he thought, *I could fry the real Kirk's insipid human face so readily.* Throwing out his chest, he roared loud enough to be heard all the way back to the Orion system. "We do as our pride and manhood demands. No surrender, not to the likes of these soft-bellied Starfleet scum!" He limped over to a control panel by the aft space door. Less than a meter of molded steel and ceramic plating separated him from the cold comfort of the void. "Are you with me?"

To their credit, not a single man called out for him to stop. That alone, he judged, should earn them all coveted berths in a heavenly *seraglio,* ruled over by some irresistible green goddess. A savvy Orion techmaster already had hacked into the control panel. Chotto needed only to press a single button. It blinked upon the panel like a winking temptress from beyond this mortal realm.

"Do it, Mister Chotto," Famrac urged him. "We're ready!"

The other men shouted their assent. "No surrender!"

His finger jabbed the button.

The enormous space door slid open. A tremendous gale filled the cargo bay as its contents, living or otherwise, was swept out into space. Massive steel drums barreled past Chotto as his failing body escaped the starship and Kirk's insulting offer of mercy. A defiant scream gushed from his lungs along with his last breath. Closing his eyes, he saw only an eternity of sultry jade eyes and olive flesh.

The icy blackness froze his hot blood.

Thirty-two

"Keptin!" Chekov said. "The Orions . . . they've opened the space door." Shock reduced his voice to a hush. "They were sucked into space!"

"My God," McCoy exclaimed, appalled. "They didn't have to do that. You offered them a chance to surrender."

"It was their choice, Bones." Kirk regretted the raiders' mass suicide, and he would have prevented it if he could, but he wasn't going to lose sleep over it. Good people already had paid the ultimate price for the pirates' greed and brutality. He wondered if Habroz would mourn his men.

Probably not.

"An unfortunate, but sadly predictable, outcome," Spock said. "You will recall that the Orions who attempted to disrupt the Federation conference on Babel also chose self-destruction over surrender."

Kirk remembered the incident well. "As did the sleeper agent they had planted among the delegates."

"Speaking of which," Scotty said, "in all the tumult, there's been nary a minute to bring this up, but I'm afraid I have distressing news for you, Commissioner." He looked mournfully at Santiago. "Seems your man, Hague, was workin' with the Orions."

Santiago stared at him in disbelief. "What are you talking about?"

"He was an Orion spy, plottin' against us," Scotty revealed. He quickly briefed Kirk and the others on what sounded like a tense encounter in the ship's cargo transport facility. "Last I saw him, before Kyle and I managed to beam me directly from the cargo transporter to the main transporter room one step ahead of some unruly Orions, that wolf in sheep's clothing was sleeping off a stun blast on the deck of the cargo bay. I immediately alerted security to his true allegiances, so I imagine he's already in custody, assuming a confused Orion didn't dispose of him for us."

Kirk was stunned by the news, which had escaped his notice while he'd been dealing with the *Navaar*. The possibility that Hague might be the mole had never even crossed his mind, although Kirk was relieved to discover that the traitor had not been among the ranks of his crew. He could only imagine how Santiago felt at having his trusted aide betray him.

"Cyril . . . a spy?" Santiago was obviously shaken by the revelation. He dropped into a vacant seat beside Scott. "I don't understand. Cyril's been my right-hand man for years now. I trusted him without reservation. How could I have not seen who he really was?"

"Trust me," Kirk assured him, "you're not the first person to be taken in by a clever spy operating under an assumed identity. We ran into a similar situation during the Babel Conference, as I said, and again on Deep Space Station K-Seven." In both instances, Kirk recalled, the sleeper agent had been surgically altered to disguise his true origins; he imagined something similar had been done to Hague. "Never underestimate the length a determined adversary will go to infiltrate the opposition."

Like being surgically transformed into a Romulan to steal a cloaking device, come to think of it . . .

Spock consulted the ship's computer. "I can confirm that Mister Hague is currently occupying our brig," he reported. "I recommend that he be placed under suicide watch, given the Orions' unfortunate predilection for self-destruction."

"Good idea, Mister Spock. See that it's done," Kirk instructed. The Orion spy during the Babel conference had taken poison prior to being exposed; Kirk didn't want a repeat of that scenario. "There's been enough lives lost over this affair."

Santiago gasped as the extent of Hague's treachery sank in. "I told him all about Seven . . . where she came from, how valuable she was." Guilt transfigured his ashen features. "This is all my fault."

Kirk went easy on him. "Hague was the traitor, not you. Don't ever forget that." His face hardened. "He was the one who brought down the Orions on us, both on Yusub and later on, and who got Seven and the others killed."

"That poor, brave lass," Scotty said. "She deserved better."

"Yes," Kirk agreed. "She did."

Hours later, Kirk felt himself winding down. Dealing with the aftermath of the battle and the invasion had been almost more exhausting than the fight itself, and without the adrenaline rush to keep him on his toes. He fought back a yawn. His stomach grumbled, reminding him that he'd only managed to grab a bite or two on the run. Briefings with damage control units had consumed his day, although he had found time to pay his respects to Captain Greer and drop in on the wounded crew members in sickbay, including Lieutenants Pierce and Robbins, who, according to Scotty, had been instrumental in getting him and Seven safely to the cargo bay. To Kirk's relief, the casualties had proven lighter than expected, which he chalked up to first-rate Starfleet training and discipline. He intended to recommend a full round of commendations for the crew serving under his command. They had certainly earned their stripes this time around.

And then some.

Still, it had been a long day. By the time Kirk finally found himself wandering down the corridors of the ship's executive quarters, it was well into the graveyard shift.

Appropriate, he thought.

He nodded at diligent technicians working to patch up the ship's war wounds. It was tempting to turn in for the night, maybe catch a few extra z's before starting up again, but he had one last call to make. Arriving at the door to Scotty's personal quarters, he buzzed to be let in. The engineer's distinctive burr emerged from the intercom.

"That you, Captain?"

"More or less," Kirk said. "Am I too late for the wake?"

"Nae, sir." The door slid open and Scotty beckoned him inside. "We're just gettin' warmed up. Make yourself at home."

Kirk entered the engineer's chambers. An antique bagpipe, hanging on a peg, personalized the suite, as did the tartan kilt mounted on one wall. A well-stocked bar made it clear that he had come to the right place. Mounds of data slates, no doubt loaded with technical journals and engineering reports, were piled haphazardly atop a desk, threatening to topple over at any minute. An open bottle of Scotch, a pot of tea, a couple of glasses, and a tray of sandwiches occupied a small coffee table. Despite the lateness of the hour, Scotty was not alone. Seated around the table were Spock, McCoy . . . and Annika Seven.

"Good evening," he greeted her. "You're looking remarkably hale for a dead woman."

"I have Mister Scott to thank for that," Seven stated. "As planned, he successfully locked onto my combadge and beamed me off the *Galileo II* an instant before the *Navaar* reactivated her deflectors, and after I had already rigged the shuttle to self-destruct."

Scotty admired the shiny Starfleet insignia pinned to her chest. "Who would have thought that badge of hers is actually a working communicator, with a stronger signal than our own handheld models? I don't mind saying, I'd like to get a pick at its innards."

"Perhaps in due time, Scotty, the future allowing." Kirk sat down at the table. "I'm just glad to see it all worked out." Although he had been privy to Seven's plan all along, he'd known that the split-second timing involved was going to be tricky. When the shuttlecraft had exploded inside the marauder, a part of him had worried as to whether Seven had truly escaped their high-tech Trojan horse in time. "So you've been hiding out here all this time?"

"Mister Scott beamed me directly to his quarters, despite the significant risks and challenges involved," she replied. "I am grateful for his accuracy, as well as his hospitality. We judged that my own guest quarters on the *Enterprise* might pose a temptation to the Orion boarding parties still at large aboard the ship." She helped herself to a finger sandwich. "I regret that we must let the rest of your crew believe that I perished aboard the shuttle, but it is safer that way. Habroz may not be the only hostile party who would consider me a valuable prize."

Kirk had to agree. "The galaxy is a safer place with you dead, no offense."

"None taken."

Dark circles under her eyes, as well as a slight-but-perceptible tremor in her hands, suggested that she was badly in need of some artificial rest. Kirk wondered if Spock could rig up an ad hoc "regeneration" apparatus in Scotty's quarters or if it would be easier to smuggle her back into sickbay and keep her in isolation from the other patients. One way or another, he was determined to do what he could to preserve her health until they reached the Beta Niobe system—and found the final component of the time-travel device.

A buzz at the door interrupted his musings.

Puzzled, Kirk looked at Scotty. "You invite somebody else to this party?"

"No, Captain. Nary a soul, aside from those already in the know."

Kirk approached the door, on guard and apprehensive. Chances were, it was just a member of the engineering crew coming to seek Scotty's advice on some particularly thorny technical issue, but after all they'd gone through, he wasn't taking any chances. How could they be sure Hague was the only Orion spy aboard?

He hit the intercom. "State your business."

"Good evening, Captain," Commissioner Santiago addressed him from the other side of the door. *"I trust Seven is well."*

Kirk was taken aback. He opened the door to admit the diplomat. "How did you—?"

"Come now, Kirk, I'm not completely guileless, despite the way my Judas of an aide played me for a fool. I suspected a ruse early on." He strode over to the table where the others were gathered. "As I mentioned before, I know your reputation, Kirk, and you usually have a trick up your sleeve . . . and Seven doesn't exactly strike me as the suicidal type."

"Survival is preferable," she conceded, "in most instances." Despite her obvious fatigue, she rose to her feet to confront Santiago. "And do you intend to expose our deception? Perhaps in hopes of turning me over to the Federation for interrogation?"

He shook his head. "No, no, I've learned my lesson. You were right all along. You and your inside knowledge of the future are too dangerous, not just to the time line, but to peace in our time as well. You're a destabilizing element and incentive to violence. It's better that that the galaxy thinks you're gone."

"I was just saying the same thing," Kirk said. "Glad to hear we're all on the same page now."

Despite the commissioner's change of heart, Kirk suspected that they could not keep Seven's continued survival a secret indefinitely. All the more reason to get her as quickly and discreetly as possible to the Beta Niobe system.

And to a planet that no longer existed.

Thirty-three

"Approaching shock wave, Keptin," Chekov reported. "Impact in approximately one minute."

Two years after Beta Niobe's explosive demise, a bubble of super-heated plasma was still expanding through space at about one-tenth light speed. At this point, the wave front was diffused enough that Kirk wasn't anticipating any serious hazards. They had already passed through similar waves of gamma radiation and high-energy particles expelled by the supernova, but Kirk didn't feel like taking any chances, especially after the battering the *Enterprise* had taken lately. "Shields on high, Mister Chekov."

"Aye, sir."

Thankfully, Scotty and his crew had gotten the main deflectors back in working order during the final stretch of their journey to the system, which had proven less eventful now that the *Navaar* had been sent running. The *Bellingham* had gone its own way, taking the treacherous Cyril Hague with it, leaving the *Enterprise* to continue its quest on its own. Kirk certainly hoped they wouldn't require any more reinforcements.

"Impact in five seconds," Chekov said. "Four, three, two, one . . ."

A bout of minor turbulence, which was nothing compared to the pummeling the ship had taken during the battle in the Neutral Zone, rattled the bridge for a moment or two before subsiding.

"That's it?" Uhura said, sounding mildly disappointed. "I was expecting something more . . . dramatic."

"The interstellar medium through which the hot gases are expanding is too tenuous to generate a shock wave of sufficient force to impact our shields," Spock explained. "What brief turbulence we experienced was purely the result of thermal and density changes."

Uhura shrugged. "If you say so, Mister Spock."

"Frankly, I can live with a little less drama after everything we've been through," Kirk said. He sipped from a cup of coffee that had slopped over the sides a bit. "Slow to one-half impulse."

"Aye, sir," Sulu said. "Welcome to the Beta Niobe system . . . or what's left of it."

Spock had briefed him on what to expect. Inside concentric bubbles of expelled plasma and radiation was an empty void inhabited only by a newborn neutron star that was all that remained of the swollen red giant that Beta Niobe had once been. The blazing crimson sun had compacted into a tiny blue sphere, only about twenty kilometers in diameter, but incredibly dense. No trace of Sarpeidon or any other satellite registered on their sensors. An entire world, with a long and storied history, had been vaporized by the supernova, only two years ago. Kirk remembered the *Enterprise* warping away from the doomed system only minutes before Beta Niobe exploded. That had been closer than any of them would have liked.

"Radiation levels?" he asked.

"High concentrations of gamma and x-rays emanating from the neutron star," Spock said, peering into his scanner. "Nothing our shields cannot withstand for a time, but I would not advise lingering in this system longer than necessary."

"Duly noted," Kirk said. "Maintain shields at maximum."

"Aye, sir." Chekov gazed out at the desolate system. The *Enterprise* occupied Sarpeidon's former orbit at a safe distance from the tiny neutron star, which was just a bright blue ball on the viewer, smaller than Kirk's hometown in Iowa. "A pity Doctor Seven couldn't make it here with us."

A mock memorial service had been held for Seven, along with Lieutenant Tang. Kirk had been uncomfortable perpetrating the hoax, particularly in conjunction with a funeral, but had seen no better option. The crew deserved closure, and Seven's survival had to be kept secret.

"I know what you mean, Ensign," he replied. "But we can honor her memory by completing the work she nobly gave her life to protect."

The "official" explanation for continuing on to Beta Niobe, even after Seven's tragic "death," was that the misplaced time traveler had been investigating the possible source of a temporal disturbance sometime in the future. Supposedly, the *Enterprise* was now confirming her theories so that the future would have the data they needed to avert the disturbance when the time came. Like the best cover stories, this was close enough to the truth to pass muster.

"But the supernova destroyed everything," Chekov pointed out. "If you don't mind me asking, sir, what is there left to investigate here?"

Good question, Kirk thought, groping for a plausible response.

Spock came to his rescue. "There is a theory, as yet unconfirmed, that the Sarpeids' ambitious use of time travel took advantage of a temporal wave created by the supernova itself, propagating itself backward through time. Our task here is to examine the surviving stellar remnant for traces of such a wave."

Kirk wondered if that was a real theory or just something Spock had manufactured for the occasion. The Vulcan's poker face made it impossible to tell.

"I see," Chekov said, mulling it over. "But where do Cheron and Gamma Trianguli VI fit into that theory? They didn't practice time travel, did they?"

"I'm afraid that's classified," Kirk said, playing his trump card. "Strictly need to know."

Chekov looked abashed. "I'm sorry, Keptin. I didn't mean to pry."

"No need to apologize, Mister Chekov," Kirk said. "You're a Starfleet officer. A healthy curiosity is part of the job description. Why else are we out here, except to find out what's lying beyond the next star or nebula?" He peered at the two-year-old neutron star before them, struck with wonder despite the urgency of their mission. "I'm sure Doctor Seven would agree."

"I am confident of that as well," Spock agreed. "And in that spirit, I suggest we proceed with our scientific investigation of this system."

"Right you are, Mister Spock." Kirk rose from his chair and headed for the turbolift. Repair teams had done wonders patching up the damage from the invasion, but a few battle scars remained. He resolved to have them dealt with at the first opportunity. "Spock, you're with me. Mister Scott is waiting in the transporter room to beam that probe of yours to the designated coordinates." He declined to mention that the "probe" in question was blonde and hailed from another era. "Mister Sulu, you have the conn."

"Yes, sir."

Scotty was indeed waiting in the transporter room, along with McCoy, Santiago, and Seven. She was already putting on an environmental suit when Kirk and Spock arrived. A torpedo-shaped probe casing, which had been used to covertly transfer her from the isolation ward to the transporter room, lay open to one side, exposing the hollowed-out cavity inside. A second space suit awaited Kirk.

"Captain," she greeted him. The protective suit was made of a flexible silver material that covered her arms, legs, and torso, beneath a more rigid unit that fit over her shoulders and chest. A bulky transparent helmet rested on a counter, waiting to be donned. The nameplate on the front of the helmet had been deliberately kept blank. "I commend you and Mister Scott for the speed at which the *Enterprise* has arrived at our destination. I am ready to conclude our quest."

"As am I," Kirk said. "How are you holding up?"

Although she had been resting more or less in peace since her "death" in the Neutral Zone, she still was looking shaky. She swayed slightly, struggling to maintain her usual formal posture. Her eyes were puffy, her skin dry and unhealthy looking, as though she hadn't slept in days. Whatever tricks McCoy and Spock had been employing to help keep her body together appeared to be reaching the limits of their effectiveness. She needed to "regenerate" soon, whatever that meant.

"I am . . . functional," she stated. Her shoulders drooped, as though weighed down by the sturdy construction of the space suit. "But perhaps another dose of stimulant is advisable."

McCoy frowned. "I know this was my idea, but I don't like how much you're relying on these injections to stay on your feet. The long-term consequences—"

"Are irrelevant, Doctor, if I cannot return to my own era before long." She cocked her head, exposing her bare neck. "The hyprospray, if you please."

"All right, damn it." He pressed the instrument against her jugular. A hiss accompanied its operation. "Here's hoping you won't need any more of these."

"I share your hope, Doctor. Believe me."

Spock helped Kirk into an environmental suit, which seemed a prudent precaution, considering.

"With any luck, we won't need these suits either," Kirk said, "provided the fragments cause us to be transported back into Sarpeidon's past . . . and not into empty space."

"I don't know, Jim," McCoy said, shaking his head. "Beaming down to a planet that doesn't exist anymore? That's one hell of a leap of faith. What if you just end up floating out in the vacuum instead?"

Kirk shrugged. "In which case, Scotty will lock onto us and beam us back aboard. No harm done, except to our mission."

"But the radiation—" McCoy began.

"Their suits will provide adequate protection for the

short time they are outside the ship," Spock said, "assuming they find themselves in space at all. Our working theory, which is supported by what we have already observed, is that they will instead find themselves transported to Sarpeidon's past, much as we ourselves have been on occasion."

It wasn't long ago, Kirk recalled, that the three of them had traveled back through time to Sarpeidon's past in search of Spock's son, conceived during their previous mission to the planet. They had successfully rescued Zar from a desolate ice age, but the young man had ultimately chosen to return to his own time in order to live and die five thousand years ago, as the history of his world decreed. Kirk had to imagine that their return to this system had stirred up plenty of bittersweet memories for his friend, not that you'd know it from Spock's stoic façade.

"Don't remind me," McCoy said.

"I would hope that would not be necessary," Spock replied, "despite the fallibility of your human memory." He turned toward Kirk. "Captain, let me point out once again that we are now in possession of *three* fragments. In theory, I should be able to accompany you and Seven on this expedition."

Kirk shook his head. "We've been through this. The *Enterprise* has already come under attack once during this affair. I'm not willing to have both of its senior officers stuck in the past of a vaporized planet if the Orions come gunning for revenge." He glanced over at Scotty. "No offense, Mister Scott."

"No worries," Scotty assured him. "I'd just as soon have ye or Mister Spock in command durin' a tight spot, given a choice. I'd rather look after my engines than be stuck on the bridge any day."

Spock persisted. "I think it is extremely unlikely that the *Enterprise* will encounter the Orions again. The deception with Seven—"

"May not be sufficient, Mister Spock." Kirk finished climbing into the suit, so that only the helmet remained to be put on. "I've made my decision. Seven and I managed on our own on Cheron. We can manage on Sarpeidon, *if* we make it back to when the planet was still in one piece."

His reasoning was sound, but Kirk privately admitted to another motive as well. He had no desire to subject his friend to the pain of revisiting, once again, the world where he had lost both Zarabeth and, eventually, their son. Kirk knew what it was like to lose a woman to the cruel vagaries of time travel . . . and to have a son you could never know. If he could spare Spock the heartache, he was going to do it. What was the good of being captain if you couldn't pull rank sometimes—for your friend's sake?

"Very well. Then perhaps a security officer," Spock suggested.

"Negative, Mister Spock. I'm not bringing another person into this circle of trust. As I just told Chekov, this is strictly need to know."

Plus, to be honest, he didn't want to risk losing another security officer on this highly unorthodox quest. Bergstrom, Jadello, Tang . . . Kirk wasn't up to sacrificing another of his crew on the altar of the future. This "leap of faith" was his to take and his alone.

Aside from Seven, of course.

"Understood," Spock assented grudgingly. "We will, of course, be monitoring the designated coordinates so that we can beam you back to the ship the instant you return from your quest."

"That's what I'm counting on," Kirk said.

Seven stepped forward. "It is possible that I shall not be returning to the *Enterprise* once I have reassembled the device that brought me to this era. That being the case, I wish to take the opportunity to thank you all for your assistance and hospitality. It has been very . . . intriguing . . . exploring this time period with you. I could not ask for better guides to the twenty-third century."

"It's been a pleasure," McCoy said, breaking out his characteristic Southern charm. "If you're at all typical of what the future has to offer, then tomorrow is looking bright indeed, at least as far as I'm concerned."

Seven was mildly surprised by his glowing endorsement. "Despite my . . . deviations . . . from baseline humanity?"

"It's not what I'm used to," he admitted, "but maybe that's not the point. Just because humanity might not be ready for your various physiological 'improvements' right now doesn't mean we won't be at some point in the future. There was a time when we weren't ready for warp travel either, but look at us now. Progress isn't always a bad thing, as long as it comes in its own time."

Spock arched an eyebrow. "You never cease to amaze me, Doctor. I was unaware that you had such an open mind."

"Damn straight I do," McCoy said. "And don't you forget it."

Seven realized now that their banter masked a deep kinship. It reminded her in some ways of the frequent verbal jousting between Tuvok and Neelix, which in no way negated the trust and loyalty between them. She experienced a pang of nostalgia for *Voyager,* which she ascribed to physical fatigue and mental exhaustion. Lack of regeneration was making her annoyingly sentimental.

"Just the same," McCoy added, "I'm still going to scrub all your medical data from the ship's computer. No need to bring on your brave new world before it's due."

"I also intend to purge the computer of any data that might compromise your time line," Spock stated. "Or warn your past self of what is to come."

Once again she realized that an opportunity existed to warn her parents against venturing into Borg space. It was not too late to prevent little Annika Hansen from being assimilated by the Collective many years hence. She could possibly change her own future and regain a normal, human childhood . . . at the risk of sacrificing the individual she had become. She pushed the temptation aside, but not without a pang of regret.

"That is for the best," she agreed.

"I'm going to keep my mouth shut, too," Santiago said. "And don't worry about that no-good aide of mine. He's looking at some pretty serious charges for espionage, not to mention aiding and abetting attacks on a Federation starship and a diplomatic conference. I'm sure he can be . . . persuaded . . . to keep silent if it means not being turned over to the Yusubi, whose brand of justice is a good deal harsher than the Federation's."

"Would serve him right to face a little old-fashioned eye for an eye," Scotty commented, "but aye, I imagine that's a powerful incentive to play ball and bite his tongue where Seven is concerned."

"Let us hope so," she said. "Regardless, I appreciate your collective discretion, gentlemen."

"It's the smart thing to do," Kirk said. "Loose lips and all that."

Spock took a moment to bid Seven farewell. "I too have valued your time about the *Enterprise*. It is reassuring to see that the humans of the future will not all be as emotional and impulsive as the good doctor. Your keen mind and resourcefulness are a credit to your own time, whenever it may be."

"As are yours," she replied. "I thank you again for sharing your meditative techniques with me. They made a difference."

"I am pleased to hear it." He raised his hand in a Vulcan salute. "Live long and prosper, Annika Seven."

She splayed her fingers likewise. A slight tremor marred the gesture. "Live long and prosper, Spock of Vulcan," she replied, knowing that he would. "And my thanks to you as well, Mister Scott. Your assistance was invaluable."

"All in a day's work," he assured her. "Godspeed, lass. Hope ye have less of a bumpy ride this time."

Seven hoped so as well. She saw no point in prolonging her exit any longer. The fourth component of the time machine awaited her, as did *Voyager* nearly a century from now. She had not forgotten the danger Captain Janeway and the rest of the away team had been facing when last she saw them. Possibly there was still a chance to save them, if she returned to the right point in time?

"Shall we proceed, Captain?" she addressed Kirk.

Her brief stint aboard the *Relativity* came to mind. "There is a saying among time travelers that strikes me as highly relevant at this juncture."

"Which is?" Kirk asked.

"There's no time like the past."

Thirty-four

Instead of the blackness of space, she found herself in an endless white wasteland. Windblown snow melted against the heated visor of her helmet. Icy cliffs, piled high with snow, blocked her view of the horizon, hemming her and Kirk in. A geriatric red sun, sinking toward the west, seemed to provide little in the way of warmth. The frozen landscape had an arctic blue tinge. The wind's mournful keening could be heard even through her helmet. Her gloved hands held on tightly to two violet wedges.

"*Welcome to the ice age,*" Kirk said via the communicators in their helmets. He gripped the third segment in his right hand. "*Seems the fragments brought us into Sarpeidon's past as expected.*" He glanced around at the glacial wilderness. A floodlight from his helmet fought against the swirling snow obscuring their vision. "*This place is a little colder than I remembered.*"

Seven had familiarized herself with Kirk's mission logs concerning Sarpeidon. "At least you are unlikely to be tried for witchcraft this time."

"*There's that,*" he conceded. "*But would it have killed these fragments to have brought us here in summer?*"

"Perhaps this *is* summer," she pointed out.

"*Now, there's a terrifying thought.*" A speculative tone entered his voice. "*I wonder, do you think we might encounter Zarabeth . . . or Zar?*"

"Unlikely," Seven stated. "Sarpeidon's glacial epochs lasted many millennia and covered much of the planet's surface. The odds that these are the same geographical coordinates, at the same time, are remote in the extreme."

"*You're probably right.*" His face was visible through the visor of his helmet. "*For all we know, we're on a different continent during a different century.*" He sighed audibly. "*Probably just as well. Yesterday's sagas should be left as they were.*"

Seven had no reason to reminisce about past visits to the planet. She preferred to focus on the task at hand. She secured the two wedges in a backpack she had attached to her suit, then she held out her hand.

"The remaining fragment, please. I would not want to misplace it in this environment."

"*That would be unfortunate,*" he agreed, handing her the component, which she added to her pack. He unhitched his phaser from his hip. "*Hold on. I want to check something.*"

He directed a short burst of phaser fire at a nearby snow bank, which evaporated into steam. He nodded in satisfaction.

"*Good,*" he said. "*It still works.*"

Seven understood his concern. Spock and McCoy had found their own phasers inoperative during their earlier visit to Sarpeidon's past. Spock had later speculated that the weapons had been automatically deactivated by the atavachron in order to prevent future technology from contaminating the past. No such problem had arisen on their return trip to Sarpeidon, suggesting that this was merely a function of the atavachron's programming and not intrinsic to time travel on this planet. Seven shared Kirk's relief that their phasers were still apparently in working order. She tested her own as well, simply to be certain.

A crimson beam vaporized a patch of ice.

"My phaser is also functional," she reported, returning it to her hip.

"Glad to hear it," he said. *"Not that I'm expecting trouble, but as I recall, this planet is not without its predators."*

"That is correct," she stated. The *Enterprise's* computer library listed several potential hazardous forms of wildlife, most notably the sithar, a large carnivorous mammal known to hunt frozen wastes of the sort surrounding them. She cast an appraising look at the snow-heaped cliffs rising up to the east and west. A sizable quantity of accumulated whiteness clung to the slopes. Fractured slabs of ice the size of shuttlecrafts appeared barely held in place, edged by a frigid glaze of rime. "We should also step lightly . . . and be on the alert for avalanches."

Kirk tracked her gaze. *"I see what you mean. Getting buried beneath a mountain of snow and ice would definitely put a crimp in our mission."*

"Precisely. I suggest we use our phasers only as a last resort."

Their environmental suits provided needed protection from the elements, but were heavy and cumbersome compared to her shipboard attire. The additional weight was already tiring Seven, who recalled that Sarpeidon's gravity was 1.43 Earth-normal, making physical activity more arduous than she would have preferred. She hoped that the final piece of the puzzle was nearby. Given her deteriorating condition, an extended hike through the wasteland was not advisable. Her limbs were already stiff and sore. Joints and implants felt out of alignment. Her organic right eye was dry and irritated.

She attempted to get her bearings. The swirling snow limited visibility, so it took her a moment to realize that the topography surrounding them was notably similar to what she had encountered on a certain nameless planetoid in the Delta Quadrant. As before, she found herself in a rugged canyon studded with fallen boulders and heaps of rubble. The only difference was the heavy coating of snow and ice on the terrain, and the terminal red sun overhead.

A coincidence?

She doubted it.

Her primitive tricorder picked up a familiar distress signal coming from farther down the canyon, much as it had on that distant planetoid. She felt as though she was retracing her steps, despite being thousands of years and countless light-years away from her starting point.

"This way," she instructed Kirk. "Follow me."

The ground was uneven, and trudging through the thick snow, which was often thirty centimeters high or deeper, added to the difficulty. Although her Borg respiratory system was more efficient than an ordinary human's, she was soon breathing hard enough to fog the visor on her helmet, making the trek even more challenging. Her head began to throb, and she had trouble keeping her eyes open.

"*Careful,*" Kirk said, tugging on her arm. He steered her away from the edge of a steep chasm running along one side of the canyon. The pervasive whiteness blurred the borders of the ravine, making them difficult to discern in the snow. "*Another reason to watch our step.*"

"I concur."

Concerned that fragile layers of snow or ice might conceal similar hazards, she devoted a portion of the tricorder's sensors to scanning for hidden ravines. By now she had a definite sense of what direction the telltale Starfleet signal was coming from, coinciding with her memories of that other canyon, so she judged she could spare some of the tricorder's computing power in the interest of ensuring the snow-covered ground before them was safe to tread upon.

Her sense of déjà vu increased as they rounded a curve in the canyon and found themselves facing a dead end. She half-expected to find another monumental bust of Kirk, perhaps encased in ice, but only a frosted cliff face lay before them, approximately seventy meters ahead. Seven was relieved that she would not have to explain to Kirk about his colossal portrait in the Delta Quadrant. Despite her fatigue, she quickened her pace, eager to reach the base of the cliff, where she had every expectation of finding another hidden entrance.

Perhaps her sojourn in the twenty-third century was truly nearing its end.

"*Spock and McCoy found refuge in a cave heated by buried hot springs*," Kirk recalled aloud. He was only a few paces behind her. "*Maybe we're looking for something along those—*"

A ferocious growl, louder even than the howling wind, cut him off abruptly. With little warning, a white shaggy beast sprang from a ledge, slamming into Kirk, who was knocked off his feet by the sithar's attack. The creature, which had to weigh at least 350 kilograms, resembled a hybrid composed of equal parts lion and musk ox. Curved horns, jutting from its massive skull, were as sharp as the claws tearing at Kirk's protective suit. A snowy mane and matching pelt blended in with the arctic terrain, providing far too effective camouflage. Any telltale musk or odor had failed to penetrate the humans' airtight suits.

Silver fabric, designed to withstand hostile atmosphere and vacuum, shredded beneath the beast's attack, although the helmet and shoulder assembly protected Kirk's face and throat from the sithar's fangs. Kirk grappled with the creature, shouting inarticulately over the comm link. They rolled across the packed snow and ice, which suddenly collapsed beneath their combined weight. They plunged from sight into a hidden chasm.

"Captain!"

Her reflexes only slightly slowed by her depleted state, Seven raced to the edge of the exposed chasm. Peering over the edge, she spied Kirk and the sithar thrashing at the bottom of the ravine, approximately fifty meters below. Only momentarily stunned by the fall, the creature remained intent on devouring Kirk, so Seven drew her phaser. Palsied tremors forced her to grip the weapon with both hands to steady her aim, but a crimson beam stunned the sithar, which collapsed on top of Kirk, practically burying him beneath its bulk. Worsening snow flurries made it difficult to tell if Kirk was still moving at the bottom at the chasm, but Seven was distressed to see traces of red seeping through the fallen snow and ice. Did sithars bleed red? Seven could not immediately recall.

"Captain? Can you read me?"

"I'm here," he responded, demonstrating that the

communicator in his helmet was still operative. *"And still in one piece, more or less. Good shooting."*

Seven experienced a surge of relief, which was quickly supplanted by the realization that Kirk's situation remained precarious. "Are you injured?"

"I've been better." A sharp intake of breath indicated that he was in pain. *"I'm pretty sure my right leg is broken, and I'm bleeding from some pretty nasty lacerations."* His teeth chattered audibly. *"I'm suddenly feeling the chill, too. Not sure if that's shock or just the cold seeping through the rips in my suit."*

Probably both, Seven thought. She glanced around the frigid landscape, facing the challenge of extricating the injured captain from the ravine. No obvious solution presented itself. There had been little reason to anticipate a need for mountaineering equipment.

She contemplated climbing down into the chasm.

"Hold on, Captain. I am endeavoring to arrive at a proper response to your predicament."

"Forget it," he replied. *"The last thing we need is both of us trapped down here, and you're in no shape to rescue me even if my leg wasn't busted."* A groan testified to his discomfort. *"You'll have to go on without me."*

Seven rejected the suggestion. "That is not an acceptable course of action."

Beyond humanitarian concerns, and her personal debt to Kirk, there was also the matter of his importance to the time line. James T. Kirk still had crucial parts to play in many events of significant historical importance, such as the V'Ger crisis and the Khitomer peace accords. He could not be lost in the past of a dead world thousands of years before his birth.

"This is not your time," she insisted.

"Maybe it is now," he answered. *"Or perhaps you can come back for me after you've completed our mission. If you climb down here with all four components, and we assemble them together, then maybe—"*

A stone-tipped spear slammed into the snow at the edge of the chasm, barely missing Seven. A second spear slammed into the neck assembly of her suit. The spearhead failed to penetrate the rigid collar, but the impact staggered her, almost knocking her into the ravine. She threw herself backward to avoid tumbling in after Kirk.

"Captain! I am under attack!"

She dropped into a defensive crouch, presenting a smaller target. Squinting up through the snow, she glimpsed a handful of fur-clad figures at the top of a nearby cliff. They brandished spears, axes, and other primitive weaponry, while shouting excitedly at each other over the wind. She was unable to make out what they were saying, but she doubted that they were friendly overtures. Had her attackers been attracted by the noise of the sithar's attack—or had they perhaps been pursuing the beast in the first place?

"What?" Kirk asked. *"Who is attacking you?"*

Seven considered the possibilities. Temporally displaced exiles, banished to the past for transgressions unknown, or simply ice-age hunters native to this era? Seven had no way of knowing, nor was this of particular relevance at the moment.

"Unknown," she replied, "but their intentions are clearly hostile."

A phaser blast stunned one of her attackers, who tumbled off the cliff into a heavy snow drift dozens of meters below. The other hunters retreated to a degree, seeking cover behind various icy outcroppings, but they continued to lob spears in her direction. Seven realized that she was in an untenable position, as her immediate surroundings offered little in the way of shelter. Her gaze turned instinctively toward the looming cliff face several meters away—and the hidden passageway she expected to find there.

"*Go!*" Kirk shouted, as though reading her mind. "*Don't worry about me.*"

She wished that was an option, but Kirk was too important to history not to be concerned with. Her options were clearly shrinking, however. Rescuing Kirk from the chasm had been a daunting challenge before, but now that they were under attack . . . ?

A snowball rolled down the side of the cliff, accumulating mass and volume along its way. Dislodged chunks of snow and ice followed after it. Seven glimpsed the hunters hacking away at the top of the cliff with their axes, while others used their spears as levers to pry loose frosty boulders and slabs of ice. They hollered and stomped their boots, almost as though trying to set off an avalanche.

Then she realized that was precisely their intention.

An efficient tactic, she conceded. The hunters could eliminate her and Kirk and later dig up their possession and carcasses with little risk to themselves. She wondered briefly if the fur-clad attackers were simply defending their territory or if intruders were considered an acceptable foodstuff before deciding that this was a question she preferred not to dwell on. She gazed with concern at the huge sheets of ice and snow suspended over the canyon. The sheer accumulation far exceeded her phaser's ability to vaporize it all in time to avoid being swept away by an avalanche.

"Seven?" Kirk demanded. *"Are you still there? What's happening?"*

Trapped beneath the stunned predator at the bottom of the chasm, injured and bleeding, Kirk was unable to witness what was transpiring. Seven could readily imagine his frustration.

"Our attackers are attempting to set off an avalanche," she informed him, hesitating only briefly before telling him the worst of it. "I am uncertain that I can prevent this."

"Then you have to save yourself before it's too late." The decisiveness in his voice overcame any hint of pain or infirmity. *"Go! Find that last fragment and get back where you belong."* He coughed hoarsely. *"That's an order, Seven. Run for your life . . . and give my regards to the future."*

"Captain . . ."

She wanted to say more, find some flaw in the merciless demands of the situation, but an ominous rumble informed her that the time for debate was over. The avalanche was coming. She had to escape if she wanted to avoid being buried alive for all time.

"Go!" he shouted. *"Now!"*

Tearing herself away from the edge of the chasm, she raced toward the towering dead end of the canyon, even as the cliff behind her lost its grip on its icy load. With a thunderous roar, the avalanche came streaming down into the canyon, carrying tons of frozen debris. Billowing clouds of powder preceded a plunging wall of snow that gained speed and momentum at an alarming pace. Huge slabs of ice knocked loose more snow and rock, propagating a dangerous chain reaction. Glancing back over her shoulder, Seven saw the avalanche bury the chasm behind her, cutting her off from Kirk. A few more moments, and she would have been buried as well.

"Captain?"

He did not respond.

Breathing hard, she reached the base of the cliff at the end of the canyon. Her muscles ached and her vision blurred, but her ocular implant located a distinctive delta-shaped insignia embedded in the stone beneath the frosty glaze. Shaking fingers operated the tricorder, transmitting the response code. Ice cracked and snow shook loose as a hidden door identical to the one on the planetoid sank into the bedrock, exposing a familiar-looking passageway leading deep into the interior of the cliff. Overhead lights clicked on before her.

"Open Sesame."

The passage beckoned to Seven, but she paused and looked back the way she had come. Her heart sank as her worst expectations were confirmed.

A mountain of fallen snow and ice filled the canyon behind her. Smaller avalanches funneled down the slope, sprinkling the top of the heap with a fresh layer of frozen rubble. In theory, Kirk's environmental suit held approximately four hours' worth of oxygen, assuming it hadn't been too badly damaged by the sithar or the avalanche, but Seven could see at a glance that there was no chance of her digging him out in time. It would take a team of Starfleet engineers to reach him. She suspected that the hunters wouldn't be able to recover their prey until the next thaw, if indeed it ever warmed enough to make that

366   Greg Cox

possible. Even if Kirk was still alive, she could not possibly recover him.

"Captain?"

Part of her wished that Kirk had been killed instantly by the avalanche. That struck her as preferable to a long, slow death beneath the ice and snow. Her exhausted mind struggled to grasp the implications of what had just occurred. James T. Kirk had been lost long before his time. The future would be forced to take another form.

Unless this past could be erased.

She heard the hunters whooping in victory. Another spear, striking the snow behind her, persuaded her not to linger. Turning her back on Kirk's glacial tomb, she plunged through the open archway into the tunnel beyond.

Kirk was gone, but her mission remained.

Panting, she staggered down a sloping corridor that bore an unmistakable resemblance to the one *Voyager*'s away team had discovered in the Delta Quadrant. The same divided-disk motif was repeated on the sloping tile floor of the tunnel, reminding her that she required only an additional red segment to complete the puzzle in her backpack, assuming she still had the strength.

Seven dragged herself down the hallway, badly in need of regeneration. Her aching muscles felt every extra percentage point of Sarpeidon's gravity. Her cheek twitched spasmodically. Her external implants chafed against the skin around them, which felt uncomfortably dry and raw. The nagging headache increased steadily in intensity. Her thoughts felt foggy, confused.

A heads-up display within her helmet indicated that the temperature within the complex was significantly warmer than outside. Gasping for breath, she removed her helmet and retrieved a loaded hypospray from a sealed pouch on her suit.

One more dose, she thought, *to get me to the end.*

The hiss of the hypospray and the accompanying stimulant instantly provided a degree of relief. She was exhausted and far from functioning with peak efficiency, but her mind felt clearer and she no longer lacked the strength to proceed. The corridor felt uncomfortably warm, and she was tempted to discard the burdensome environment suit, but then she recalled that she might well end up back in space in the twenty-third century, so she refastened her helmet. She reached out to steady herself against the wall, then she yanked her hand back before it came into contact with the polished stone. Now was no time to carelessly risk triggering another booby trap, so she kept her hands to herself.

The corridor led, as before, to a spacious chamber deep within the complex. Once again, graceful columns supported a vaulted ceiling, but instead of a central sarcophagus, a tiered circular platform occupied the center of the chamber. Three levels of wide concentric circles, stacked atop each other like an ancient Terran wedding cake, led to the topmost pedestal, roughly at the level of her waist, where the fourth and final component rested within a circular depression. The negative space within the depression clearly awaited the three segments Seven had collected throughout time and space. Now it was only a matter of completing the design—and reassembling the time-travel device.

Could it be that simple?

She cautiously approached the platform. A quick

visual survey of the chamber failed to discover any scattered corpses, but she remained wary of booby traps. Seven watched her step, not wanting to repeat Neelix's mistake, and avoided touching anything if she could avoid it. Unfortunately, her arms were not long enough to reach the central pedestal without mounting the surrounding steps, so she had no choice but to take another leap of faith. Holding her breath in a manner unbefitting a Borg, she gingerly set foot on the lower level. If there was a booby trap in wait, she would likely discover it soon.

To her relief, however, no chroniton burst assailed her, nor was she inexplicably transported to yet another era or world. Hope spread within her, like an expanding wave front, as she climbed the steps until the top of the upper tier rested before her like a transporter control console. Removing the three captured fragments from her pack, she placed them, one by one, within the recessed area so that they matched the design seen throughout the complex. The segments fit together perfectly, filling the circular depression as though they belonged there, until only one last piece remained to complete the design. She braced herself for—what?—as it clicked into place.

She expected to be transported elsewhere, perhaps back to Sarpeidon's empty orbit, perhaps back to the Delta Quadrant, but instead a figure materialized atop the pedestal like someone arriving on a transporter pad. Seven backed away prudently, stepping down from the platform. She regarded the figure intently.

He was humanoid in appearance, with dark skin and a fringe of silver hair around a bald pate. A lean face had been lined by care and time. A violet robe with crimson trim was draped over his slender frame, which was slightly stooped with age. Seven could not immediately place his species or planet of origin. He could have been Terran or Sarpeid or any of a number of indistinguishable humanoid races. Deep blue eyes regarded her thoughtfully.

"Greetings, pilgrim," he addressed her. "You have come a long way."

"That is an understatement," she said with a flash of irritation. Now that her quest appeared to be nearing its end, she resented being made to follow such a circuitous route for no clear purpose. She hoped the answers would prove satisfactory. "Who are you?"

"Nehwa of Sarpeidon," he identified himself. "Or rather a replica of same."

She made a reasonable supposition. "You are a hologram?"

"That is correct. You are familiar with such entities?"

"Quite." She recalled that Kirk and his companions had encountered a librarian with multiple replicas during their first visit to Sarpeidon. "And where is the original Nehwa?"

"Long dead, many ages and light-years from here. I suspect you discovered my tomb in that distant region of the galaxy."

She nodded, putting the pieces together. "Those were your remains in the sarcophagus."

"Yes," he confirmed, "assuming certain postmortem arrangements were carried out as instructed by another replica." He spoke calmly of the death of his original, apparently untroubled by the notion. "And I may ask your name, pilgrim?"

"My designation is Seven of Nine." She clasped her hands behind her back, in part to keep them from shaking. "I desire answers."

He nodded. "If you have found your way here, you deserve nothing less. What would you ask of me?"

"The clues you planted throughout space-time, leading me to this moment," she began. "Explain."

"My story began many millennia from now, when, as a scientist, I made the breakthrough that led to the creation of my first great invention: the atavachron. Young and naïve, I was inordinately proud of my accomplishment, which promised to open a new frontier in temporal exploration, but I was swiftly disillusioned by the speed with which my discovery was abused to banish political prisoners, dissidents, and those whose families had merely fallen out of favor to eternal exile in the past. My work—my genius—had become an instrument of oppression."

The replica seemed to share his original's sense of remorse. Regret tinged his artificial voice. Guilt shadowed his gaunt features, giving them a melancholy cast.

"And yet the atavachron ultimately proved your people's salvation," Seven pointed out, "allowing them to escape the supernova that destroyed your world."

"That is a great consolation," he admitted, his somber tone lifting to a degree. "Nonetheless, I had learned a bitter lesson. Although I continued my research, unable to curb my restless curiosity, I hid the fruits of my work from those who would put them to dubious purposes, so that when I devised my ultimate creation—a mechanism that could transport living beings across vast gulfs of time *and* space—I kept this a closely guarded secret, known only to myself."

"And your replicas," she assumed.

"Indeed. And yet, as my life drew to a close, I found myself faced with a thorny dilemma: What was to become of this device that I had created? To whom could I entrust this legacy and responsibility? For years I traversed the known and unknown universe, journeying backward and forward through time, in search of a species or civilization that I could trust to use the device wisely. But everywhere I went I was reminded that folly and corruption were as inevitable as hope and progress, or so it seemed to me. Nowhere could I find a worthy custodian of my legacy . . . and yet I could not bring myself to destroy my life's work.

"So I chose to scatter the pieces throughout spacetime in the hopes that someday an individual of sufficient intelligence and resourcefulness would reassemble the device. And have the wisdom to know what to do with it."

Seven grasped his intent. "This was a test. A puzzle to be unraveled in order to claim the device."

"A quest, to be precise, full of challenges and riddles to overcome."

Spoken like a wizard, she thought, realizing that Nehwa was surely the enigmatic traveler of whom the legends of the Delta Quadrant told. "I prefer a less fanciful description."

"A test, then . . . and lessons."

She failed to comprehend his meaning. "Lessons?"

"Think about what you have witnessed and experienced on your journey. Do you truly suppose that the stations of your pilgrimage were chosen at random?"

Understanding dawned, despite her fatigue.

"Gamma Trianguli VI, Cheron, even Sarpeidon . . . they were all warnings. Cautionary examples."

He nodded gravely. "Of the dangers of technology abused . . . and the potential darkness lurking in every sapient species. You have seen minds enslaved to serve a machine, an advanced civilization destroyed by racial conflict, and a world that turned its own history into a prison and a punishment. And all found within the voyages of a single bold explorer. . . ."

"Kirk," she realized. "Why Kirk? He is not of Sarpeidon. Why build your puzzle around him?"

The hologram shrugged. "Every code needs a key. Every map needs a legend. And what more suitable starting point than the last traveler to set foot on Sarpeidon . . . and a historic figure whose fabled exploits poignantly illustrate both the dangers and rewards of voyaging through time."

Seven thought of Kirk, buried alive millennia before his birth. Even before the (literally) untimely fate that had just befallen him, Kirk had demonstrated a profound appreciation of the Temporal Prime Directive, despite his reputation to the contrary. Nehwa was not wrong in thinking that Kirk embodied both the perils and promise of time travel. By traversing time, he had saved planets and endangered history, often at the same time.

"But Kirk is not here," she stated. "I am. What now?"

"That is for you to decide. You may claim the device, use it as you will, or you may make what is possibly the wiser choice."

By now, his meaning was clear.

"You want me to destroy the device."

He nodded. "Destroy it in the past . . . so that it will

never exist in the future. As I said, I could not bring myself to destroy my life's work, nor even program my replicas to carry out the task. They . . . we . . . I . . . were too close to the dilemma to see it clearly. Our work was too much a part of us. But perhaps a stranger, capable of completing our quest, would have the strength and understanding to make the right choice. . . ."

"I see," Seven said.

She contemplated her options. She could, as planned, use the completed device to return to the Delta Quadrant to rescue Captain Janeway and the rest of the away team. Beyond that, she could conceivably adapt the future version of the device, the one inside Kirk's monument, to transport *Voyager* back to Earth many years ahead of schedule, delivering Nehwa's revolutionary space-time technology to Starfleet.

But what then? Would some twenty-fourth-century equivalent of Commissioner Santiago insist on harnessing the device for the good of the Federation? Seven thought back on her debates with Santiago regarding the Temporal Prime Directive and wondered how she could possibly guarantee that Nehwa's technology would not prove a threat to the time line and galactic peace. Her own trip through time had already resulted in chaos, bloodshed, deceit, death, and the premature loss of James T. Kirk. What could be the consequences of introducing the device to her own time?

"Choose wisely," the hologram advised her.

Destroying the device would trap her in the past—or would it? Her memory, which remained functional despite everything, played back Nehwa's words to her. She noted the precise phrasing of his suggestion:

"*Destroy it in the past . . . so that it will never exist in the future.*"

But if it never exists in the future . . .

Her legs buckled as her long ordeal caught up with her. The last dose of stimulant was already wearing off, leaving her almost too weak to take any action at all. The Borg in her was in desperate need of regeneration. Her implants were shutting down, beyond the ability of her nanoprobes to restore them. Her vision blurred even more severely than before. Random muscles twitched. Involuntary neural surges caused her assimilation tubules to extend and retract spasmodically, poking holes in the glove of her environment suit. Alternating waves of hot and cold left her shaking and sweating simultaneously. Her head felt as though there was a warp core breach inside it. Darkness began to infringe on the periphery of her vision. She was becoming inoperative.

"What is it?" the hologram asked in alarm. "What's wrong with you?"

It required considerable effort to reply. "I am out of time."

The irony was not lost on her.

"No!" the hologram protested. "You can't die yet. You have to choose!"

She did so.

Drawing her phaser, she set it on disrupt and opened fire on the pedestal. The device flared red before dissolving into nothingness. In an instant, its future went away.

And so did Seven.

Thirty-five

The control booth inside Kirk's monument was precisely as Seven remembered it—with a single notable exception. Glancing down at the floor of the booth, she saw only a flat circular depression where the device had once been, or would have been had she not just destroyed it in the past, so that it had never sent her back in time in the first place. . . .

The paradox was enough to make her head swim, even though she was no longer on the verge of passing out. Her extreme exhaustion had vanished along with the twenty-third-century space suit she had been wearing only seconds before, thousands of years ago. Aside from her memories, no evidence remained of her extended "quest" through space-time. No doubt that was as Nehwa intended.

Her chronometric node, which was no longer in desperate need of regeneration, confirmed that only a heartbeat had passed since she had first set foot in the booth. She heard Captain Janeway moaning in pain in the adjacent burial chamber and realized that she could grapple with any slippery temporal conundrums later. More pressing matters, in the here and now, demanded her attention. The control panel allowed her to deactivate the force field.

She tapped her combadge.

"Seven of Nine to *Voyager*. I require immediate assistance."

"Chakotay here," he responded. *"What's your situation?"*

It was unexpectedly reassuring to hear his voice again. "The captain and the rest of the away team have been seriously injured. They need to be beamed directly to sickbay."

He did not waste time pressing her for details, although she heard a new edge to his voice. "We're on it. Stand by."

He responded with admirable efficiency. Mere moments passed before a transporter beam locked onto her and beamed her away from the planetoid. A keen sense of anticipation washed over Seven as she dematerialized.

She could not return to *Voyager* soon enough.

Hours later:

Seven could not help comparing *Voyager*'s spacious, state-of-the-art sickbay to the more rustic version she had occupied aboard the *Enterprise*. Doctor McCoy had been most hospitable, but she had always felt distinctly out of place in that primitive, frontier environment. By contrast, the familiar sights greeting her as she entered sickbay proved more tonic than any hypospray.

In short, she was glad to be home.

"Seven?" Janeway called to her. "Come on over. I can use the company."

The captain was resting, somewhat impatiently, in the primary biobed. A detachable decontamination unit was clamped over the patient, covering her torso, while an insulated blanket kept her warm. The bed itself occupied its own separate chamber, apart from the larger recovery ward, where Tuvok and Neelix were sleeping in side-by-side standard biobeds. At least they appeared to be sleeping; Seven would not have been surprised to discover that Tuvok was merely feigning sleep to avoid being a captive audience for the often chatty Talaxian. She thought briefly of Spock and McCoy and how they seemed to amuse and irritate each other in equal parts. Did Neelix and Tuvok enjoy a similar dynamic? She resolved to make a closer examination of their byplay for purposes of comparison.

Later.

"Captain." She approached Janeway's bed, which was tilted upward at a forty-five-degree angle to better facilitate conversation. Seven was relieved to note that the captain already appeared much recovered. Not only was she conscious and alert, but the radiation burns on her face and hands were fading thanks to the Doctor's assiduous treatment. A nearby monitor displayed Janeway's vital signs, which were improving significantly. "You seem to have survived."

"Tell that to the Doctor," Janeway said. "He insisted on yet another decontamination session to make sure my cells are completely free of chroniton radiation." She squirmed restlessly beneath the bulky apparatus. "Damn thing tickles."

"It is a reasonable precaution," Seven said, inspecting the readouts on the unit's display monitors. Only trace amounts of chronitons, well below toxic levels, remained to be neutralized. "A full recovery is indicated."

"Thanks to you," Janeway said. "From what I hear, it was your quick thinking and prompt actions that got us out of that deathtrap in time for the Doctor to work his magic." She smiled warmly at Seven. "Good work."

Seven shifted uncomfortably. "My response may not have been as rapid as it appeared."

Janeway picked up on the tension in Seven's voice. Her eyes narrowed.

"What do you mean by that? Is there something you're not telling me?"

"Perhaps, but it is not for other ears."

Seven walked over to a control panel by the entrance to the ward, which was equipped with a force field that could be employed to quarantine the chamber or confine an unruly patient. She activated the barrier to guarantee their privacy and set it to block even sonic wavelengths so that they would not be overheard. This was not a conversation she wished to share with others.

"Okay, now you've got me really intrigued," Janeway said, "and a little worried." She took charge of the conversation. "Spill."

"Very well."

Seven had seriously debated whether she should speak of her extended detour through the twenty-third century at all, but she had ultimately decided that she was obliged to give Captain Janeway, at least, a full account of what had transpired in the past. It was a matter of duty, as well as the most efficient way to forestall any further investigation of the monument on the planetoid. The captain's curiosity would surely require some explanation for the edifice's puzzling existence before *Voyager* could continue its long trek back to the Alpha Quadrant, and the truth struck Seven as more convincing than any flimsy fabrication.

Or perhaps she simply needed to talk about it to someone she trusted.

"It involves time travel," she began.

Janeway listened intently, only occasionally interrupting to clarify a point, while Seven recounted the entire experience, ending with her return to the present. Janeway took a few moments before responding, as though she required a short interval to process all that Seven had just informed her. She expelled a deep breath.

"So let me get this straight. Because you destroyed the device in the past it no longer existed in the present, so you were never sent back to the past, where you destroyed the device?" Janeway groaned and rolled her eyes. "My head hurts already. Have I ever mentioned how much I hate time travel?"

"Frequently." Seven considered the matter, having received a thorough briefing on the wide varieties of temporal phenomena during her stint aboard the *Relativity*. "This appears to be a variation on a Pogo Paradox: a self-contained time loop that circles back on itself so that its end is its beginning. That I still retain my memories of the experience can perhaps be attributed to the distinctive peculiarities of the Sarpeids' singular mode of time travel."

Mister Spock, she recalled, had undergone an unusual psychological regression while using the atavachron, which suggested that the process had a cerebral component. She had not regressed while using Nehwa's later device, but the events were clearly imprinted in her memory.

"Peculiar is the word for it, all right," Janeway said. "And better you than me."

At the moment, Seven was less concerned with the mechanics of the paradox than with the consequences of her choice back on Sarpeidon. "I hope you are not disappointed by the decision I made regarding the device."

Janeway mulled it over, giving the issue the consideration it deserved, before answering.

"I can't deny that part of me regrets losing that technology and a shortcut to home, but I respect that you had to follow your conscience. And who knows? You may have made the right call. From the sound of it, everything turned out exactly the way it was supposed to."

"So it appears," Seven said, wondering if that was why the *Relativity* had not, in fact, intervened in the situation. "Since my return, I have begun a survey of the historical records regarding James T. Kirk and his crew, in search of any significant changes to the time line."

Janeway nodded. "And?"

"There do not appear to be any lasting deviations, nor any surviving records of my time aboard the *Enterprise*. 'Doctor Annika Seven' seems to have been thoroughly expunged from the historical record."

"Probably just as well," Janeway said. "I suspect I'd do the same in Kirk's position." She sounded relieved by Seven's failure to detect any changes to history. "So you didn't turn up anything odd in your research?"

Once again, Seven considered keeping silent, but decided against it.

"There was one unexpected discovery," she admitted. "Lieutenant Elaine Bergstrom, the Starfleet security officer killed during the firefight on Yusub . . . it seems she was my grandmother, on the maternal side."

Janeway's eyes widened. "Your grandmother? But if she was killed before your mother was born . . ."

"There is no record of her dying on Yusub. Starfleet personnel records have her surviving until 2349, a year before I was born." Seven regretted that she had no memory of the woman. "This does not coincide with what I witnessed on Yusub."

"Another paradox?" Janeway speculated. "I admit I'm at a loss here. You had better page the Doctor. I'm definitely going to need something for this headache." She leaned back against the biobed. "Still, it sounds like you had quite the adventure."

"It was . . . memorable," Seven conceded.

"I'll bet. I definitely want to hear more about what James T. Kirk was like in the flesh." She lowered her voice to a conspiratorial whisper. "So, did he *really* meet da Vinci?"

Thirty-six

"A most thoughtful and appropriate gift," RoMusscu Dihana declared, warming to Santiago somewhat, "which speaks well of your Federation and its intentions." The Yusubi chieftain opened the star chart to admire it once more. "You will have to show me where to find your respective homeworlds on this—"

"Watch out!" Kirk shouted, shoving her to one side. He drew his phaser and fired at the Orion sniper even as the would-be assassin rose from the silvery pool at the center of the oasis. A stun beam sent the sniper toppling back into the water. "Bergstrom! Multiple hostiles in the pool!"

"I see them, sir!" The redheaded security officer sprang into action, stepping between the startled diplomats and danger, while targeting the submerged Orions the moment they broke the surface. "Get back!" she warned Santiago and Hague. "And keep your heads down!"

"I don't understand," Dihana exclaimed, even as Yusubi bodyguards rushed to defend her. "What's happening?"

"Orion raiders," Kirk explained quickly, "working with Yusubi allies to disrupt the conclave." His memory flashed back to what felt like several days ago. "There's a ground vehicle, equipped with a transporter, hidden in a dune just beyond the tents." He pointed in the right direction. "Over there!"

"We'll find it," a Yusubi warrior snarled. He shouted to his cohorts, leading them in a charge toward the dunes. "Root out those who would violate our sacred hospitality!"

Kirk wondered if the traitors lurking in their ranks would show their true colors or simply blend in with the defenders now that their plot had unraveled. He suspected that the smart ones would know better than to expose themselves.

Dihana gazed at him in wonder and confusion. No disruptor blast had claimed her life. "But how do you know these things?"

"It's a long story," Kirk said.

That was putting it was mildly. One minute, he had been buried alive on ancient Sarpeidon, wounded and bleeding beneath a stunned sithar and several tons of fallen snow and ice. A heartbeat later, he had found himself back on Yusub right where it all began. He had to assume that this meant that Seven had somehow succeeded in her quest, with unexpected results.

Good for her, he thought.

Lieutenant Jadello, still very much alive as well, lowered her phaser. "I think we've sent them running, sir, although we may have to fish a few stunned pirates out of the pool."

"Nice shooting," he commended her. "I must say, it's good to see you in action."

She gave him a puzzled look. "Sir?"

"Never mind, Lieutenant. Carry on."

Santiago approached Kirk, looking equally baffled. "Kirk! What's this all about? Did you have advance intelligence on this attack? Why wasn't I informed?"

"Ask your aide," Kirk said coldly.

"Me?" Hague fell back. He tugged nervously on his collar. "I'm sure I don't know—"

Kirk blasted him with a stun beam. The exposed sleeper agent collapsed onto the sandy floor of the oasis. Santiago gaped at Kirk in shock.

"I'll explain later," the captain promised.

"Tell me, Spock. Does the name 'Annika Seven' mean anything to you?"

"Not that I recall, Captain. Should it?"

The Vulcan had beamed down to Yusub to assist in the cleanup operation, bringing with him enough Starfleet security personnel to discourage any further resistance on the part of the Orions and their allies. Kirk watched with satisfaction as his people, including Bergstrom, Jadello, and Tang, turned Habroz and his soggy assault team over to the Yusubi forces. Kirk noted that K'Mara was not among the captives; he guessed that the ruthless female pirate had just inherited command of the *Navaar*. He'd have to alert Starfleet to be on watch for her.

"I guess not," Kirk said.

From what he could tell, Seven's entire stay aboard the *Enterprise* had been erased from history, so that only he recalled it. Kirk wondered if that was because he had traveled back through time with Seven when she had finally completed her mission. That was the only explanation he could think of.

But her presence had not been without consequence.

Thanks to that hiccup in time, he'd had a second chance to fix things on Yusub. Bergstrom was alive, Habroz was in custody, Hague had been exposed, the conclave was back on track, and, judging from the reaction of Dihana and the other chieftains, the Orions were not going to be welcome on Yusub much longer. All in all, a good day's work, even if it had actually involved a lengthy trek through time and space.

Granted, he had arguably tampered with history, but from where he was standing, the future remained an undiscovered country. *Changing the past is one thing,* he reflected, *but we shape the future with every choice we make.*

He could live with that.

He watched as Bergstrom retrieved the idol from where she had dropped it in order to defend Santiago. "Excuse me, Lieutenant," he called to her. "Please bring that over here for a moment."

"Aye, sir." She carried the idol to where Kirk and Spock were standing. "It seems to have survived the excitement, Captain. Shall I take it back to the *Enterprise* for you?"

"All in good time, Lieutenant." He turned to Spock, whose tricorder was slung over his shoulder. "Do me a favor and scan this artifact for any unusual contents or readings."

Spock arched an eyebrow. "Captain?"

"Indulge me," Kirk said.

Spock scanned the idol with the tricorder. "I am detecting nothing unusual. This object appears to be simply what it seems: a ceramic sculpture of questionable aesthetic merit."

"I suspected as much," Kirk said. Now that the fragments had been retrieved, they no longer existed in the time line. "Just checking."

Spock regarded Kirk quizzically. "I confess, Captain, that I am puzzled by your seemingly prescient knowledge of events, as well as by your rather cryptic comments and behavior. Perhaps you would care to enlighten me?"

"I promise to give you the full story, Mister Spock, at the right moment."

Off the record, of course.

"Which would be?" Spock asked.

"Sometime in the future," Kirk replied. "When else?"

Acknowledgments

Because I wrote my one-and-only *Star Trek: Voyager* novel, *The Black Shore,* way back in the early days of the TV series, before Seven of Nine joined the crew, I've always regretted that I never had a chance to write everyone's favorite Borg crew member—until now. But I would have never had this opportunity without the help and encouragement of various parties who deserve my full and appreciative thanks, including:

My editors, Ed Schlesinger and Margaret Clark, who helped guide this book from proposal to print. Truth to tell, it was Margaret who first suggested that it might be interesting to throw Seven of Nine and James T. Kirk together. Needless to say, I knew a good idea when I heard one.

John Van Citters at CBS and Paula Block, who offered valuable input on both the original proposal and the eventual manuscript.

My agent, Russell Galen, who, as always, kept the business side of things running smoothly.

My friends and colleagues, John Ordover, Marco Palmieri, Dayton Ward, Scott Pearson, and Christopher Bennett, who let me pick their brains when I required help with some sticky plot point or esoteric bit of *Star Trek* lore . . . or just needed to talk out various crazy theories concerning explosive rocks, duotone aliens, and other vital matters. And the late A. C. Crispin, whose previous novels, *Star Trek—Yesterday's Son* and *Star Trek—Time for Yesterday*, about the planet Sarpeidon were required reading. She will be missed—and remembered.

Writers Max Ehrlich, Jean Lisette Aroeste, Oliver Crawford, and Lee Cronin for penning the three classic Original Series episodes that I mined heavily in this novel. All modern *Star Trek* fiction builds upon the vast edifice created by innumerable talents over the last forty-plus years, but these three episodes were of particular inspiration on this project—and gave me plenty of great material to work with.

And, of course, my girlfriend, Karen Palinko, and our four-legged family members—Henry, Sophie, and Lyla—who put up with me locking myself in my office for hours at time—and constantly watching *Star Trek* DVDs in my down time!

About the Author

Greg Cox is the author of numerous *Star Trek* novels and short stories, including *The Weight of Worlds, The Rings of Time, To Reign in Hell, The Eugenics Wars (Volumes One and Two), The Q Continuum, Assignment: Eternity,* and *The Black Shore.* He has also written the official novelizations of such films as *Godzilla, Man of Steel, The Dark Knight Rises, Ghost Rider, Daredevil, Death Defying Acts,* and the first three *Underworld* movies, as well as books and stories based on such popular series as *Alias, Buffy the Vampire Slayer, CSI: Crime Scene Investigation, Farscape, The 4400, Leverage, Riese: Kingdom Falling, Roswell, Terminator, Warehouse 13,* and *Xena: Warrior Princess.*

He has received two Scribe Awards from the International Association of Media Tie-In Writers. He lives in Oxford, Pennsylvania.

Visit him at: www.gregcox-author.com.